The Banker Trilogy

Martin Lundqvist

Published by Martin Lundqvist, 2021.

This is a work of fiction. Similarities to real people, places, or events are entirely coincidental.

THE BANKER TRILOGY

MARTIN LUNDQVIST

SCI-FI THRILLER

THE BANKER AND THE DRAGON

WHEN A NEW VIRUS EMERGES,
ONE MAN IS SET TO CHANGE THE FUTURE.

Chapter 1: The Honey Dragon, 2nd March 2021.

'Turkish Elvish Honey'

Chairman Jing Xi of the Columnist Party of China, CPOC, studied the jar in anticipation. He was a man of extravagant taste, and it didn't get fancier than this, buying honey that was worth its weight in gold. Jing smelled the honey, and the sensation took him a bit closer to heaven. He closed his eyes and Jing pictured himself on the top of the world, listening to serene music in a Tibetan temple on the top of a mountain.

The association with Tibet surprised Jing. He didn't care for the monks and their music. Furthermore, the party he oversaw, had brutally subjugated the Tibetan people some decades earlier. 'Am I getting soft as my age advances?' Jing thought for a moment.

Jing brushed off the notion. He was approaching 67 years of age, but he was still a man of power, and in many ways in the prime of his life. The longest living emperor, the Qianlong emperor who had lived in the 18th century had lived until the age of 87. Jing, who had expertise in both Chinese medicine and modern medicine, strived to outlive that legendary emperor.

Jing grabbed a spoon and ingested a spoonful of the exquisite honey. It tasted as amazing as it smelled, but as the taste faded in his mouth, Jing felt dissatisfied and restless. Eating honey that cost more than the average annual salary in China hadn't resolved the issue that kept frustrating Jing and filled him with anger.

Jing felt that the people should worship him like they had worshipped the ancient emperors. Instead, his subjects were busy slandering him behind his back. How did the ungrateful masses dare to treat him like this?

They should deify him for his leadership. During Jing's reign as the Chairman of the Columnist Party, China had risen to its rightful place as the centre of the world. Yet the topic of this month's column was an insult to his person. The WeChat voters had decided that this month's topic should be: 'How I intend to improve my character during the year of the Ox.'

This topic was nothing but dissent towards his leadership, and it was a dangerous column to write. He couldn't admit having character flaws, as he represented the state, and the state was faultless. But he couldn't be too arrogant either as that would contravene his promise to the people. Jing had promised the Chinese public a change when he reformed the Chinese Communist Party, CCP, into the Columnist Party of China, CPOC.

The name change of the party was Jing playing lip service to the Western world. This was to secure international trade that was crucial for his ambitions. Nothing had changed under his leadership, but at least he had given the people the chance to vote. Although Jing had restricted the popular vote to entail the topic of his monthly column in China Daily. This cosmetic change hadn't caused him any grief until this month.

Jing closed his laptop. He wouldn't write that article; the topic was beneath him. Instead, he would have sex to release his frustration. Jing's latest concubine, the 23-year-old winner of the National Chinese pageant, the stunning Min Li, had improved Jing's life in that aspect.

Jing summoned Min Li, and she told him that she would arrive in 30 minutes. Having summoned Min Li, Jing experienced restlessness and anticipation. He was 67 years old, and he was under a lot of stress. He needed to get a proper release, and he didn't want any violent mishaps. Covering up his violence towards previous concubines had stolen a lot of energy.

Jing took out a Ziplock bag, which contained a powder. The powder was a mixture of Viagra and ground rhino horn, and it always worked on him. Jing believed in mixing the best of Chinese and western medicine, and he followed this thesis in many aspects of his life.

30 minutes later, Min Li entered Jing's residence, and she kneeled at his feet.

Min Li:

- You summoned me, Heavenly Master. How can I serve you?

Jing:

- I didn't hire you for your intellect. So, shut up and use your
mouth for something useful.

Min Li hesitated. She hated the way Jing treated her, but she didn't dare
to argue with the supreme leader. Reluctantly, she kneeled next to the Jing
and unbuttoned his exquisite silk pants.
Jing:

- Good dog. Obey your master.

Having said this, Jing sighed as his young mistress gave him fellatio. If
it could only release his anger, but it was in vain. Jing wanted to punch the
bitch for doing it wrong, but he controlled himself. Instead, he took her
from behind and he felt relieved when he came. Now, he could send her
away while keeping his self-respect.
As he had finished, Jing threw Min's clothes to her and spoke:

- Wash up and make sure to look good for tomorrow's photo-
shoot. I don't want any more stuff-ups!

- Dismissed.

Min Li, who struggled to contain her tears, got dressed and rushed to
leave Jing's residence.
Jing got seated by his computer. He checked if the advanced AI that supervised the Chinese population had found any new enemies. It had. Jing
cursed at himself. Of course, there would be dissenters in a country with 1.4
billion inhabitants. The ancient emperors were wise, secluding themselves
in their forbidden cities. That way, they had never faced the opinions of regular citizens. Jing knew that he shouldn't look, but he couldn't help himself.
Knowing which enemies, the AI had identified, was his drug, and he could
not break the vicious addiction.
Jing's eyes got fixated on the file of Eileen Lu. Her file said that she was
a 28-year-old lawyer and civil rights activist. Eileen had recently got one of

his enemies, Ming Shebao, acquitted in the people's court of Xuwan. It was unbelievable that the courts in HIS country had acquitted one of his enemies, but it was an issue he needed to deal with. Jing stared at Eileen's photo for a long time.

Eileen's beauty captivated Jing, and he knew that he needed to own her. Yet, Jing's power wasn't absolute. While he could eliminate the enemies of the republic, he couldn't kidnap and rape people on his whim. The rest of his party would never allow it. But he would own Eileen one way or the other, and she would regret defying him. Filled with rage, Jing picked up his expensive jar of honey and threw it against the wall, splashing honey across the room.

Chapter 2: Another Win for Freedom, 5th of March 2021.

"**...A**nd because of the disclaimer regarding fictional content, Mary Sheng didn't break any laws when she drew a sad bear looking at an empty honey jar."

Eileen Lu finished her statement and she corrected her glasses. She wore the glasses as a fashion statement, and because she knew that the judge on the case, Feng Woo, liked goofy women. Eileen looked at Feng and gave him a pretence innocent-look, knowing that she had him in her back pocket.

Feng Woo cleared his throat and spoke.

- You raise some valid points, Miss Lu. I am willing to drop this case if Miss Sheng, apologises to Chairman Xi about the resemblance between the sad bear and our Supreme Leader.

"Please don't make a scene!" Eileen thought as she leaned over to her client and whispered in Mary Sheng's ear.

- Please take the plea bargain. I have done everything I can to save you.

Feng Woo:

- Don't whisper to your client. Everyone deserves to hear the advice you are giving your client.

Eileen:

- I am sorry for my insolence, Magistrate Woo. I merely recommended my client to accept your gracious offer.

Feng Woo:

- But, if that is the case, how can we be sure the client shows remorse for her thoughtlessness?

Mary Sheng interjected:

- Please, Magistrate Woo. I want nothing more than letting the Chinese people know how sorry I am.

Feng smirked at Mary and replied:

- Good. How fortunate we have a camera crew filming the proceedings

- Read these lines. We will record until you get it right. I want to see heartfelt remorse on the video. I don't want to see a woman who is lying to save her life. Can you do that?

Mary nodded, and one of Feng's aides handed Mary a note. Mary read the note a few times, and she started crying. Mary:

- I am ready to film.

clap clap
Feng clapped his hands and he taunted:

- Excellent. Get ready, team. Let's produce a new masterpiece.

An AV-crew entered the room and they rigged a video shoot. A few minutes later, Mary was ready to confess. Mary looked into the camera with her teary eyes and spoke:

- I want to say sorry to all the people of China who I offended with my talentless drawing. Being a true patriot, I cannot stop thinking about Chairman Xi and it influenced my drawing. The empty jar symbolises how poor China was, before our saviour lifted our people out of poverty. I am truly grateful for how merciful the court has been towards an old woman like I.

Feng:

- Cut!

- Such terrible acting. But I cannot back down on my word. Get out of here you wretched cow! Dismissed!

Eileen acted decisively and pulled Mary out of the room to avoid a confrontation. When they were outside of the courthouse Mary shouted at Eileen.

- You destroyed my legacy, Eileen. I should have stood strong and taken my unjust punishment. Instead, I looked like a snivelling coward, praising Jing Xi and this travesty of a court.

- I'd rather spend some time in prison, but you stopped me. Why?

Eileen:

- I saved your life. While the court sentence wouldn't have killed you, you would have had an accident within the next year. As is customary for people angering Jing Xi.

- Faking an apology was the only way to save you.

Mary Sheng calmed down and she covered her face with her hands. After a while she spoke:

- You're right, Eileen. Thank you for saving my life.

Eileen smiled and replied:

- That's my job. As your lawyer, I am here for you.

Mary:

- You were the only one. Of the millions that saw and liked my drawing on WeChat, you were the only one who protected me when things got tough.

Eileen:

- That is, unfortunately, human nature and the reason Chairman Xi can continue his tyranny.

- What are your plans now?

Mary:

- I'll go home to Xuwan. I'll delete my online presence and spend my last year's nursing my grandchildren.

Eileen:

- Best of luck to you. I'll come to visit you, Xuwan is beautiful in spring.

Mary:

- Don't worry about this old hag!

- Focus on yourself, Eileen. Find a rich handsome man, and raise a happy family.

Eileen didn't reply and Mary entered a cab that took her to the train station.

Eileen went home and she poured herself some herbal tea. She felt empty. While she had won in the sense that she had saved her client, she had destroyed Mary's sense of pride and bowed to the tyrant Jing Xi. Most of all she felt shame. Like everyone else, she loathed and feared the dictator. Yet, she did nothing and she instructed her clients to bow to the tyranny. Eileen wished that her time for bravery would come, but for now, she could only focus on her life and finding her prince charming!

Chapter 3: Royal Casino. 7th March 2021.

Jared Pond was pulling his hand through his long blonde hair while sipping his Espresso Martini. Jared's expensive brand name tuxedo was getting tight and he knew that he needed to go back to Australia for training and detox soon. It didn't cut it, to be an agent for the Royal Australian Kangaroo Intelligence (RAKI) while being unfit.

The lack of fitness came with the territory. Jared's greatest strengths lay in his sharp observation ability, and poker skills. His assignment here at Royal Casino in Monaco combined those strengths. While the poker playing was a way to pass the time, Jared also had a mission in Monaco. He needed to investigate if the leader of the Global Health Association (GHA), Theodore Ahmadi, took bribes from the Chinese government.

Jared got distracted from the poker when his latest fling, the Italian femme fatale Celeste Florentino tapped him on his back.

- Hi Jared, how nice to see you again. Are you winning at the tables today?

Jared:

- I think I just did.

Jared turned towards the others, gathered his chips, and spoke:

- Well played, gentlemen. I need to focus on the lady now.

Jared got up and smiled at Celeste:

- Would you like some Dom Perignon to celebrate the occasion?

Celeste smiled seductively at Jared and replied:

- Of course, there is not a better way to get a woman excited for the evening.

'I wish there was,' Jared thought to himself, but instead he replied:

- Come with me, Celeste.

Having said this, Jared put his hand on Celeste's back and he walked her to the bar. "Keep the change!" Jared said as he paid for the exquisite champagne with a 500-euro gambling marker.
Celeste:

- That's a very generous tip, Jared.

Jared:

- I can't bring money to the grave, and in my line of work, one never knows when the grave is due.

Celeste:

- What exactly do you do for work, Jared?

Jared:

- Shh, we are too early in our connection to ruin the mystique.

Hearing this, Celeste grabbed one of the strawberries that came with the champagne, and bit it seductively.

- I agree. You know how to behave yourself, Mr Pond.

Jared reflected over why Celeste addressed him by his last name, but he soon found a more pressing matter. His target, Theodore Ahmadi, entered the casino, and he got seated by a table occupied by a Chinese businessman.

Jared had seen the same procedure take place several times in the last week. Every day, Theodore got seated at a table and won a large sum from a Chinese man, who subsequently left the casino. Since it had happened five days in a row, it was not a coincidence.

Jared decided to observe the transaction while sitting at the same table, he handed Celeste his room key and spoke.

- I got to work, honey. Meet me at my room, 407, in one hour.
Keep the champagne cool and everything else hot.

Celeste:

- You can't treat me like that. I am not a prostitute!

Jared pretended to drop 1000 euros in chips and he replied:

- Oh, how clumsy of me. I just dropped a thousand Euros. They
are yours if you pick them up.

Jared looked at Celeste in disappointment as she got down on the floor and picked up the chips. She had failed both his tests, and he realised she wasn't the one for him. On the bright side, her body was luscious and she would keep him busy tonight. This wouldn't have happened if she had splashed the champagne in his face and taken off.

Jared walked over to Theodore's table where the Ethiopian had won 50,000 euros from the anonymous Chinese businessman who was getting ready to leave.

Jared approached Theodore and spoke:

- Do you mind if I join you?

Theodore:

- I was about to leave.

Jared:

- Don't be like that. You just arrived and luck is favouring you tonight.

While saying this, Jared glanced at the Chinese man who was rushing to get away from the table.
Theodore seemed hesitant, but at last, he decided to stay:

- Very well, Mr?

Jared:

- Pond. Jared Pond.

Theodore:

- Ahmadi, Theodore Ahmadi.
- I will play you, Mr Pond.

Jared:

- May the best man win.

Jared and Theodore played for a while until Jared started missing Celeste's warm body and decided to lure his Ethiopian adversary into a trap.
Theodore flustered when he realised he had lost 100,000 Euros.
Theodore:

- Fuck. Well played Mr Pond. I shouldn't have overextended my luck!

Jared smirked at Theodore and replied:

- I am sure money will drop down from the sky for you again. If not, you still have the 200,000 that you won from the other Chinese gentlemen. I bid thee farewell.

Jared got up, collected his chips, and bowed theatrically as he walked towards the cashier to deposit his winnings. After that, he walked up to room 407, for a steamy night with Celeste. She had failed his tests so far, and she was unlikely to win his heart. But with a body like hers, she had won his body for the night!

Chapter 4: Pierre Beaumont is Planning his Ascension. 10th March 2021.

The World Bank deputy director, Pierre Beaumont, was enjoying a sumptuous dinner at the 'Le Comer Paradise' restaurant in Hague. World Economic Forum was coming up in a few days, and Pierre had an urgent matter on hand. The world had cooled down, as the sun had entered a Global Solar Minimum which had lowered the average temperature by 0.2 degrees.

This caused Pierre a headache as he had planned to become the CEO of the World Bank through his active stance against climate change. This issue would become less important if the global temperatures were falling. However, Pierre had a solution to his predicament. Pierre had convinced the fool Martin Orchard, to murder Pierre's rival at the World Bank, Chakri Apinya. Pierre planned to blame the murder on the Buddhist leader Arhat Somchai. Because the world needed distractions so no-one asked about global warming!

Pierre stroke his balding head, and he studied CIA Agent James Winter who approached him. James was tall and muscular, with a perfect set of light brown hair and lively eyes. Compared to Pierre he looked like a Greek god. Pierre brushed off his complex, Pierre was wealthy and he had unmatched intellect. Particularly since the incident in Nepal, the previous year.

In Nepal, Pierre, James and a group of travellers had lost their way during a blizzard and found an ancient alien temple. In the temple, they had found alien technology that elevated their intellects and gave them impressive abilities. The monocle that Pierre often wore, contained this alien technology.

James got seated and Pierre whispered.

- We should not both wear the monocle at the same time. It looks too conspicuous.

James shrugged his shoulders and replied:

- Who cares? People are too busy staring at their phones, following the vain celebrity culture, to notice.

Pierre felt irritated by James' reply, but he didn't say anything. He considered taking off his monocle but he decided against it. Pierre was the vice director of the World Bank, soon to be director, and he couldn't give in to a lowly CIA agent. Pierre changed the topic.

- Our subsidiary, Xeng Fao Technologies, won the tender to maintain the new 'Eternal Safeguard" AI in China.

James:

- Perfect. Jing Xi is obsessed with using AI to control his population. If we control China's AI, we control the World.

Pierre:

- Exactly. We need a new crisis, by the way.

James:

- What's wrong with Climate Change?

Pierre:

- The sun has entered a Grand Solar Minimum, and Earth is getting colder.

James:

- That won't last forever. I am sure it will get hotter at some point.

Pierre:

- I'd rather not wait for that to happen.

James:

- So, what do you suggest? Should we start another war in the Middle East?

Pierre:

- Wars are a risky business. I don't want to destroy the world that I seek to dominate.

- Regardless, the World Bank cannot win a regular war. Our best hope is economic warfare.

James:

- How do you intend to conduct economic warfare?

Pierre:

- I am not sure, yet. But opportunities will arise, as they always do, when I am looking for them.

A waiter attended the table, and James ordered a Budweiser with his thick American accent. When the waiter had left, James turned towards Pierre and spoke:

- So, Pierre. Tell me about your plan for disposing of Chakri Apinya?

Pierre smiled. He didn't expect to need the assistance of the CIA on this matter, but It was always good to have a backup plan. For the next 20 minutes, Pierre hinted James about his plan, without revealing the exact details. While the CIA was a useful ally, Pierre wasn't foolish enough to trust them!

Chapter 5: The discovery of the Hei Bai Virus, 27th March 2021.

Chairman Jing Xi, was finishing his monthly column for the China Daily. He emailed the document to the editor, and he slammed his computer against the floor in frustration. He had hated writing the column about how he intended to improve his character traits in 2021 but it was part of the societal contract. One of his obligations as the chairman of the Columnist Party of China was to write an article that the people requested, once a month. Jing's promise for self-improvement was to stop importing expensive honey and instead ensure that China produced the best honey in the world.

To produce the best honey in the world, Jing had travelled to Elephant Hill in the Guilin region of China. The caves, vegetation, and climate of this location should create the perfect blend of honey. Jing closed his eyes and he envisioned how this perfect blend would taste.

Jing's secretary, Biyu Sang, interrupted him in his thoughts.

- Chairman Xi. Theodore Ahmadi from the Global Health Association will meet with you shortly.

Jing:

- Why is that dog coming? Why didn't you cancel the meeting?

Biyu:

- I couldn't cancel it as you told me about your Guilin trip yesterday, and Theodore was already on his way to China.

Jing:

- Very well. I forgive your incompetence. But keep making mistakes and it will cost you dearly.

Biyu:

- Thank you for having mercy on this dumb and useless woman.
You are the most gracious leader China has ever seen.

Biyu bowed, turned around and quickly left Jing's office. 'Pathetic woman. She fucked up, I forgave her, and yet she cried.' Jing thought.

Jing leaned back in his massage chair and he turned on some meditative music. Jing recalled that he was meant to discuss China's aid in alleviating an Ebola outbreak in central Africa. But this was of no concern to Jing, so instead, Theodore would have to accompany him during his pursuit to find for the perfect honey making location. The only way to make his lapdog obey him, was to treat him as such. Jing leaned back into his chair and fell asleep.

BIYU SANG

- Chairman Xi, Theodore Ahmadi has arrived.

Jing opened his eyes, Biyu was standing on the other side of the desk. She looked tense, as if she was anticipating that Jing would attack her. This didn't come to pass, Jing had experienced great dreams, envisioning a honey degustation while his concubine Min Li was massaging him. He couldn't be angry after such a pleasant dream. Jing Xi spoke

- Very well, let him in.

Theodore entered the room, and Jing struggled to hide his contempt for the scruffy African man, whom he would have to interact with for the next few hours. Jing had preferred to appoint a Chinese citizen to be the GHA director, but an African would have more credibility among Jing's western enemies. Theodore spoke:

> - Greetings Chairman Xi. Can I expect China's help to resolve the Ebola epidemic in Central Africa?

Jing:

> - Is this a real epidemic or are you merely trying to extort more money?

Theodore:

> - It is a real epidemic. I wouldn't bother you otherwise. You have been very generous to me and my country.

Jing:

> - Very well. I want you to get down on the floor, begging me for the money.

Theodore:

> - I cannot do that. I am the leader of an important global organisation. We are equals.

Hearing Theodore's objections, Jing lost his temper. He picked up a vase and he threw it at the floor next to Theodore. As the vase shattered, Jing roared:

> - You are nothing but my dog. I put you where you are and I can put you somewhere else. No-one will ever know what happened to you!

> - Now kneel and beg for my forgiveness.

Being a pathetic and corrupt lapdog, Theodore got down to the ground, kissed Jing's shoes and pleaded:

- Please forgive me, Heavenly Master Xi. Please have mercy on the poor souls in Central Africa who cannot develop enough, to deal with their local diseases.

Jing spat next Theodore and replied:

- Get up, you dog. You have swayed my heart. Speak to my ministers and the Chinese Empire will save your sorry continent, for now.

Theodore:

- Thank you, Master Xi. God bless your kindness and grace.

Jing:

- I care little for deities and other superstitions.

- But since you are here, you'll follow me on an important mission today.

Theodore:

- What do you need me to do, Chairman Xi?

Jing:

- You're coming with me to the caves near Elephant Hill. You can fill me in on your Ebola epidemic while we are in the car.

Jing picked up his phone, organised his car, and left his office, with Theodore as his obedient dog in tow.

JING WAS ENJOYING THE view from the Elephant Hill lookout. He would make sure to get photos of him and Theodore, that could accompany the official narrative. Jing cringed as the burst of photo flashes struck his face, and he had to pretend to smile and treat Theodore as his equal. In the past, the emperor of China had been revered like a god, yet Jing had to pretend to be equal to his African henchman.

"Don't get any ideas!" Jing whispered to Theodore, who looked away. After finishing the press conference, Jing and his entourage started walking to a nearby cave. The cave was perfect. Jing had never been to the cave where the Turkish Elvish Honey was made, but his intuition told him this place would do the job. As Jing and Theodore traversed deeper into the cave, Jing heard a cough echoing. This was followed by a male voice wheezing "Help me."

One of Jing's bodyguards, Chao Li, approached him and whispered into his ear:

- Chairman Xi. We found a very ill man. This place is not safe. We better get you back to safety.

Jing gave Chao a stern look and replied.

- I am the master of this country. The truth cannot be concealed from me. I want to see the man who is wheezing.

Chao:

- Understood. Put on this facemask and follow me.

Jing put on his facemask, turned towards Theodore and spoke:

- Come with me. As the leader for the Global Health Association, you can help with the diagnosis.

Theodore:

- But I don't have a facemask.

Jing:

- Well, that's a shame. Shouldn't the leader for the GHA always have one in his pocket? Pray to your gods that the disease is not infectious.

Jing didn't wait for Theodore's response. Instead, he ventured forth until he reached the source of the wheezing.

Jing stared in shock and awe at the sick man. The man had a layer of fungus covering his body and gave off the impression that he was covered in bark. The man's eyes were blood sprained and he smelled of faeces.

The diseased man got up on his feet and tried to approach Jing:

- Chairman Xi. You must help me. The pain is unbearable.

Jing didn't have the time to respond as a multitude of bullets ended the disease-stricken man's life. Jing turned around and gave Chao a disapproving look:

- Why did you shoot that man, Chao?

Chao:

- He was posing a threat to you, Heavenly Master.

Jing:

- Bloody fool. You could have knocked him out. We lost an excellent opportunity to examine this man for our biological weapons program.

- Anyways. Let's get out of here. Get our scientists to come here and examine the man and the cave. Leave no stone unturned.

Having said this, Jing left the cave. As his car drove him and Theodore back to the banquet hall, for a state dinner, Jing spoke:

- I hope you realise that nothing of this happened?

Theodore:

- As far as I am concerned, you took me to a beautiful lookout and then you shared your passion for honey-making with me. Nothing else happened.

Jing:

- We are on the same page. Keep being on the same page, so I don't have to close your book.

Having said this, Jing plugged in headphones to listen to meditative music and ignored Theodore for the rest of the drive.

Chapter 6: Jing finds out about his Hei Bai virus infection, 4th April 2021.

- I have some bad news and some good news.

Jing's personal doctor, The Chinese Minster for Health, Dr Song Bao, revealed.

Jing studied his doctor. As if it wasn't bad enough to be back in the polluted shithole Beijing, he now also had to face some bad news? Jing spoke:

- Tell me the good news first. Anything to lighten up my life in this dreary city!

Song:

- We found the cause of death for the man who died in the cave near Elephant Hill. We have isolated a sample of the virus. We have never seen anything like it!

Jing:

- Excellent. This will be invaluable to our future bioweapon research!
- What is the bad news?

Song:

- The blood samples we took from you and your entourage, show that you are all infected.

Hearing this, Jing sunk in his seat and despair overwhelmed him. He had seen the agony of the dying man in the cave, and this was not the way he wanted to go. But what if he was immune? Like the vast majority had been during the previous year's Coronavirus outbreak? Jing decided to hope for that outcome. If he was immune nothing would happen, and if he was infected, he would be gone. In that case, it didn't matter to him if he brought a lot of others with him to the afterlife.

Jing:

- Doctor Bao. Make sure to quarantine everyone that was in the Elephant Hill cave. Don't tell anyone else about this.

Song:

- Understood, Chairman Xi.

Jing:

- Has anyone gotten any symptoms from the virus yet?

Song:

- No, everyone is healthy so far.

Jing

- Good. Extract and prepare a large batch of the virus. We need to test it on our Uighur prisoners, to find out more about it.

- Dismissed, Doctor Bao.

As Song Bao left the room, Jing experienced mixed feelings of anticipation and worry. He worried that he would succumb to the terrible fate that befell the man in the cave. But at the same time, he felt excitement. With a bit of luck, he could weaponise this new virus and use it to destroy the Western economies once and for all.

Chapter 7: Jared Pond receives a new mission, 10th April 2021.

Jared Pond was finishing another gruelling fitness session at the HMAS Kuttabul navy base in Sydney. Since his return to Australia, a few weeks earlier, he had pushed himself to the limit every day. The results were starting to show. Yet again, Jared looked like an agent from the movies, rather than an alcoholic with a gambling addiction. Speaking of gambling, the commander of the base had forbidden Jared from playing poker, as his many wins caused a lot of tension among the men.

Jared felt surprised when his commander at RAKI, Greg Steel, approached him at the gym.

Greg:

- Hi Jared. I got a new mission for you.

Jared:

- Why are you telling me like this? Wouldn't a meeting at your office be more appropriate?

Greg:

- I am going to New York tomorrow morning, and you're coming with me.

Jared:

- What is this about?

Greg:

- There are rumours about the Chinese dictatorship conducting medical tests on their Uighur prisoners.

Jared:

- I am sorry, but I wouldn't be suitable for a mission in China. I am not Chinese, and I don't speak the language.

Greg:

- I know. That's why you are coming with me to New York. We tracked the person who posted the accusations against the Chinese government.

Jared:

- Was the source believable or was it another tin foil conspiracist?

Greg:

- That is your mission to find out. The woman who posted the article was Eileen Lu. She is a Chinese civil rights lawyer who is currently attending a UN civil rights conference in New York city.

Jared:

- I see. And what would my mission entail?

Greg:

- You do what you do best. Seduce her and get her to share her secrets with you. Only then can we know whether she is trustworthy or not.

Jared sighed:

- Hey Greg. Stop treating me like a man-whore, please.

Greg smirked:

- Isn't that how you have treated yourself for the last decade?

Jared:

- Fair call. At least tell me if she is a good sort.

Greg:

- I leave that for you to decide.

Having said this, Greg handed Jared a photo of Eileen. Jared studied the photo for a while. Eileen looked cute and quirky, but would she be the kind of woman that would fall for his charms? Jared pushed the thought aside. He had an obligation to use his talents to serve his country and save his fellow citizens. Whatever the Chinese dictatorship was planning, the world needed to know and prepare for the worst.
Jared:

- Very well, I'll come with you to New York. Hopefully, I can work my magic on this Eileen woman.

Greg:

- Excellent. See you tomorrow for the 9 AM flight to New York.

After saying this, Greg left the building and Jared prepared himself mentally for the upcoming mission. He stared at Eileen's picture even though he knew he shouldn't. He needed to stay calm and collected for the mission ahead of him, otherwise, things could end badly. Jared went home, showered, packed his bag, and went to sleep early to be ready for the next mission.

Chapter 8: Pond, Jared Pond. 12th April 2021.

Eileen Lu stared at her computer screen. There were no new emails, which was a relief. A lot of emails would be an indication that she had been exposed. It would be dangerous if people on the Internet, as well as the CPOC, knew she had spread leaked videos from the Uighur concentration camps. The world needed to know what was going on, but Eileen loved living too much for the Columnist Party of China to know she had exposed them. All governments hated when people exposed their crimes, but the CPOC hated it more than most governments.

Eileen looked at the asylum request she had written to the American government. She was certain they would grant her request because of her relative fame as a human rights advocate. But if she sought asylum in the USA, she would abandon her people and become a mouthpiece for American propaganda. Eileen didn't want to help the USA against her mother nation, she wanted to liberate the Chinese people from Jing's tyranny.

Eileen made up her mind. She threw her asylum application in the bin, and she prepared herself for today's seminary. Open dialogue and genuine discussion were the only ways to progress humankind and Eileen wanted to play her role. Eileen closed her laptop, put it in her bag and started walking towards the Downtown Conference Centre in New York.

As Eileen left her hotel, she noticed the man who observed her from across the road. He was athletic, had long blonde hair, and he looked like your run of the mill superhero from the movies. Eileen would have loved if he approached her in a cocktail bar, but having him stalk her at 8 AM was outright creepy. Had someone sent this man to hurt her? Eileen shook off the notion. The man didn't look like he a Columnist Party henchman, and besides, he stood out too much to be a suitable assassin.

Eileen stopped staring at the man, and she set out to walk her conference. She got to a pedestrian crossing, and the red light stressed her. Eileen was giving a presentation in the morning, and she would hate to be late. Worse yet, she couldn't shake off the feeling that people were following her.

Splash

Someone bumped Eileen from behind and splashed warm latte over her white blazer. 'Fucking hell, why today out of all days?' Eileen thought and turned around. What she saw petrified her. The blonde man, which she had noticed before, was the one who had bumped her.

Jared:

- I am so sorry, how clumsy of me!

Eileen shook her head and sneered at Jared:

- Clumsy? I saw how you were checking me out when I left the hotel. Is this how men try to connect with women in New York City?

Jared leaned in and whispered:

- I am sorry, Eileen. My name is Pond, Jared Pond, and I need to talk to you. It's important.

Eileen wouldn't have it and she replied:

- Okay, Mr Pond Jared Pond. I have to give an important presentation in one hour. And you ruined my blazer. Buzz off and book an appointment like everyone else.

The light turned green, Eileen slapped Jared, and she rushed to cross the street.

Eileen's rejection left Jared dumbfounded. Eileen's slap had stung but the rejection had stung more. Had he lost his touch with women after all these years, or was Eileen a special case? On the bright side, she had told him to book an appointment, so that was what he would do.

JARED POND WAS SIPPING an Espresso Martini in the upmarket cocktail bar, The Aviary NYC. His tailor-made tuxedo emphasized his great physique and sophisticated style.

"You cannot enter this establishment with those clothes. Please refer to our dress code, madam" Jared heard the doorman say this to some uncultured peasant. Jared looked in the direction of the entrance and he realised that the uncultured peasant was his appointment for the evening. Somehow, Eileen Lu thought it was suitable to enter an upmarket venue dressed in jeans, sneakers and a T-shirt with a cartoon character.

Jared ran towards the entrance and intervened:

- It's okay, Michael. Eileen is with me. Please let her in.

Michael the Doorman:

- Sorry, Mr Pond. I need to uphold the dress code of this establishment.

Jared:

- But don't you have any suitable attire for the lady in the coatroom?

Michael nodded and ran off. A minute later he returned with an expensive ladies' fur coat.

Michael:

- Please wear this, Ms Eileen.

Eileen shook her head, but she agreed to put on the fur coat, which had been there since the winter months.

Jared:

 - Can I get you a drink, Eileen? This place has a great selection of champagnes and cocktails.

Eileen:

 - I would like a peppermint tea. I won't be staying, and I don't drink when I need to work the next day. Thanks for offering Mr Pond Jared Pond.

Jared:

 - It's just Jared Pond.

Eileen:

 - Why didn't you say it like that before then?

Jared:

 - Never mind.

Jared walked up to the bar and he ordered two teapots with peppermint tea. He couldn't recall the last time he drank tea, but he had to be flexible and drink what the situation required.

As the waiter arrived with the tea, Jared poured tea for himself and Eileen. As Eileen sipped the tea, she spoke:

 - So, Mr Pond, who are you working for and what do you want?

Jared realised he had lost his touch and he decided to give an honest reply:

 - I am working for RAKI and I am investigating whether you are a credible source when it comes to the Uighur camps.

Eileen:

- Excuse me for not knowing every abbreviation in the spy community. RAKI?

Jared:

- Royal Australian Kangaroo Intelligence.

Eileen:

- For future reference, you should probably use the full name instead of the abbreviation.

Jared didn't comment on Eileen's statement. Although it was a bit hurtful that she didn't recognise the fame of his workplace, he had to focus on the mission.
Jared:

- So, the videos you uploaded. Who is the source and do you know what the Columnist Party injects prisoners with?

Eileen:

- I do trust the source but I won't reveal him to a spy. There is no reason for me to trust that the Australian government wouldn't sell him out to Jing Xi, as your spineless prime minister is licking Jing's boots. As for the injections I have no idea. But I doubt it is for the benefit of the prisoners.

Jared reflected over Eileen's statement. Eileen mistrusting Australia's prime minister Scurry Morrissett, also known as Scummo, proved that she was of sound character and a sane mind.
Jared:

- Very well. I think this is all for today. Let's keep in touch. While I cannot speak for our prime minister, I am an advocate for protecting the Chinese people against Jing's tyranny.

Eileen shook her head:

- I rather not keep in touch. I don't want the Columnist Party
to use my connections with an Australian spy to discredit me.
Thank you for the tea, Mr Pond.

Pow
Jared was about to reply, when a punch knocked him off his chair.
Seeing the stars, Jared recognised his opponent, Marcel Blanco, a drug
smuggler for the Colombian Juarez Cartel.
Marcel yelled at Jared:

- Puta de Madre. Why did you fuck my wife!

Jared reflected over Marcel's statement for a second. He didn't know
who Marcel's wife was, but presumably, the act of copulation was to satisfy
his own raging masculine needs.
Jared sprung to his feet and replied:

- I am sorry, but who is your wife?

Marcel screamed:

- You motherfucker! I'll kill you!

Having said this, Marcel swung a bottle after Jared.
Jared dodged the bottle, and then he kicked Marcel at the side of his
knee. This dropped Marcel to a crouching position. Jared picked up a chair
and swung it at the head of Marcel, knocking the Colombian unconscious.
Jared shouted at the unconscious Marcel:

- I still don't know who your wife is, Marcel!

After this, he corrected his bowtie and ran after Eileen. He caught up
with her at the elevator.
Jared:

- Sorry about that. How are you spending the rest of your night?

Eileen:

- As far away from you as possible!

Jared:

- I just saved your life. That man attacked us.

Eileen:

- He attacked you. I had nothing to do with it. You are nothing but trouble. Goodnight, Mr Pond.

As Jared was driven to police custody, he reflected over Eileen's words. Was he the greatest agent Australia had to offer, or was he a sex-addicted jerk who ended up in stupid fights? He couldn't answer that philosophical question, but he did know one thing. He had a terrible headache.

Chapter 9: What an Embarrassment, Jared! 14th April 2021.

Jared Pond was sitting on a Qantas flight back to Australia. His mission had been a failure. He hadn't managed to seduce Eileen, and he had got himself arrested due to the altercation in the cocktail bar.

Jared's boss, Greg Steel, who sat next to him in the business class of the flight, decided to discuss the matter. Greg:

- What a debacle, Jared. All this because you couldn't keep your dick in your pants!

Jared:

- Stop moralising. You were the one who sent me to seduce Eileen in the first place.

Greg:

- That didn't work out, did it?

- Instead, you got into a bar fight because of your latest indiscretions with that Celeste Florentino woman.

Jared:

- You should be thankful that I wasn't seriously injured.

Greg:

- Well, then I wouldn't have to call Scurry Morrissette and plead him to call Deidrick Dump to get you out of jail.

- We are a secret intelligence service. The secrecy part fails if I have to get you out of jail because of your stupid private fights.

Jared:

- I apologise, Greg.

Greg:

- Too little and too late. We will have to reconsider your position with RAKI.

Hearing this, came like a heavy burden on Jared's chest. Serving Australia was all he knew, and he didn't know what he would do with himself if he lost the job. He had no remaining family, he was unable to keep a long-term partner, and he would get restless without the danger of his job.
Jared:

- Please give me another chance, Greg. I live for this job.

Greg:

- I will discuss your employment with Scurry when we return to Australia. For now, don't discuss this debacle with anyone.

Jared sighed and sat silent for a while. He closed his eyes, and he saw the cute and quirky smile of Eileen Lu. He knew she was genuine and telling the truth and he couldn't get her out of his mind. Eileen's rejection of him was a testament of her integrity, and Jared needed her.
Jared:

- Eileen is telling the truth. Jing Xi is up to more villainy.

Greg shrugged his shoulders and replied:

- Oh really? What a shame you stuffed up your mission so we won't get the chance to verify it.

- We have a sixteen-hour flight ahead of us. Please be quiet. I am intending to get some sleep.

Having said this, Greg put on a set of noise-cancelling earphones and a blindfold to ignore Jared.

Jared sighed. What a terrible mission. He was about to lose his job, and worse yet, he had become obsessed with a woman who rejected him. Following Greg's example, Jared put on his noise-cancelling earphones, started a playlist with jazz music, and closed his eyes.

Chapter 10: Jing has a realisation about the Hei Bai virus. 20th April 2021.

Jing Xi was experiencing mixed feelings. As it turned out, none of the 50,000 Uyghurs that his men had infected with the virus had developed any symptoms. On the bright side, this meant his infection was unlikely to kill him.

Jing studied his latest blood test. The Hei Bai virus was still dormant in his body, but it seemed to not do anything to him. On the other hand, he hadn't developed antibodies to it either. What a bizarre virus.

Jing put his blood test aside, and he opened a bag of Brazil nuts. He hadn't eaten Brazil nuts for years, but it was good thing to have some variety in his diet. Jing picked up a handful of nuts and he started chewing on them, when his secretary, Biyu Sang, called him over the intercom.

- Chairman Xi. Vice-Chancellor Chi Wang requests that you come with him to the cabinet finance meeting.

Jing got irritated with Biyu. She needed to learn her place and not speak to him like that. Jing calmed down. He knew Biyu was stuck between a rock and a hard place as she couldn't reject the Vice Chancellor's commands. Thus, it was Chi Wang that he needed to put into place! Jing put away the nuts and replied.

- Tell him that I am on my way.

Having said this, Jing picked up a flower vase and chucked it into the wall. On his way to the meeting, he spoke to Biyu:

- Biyu, you better clean up the vase you made me break. Don't anger me any more today!

JING LISTENED TO CHANCELLOR Chi Wang who described how the previous year's Coronavirus outbreak had benefitted the Chinese dictatorship. The crisis had been a stroke of genius. Shortly after the virus had struck China. Jing and his comrades had found out the truth, that the virus was extremely contagious but not very virulent. By concealing this fact, Jing and his politburo had declared that China had conquered the epidemic. They had quadrupled their wealth through trading on the international markets, which had collapsed due to unfounded fears.

But the Coronavirus outbreak was over, and the world would be sceptical if a similar virus were to arise. Jing needed a new plan to enrichen himself and weaken his enemies.

Chi Wang:

- So, by selling our US treasury bonds on the 23rd of March 2020 and buying shares at the same time, we doubled our wealth.

Suddenly, Jing felt sick. Had anyone in the politburo poisoned him? He realised that he hadn't touched any of the food or beverage in the meeting room. Jing coughed violently and got up.

Chi Wang:

- Chairman Xi. Are you okay? Should I call our doctors?

Jing shook his head, and he exited the room. "I need to get to my office and contact Dr Song Bao," He thought. This was easier said than done. Jing was struggling to walk upright and the room became blurry. On top of that, his skin had a burning itch.

"Where is Biyu?" Jing thought, and he soon found his answer as he stumbled over Biyu in his office. Biyu stared at Jing in terror:

- Chairman Xi. What is going on?

Jing:

- Biyu? What the fuck are you doing in my office, you stupid cow? Call Dr Song Bao and tell him to get here immediately.

Biyu:

- But Dr Bao is not in Beijing today. Can I get someone else?

Jing:

- No! It has to be Dr Bao. Call him and get him to come here. Send a helicopter to his location and pick him up. Now leave!

Biyu did as Jing instructed and she rushed out of the room. "The bastards have poisoned me. I need to purge!" Jing thought and he crawled to the rubbish bin, put his fingers in his throat, and purged. After that, he passed out.

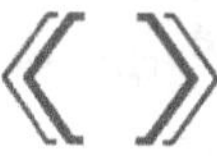

JING XI WOKE UP IN his private residence. Dr Bao and Jing's wife Lan Peng stood by his side. Lan sighed of relief:

- Oh, thank god you are awake. Dr Bao and I have been so worried about you.

Jing processed Lan's statement. He knew it was a lie. His wife didn't give a shit about him, and he was certain she had an affair with Chi Wang. Jing had been too busy scheming against the world and copulating with the beautiful Min Li, to verify the suspicion, but it was on his 'to-do' list.
Jing:

- Don't waste our time with this charade, Lan. Please leave the room. I need to speak to Dr Song Bao.

Lan Peng got up, and she left the room without saying a word. As she left the room, Jing turned towards Dr Song Bao and spoke:

- So, what happened to me? Did someone poison me?

Dr Bao shook his head and replied:

- I am afraid your Hei Bai virus infection has activated at last. We might need to prepare for the worst. I have brought opioids to alleviate your pain.

Jing shook his head:

- I don't need to ease any pain. I am a fighter and I won't go down without a fight.

Dr Bao:

- As you wish, Chairman Xi. I will be nearby if you change your mind.

Jing:

- Dr Bao. Do you know if anyone else from the group has fallen ill yet?

Dr Bao:

- Not as far as I know. But I will find out for you.
- We don't have a cure against this virus, so what do you want me to do?

Jing:

- Stay in the background for now. I need to feel this virus myself. Only then can I understand it and learn from it.

Dr Bao:

- Understood. Just press the emergency button, and I will come.
Best of luck, Chairman Xi.

As Dr Bao left the room, Jing started writhing in pain. His skin felt like he was on fire and he had to use his iron will to not scratch himself. He pulled himself together and he pulled off his shirt. Jing made his way to a mirror. He stared in horror as bark like streaks were spreading across his body. "I have to come up with something or I will die," Jing concluded.

Jing wouldn't call his doctor. The fool had suggested opioids to reduce the pain, but that wouldn't do anything against the symptoms. "Something I ate must have triggered the virus!" Jing thought. Could it be the Brazil Nuts? Jing decided to try an extreme measure to get out of his predicament. He would need to cleanse his body from toxins through sweating and shitting it all out. If he was wrong, he would die, but at least he would have died as a fighter. Jing pressed the emergency button and Song Bao rushed in.
Jing:

- Dr Bao. Bring me laxatives and ghost chilli at once.

Dr Bao stared at Jing's skin rash that was growing as he watched it and he protested against the order:

- Are you insane? You cannot put your body under more stress.
It will kill you.

Jing:

- So would your bloody opium. The white devils used opium against us during the 19th century. I will never succumb to such foreign influences. Now, do as I request. You might be my personal doctor, and the health minister, but I am the Chairman of CPOC!

Dr Bao:

- Understood, Heavenly Master.

Having said this, Song bowed and ran away to procure the supplies.

Dr Bao came back ten minutes later, and he handed Jing the laxatives and the ghost chilli. To his amazement, Jing skolled the bottle of laxatives and ate several of the super-strong chillies.

Jing:

- Please leave, I doubt the coming hours will be pleasant.

Dr Bao did as Jing instructed and he hurried to leave Jing's private quarters. Jing rushed to the bathroom and braced himself for several unpleasant hours.

A FEW HOURS LATER, Jing emerged from the bathroom. He was severely dehydrated and covered in sickly stinking sweat. But it was worth it. The skin rash had reversed and it no longer pained him much. He pressed a button and Song Bao entered the room.

Dr Bao stared at Jing. Jing was pale, dressed in his underwear, and a thick layer of rancid sickly sweat covered his body. Jing smiled and spoke:

- I did it. I beat the Hei Bai virus. I would have died if I followed your advice.

Dr Bao:

- I don't understand. How could laxatives and chilli reverse your skin condition?

Jing:

- I thought about my day. The only thing I did differently today was that I ate a handful of Brazil nuts. Brazil nuts have a very high selenium content. Thus, selenium must be what is activating the Hei Bai virus. So, I drank heaps of laxatives and I ate a lot of chillies to excrete the selenium. It was hell, but at least it saved my life.

Dr Bao:

- This is amazing, Chairman Xi.

Jing:

- Yes. Get some medical staff here. I need a saline drip to recover. Also, send a large shipment of Brazil nuts to the Lop County concentration camps. We need to find out whether selenium is what triggers the virus.

Dr Bao:

- Understood, Chairman Xi. I will do your bidding.

After saying this, Dr Bao left the room while a medical team rushed in to attach Jing to a saline drip. Realising that he needed to recuperate, Jing didn't leave the bed for several days.

Chapter 11: Eileen receives a terrifying video. 1st of May 2021.

Eileen Lu was back in her home in Shanghai. She felt anxious knowing that Jing's AI monitored her. Fortunately, she had found a way to secure her laptop from government interference. At least she hoped the government couldn't check her computer.

Eileen opened her email application. There was a message from Ming Shebao, a human rights activist, she had defended in a recent court case. Ming's emails annoyed her. He was putting her at risk by sending her information. Knowing too much was dangerous, and although Eileen wanted to oppose the dictatorship, she also wanted to live.

Eileen couldn't contain her curiosity and she opened the video. It was terrifying. In the video, a dozen half-naked prisoners were screaming in agonizing pain. A bark-like rash was growing on their backs and spreading rapidly. At the end of the video clip, guards in hazmat suits came in and burned the prisoners alive with flamethrowers.

Eileen closed the video. She didn't know what to believe. The video didn't make sense and it was very likely to be fake. But why would Ming Shebao send her fake video? Perhaps Ming Shebao had swapped sides, and the Columnist Party wanted to discredit her movement. If she released a video that was later proven to be false, the Chinese dictatorship would use this as an argument against the civil rights movement.

Eileen closed Ming's email, and she was about to head out when another email hit her mailbox. It was from Jared Pond, the goofy Australian spy, who had failed to seduce her. What did he want? Eileen opened the email. It read:

"Hi, Eileen. I am visiting Shanghai at the moment. I recently resigned from RAKI, so you don't need to worry about what I do for work anymore. I bought some tickets for Moulin Rouge playing at the Pearl tomorrow night. Would you like to accompany me?"

Eileen shook her head. She couldn't think of a worse way to spend her time than going on a date with the boofhead that had hassled her twice in New York. The first time they met, he had spilled coffee on her, and during their second meeting he got into a fight and ended up in jail. What a loser!

But then an idea struck Eileen. What if she could give Jared a USB memory with the video Ming had sent her, and ask Jared to post the video online? If the video was authentic, it was crucial that the world found out. If the video was fake, Jared would look like an idiot and Eileen's movement would not be discredited. Eileen sent the following reply:

"I would love to see the Moulin Rouge with you tomorrow. See you at the Pearl at 6 PM. Cheers Eileen."

Having sent her reply, Eileen put her phone in her handbag and she went to her workplace.

Chapter 12: Jing Xi Gets the Results from the Hei Bai Virus Testing. 2nd May 2021.

Jing Xi was sitting in his office when his health minister Dr Song Bao and Jing's security advisor Tzi Cheng entered his office. Dr Bao approached Jing, handed him a document and spoke:

- Chairman Xi. We have conducted the requested tests on the Uighurs at the Lop County Uighur concentration camp.

Jing:

- A bit slower than I had anticipated, but never mind. I needed to recuperate from my illness.

- What did you find?

Dr Bao:

- We found out that your hypothesis was correct. Selenium does trigger the virus.

Jing:

- Lucky, I didn't give in to my weakness and took the morphine. What exactly did you find?

Dr Bao:

- The virus becomes active and the carrier contagious at a daily intake of 100 micrograms of selenium. At 300 micrograms, serious symptoms appear. That's when a burning skin rash starts covering the back of the carrier. At a 500-micrograms intake of selenium, a person's entire body is covered by the skin rash. In this instance, the individual experiences prolonged excruciating pain, which often kills the carrier.

Jing:

- Excellent. How much selenium is there in a Brazil nut?

Dr Bao:

- About 80 micrograms, Heavenly Master.

Jing:

- So, with this virus: Two nuts would make someone contagious; four nuts would make someone sick, and six nuts would kill someone.

Dr Bao:

- Well, individual tolerances to the virus can differ, but on average yes.

Jing thought back on his virus episode. He tried to recall how many nuts he had eaten before the cabinet meeting. He thought the number was three, which meant that his 'cure' consisting of laxatives and chillies had not affected his outcome. Jing didn't want to admit that luck had saved his life, and instead, he asked:

- So, what about antibodies towards the virus. Can someone build tolerance through gradually increasing the selenium intake?

Dr Bao:

- Survivors do get antibodies while the virus remains dormant in the body. We haven't tested your hypothesis about increased tolerance towards the virus yet, Chairman Xi.

Jing:

- Well, then you should. We must learn about the virus before using it against our enemies. And see if you can figure out a way to make people eat selenium. I doubt we can convince our enemies to eat heaps of Brazil nuts while we release the virus.

Dr Bao:

- Understood, Heavenly Master.

Jing:

- Dismissed, Dr Bao.

Hearing this, Dr Song Bao bowed to Jing and left the room. Jing turned towards Tzi Cheng.

- What do you have to report, Security Advisor Cheng?

Tzi Cheng:

- Someone leaked a video of our experiments to our enemy, Ming Shebao.

Jing:

- Really? I hope you have Ming Shebao in custody.

Tzi Cheng:

- Yes. We have him in a secure facility nearby.

Jing:

- Excellent. I am coming with you. We need to find out who he has told about this!

Tzi Cheng:

- You don't need to come, Chairman Xi.
- We can torture him and find out what he knows.

Jing smirked and replied:

- I know. But when it comes to Ming Shebao, I want to see him die.

Tzi Cheng:

- As you wish, Chairman Xi. I'll take you to our Ministry of State Security prison now.

After saying this, Jing and Tzi Cheng left the room. They travelled to the prison where Jing's infamous secret police kept and tortured their prisoners.

A WHILE LATER, JING and Tzi Cheng arrived at the interrogation room where they kept Ming Shebao. Jing studied Ming Shebao through a one-sided mirror. Ming Shebao was battered and bruised from the interrogation but worst was yet to come for him. Jing smiled. It would be a pure delight to watch his enemy die from the Hei Bai virus.

Jing looked at Tzi Cheng and said:

- Stay here, Tzi Cheng. Watch what happens if I give him these.

Jing grabbed a bag of Brazil nuts and entered the interrogation room where Ming Shebao was chained to a chair. Jing's appearance shocked Ming and he exclaimed.

- Chairman Jing Xi! I would never believe you would come here yourself. Have you come to torture me?

Jing scoffed:

- Don't be silly. I have others to do that for me. I just wanted to talk to my long-term critic. I would be a fool if I didn't take the opportunity to learn from my enemies.

Ming Shebao:

- And what do I gain from allowing you to learn from me?

Jing:

- Ah, you're looking after yourself. I like it. But before we discuss business, let's chat a bit first, shall we? I brought some beer and some nuts.

Ming Shebao looked sceptically at Jing and replied:

- What is going on? First, you sent your men to torture me, and now you are offering me beer and nuts.

Jing:

- The torture wasn't my intention. Some of my men are overzealous and take their own initiatives. It's difficult to govern a nation of 1.4 billion souls after all.

Jing took one of the nuts and he chewed it slowly. According to Dr Bao, he would be infectious after two nuts. After that, he would watch as the starving Ming Shebao ate the remaining nuts, and the Hei Bai virus took hold of his body.

Jing clapped his hands and shouted out:

- Tzi Cheng, bring in a TV. We are going to watch Beijing against Shanghai in the Chinese Super League.

Ming Shebao stared at Jing in surprise as Tzi Cheng rolled in a TV on a stand and then left the room.

Jing:

- Don't look so surprised, Ming. What better way to bridge our differences than watching soccer together? I like Beijing and you like Shanghai. Yet we are both linked together by our love for the sport.

Ming Shebao:

- Is this your metaphor for how we both love China despite our political differences?

Jing:

- Exactly. But for now, just eat the nuts and drink the beer. You must be starving.

Having said this, Jing picked up his second nut and smirked. He would feel an itch but Ming Shebao would feel like he was being burnt alive.

Ming Shebao relaxed and he started eating the nuts and drinking his beer.

Jing smirked:

- Don't be shy. Have the rest of the nuts. I am saving myself for dinner.

Jing smiled as Ming devoured the remaining nuts, and then the two men sat silent for a while watching the game. In the halftime break, Jing turned to Ming, whose infection was taking hold of him:

- I know that you filmed our Lop County concentration camp. You must have been wondering what happened to those prisoners. You are about to experience it firsthand.

Ming:

- What? Have you poisoned me? How? We are eating the same nuts and drinking the same beer.

Jing:

- Not poisoned. Infected. I am carrying the same virus those prisoners had. The selenium in those nuts activates the virus. The two nuts I ate is enough to make me contagious. Six nuts plus the virus is enough to kill a man. You ate a dozen nuts. Let's just say you are in a for a world of pain. Muahaha.

Ming didn't reply. The pain was overwhelming him and he collapsed to the floor together with the chair he was chained to.
Ming:

- Ahh! It is so painful. Please make it stop. I'll do anything

Jing:

- That's what I want to hear. Who did you show the video from the Lop County camp? Why hasn't anyone tried uploading it on our Internet?

Ming:

- It's already on the Internet. I will expose your crimes against humanity, Jing.

Jing:

- No, it's not. Our AI would have found it.

- The most interesting part about the Hei Bai virus is that when the rash reaches its peak it feels like you are being burned alive. That's why our prisoners didn't even react when our guards with flamethrowers set them alight. As a matter of fact, being burnt alive was preferable to suffering the consequences of the virus.

Ming squirmed in pain on the floor. The pain was too much for him and he passed in and out of consciousness. Ming pleaded:

- Please make it stop. I'll do anything.

Jing clapped his hands and Tzi Cheng entered the room. Jing:

- Our prisoner is ready to confess his crimes. Shoot him and end his life on my signal.

Tzi Cheng nodded and he aimed his pistol towards Ming. Jing turned towards Ming:

- Give me a name and your pain will be over.

Ming wheezed:

- Eileen... Eileen Lu.

Tzi Cheng looked at Jing:

- Chairman Xi?

Jing shook his head:

- Don't waste a bullet, Tzi. This man is a goner. We have a job to do. Find someone to abduct Eileen Lu for me.

Tzi Cheng looked at Jing in bemusement:

- Abduct? You are the leader of China. Your word is the law. You can have the police arrest her.

Jing:

- No. Arresting her would complicate what I have in mind for her. Abducting her would suit me better. Muahaha.

Having said this, Jing left the room where Ming was dying an excruciating death. Jing smiled to himself. He couldn't wait to first have his way with Eileen and then send her off the same way Ming Shebao died!

Chapter 13: Pierre Beaumont books a meeting with Jing Xi. 3rd May 2021.

Pierre Beaumont was studying the discussion between Jing Xi and Dr Song Bao, while he was sitting at his office in Switzerland. Having one of his proxy companies, Xeng Fao Technologies, which had won the contract to creating the 'Eternal Safeguard" AI that supervised China was valuable, as it gave Pierre a backdoor into the system. This allowed him to spy on important Chinese government meetings.

From listening to Jing, Pierre knew he had struck gold. If he could acquire a controllable virus, he would rule the world. And once he ruled the world, he would develop the cure, to bereave Jing Xi of his weapon. But first, he needed to retrieve the virus, and Pierre had an idea. It was a risky idea, but fortune favoured the bold. He needed to meet with Jing Xi so he could get hold of the virus and infect himself with the dormant but otherwise harmless virus, as it could only trigger its toxins when he has ingested selenium. If he had the virus in his bloodstream, he could extract it from his own blood. Then he would use the enhanced intelligence bestowed upon him by the Zetan monocle, to figure out how to use the virus.

Pierre picked up his phone and called Jing's office. Biyu Sang responded. Pierre felt irritated that he didn't have Jing's direct number. This was because Pierre hadn't been the CEO of the World Bank when they last met.

Pierre spoke:

- Hello. This is Pierre Beaumont from the World Bank. I need to speak to Chairman Jing Xi.

Biyu Sang:

- Chairman Xi is not in his office. Call back tomorrow.

Pierre frowned. He was one of the most influential men in the world and when he called someone, he expected them to receive his call. Pierre reprimanded Biyu:

- The CEO of the World Bank does not call back tomorrow. You better call your boss straight away to avoid dire consequences for your well-being.

Biyu:

- Okay. Please hold the line.

Biyu sighed. Pierre Beaumont sounded important so ignoring him was dangerous. But if he turned out to be unimportant, Jing would scold her for disturbing him! Biyu called Jing's private phone, and he sounded happier than usual.
Jing:

- Hi Biyu. What's on your mind?

Biyu:

- Pierre Beaumont from the World Bank called. He insisted on speaking with you straight away.

Jing:

- Very well. Forward his call to me.

The situation puzzled Jing. What could the French-speaking faggot Pierre Beaumont want? And who did he think he was, demanding to speak to Jing straight away? Jing was the most powerful man on the planet and Pierre was a money-grubbing poof. The phone connected and Pierre spoke:

- Chairman Xi. We need to meet tomorrow. My private jet will land at Beijing airport at 9 AM. I expect an appropriate reception.

Jing was about to scream obscenities and smash his phone but he stopped himself. Although Pierre was a rude peasant, and not as powerful as Jing, he was too powerful to mistreat. Instead, Jing replied:

- I am busy. But I expect to see you at the World Economic Forum in two weeks.

Pierre:

- Oh, that's a shame. I wanted to discuss the bank account of 'The Honey Dragon Inc.' at Credit Suisse. The Swiss Government is about to absorb its $5 billion balance.

Jing:

- You stay away from my money!

Pierre:

- Oh, so it is your money? We better meet up tomorrow and discuss the matter. I'll be landing at 9 AM at Beijing International Airport. Make sure I am well-received.

After saying this, Pierre hung up the phone. Jing, who was about to leave the secret prison was furious. Jing turned to Tzi Cheng and exclaimed.

- Give me your pistol. I need to blow off some steam.

Tzi handed Jing his pistol, and Jing rushed into the cell where Ming Shebao was dying from the Hei Bai virus.
Jing:

- Fuck you, Dog!

After screaming this, he shot Ming Shebao with 15 bullets emptying the magazine of the gun!

Chapter 14: A Disrupted Date. 3rd May 2021.

Eileen Lu was studying herself in one of the grand mirrors at the Pearl in Shanghai. She had agreed to meet up with Jared Pond. To wrap him around her finger, she had dressed according to his preferences. The velvet red ballroom dress made Eileen stand out like a beacon in the crowd. Eileen smiled. Eileen liked to look beautiful, but she preferred when people measured her on her intellectual attributes.

Eileen felt bemused that she had agreed to meet with Jared. He was a buffoon, who believed himself to be every woman's dream. But she needed an ally. She needed someone who could post the video from the Uighur concentration camps online, without drawing attention to her. Jared was that someone.

Eileen saw Jared approaching. He was casually dressed, like she had been when they met at the cocktail bar in New York. Eileen smiled. It seemed like they had second-guessed each other.

Eileen walked up to Jared and seduced:

- Hi Jared. You look great today. Are you having a casual evening?

Jared:

- Well. I didn't know you'd look so stunning today. I thought we could meet up as friends.

Eileen teased:

- So, are friends what we are?

Jared:

- Well, unless starstruck lovers is an option?

Eileen:

- It might be.

- Let's head to the bar. I would love you to educate me on cocktails and champagnes!

Jared:

- People have told me that I am a great teacher.

Eileen:

- Of that, I am certain

After saying this, Eileen took Jared's hand as she allowed him to lead her to the bar section of the venue.

They got seated at a table, and the waiter delivered their drinks, a mojito for Eileen and a whisky sour for Jared. Eileen smiled at Jared:

- So, what brings you to Shanghai, Jared?

Jared:

- Isn't the performance and your lovely company good enough reasons?

Eileen:

- Yes. But you came here yesterday. Before I had accepted to meet you.

Jared:

- Yesterday, I was in Macao skimming some rich Chinese businessmen in poker.

- Would you like another drink?

Eileen:

- Yeah, I'll have what you are having.

Jared:

- Excellent choice, Eileen.

As Jared walked up to the bar, Eileen felt tipsy. She wasn't a big drinker, so the cocktail had got her gears moving. She needed to get Jared away from the crowds so she could experience him on her own. Eileen felt silly. Until now she hadn't even liked Jared, and yet she felt attracted to him? Perhaps it was a physical need she needed to fulfil, to get away from all the stress and paranoia the concentration camp video had caused her.

Jared returned with their cocktails and they got involved in some more idle chatter until a bell rang.

Jared:

- The show is about to begin.

Eileen was getting intoxicated and she slurred:

- How about we head straight to your hotel room?

Jared smiled and teased:

- Business or pleasure?

Eileen:

- I need to show you something. After that, I am very much up for pleasure.

Jared:

- Very well. Come with me, and I'll teach you how to spend a full night of passion.

EILEEN WAS RIDING JARED with wild enthusiasm when she realised that she hadn't told him about the virus testing video. She paused for a second. She hadn't had sex since the separation from her fiancée a year earlier. Part of her would love to have that fourth consecutive orgasm, but she needed to focus on her duty to her country.

Jared smiled at Eileen and teased:

- Are you getting tired already? It's only been twenty minutes.

Eileen was collecting herself from the exhilarating experience. She was about to reply when the door opened and two shady Chinese men ran in.

One of the men rushed to Eileen and punched her in the gut, knocking her to the ground. The combination of shock, physical trauma and alcohol knocked Eileen out.

"I should not have taken all that Viagra. This is awkward." Jared thought.

Jared got up from the bed. He wore no clothes, and he was sporting an erection. This was his first fight for survival while being naked, and hopefully, there wouldn't be many too follow.

One of the attackers kicked Jared on the balls and was amazed as Jared hardly flinched. Being a prominent womanizer, Jared had developed a tolerance to ball-busting kicks, and it would take more to put him down. Jared responded in kind, and the first attacker was gasping for air on the ground, with his prospect of future fatherhood diminished.

"Don't come uninvited!" Jared exclaimed. Jared rushed over to the second attacker, punched him in the face, and then dropped a TV over him. After this, Jared ran back to the first attacker and knocked him out with a knee to the face.

Jared put on his pants, and he checked on Eileen.

Eileen:

- Uh. What happened?

Jared:

- Some intruders decided to interrupt our lovely evening. But we shouldn't let them. Let's head over to your place and continue from where we were.

Eileen:

- So, you want to have more sex after men attacked us?

Jared:

- What better way to relieve stress?

Eileen:

- Okay. I have booked a cab to my place.
- Let's get out of here.

Having said this, Eileen and Jared hurried to grab their stuff, and they left the room before their attackers woke up.

THE NEXT MORNING, EILEEN woke up with a terrible headache. She had drunk too much alcohol and getting assaulted by assassins didn't help. Furthermore, her marathon session with the tireless Jared Pond had dehydrated her. She made her way to the kettle and boiled some tea. She diluted the hot tea with tap water so she could drink it quickly. After a few cups, she remembered the USB with the video. She tapped Jared on the shoulder and he woke up with a smile:

- Good morning, sunshine. Are you ready for another session?

Eileen shook her head and replied:

- As lovely as that would be, we agreed on business and pleasure. And we haven't dealt with the business part yet.

Jared sighed:

- I see. What do you want to discuss?

Eileen opened her laptop and showed Jared the video from the Uighur concentration camp. Jared looked at the video sceptically for a while and replied:

- Where did you get this video from?

Eileen:

- One of my former clients sent it to me. I cannot disclose who it was.

Jared:

- Was it Ming Shebao?

Eileen gave Jared a worried look and held her tongue.
Jared:

- Don't worry, Eileen. I am a former spy. This is what I do.

- Ming Shebao doesn't have the best reputation overseas, due to making erroneous claims in the past. But I am sure you know about this already?

Eileen nodded.
Jared:

- So, I take it you want me to publish these claims? In that case, I would need to verify them with RAKI first.

Eileen:

- But didn't you quit?

Jared:

- Yes, but this video is explosive stuff. I need to verify it before I release it on the Internet. I am not a conspiracy theorist that releases anything I get hold of.

Eileen:

- I understand. Don't take too long. People are suffering and we cannot know what more crimes Jing Xi is planning against humanity.

Jared:

- Agreed.

- Did you recognise the men that attacked us last night? I think you were the one who got us in trouble this time!

Eileen shook her head and replied:

- Well, they didn't come here, so it must have been you.

Jared:

- Just my luck. We should leave China to be safe.

Eileen shook her head and replied:

- You should leave, but I am not going anywhere. I need to congregate with our civil liberties movement and celebrate the second Qingming festival in Xuwan.

Jared:

- Isn't the Qingming festival in April?

Eileen:

- You know a lot about China, Jared.

- The second Qingming festival is not a real event. We are gathering to honour the ones who fell in the last stand against tyranny in 1989. We are not allowed to commemorate those heroes, so we created the second Qingming festival instead.

Jared:

- Very well. I better head back to Australia. It would be lovely if you decided to visit me there, after your celebration.

Eileen felt sorrow gripping her mind. She would love to move to Australia and leave this mess behind her. But she couldn't let Jing Xi go unchecked. If she did, his tyranny would spread, and he would subjugate the whole world. Eileen:

- Thank you, Jared. I hope to see you soon. Make sure to spread my video.

Jared nodded, kissed Eileen goodbye, took a taxi to the airport and boarded the next flight back to Australia.

Chapter 15: A Frosty Meeting. 4th May 2021.

Pierre Beaumont exited his limousine outside the presidential palace of China. He wasn't particularly impressed. While China had experienced impressive economic development, it was still a polluted shithole. Nothing compared to Switzerland, which had great cities and beautiful mountains just a short drive away!

Pierre reminded himself of his plan. He had added a grain of selenium hydride to a jar of Elvish honey. It was a dangerous plan. Pierre needed to get Jing Xi to ingest enough selenium to become infectious, but not so much so he got the symptoms. Making Jing eat the right amount of selenium added honey to get the right level was almost impossible. Pierre sighed. He would have to settle for making Jing eat Brazil nuts. It was a risky and conspicuous plan, but it was the only way to get the dosage right.

Pierre reached the reception area of the presidential palace, where an attendant told him to stay and wait. Pierre looked at his luxurious Swiss watch. He would get upset if Jing kept him waiting. Pierre was certain Jing would keep him waiting. They didn't like each other, and for now, Jing was the more powerful of the two, although that was about to change. Pierre smiled when he thought about how he would reform the world and enrichen himself.

JING XI FELT JITTERY and frustrated. The men he had sent to kidnap Eileen Lu, had failed miserably and had ended up in the hospital. Eileen's contact, the Australian agent Jared Pond, had evaded the country, no doubt carrying a copy of the virus testing video. Jing thought of his next step. It would be easy for him to have Eileen arrested and killed, but he desired her body, which he couldn't have if she was officially arrested. Jing had evil thoughts about Eileen. Raping her and then letting the Hei Bai virus kill her would be a great pleasure. But first, he needed to deal with Jared Pond. Jing walked over to Tzi Cheng and whispered:

- Contact our Australian friends and make sure Jared Pond doesn't release the virus testing video on the Internet.

Tzi Cheng nodded and rushed away to make the arrangements. One of the palace attendants approached Jing:

- Chairman Xi. Pierre Beaumont has arrived and he is waiting for you in the sun dragon room.

Jing:

- Good. I'll be there shortly.

Jing reflected over his options. On the one hand, he wanted Pierre to wait for him. Pierre was a lowly banker, and as such he should wait for the emperor. But on the other hand, Jing had nothing else to do, so wasting his own time to make Pierre wait for him was irrational. Jing sighed and realised that he was better off meeting Pierre straight away. That way he would get this issue dealt with.

PIERRE FAKED A SMILE as Jing greeted him. This would be difficult, but he had to overcome the difficulties.

Pierre:

- Thank you for seeing me on such a short notice, Chairman Xi.

Jing:

- Extraordinary circumstances require extraordinary measures. How can I resolve this problem with my Credit Suisse account?

Pierre:

- As the CEO of the World Bank, I can call them and make them reactivate the account.

- But first, let's exchange gifts. I brought you this jar of honey and these Brazil nuts. I have heard that nuts dipped in honey is a delicacy.

Having said this, Pierre froze for a second. What if the combination of the contaminated honey and the brazil nuts would cause a full virus outbreak in Jing's body? Pierre shook off the thought, he was here now, and he could only roll with it.

Jing looked at Pierre for a while and then he dipped one of the brazil nuts in the honey and smiled:

- You are right, Pierre. Nuts and honey are a great combination.

Pierre:

- Yes of course. Let's have one more but without the honey flavour. They have a great and unique flavour, don't they?

Jing picked up another nut, hesitated for a while, ate the nut, and replied:

- Yes. They are a favourite of mine. But we can't have more than this, we need to save ourselves for morning tea.

After saying this, Jing pointed in the direction of a set table. He handed his attendant the nuts and honey and they walked to the table.
Jing:

- Traditional Chinese breakfast.

Pierre looked at the food and taunted:

- Oh, I was hoping for bat soup. Nothing beats the emergence of another virus.

Jing's gaze blackened but he contained his anger. Jing:

- So, why did you insist on meeting me today?

Pierre:

- I wanted to discuss some changes to your Silk and Belt Road project. It is clashing with our Human Rights Project in Almaty, Kazakhstan.

Jing:

- Since when does the World Bank care about human rights?

Pierre:

- I don't care about human rights per se, but they are a great tax write off and good for the reputation of the bank.

Jing:

- Bah. When China first became wealthy, we thought we needed to pretend to care. But we soon realised that no-one gives a shit about human rights, as long as the money flows.

Pierre:

- Interesting approach, but let's discuss how we can synchronize our projects in Almaty. The world will be a better place if we co-ordinate our efforts.

Jing nodded and they discussed their business interests in Almaty for half an hour. After half an hour, Jing was getting itchy. He thought about whether he had inadvertently activated the Hei Bai virus. It couldn't be the case. He had antibodies to the virus in his body now, so his selenium tolerance should have gone up. He rushed back to his office and he told Biyu to summon Dr Bao.

DR SONG BAO:

- Your blood test shows that you have ingested over 300 micrograms of selenium. Lucky you already had some tolerance to the Hei Bai Virus.

Jing:

- How is that possible? Those nuts should have contained less than half of that.

Dr Song Bao:

- Perhaps there was something special with the nuts. Do you still have the bag?

Jing:

- No, I gave it to one of the attendants, Mie Yung. I told her to throw it away.

Dr Song Bao:

- Well, I better find her and retrieve the contents of the bag. You stay here and recover. The virus is receding and your excess selenium should be depleted in a couple of hours.

Jing nodded. While he hated hiding away in his office, he could not show himself in public until his terrifying skin rash had disappeared.

PIERRE BEAUMONT WAS back in his mansion in Switzerland, which had a small research lab in the basement. He had extracted some of his blood, and his plan had worked. There were traces of dormant Hei Bai virus in his blood, which he had received from the encounter with Jing Xi. Pierre Beaumont studied the virus in a microscope. He had taken a huge risk, travelling to China and getting himself infected by Jing Xi. But it would be worth it. He had the virus dormant in his blood stream and with a controllable virus in his hand, he could control the world markets and the world economy. Once Pierre had set his plan in motion, the future was his.

Chapter 16: Greg Steel arrests Jared Pond at Sydney Airport. 5th May 2021.

Jared was sitting in the business class of the Qantas Flight 130 from Shanghai headed to Sydney. He looked at the virus testing video from the Uighur concentration camp. It was full of terrifying images and Jared couldn't get over the hunch that it could be real. But he needed to verify the content with his former colleagues at RAKI before he spread it. Tensions were still large in the world after the Coronavirus plandemic, and more villainy from China could cause outright war. Thus, Jared needed to be on the safe side before acting.

A thought struck Jared. What if Greg Steel would confiscate and delete the videos? There was a possibility, particularly if Scurry Morrissett prioritised licking Jing Xi's boots over doing what was right. Jared came up with the solution. He would upload the video on a lot of official and secret platforms on the Internet. Then he would set the video to publish in 14 days unless he cancelled it. This way, he had plenty of time to determine whether the video was fake or real, and the Australian government couldn't silence him to please China.

Having decided on a course of action, Jared spent the flight back to Sydney, implementing his plan. Once he had finished, he formatted his computer and mobile phone to stop his colleagues from tracking his steps. He leaned back into his seat, and he fell asleep.

WHEN JARED ARRIVED in Sydney, Greg Steel and a host of federal police officers were waiting for him at the gate. Greg approached him:

- What were you doing in China, Jared? Our Chinese friends have sent a warrant for your arrest.

Jared:

- I am no longer working for the RAKI, so it's none of your business. But I had a rendezvous with the beautiful Eileen Lu.

Greg:

- Yes. But why did you assault two security guards at the Shangri-la Hotel in Shanghai?

Jared:

- When people storm into my room in the middle of the night, I would classify any violence against them as self-defence.

Greg:

- Well, the Chinese doesn't. They have requested that we send you back. But first, we need to interrogate you to find out the truth. Please come with us.

Jared:

- Sure. But please analyse this critical piece of evidence that I found. I got this video from Ming Shebao and it shows how the Chinese government is testing a new virus on prisoners.

Greg:

- Thank you, Jared. I will look into this.
- Officers, please bring Jared to the RAKI holding facility in Pyrmont.

Having said this, Greg seized Jared's USB memory, phone, and laptop. After this, he headed back to his office to decide his course of action.

A FEW HOURS LATER, Greg Steel was talking to Jing Xi over the phone
Greg:

- It's a great honour to speak to you, Chairman Xi.

Jing:

- Spare the pleasantries. Tzi Cheng told me you had some alarming news.

Greg:

- Yes. Jared Pond carried an incriminating video. It shows how the Chinese government is testing a deadly pathogen on prisoners.

Jing:

- Jared Pond is a criminal who colluded with the fraudster Ming Shebao and assaulted security guards.

Greg:

- And what about the video?

Jing:

- The video isn't real and the Hei Bai virus doesn't exist.

Greg:

- Why do you have a name for it, if it doesn't exist?

Jing:

- Bah. Our AI analyses all the communications of Chinese citizens. We know what the enemies of the nation are discussing amongst themselves.

Greg:

- Understood. There is one more problem. Jared had formatted his phone and his computer. I believe he anticipated arrest and uploaded the videos all over the Internet.

Jing:

- That would be unfortunate. We need to access his computer and phone. Our AI can restore everything Jared is trying to hide. Also, please send our men a log of all the WIFI usage from QF130.

Greg:

- Understood. What are we going to do with Jared?

Jing:

- You need to bring him to me.

Greg:

- That would be difficult. Australia is not extraditing prisoners to China. Should I ask Scurry Morrissett for an exception?

Jing:

- No. Find a way to do it covertly. There will be a $20 million reward for your troubles.

Greg:

- Understood, Chairman Xi. I will contact Tzi Cheng about our arrangements.

Jing:

- Great. Discuss all further arrangements with Tzi Cheng. Dismissed, Colonel Steel.

After finishing the conversation with Jing, Greg leaned back into his chair and rubbed his hands. After serving his country for many years, it was finally time to serve himself!

Chapter 17: Pierre Beaumont Plans for a Controlled Virus Outbreak. 6th May 2021.

Pierre Beaumont was at home in his mansion overlooking Lake Geneva in Switzerland. He put through an order for 20 kilograms of selenium hydride. He sent it to the New York office of Jing Xi's shelf company "The Honey Dragon Inc.". While Pierre had shelf companies of his own, it was better if the blame for the outbreak fell on China when it was all over. Pierre suspected that Jing Xi planned to strike during the World Leader Summit at the United Nations Headquarters in New York. Jing seemed to be planning for a minor outbreak at the United Nations to cover up the real attack on the Civil Rights movement in Xuwan. Pierre, however, had another goal. If he could wipe out the majority of the world leaders, the global markets would collapse. Predicting the crash, he could short every share of the global economy, using the World Banks wealth as collateral. Once the dust had settled, Pierre would be the wealthiest person on the planet.

Vladimir Kravchenko entered Pierre's residence. Pierre studied the thuggish Russian who was both Pierre's occasional lover as well as Pierre's most accomplished assassin. Pierre found Vladimir both attractive and terrifying at the same time. Aided by the same alien technology as Pierre, Vladimir had super-senses that made him the most accomplished covert operative in the world. Pierre feared Vladimir's lust to murder and torture people. While Pierre didn't mind if people died as long as he benefitted, he saw no value in needless suffering. Vladimir was different. He didn't care about money, but nothing meant more to him than the opportunity to maim and torture people to fulfil his sadistic needs.

Vladimir:

- You summoned me, Pierre. Is this about business or pleasure?

Pierre:

- Are they not one and the same?

Vladimir nodded, Pierre gave him a USB memory and spoke:

- I summoned you about business. I have ordered 20 kilograms of selenium hydride to an address in New York. I need you to collect the selenium and contaminate a water processing plant. This plant provides the United Nations headquarters with drinking water. I plan to attack the UN summit on the 14th of May to cause mass panic and crash the markets to enrichen my-self.

Vladimir focused for a while as the monocle gave him an estimate of casualties such an attack would cause. Eventually, he spoke:

- What's the point of that? Selenium is only dangerous if you in-gest more than 5 milligrams a day. The delegates would have to drink 10 litres of water for that to happen.

Pierre smiled and replied:

- Good thinking, Vladimir. But I am not aiming to kill anyone via selenium poisoning.

Vladimir looked at Pierre in confusion and replied:

- So, what is the point of this then?

Pierre:

- Behold the Hei Bai virus, Muahaha.

Pierre showed Vladimir a model of the Hei Bai virus. Vladimir shook his head and replied:

- Who cares? Why are you showing me this virus, Pierre?

Pierre smirked and turned on the video of the Hei Bai virus testing in the Uighur concentration camp in China. Vladimir studied the video and marvelled at the pain and the suffering of the prisoners. He almost orgasmed when he saw how the guards torched the prisoners with their flamethrowers.

Pierre:

- That is the Hei Bai virus, Vladimir. A high dosage of selenium in the body activates the virus. I estimate that everyone who drinks more than one litre of contaminated water will get serious symptoms and die at the meeting.

Vladimir:

- Excellent. But some of them will survive?

Pierre:

- Viruses don't kill everyone infected. It will look more natural if there are survivors. Besides I am only after the market collapse to enrichen myself.

Vladimir:

- I like your plan. Let's fuck!

Pierre shook his head and replied:

- We'll only fuck after you have completed the mission. But don't worry. I have organised a new victim for you. Aleksei has kidnapped another street urchin, a Syrian refugee. That will have to suffice for now.

- I'll meet you in New York on the 14th of May.

Vladimir licked his lips and replied:

- Ah. I love the young Syrian refugees. I'll enjoy my evening and then I'll travel to New York to prepare for the attack.

Pierre:

- Great. Enjoy your night.

After hearing this, Vladimir walked up to Pierre's computer and pressed a few commands. Pierre shouted:

- Stay away from my computer, Vladimir. We are close but not that close!

Vladimir smiled maliciously and replied:

- Of course, Pierre. I will follow your command.

Having said this, Vladimir left Pierre's residence while whistling a joyful tune.

Chapter 18: Greg Steel abducts Jared Pond and ships him off to China. 7ᵗʰ May 2021.

Jared Pond was staring at the wall of his prison cell. He didn't like the fact that Greg had locked him up in a secret RAKI facility instead of in a normal jail cell. Something was amiss and he wondered what he would do. He wouldn't tell anyone which websites he had posted the video on. The world needed to know and the video was real, there could not be any other explanation to his imprisonment. But was Jared's imprisonment Greg's idea, or was Scurry Morrissett behind it all?

"Speaking of the devil!" Jared thought when Greg Steel and Michael Walker entered the cell. Greg spoke:

- Good news, Jared. You are free to go. Scurry doesn't want to hand you over to the Chinese government.

Jared:

- What about the video? Did you analyse it yet?

Greg:

- That is a question of national security I will not disclose to civilians.

- Follow me. I'll escort you out.

Jared sighed of relief. Once he was out of this mess, he would hide in the outback for a while, staying out of sight from Chinese agents. It had been a while since Jared was camping by himself in the wilderness. There was something cleansing about enjoying the clear night sky of the Australian outback. Jared's thoughts didn't get much further than that. He felt a pinprick in his neck when Michael injected him with a sedative. Jared tried to stand up and fight, but he didn't get far and he collapsed unconscious to the floor.

WHEN JARED WOKE UP, he was on a private jet. He was bound to a chair and surrounded by four Chinese agents and Greg Steel.

Jared felt dizzy and he mumbled:

- Greg? What is going on?

Greg taunted Jared:

- Isn't that obvious? I am selling you to the Chinese Ministry of State Security.

Jared:

- Why? I thought we were friends?

Greg:

- Friends? You were my disrespectful subordinate. I accepted your philandering and gambling as you delivered results.

- But Jing offered me something better. USD 20 million for delivering you to China.

Jared:

- He is never going to pay you! You are being duped.

Greg:

- He has already paid me. Besides we are refuelling the plane in Singapore. I'll get off there.

Jared:

- You'll never get away with this!

Greg:

- Oh, I am sure feckless Scurry will fire me for this. But what else can he do? Issue an international arrest warrant and cause a diplomatic crisis with China? You don't think he cares that much about your well-being, do you?

Jared:

- Fuck you, Greg. You'll pay for your crimes. I'll come after you myself.

Greg:

- No, you won't.

Having said this, Greg electrocuted Jared with a Taser. Then he gagged Jared to avoid listening to Jared's ranting. The plane landed and Greg got off. Jared could hear that the employees outside was refuelling the plane. He tried to scream but he was gagged so it was to no avail. "Oh, if I only had one of those Bond gadgets," Jared thought, but he didn't. One of the Chinese agents injected some more sedatives into Jared's body, and he fell unconscious.

Chapter 19: Tzi Cheng interrogates Jared Pond. 8th May 2021.

Jared was sitting in a gloomy interrogation room in a Chinese Ministry of State Security facility in Beijing. He had been in trouble before but this was it. Being locked up in the Chinese dictatorship's facilities was a death sentence. Jared knew the only reason he was alive, was so they could find out where he had posted the virus testing video. Jared damned Greg for betraying him and the world to Jing's tyranny.

The door opened and Tzi Cheng entered the room. He was a muscular and stout man with a dangerous appearance. A large scar ran along the left side of his face. Without a word, he walked up to Jared and punched him in the face. Jared dropped to the ground and two soldiers ran in to tilt the chair that bound Jared, to an upright position.

Tzi Cheng:

- Welcome to China, foreign scum!

Jared:

- Thank you. Can you tickle my chin again? I think I got a mosquito bite there.

Tzi Cheng:

- There are better ways for me to inflict pain on you, than punching you. As a matter of fact, I have developed a whole array of torture methods under Jing's glorious leadership.

Jared:

- Well, I must be pretty important if Jing's top security advisor, Tzi Cheng, comes down to torture me.

Tzi Cheng:

- You have done your research, Mr Pond.

- You are only a speck of dust to the Chinese government. But the fake video that you posted online is dangerous and we must take it down before it spreads.

Jared:

- How can a fake video threaten your authority? The real threat for you is that the video is real and you don't want evidence against you when you release the virus.

Tzi Cheng:

- Very well. The video is real. But you are not getting out of here alive in any case.

Jared:

- Good to have cleared that out. So, why would I help you then?

Tzi Cheng:

- Because I have a vast array of torture methods I would like to test on you. Let's start with electricity.

Having said this, Tzi Cheng electrocuted Jared with a cattle rod, multiple times, while he laughed in delight.

A FEW HOURS LATER, Tzi Cheng reported his progress at Jing's office.
Jing:

- So, what have you found out?

Tzi Cheng:

- Our torture of Jared hasn't worked so far. But we found all the sites he posted the video on through studying the Wi-Fi usage on his flight.

Jing:

- So, did you take them down?

Tzi Cheng:

- We got most of the major sites to take them down. The threat of economic sanctions from China was enough to make most of the major video sites bending over backwards. Jared set the videos to release on the 19th of May.

Jing:

- This is excellent. That gives us ample time to exert pressure on all the sites to have the video removed. It also explains why our AI hasn't detected and warned us about the video.

- Why do you reckon Jared set the videos to release on the 19th?

Tzi Cheng:

- I reckon he trusted Greg enough to wait for his input, but he still made copies of the video as an insurance policy.

Jing:

- You might be right. Don't worry about Jared for now. Leave him in a cell and don't kill him.

Tzi Cheng:

- Why do you want to keep him alive?

Jing:

- Because I will blame him, Eileen Lu, and the civil rights movement for the outbreak that will take place in Xuwan next week. I can't use him as a scapegoat if I kill him now, can I?

Tzi Cheng:

- So, do you want me to release him?

Jing shook his head:

- No. Wait until the 15th of May. Then release him in Xuwan and entice him to find Eileen Lu. It's time to crush the civil liberties movement, once and for all.

After saying this Jing feasted on a jar of expensive honey and laughed maliciously for an extended period of time.

Chapter 20: Pierre Gets a Copy of the Virus Testing Video. 8th May 2021.

Pierre woke up as his monocle was beeping. He had set the Zetan Monocle and it's intuitive advanced AI to wake him up if there were any important developments in the world. Pierre smiled when he saw the video with the conversation between Jing and Tzi Cheng. If he could acquire the virus testing video, he would have ample evidence to frame the Chinese government. If he played his cards right, he could crush China and increase his power. It was the opportunity of a lifetime for Pierre.

Pierre downloaded the list of websites that had refused to take down the virus video. He started contacting the website administrators. After a few hours, Pierre reached King Mwanza from a Nigeran herbal medicine website.

King:

- Hey, who is this?

Pierre:

- This is Chi Wong. I am interested in a video of yours.

King:

- Are you talking about the Chinese video? I am not taking it down unless you pay me a lot. That video could make me a fortune from selling herbal remedies to the disease in the video. I am already scaling up production.

Pierre:

- How can you have a treatment when you don't even have a sample of the virus?

King:

- I don't need one. I operate on faith. My followers believe in my herbal remedies. Faith trumps science.

Pierre:

- And money trumps both.
- I have an offer for you.

King:

- I am not removing that video.

Pierre:

- I don't expect you to. As a matter of fact, I want a copy of the video sent to me. I am willing to pay you USD 10 million for the video.

King:

- Who are you?

Pierre:

- A friend wanting to do the right thing. So, do we have a deal?

King:

- You need to pay me upfront, man.

Pierre:

- That can be organised.

- I'll send you the money on an anonymous Swiss bank account. I expect you to transfer me the video, to avoid 'unfortunate' accidents from happening.

King:

- You got it, man. I will send you the file as soon as you have paid me. You know how to reach me.

Having said this, King Mwanza hung up the phone. Pierre logged in to Credit Suisse and paid Mwanza with Jing's hidden bank account. Pierre smirked. Jing was too afraid of losing his hidden bank account to ask the real question, how Pierre knew about the account in the first place!

A few minutes later, Pierre received the virus testing video. After securing the video Pierre instructed the monocle to upload the video everywhere under 100's of different user names. He would release the video on 16th of May. Then Pierre took off the monocle, put it close to the Wi-fi router and went to sleep. Pierre dreamt about his rise to become the true puppet master of the world.

Chapter 21: Jing Xi Travels to New York. 10th May 2021.

J ing Xi boarded the Chinese government plane that would take him to the United Nations summit in New York on the 12th of May. Everything was going according to plan. Jing would cause a minor outbreak at the United Nations summit to divert media attention from the Xuwan outbreak. The Chinese civil rights movement was congregating in Xuwan, and what better way to get rid of them than causing a massive outbreak? Jing would then lock down the city and have his secret police murdering everyone that opposed him. In the aftermath, Jing would claim that the Hei Bai virus caused their deaths.

To create the Xuwan outbreak, Jing had transferred infected Uighur prisoners to the city. Furthermore, he had ordered Tzi Cheng to contaminate the water supply with large amounts of selenium hydride. The selenium would activate the dormant Hei Bai virus and make millions sick within a matter of days. Thousands would die from the virus, but many more would die from the purges that Jing would put through during the lockdown. Likewise, Jing would cause minor outbreaks in other cities, to motivate lockdowns there. In the end, everyone the AI had identified as his opponents, 1.2 million people, would be wiped off the face of the Earth. After the genocide, the Columnist Party of China would reign supreme and people would have to deify Jing.

When it came to the summit in New York, Jing would pick a more careful approach. He had ordered the caterer, which he owned, to supply Brazil nuts at most of the conference tables. Some people would undoubtedly get sick, which would steal all the media attention. But most delegates wouldn't touch the nuts and wouldn't get sick. Furthermore, Jing had ordered the caterer to serve the important delegates other snacks to avoid triggering the virus.

Jing called his right-hand-man Tzi Cheng:

- Is everything ready?

Tzi Cheng:

- Yes. We have transferred Jared and the infected Uighurs to Xuwan. We will release them and contaminate the water supply in two days.

Jing:

- Excellent. Have you organised the minor outbreaks and the lockdowns of our other major cities?

Tzi Cheng:

- Yes. We are ready to move in and seize all the enemies of China during this glorious time of our history.

- It's a shame that you cannot lead us through the great purge.

Jing:

- Yes. But I have to visit the United Nations. I have to get infected myself to prove my innocence and that the enemies of China are behind this.

Tzi Cheng:

- Yes. I know. Best of luck, Chairman Xi.

Jing:

- For China and the rise of the dragon! Dismissed, Tzi.

After saying this, Jing hung up the phone. He felt uncomfortable knowing that he would have to get sick with the Hei Bai Virus to create an alibi for himself. But it was a risk he was willing to take. When it came to strengthening the power of himself and his party, no risk was too high.

"Bring me some honey liqueur, slave." Jing shouted to Biyu, and he leaned back in his chair full of joy, as the sweet drops satisfied his taste buds, and the alcohol calmed his senses.

Chapter 22: Pierre Beaumont Travels to New York. 11th May 2021.

"I would like a glass of Penfolds Grange Shiraz 2015." Pierre said with a smug voice. Pierre sat on board his private jet, headed from Geneva to New York and he felt amazing. He sipped the wine. It didn't taste as good as the 2012 vintage despite costing $200 more. Regardless of this temporary setback, Pierre felt excited. He would soon become the richest man on the planet and he would never need to worry about money again.

Pierre had considered whether he needed to travel to New York at all. He could do all the trading from the safety of his home in Geneva. He had decided that his presence in New York was advantageous. Pierre was a control freak, and he couldn't relinquish control of the entire operation to Vladimir. He needed to be there himself. Pierre had invested billions in CFD-s and shorting the market. He had used the World Bank's money as a security for all the anonymous letterbox companies he had set up. If the outbreak didn't happen, he would have lost most of the money he had invested, and the entire world would come after him. Even with his heightened intelligence, Pierre would be in serious trouble under such a scenario.

Struck by his fear of failure, Pierre lashed out at his servant:

- 2015 is not a good vintage. Bring me a glass of 2012 vintage.

Servant:

- I am sorry, sir. We didn't bring any 2012 vintage. Can I suggest 2014?

Pierre:

- 2014? I'd rather drink this cat piss you served me. Go away.

The servant rushed off without a word.

Pierre felt remorseful. While he didn't mind the prospect of murdering thousands to enrichen himself, he shouldn't treat his staff like they were dogs. Such was the behaviour of the brute and simple idiot Jing Xi, but Pierre was a superior human. A superior human didn't allow minor setbacks to change his behaviour to that of a lesser animal.

Pierre took out a few 100-swiss-francs banknotes and he got up from his seat. He walked over to his servant and spoke:

- I am sorry, Michelle. Your transgression didn't warrant such a brutish behaviour from me. Here is a token of appreciation. Buy your daughter Eva a present from me.

Michelle:

- Thank you, Pierre. That is very generous of you.

Pierre:

- But don't allow complacency. We will return to Geneva in two days, and I need you to get me the 2012 vintage by then. Money is, as always, not an issue.

Michelle:

- Thank you, Pierre. I will do everything I can to satisfy your request.

Pierre nodded and didn't reply. A minor dilemma struck him. He didn't want his servant to die, but he worried that he would expose himself if he warned Michelle. He shrugged off the notion and decided that he could save his servant while maintaining his alibi at the same time.

Pierre:

- Just a heads up. I have heard that New York tap water is unsafe to drink. Only drink bottled water from our Swiss Alps while you are there. Take enough bottled water from the plane to last for two days.

Michelle:

- Thank you, Pierre. I will.

After warning Michelle, Pierre felt a bit worried. What if warning Michelle would affect his plan? Pierre shrugged off the notion. A lot of people had warranted and unwarranted objections towards drinking tap water. As long as he didn't tell Michelle why the tap water was dangerous to drink, his statement would not implicate him.

Pierre calmed down and took another sip of the red wine. On second thoughts, Penfolds Grange Shiraz 2015 was a good vintage, even better than 2012. But he wouldn't tell Michelle about his new conclusion. Pierre had already given an order, and for this command, Pierre was ready to live with the consequences.

Pierre smiled as he anticipated his 'suffering' on the way home. Life could be worse!

Chapter 23: The UN summit outbreak. 13th of May 2021.

Pierre Beaumont chewed a few Brazil nuts and got on the stage in front of the assembled delegates. It was time to shine. Pierre was giving a presentation on how the World Bank was going to 'help' developing countries affected by the Coronavirus lockdowns that occurred the previous year. In reality, the World Bank had never, ever, helped any country, and the places that received their subsidies stayed poor indefinitely. Pierre's speech slurred, as he feared he had revealed the World Bank's true intentions. Judging from the lack of reactions from the crowd he hadn't. Or maybe they already knew, but they didn't care, as long as they could enrichen themselves. Pierre studied the gathered world leaders. All the prominent ones were present.

- Chairman Jing Xi from China
- President Deidrick Dump from the USA
- Chancellor Angela Mittler from Germany
- Prime Minister Scurry Morrissett from Australia.

Would any of them survive the outbreak? It was crucial that Jing Xi survived. It would be hard to pin the blame on him for the outbreak if he died.

Pierre feared that the outbreak could cause a nuclear war. Neither he, nor the World Bank would win if things escalated to a nuclear exchange. An economic collapse was what Pierre needed, but people were unpredictable and things could go out of hand. For a second, Pierre thought about contacting Vladimir and tell him to not contaminate the drinking water. But if he didn't move ahead with the attack, he would lose all his money and owe billions. In such a scenario, jail time was the best possible outcome for Pierre.

Pierre made up his mind. He would proceed as planned. The fear he experienced was only his conscience messing with his mind. After a bit of mumbling, he continued his presentation.

JING XI WAS LISTENING to Pierre Beaumont's presentation. He wondered what the bloody idiot was talking about. Pierre didn't follow the presentation notes, and he was rambling incoherent nonsense. Jing shrugged his shoulders. He didn't care about the presentation. But the number of diseased people among the crowd would be a good distraction from the main event that was to take place in Xuwan. Jing ate his fifth nut and coughed loudly. Since the Hei Bai virus was airborne and extremely contagious, this would be enough to infect everyone in the room. Once the outbreak began, it would implicate the USA as Deidrick Dump wouldn't get infected while other world leaders, who were against Dump, would.

Pierre paused his presentation and spoke to Jing:

- Chairman Xi. Are you okay?

Jing:

- No, I am not. I need to return to my hotel at once!

Everyone in the room stared at Jing as he got up and walked out of the room. Jing braced himself. The rash was getting painful, but it wasn't dangerous to him as he had antibodies from several other Hei Bai virus episodes.

"Get me to my hotel suite, and make sure the camera crew are ready for my statement," Jing commanded his bodyguards and he left the UN headquarters together with them.

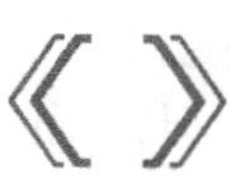

PIERRE FINISHED HIS presentation and he hurried to leave the venue. What a disaster the presentation had been. Pierre brushed off some imaginary dust from his jacket. Although he felt like a fool, he would feel marvellous once his plan had come into fruition. Pierre texted Vladimir. "Did you complete the mission?" A few minutes later he received a "Yes."

Pierre got up. He needed to attend a meeting at the Federal Reserve, where the real power resided. Besides, Pierre didn't want to be at the UN headquarters when people started collapsing around him. When the outbreak took place, Pierre would much rather follow the figures on his trading screen. He got excited thinking about how his shorting of the market would propel him towards unparalleled wealth. Pierre got into the limousine that took him to the Federal Reserve.

PIERRE WAS ATTENDING a seminar at the Federal Reserve Bank of New York. Angus Brothschild was explaining how the federal reserve could print more money and give to the wealthy to stimulate the economy. Pierre agreed with the notion but he found listening to Angus dull and boring. Angus was an intellectual lightweight. The only reason he was the head of the Federal Reserves' New York branch was because he was heir to the Brothschild throne. Pierre wasn't a fan of the hereditary transition of power. It allowed imbeciles to rise to the top instead of promoting talent. Pierre wasn't born wealthy. He had clawed his way to the top, reaching the top spot through murdering his rival Chakri Apinya. That was the true spirit of nature, to do anything to reach one's goal!

Pierre got interrupted from his daydreaming when the man next to him, the vice-chancellor of the European central bank, turned sick. Was the man infected by the Hei Bai virus? How could that be? While Pierre could have infected him, he hadn't seen the man eat any selenium-rich food to activate the disease.

Angus:

- Are you okay, Jurgen?

Jurgen:

 - My back. It is on fire.

"Oh shit. Here we go." Pierre thought. But how had this happened? Had Jurgen eaten some high-selenium food before attending the meeting? That would be some bad luck! Suddenly, the man opposite Pierre collapsed to the floor as well. "I feel so hot, please help me."

Pierre realised that he needed to get out of the room. His intention had failed and somehow, he was killing his fellow bankers. Even though he didn't care about their lives, he didn't want to end up in quarantine. It was crucial that he didn't. He couldn't implement his trading schemes if he was in hospital lockup and all his plans could come to naught.

Pierre rushed out of the room and into the bathroom. He inserted his Zetan monocle, set it to avoid confrontation, and left the Federal Reserve building.

"Vladimir, meet me at the airport at once. We are heading back to Geneva straight away." Pierre texted. Pierre got back to his limousine. His driver was lying on the ground next to the car, screaming in pain. "Fuck this shit." Pierre thought and shouted:

 - Give me your keys now. I need to get back to the airport straight away.

Driver:

 - Please help me. The pain is unbearable!

Pierre:

 - Give me the keys, and I'll drive you to the hospital.

Driver:

 - Here. Take them.

The driver handed Pierre the keys. Pierre scoffed at him.

- Bloody useless. Did you really think I would drive YOU?

The driver wheezed something in return but Pierre didn't bother to respond. Instead, he drove as fast as he could to the airport. It wasn't easy. The city had descended into complete chaos. Dead and dying were lying everywhere. How had this happened?

JING XI HAD FINISHED recording the video showing how the Americans had poisoned him when he suspected that something was amiss. The endless sirens of emergency vehicles and screaming were making the city surreal. Jing looked outside the window. There were several Hei Bai virus infected people outside on the street and it seemed like the army was gathering in hazmat suits.

Jing turned on the TV. The news reporter said. "There is a biological warfare attack in New York. Most world leaders attending United Nations summit confirmed dead, including the US president Deidrick Dump."

Jing turned off the TV. This was a disaster. Jing had hoped to infect a few leaders who were enemies of the United States. This would have implicated the USA was behind the biochemical warfare attack that would take place in Xuwan. Jing called Tzi Cheng:

- Tzi Cheng. Something is amiss. New York has been hit hard by a Hei Bai virus attack. There is a change of plan. You have to abort the attack on Xuwan. We can no longer blame the US for an attack on China since the US president died himself from the virus. This is an atrocity!

Tzi Cheng stayed silent for a while and replied:

- It is too late. We have already contaminated the water supply in Xuwan a few hours ago.

Jing:

- Turn off the water in the city. Let's minimise the outbreak.

Tzi Cheng:

- If we close down our water supplies in Xuwan to stop the virus, the Americans will know that we released the virus in New York.

Jing sighed. Someone had played him and he was in trouble. But the situation was still salvageable. After all, Jing had been infected himself from the outbreak and the virus struck one of China's cities as well. Jing hoped he could implicate a third party. Jing:

- Okay. You're right. Do nothing with the water supply. Release Jared next to Eileen's rally. He will seek her out. Then arrest them and everyone else opposing us once the outbreak starts.

Tzi Cheng:

- Understood, Heavenly Master. I recommend that you leave the United States as fast as possible. Things are going to get nasty in New York.

Jing:

- Yes. I will get out of here straight away.

Jing hung up the phone, and he turned to his bodyguards:

- What are you waiting for, you idiots? We are leaving New York at once. Take me to the airport. And whatever you do, don't drink anything from the tap!

Having said this, the group got up and they all rushed towards the air-port.

PIERRE BEAUMONT GOT on the plane, and he noticed that the pilot hadn't arrived. This was bloody inconvenient. He had saved his servant by warning about the tap water, but he hadn't saved his pilot. "That was a stupid way to prioritise!" Pierre muttered to himself.

Vladimir arrived at the aircraft and he looked happy, happier than Pierre had ever seen his Russian assassin and booty call. Pierre looked at Vladimir and spoke:

- What happened? Why was there an outbreak in the entire city?
I only intended to infect the United Nations summit.

Vladimir smiled maliciously and replied:

- I went above and beyond your orders, Pierre.

Pierre stared at Vladimir with a mixture of terror and admiration. Pierre:

- WHAT exactly did you do, Vladimir?

Vladimir smirked:

- Well, after you told me about the mission, I had a thought. I thought: Why kill 500 when I can kill 500,000?

- So, I ordered 5 tonnes of selenium hydride, and I dumped it straight into New York's water supply.

- Then I walked around in the city and coughed at everyone while being infectious. You know how contagious this virus is. Muahaha!

Pierre:

- Bah, I don't advocate for needless killing. Killing 500 world leaders would have made me the same amount of money.

The intuitive interface of Pierre's monocle revealed that Michelle had overheard the conversation. "Fucking hell, such a hassle it will be to train a new waitress!" Pierre thought and shouted:

- Vladimir, Michelle overheard us. Seize her.

Michelle tried to escape from the dangerous Russian, but it was to no avail, and Vladimir subdued her.
Pierre:

- Drag her onto the plane. We'll deal with her there.

Vladimir dragged Michelle onto the plane. As they reached the inside of the plane, Michelle whimpered:

- Please spare me. I won't say anything. Think about my family.

Pierre shrugged his shoulders and replied:

- I am sorry, Michelle. You have been a good servant and I would love to spare you. But I am not willing to take the risk. Instead, you'll die from the Hei Bai virus like most of Manhattan. It will be painful and unpleasant, but I need an alibi.

Pierre took out some selenium hydride and dissolved it into a bottle of water. He handed the bottle to Vladimir and spoke.

- Michelle must be thirsty. Let's give her some water.

After that, Pierre and Vladimir force-fed Michelle from the bottle. Due to the extremely high selenium content in the water bottle, Michelle's symptoms spread fast. When Pierre was satisfied that Michelle would die, they threw Michelle out of the plane, closed the door and prepared for take-off. Pierre used the Zetan monocle to start the plane and took off. He didn't even bother to contact air traffic control to get permission to leave. The city had descended into chaos anyway.

JING XI ARRIVED AT the same private airport in New York. He saw how Pierre and Vladimir threw out the body of Michelle from their plane and then took off. Jing didn't reflect much over it. He needed to get out of the city himself.

Jing:

- Get my plane ready.

Jing's bodyguard, Ma Tin, shook his head and replied.

- I have tried calling our pilots. None of them is picking up. The outbreak must have infected them.

Jing panicked. He couldn't be stuck in this city. It was way too dangerous. Because after the deaths from the virus had subsided, the city would collapse into anarchy with the death of the US leadership. Jing:

- Come with me. We need to use the airport's public announcement system to look for a pilot.

Jing and his bodyguards entered the airport terminal. Dead and dying were littering the corridors. Jing approached the air traffic control room. The door was locked. Ma Tin took out his pistol and shot the lock to pieces. After that, he kicked in the door. Jing walked up to a microphone and made an announcement.

- Hello. This is Jing Xi, the president of China. I am willing to pay $1 million to any pilot who can pilot our plane away from this city. Please come to gate 12 to declare your interest.

Jing felt a deep sense of relief when a pilot showed up a few minutes later. He felt so relieved, so he didn't even object when the pilot insisted on flying to London instead of Beijing. After agreeing on the pilot's terms, Jing hurried to the plane to get away from the disaster-struck New York City.

Chapter 24: Go see your girlfriend, white devil! 14th of May 2021.

"Go see your girlfriend, Gweilo!" the Chinese soldier shouted at the Australian agent as he pushed Jared Pond out of the white van.

Hitting the asphalt with speed, Jared scraped his arms and knees, destroying his clothes and causing him to bleed profusely. Jared felt confused. He had never anticipated the CPOC operatives would let him out of this alive.

As Jared's arms and legs were bound with cable ties, Jared wriggled until he could find a sharp surface. Jared rubbed the cable ties against the curb until they broke and he was a free man.

Jared got up. He thought about what the guard had shouted to him. Why did the Columnist Party want him to find Eileen Lu? Jared realised he had to play along with the dictatorship's plan. He was wounded and carried neither money nor a passport. This was hardly ideal circumstances, especially since he didn't even know where he was!

Jared walked up to a group of people playing mahjong and spoke:

- Where am I?

The people shook their heads, picked up their game, and left without acknowledging Jared. Jared couldn't blame them. They must have seen how the secret police had thrown him out of a moving vehicle and had assumed that any contact with him was dangerous. Jared was close to collapsing in self-pity when he heard a familiar voice:

- Jared, what happened to you?

Jared looked up and saw the angelic features of Eileen Lu. He felt dizzy and blissful at the same time. He had assumed that he would never get out of captivity alive, and yet here he was, together with Eileen. Jared:

- My boss betrayed me and sold me out to the Columnist Party. I don't know why they let me go.

Eileen:

- Oh my god, Jared. What did those monsters do to you? We need to get you out of China.

Jared:

- But I have no money and no passport.

Eileen:

- Come with me. I'll help you get to the Australian Consulate in Shanghai after the rally.

Eileen turned to one of her associates and spoke:

- Chen Lan, please help Jared. He'll need to walk with us, and then I'll take him with me to Shanghai.

Chen nodded and she helped Jared get back to his feet. As Jared got up, Eileen kissed him and spoke:

- I need to hurry to the rally. I am giving a speech. Chen will help you, and I'll meet you afterwards.

Jared:

- Thank you, Eileen.

Eileen rushed off to make her way to the civil liberties rally, while Chen helped Jared to a nearby apartment.

JARED WAS SITTING IN an apartment overlooking the main square of
the city of Xuwan. Jared was listening to Eileen's speech, while Chen Lan
was patching up his wounds. Chen:

- Do you want some tea?

Jared:

- No, thank you.

Chen:

- Okay. This is my third cup. I love tea.

Saying this, Chen went to the kettle and filled her cup with some more
tea. Jared sighed. He couldn't understand why CPOC had released him
and he worried that something was amiss. Why did Jing's goons want him
to meet with Eileen?

- AH! My back is burning!

Jared turned towards Chen who was lying on the floor, screaming in
pain. Jared:

- Get on your stomach and stay still.

Jared got up, grabbed a pair of scissors and cut up Chen's blouse. Chen's
back was full of a fast-spreading bark-like rash. Jared had an epiphany; this
must be the same virus he had seen in the video from the Uighur concentration camp. 'So, this is why they released me. To frame me for the outbreak!'
Jared realised.

Jared realised he needed to warn Eileen and the others for the outbreak
before it was too late.

Chen wheezed:

- Help me. Don't leave me.

Jared looked at her for a brief moment, turned around, and left the apartment. He felt terrible for abandoning the woman who had patched up his wounds. Yet, if the Columnist Party aimed to murder the civil rights movement with the virus, there was no time to waste.

Jared got out from the apartment complex, and he ran towards the stage. When he was halfway to the stage, a man next to him collapsed to the ground. He was too late, but he had to save Eileen.

He got on the stage and shouted at Eileen:

- Chen is dead. Everyone needs to leave. The Columnist party
  has unleashed the Hei Bai virus on the crowd.

Eileen:

- What are you talking about?

Jared didn't have the time to answer, as one of the other civil rights leaders on the stage collapsed.

Eileen:

- Zhang Wei! What's happening to you?

Jared:

- Eileen! Tell everyone that they need to leave now. The Columnist Party is attacking us with biological warfare.

Eileen shouted out the message to the crowd, but they didn't get far. Hundreds of white vans and soldiers in hazmat suits arrived and sealed off all the exits to the square.

Some of the soldiers ran up to the stage and subdued Jared and Eileen, and threw them into an unmarked white van.

Chapter 25: Jing Xi kills his wife with the Hei Bai virus. 15th May 2021.

Jing Xi was back at his presidential palace in Beijing. The world was in an uproar after the Hei Bai virus outbreak in New York and Xuwan, and the global death toll was approaching half a million. Jing Xi had declared a national lockdown and it was time to wipe out the 1.2 million dissenters that Jing's AI had identified. They would all 'die from the virus' and the Columnist Party would add them to China's death toll during this 'tragic' time of Chinese history.

Even though everything was going according to plan, Jing felt worried. He could not be certain that the virus testing video was deleted from the internet. Jing needed a way to gain sympathy, a way to prove he was not the mastermind behind the virus outbreak. Jing pulled his hair. He worried about the massive New York City outbreak. Jing hadn't ordered the contamination of New York's water supply, so who was behind it?

Jing tapped up a bath and added some bath salts. A nice, warm, oily bath would soften his limbs and put his mind at ease. He thought of summoning Min Li. Jing intended to meet her for her company as he was too tense to think about sex. Jing sunk his fat body into the warm water and for a short moment, he felt at peace. The shrieking voice of his wife, Lan Peng, broke the peace.

- Honey. Are we still going to the Shen Yun dance show?

Jing took a deep breath. Why would he even consider visiting the Shen Yun dance show? Jing's enemies, The Falun Gong movement, sponsored the Shen Yun performers. Jing:

- Are you fucking insane? Why would I visit the dance show run
by my enemies during a nationwide lockdown?

Lan Peng:

- Do we need a lockdown every time you hype a flu virus? Lah?
Last year was so boring!

Jing:

- 200,000 people died in Xuwan yesterday. It is not hyped this
time. You stupid bitch!

Lan Peng:

- Whatever, lah. I'll ask Chancellor Chi Wang to summon the
Shen Yun troupe for a private show. He knows how to treat me.

Hearing this, reminded Jing of his suspicions that Lan Peng was cheating on him with Chi Wang. He had suspected it for years, but he had never bothered investigating. After all, he was too busy having sex with his young and beautiful concubines to pay his wife's sex life any attention.

But, since Lan Peng was cheating on him, he had a reason to murder her. If she were to die from the Hei Bai virus, Jing could showcase his tragedy to the world. That would deflect suspicions elsewhere. Jing smiled. It was time to fulfil the 'until death do us apart' part of his wedding vows and send Lan Peng off to the afterlife!

JING XI APPROACHED Lan Peng as she was preparing her make up for her private Shen Yun dance show. He gave her a cup of tea laced with selenium and spoke:

- I am sorry, honey-boo. You were right. I would be happy to
watch the Shen Yun show together with you.

Lan Peng:

- Oh really? What made you change your mind?

Jing:

- I am not a fan of leaving you alone with Chi Wang. He might make a fool out of himself swooning over your beauty.

Lan Peng scoffed:

- Bah. When was the last time you called me beautiful?

Jing:

- I just did. Now stop arguing.

Lan Peng:

- What about Min Li and your other whores?

Jing:

- You cannot expect the Emperor of China to settle for one old hag. Now drink your tea and we'll head to the show. I am not going to ask again.

Lan Peng thought of objecting but she didn't. Instead, she had a few sips of the tea and replied:

- Thank you, for giving me the tea, Heavenly Master.

Jing smiled as Lan drank the tea, he watched her for a while. Eventually, he spoke:

- I know what you did. I know you have been fucking Chi Wang behind my back for years.

Lan Peng:

- So, what is it to you? Since when do you care about my fidelity?

Jing:

- It's not about fidelity. It's about power. I cannot have my chancellor fuck my wife.

- On the bright side, you will realise that the Hei Bai virus is very real, as it ends your life in terrible pains.

Lan was about to slap Jing when the virus took hold of her and she collapsed to the ground in severe pain. Lan shouted:

- What did you do to me, monster?

Jing:

- I infected you with the Hei Bai virus.

- I'll use your death to my advantage. I'll get my revenge for your affair with Chi Wang, and I can use your passing as a distraction. I will fill all the newspapers with stories about how I am mourning your tragic death.

Lan Peng couldn't argue against Jing Xi. Her excruciating pain took hold of her senses and all she could do was to scream in pain. After a few minutes, the pain put Lan into shock. She slipped into unconsciousness never to wake up again.

Chapter 26: Pierre Beaumont witnesses Lan Peng's murder via the hacked AI. 15th May 2021.

Pierre Beaumont was lying in bed with his assassin and occasional lover, Vladimir Kravchenko. Pierre studied the naked body of his dangerous and muscular lover. A chilling thought struck Pierre: Vladimir had killed 100's of thousands in New York and nothing stopped him from murdering Pierre as well. Pierre thought of striking first. There would never be a better opportunity to kill the cold-blooded Russian than now, and Pierre had a good motive. Vladimir's action had caused two of Pierre's fellow bankers at the Federal Reserve meeting to die.

Pierre looked at the pistol that lay on the bedside table next to Vladimir. With a bit of luck, he could reach the pistol and shoot Vladimir in his sleep. There was, however, a problem. Vladimir had his Zetan monocle connected and its intuitive processing would alert Vladimir if Pierre became a threat. If it came to violence, Pierre would be dead. Vladimir had carried out hundreds of assassinations in the last year, while Pierre had been counting money in his ivory tower.

Pierre shook off his murderous plans and checked his trading accounts. The attack on New York had turned Pierre into a trillionaire. It wasn't his personal wealth. It was the wealth of the letterbox companies that he controlled, which was just as well. Pierre pondered whether he was the wealthiest man on the planet. It was hard to tell, as many wealthy individuals hid their wealth using trusts, offshore companies, and other instruments.

Pierre's Zetan Monocle beeped and Pierre connected it to his eye. Pierre rejoiced over what he saw. A video showed how Jing Xi murdered his wife in cold blood. This was excellent news. With even more evidence against China and Jing Xi, Pierre could soon crush Jing Xi, and get away with his crimes. The demise of China would make him the richest and mightiest person in the world and everyone would bow to him.

Pierre slapped Vladimir and exclaimed:

- Vladimir! Wake up, you big bear! Check out the latest video from China. My great plan is coming into fruition.

Vladimir watched the video and shook his head:

- Why do I care if Jing Xi killed his wife?

Pierre:

- Because these are damning evidence against Jing. Combine this with the virus testing video and Jing and the Columnist Party leadership will fall.

Vladimir:

- If they fall, they will bring the world down with them. Do you want a nuclear war?

Pierre took a deep breath and walked a few steps away from the bed. Vladimir was correct. If he exposed the crimes of the Chinese leadership the nuclear option would be on the table, and all his hard-won victories would be for nothing. He would need to eliminate the Chinese leadership, and Pierre had an idea.

Pierre turned to Vladimir and spoke:

- Vladimir. Head to the airport at once. I have a mission for you in China. There is someone I need you to meet.

Vladimir:

- Understood. I'll leave at once.

After saying this, Vladimir got dressed and headed towards the airport. Meanwhile, Pierre remained in his mansion and prepared the next step of his plan.

Chapter 27: Jing Xi is taunting Eileen when he gets an urgent reminder. 16th May 2021.

Eileen Lu was confined in a damp and dark prison cell, in a Ministry of State Security facility in Beijing. She realised that she wouldn't get out of this alive. However, what worried her the most was the carnage she had witnessed before the secret police had arrested her. Several people in her movement had collapsed to the ground showing symptoms of the Hei Bai virus. Had Jing Xi unleashed a deadly virus on the Chinese population? That was a new low, even for him.

Eileen heard some ruckus from the outside corridor and the door opened. A group of guards pushed a bruised and battered Jared into the cell. Tzi Cheng:

- We fetched your boyfriend for you, Eileen.

Eileen:

- What did you do to him?

Tzi Cheng:

- We gave him a taste of Columnist Party hospitality.

- Freshen up, Eileen. Chairman Xi is coming and he doesn't like dirty people.

After saying this, Tzi Cheng and the guards left and slammed the door behind them.

Eileen rushed over to Jared who was delirious and passing in and out of consciousness. Eileen:

- Jared. What did they do to you?

Jared slurred:

- Eileen? I don't know, but I feel dizzy. At least we'll die together.
I love you.

After saying this, Jared passed out and Eileen had to face her fears alone.

JING XI AND TZI CHENG entered the cell an hour later. Jing looked around in the cell and scoffed at Tzi Cheng:

- I cannot fuck her in here. Bring them to a nice cell.

Tzi Cheng shouted:

- Guards. Bring them to the rape room.

A few sturdy guards came in and they dragged Eileen and Jared to a much nicer cell. Once they were in the luxurious prison cell, Jing spoke again.

- Awaken the Australian spy. I want him to be fully aware.

Tzi Cheng injected Jared with a shot of adrenaline and Jared woke up with a shock, gasping for air. Jared stared at Jing and spoke:

- Dictator Jing Xi? Why on Earth are you here?

Jing nodded at Tzi Cheng, and Tzi Cheng punched Jared's in the kidneys. Tzi Cheng:

- It's chairman Jing Xi. Say it right, Australian dog.

Jared realised that debating Jing's title wasn't worth another punch to the kidneys so he replied:

- Chairman Jing Xi. What brings me the honour.

Jing smirked:

- I have no interest in you, dog. The beautiful and fiery Eileen Lu is the reason I am here. I will tame her like I tame everyone else.

Eileen:

- Don't touch me, you fucking creep.

Jing punched Eileen in the face and then he laughed:

- How funny is that? This girl is giving the chairman of China orders? I don't think so.

Eileen didn't reply and Jing spoke again:

- I was going to present you with good news. As your host, I will provide you with fresh food and drinks.

- Yet, there is a slight problem. We have contaminated the food and drinks with selenium. So, if you eat or drink, you'll activate the dormant Hei Bai virus in your bodies. If you don't, you'll thirst to death.

Eileen shouted at Jing:

- Do you want me to beg for mercy? It's never going to happen. Just kill us already, you evil monster!

Jing:

- I am not going to kill you yet. I have been longing for months to force my manhood upon you. The time has finally come. Make yourself ready, Eileen.

Tzi Cheng and the other guards chained Eileen against the bed with her facing down. Jing snorted some Viagra and was about to rape Eileen when an urgent message popped up on his phone. The AI had identified Chancellor Chi Wang to be an enemy of Jing and the Columnist Party. Jing showed Tzi Cheng the notification and Tzi Cheng nodded. Jing turned to Eileen and spoke:

- We'll have to make love later. I have an urgent party business to attend to.

Having said this, Jing and Tzi Cheng left the room in a hurry.

Chapter 28: Enemy of the State. 16th May 2021.

Jing Xi, Tzi Cheng, and a group of bodyguards were heading for Chancellor Chi Wang's office in the Chinese Presidential Palace. It was imperative to deal with Chi Wang at once. If the second most powerful person in the country had turned hostile, the whole nation was at risk.

As Jing entered the office, Chancellor Chi Wang and a group of bodyguards stood ready. They aimed their pistols at Jing's group who followed suit, and it all ended in a deadlock. Chi Wang screamed at Jing Xi.

- I saw the video. You murdered Lan Peng through infecting her with the Hei Bai Virus.

Jing:

- Don't lie. The death of my wife was a great tragedy that has shaken me to the core. Don't deflect the fact that the AI identified you as an enemy of the state.

Chi Wang:

- It has also identified you as an enemy of the people, so that means nothing. Don't let a stupid AI determine who is right and who is wrong.

Jing:

- Really? Show me where it says that I am an enemy of the people.

Chi Wang:

- It's all in the system.

After saying this, Chi Wang handed Jing a tablet, which was logged in to the core system of the AI supervising China.

Jing pretended to look at the tablet for a few seconds, and then he shouted "Now!". Hearing this, Tzi Cheng swiftly shot Chi Wang and Chi Wang's bodyguards. Jing picked up the tablet again, and he overrode the code that classified him as an enemy of the people. Jing turned to Tzi Cheng and spoke:

- Check if he is still alive.

Tzi Cheng kneeled beside Chi Wang, checked his pulse and nodded:

- Yes, Chairman Xi. The traitor Chi Wang is still alive.

Jing dissolved some selenium hydride in a water bottle and replied:

- Give him something to drink. It is better if Chi Wang dies as an unfortunate victim of the Hei Bai virus.

Tzi Cheng did as Jing instructed and infected every enemy that was still alive with the Hei Bai virus. As Jing watched Chi Wang die from the Hei Bai virus he called Dr Song Bao:

- Chancellor Chi Wang has fallen victim to the Hei Bai virus. I command you to come and verify the cause of his death. Don't bring anyone else.

Dr Song Bao:

- Did he really die from the Hei Bai virus?

Jing:

- He died with the Hei Bai virus in his body. Wasn't that how we agreed to count Coronavirus deaths that we dispersed last year?

Dr Song Bao:

- Understood, Chairman Xi.

Jing hung up the phone and turned to Tzi Cheng:

- Investigate why Chi Wang accused me of murdering my wife. I fear someone is trying to sow dissent in the Columnist Party.

Tzi Cheng:

- Did you murder your wife, Jing?

Jing gave Tzi Cheng a cold dead stare and replied:

- Yes. She was fucking Chi Wang behind my back. But I want to know how he found out about it.

Tzi Cheng:

- Understood. We will investigate his phone and computer.

Jing:

- Good. Make sure to be discrete. This situation could lead to the fall of the Columnist Party. If the party falls, so will you, Tzi Cheng!

Tzi Cheng nodded and replied.

- You'll have our discretion.

Jing:

- Good. I am heading home. I am an old man and I need to drink some tea with honey to relax from all this stress.

After saying this, Jing left the murder scene and headed home. On the way home, worries filled Jing's mind. How did Chi Wang know about how Jing murdered his wife, and why had the AI tagged Jing as an enemy of the people?

Chapter 29: We need to save Eileen Lu from Columnist Party detention. 16th May 2021.

Pierre Beaumont was drinking a glass of Chateau Margaux 2000 red wine and listening to Chopin - Nocturne op.9 No.2 in front of the fireplace in his mansion. It was a warm evening and it was ridiculous to run the air-conditioning and the fireplace at the same time, but Pierre enjoyed the setting. Pierre had his Zetan monocle lying on the coffee table. While he enjoyed the heightened intelligence it provided, he needed to unwind every now and then and have the mind of a human, a lesser species.

The monocle beeped to warn for danger, and Pierre was about to insert it, but he was too late. "Freeze! Hold it right there!" An American voice commanded.

Pierre got startled, spilled wine over his shirt, and turned around. CIA agent James Winter was aiming a silenced pistol at him. Pierre:

- Did you injure my guards?

James:

- There was no need. I hacked the house's security system and my monocle made it easy for me to infiltrate the house undetected.

Pierre:

- That's a relief. It's such a pain to find good employees these days.
- Why are you here, James?

James:

- I want you to tell me about your involvement in the biological weapon attack on New York.

Pierre:

- I don't know what you are talking about.

James:

- Yes, you do. I know that you and the World Bank made an absolute fortune from shorting the international markets before the attack.

Pierre sighed. He realised that he hadn't hidden his tracks well enough if James Winter had found out. However, James had heightened intelligence via his Zetan Monocle, so Pierre hoped that the other dimwits wouldn't realise. Pierre:

- You are right, James.

- I knew about the attack in advance and I chose to benefit from it. But I was never involved in the attack.

James:

- So, who is behind the attack?

Pierre:

- Jing Xi and agents from the Columnist Party.

James:

- Do you have any evidence?

Pierre:

- Yes. I have these videos. I also have reports showing that Jing Xi bought five tonnes of Selenium Hydride to contaminate the New York water supply.

James:

- How do you know all this?

Pierre:

- I own the company that is maintaining the Chinese government's surveillance AI. I have backdoors into their systems and I know everything they are up to.

James:

- Wow. This is amazing.

Pierre:

- Yes. Now put that gun away. You are making me uncomfortable.

James put away the pistol and looked at the files and videos that Pierre had provided him with. James' Zetan monocle indicated that the documents and videos were genuine.
After a while, James sighed:

- Wow. This is explosive stuff. I would have hoped that some less powerful terrorist group had released the virus. A biological warfare attack from China. This will lead to war.

Pierre:

- I didn't know the CIA was so afraid of war. You have started quite a few in the last few decades.

James scoffed:

- Bah. That's different. Bombing Iraq, who didn't have any weapons of mass destruction, is a lot less risky than attacking China. China is armed to the teeth and has a large nuclear arsenal!

Pierre:

- What if I can help you out?

James:

- What would you do?

Pierre:

- I can access the Chinese AI and designate Jing Xi and other top-ranking Columnist Party officials as enemies of the state. Then we can watch as they kill each other.

James:

- Hmm. Any chance you can free Eileen Lu from her imprisonment?

Pierre:

- Eileen Lu? Who is that?

James:

- Eileen Lu is the most prominent leader in the Chinese civil rights movement. I suspect that the Columnist Party arrested her during the outbreak in Xuwan.

Pierre:

- And why do you want to free her?

James:

- Because if we can make her the president of China, China will become a weak pushover. Eileen is meek and a lot of the old guard would hate her. She would be completely dependent on foreign help to stay in power. Wouldn't that suit the Bank?

Pierre reached for his monocle and he inserted it. He pulled up Eileen's file and analysed it. James was correct. Pierre had never considered installing a weak president in China to strengthen his power. His original plan had only entailed carrying out the bioweapon attack on New York to crash the markets and expand his wealth. But James had brought a new interesting scenario to the table.

Pierre accessed the Chinese AI and he found a video feed of Eileen in a prison cell together with the Australian spy, Jared Pond. Pierre didn't know why the Chinese had placed them in the same cell, but it wasn't particularly important. Pierre spoke:

- I am in on your plan. I'll instruct my agents to save Eileen. Furthermore, I will mark all the Columnist Party leadership as 'enemies of the state' in their AI. Then we can watch from afar how they are killing each other hoping to rise to power!

James:

- Excellent. I am sure this will please President Mitchell Cent, who replaced Deidrick Dump when he died.

- Are you going to release the documents proving China's guilt?

Pierre:

- Yes. The compensation claims will drive them bankrupt and the Dragon will fall.

James:

- And the Banker will rise?

Pierre:

- Exactly!

James:

- Are you sure you had nothing to do with the New York outbreak?

Pierre:

- Don't ask questions you don't want answered. Now get out of my house. Leave via the front door this time!

Pierre pressed a button on his phone and two bodyguards arrived.
Pierre:

- Gerard, Philip. Escort James from my property. He is overstaying his welcome.

For a second, Pierre noticed how James' threat level increased to 'moderate', but he quickly returned to 'low'. Without a word, James got up and followed the guards away from Pierre's residence.
Pierre called Vladimir:

- Vladimir, we have a new objective. You need to get Eileen Lu out of the Ministry of State Security facility in Beijing.

Vladimir:

- Do you want me dead, Pierre?

Pierre:

- Yes. But that's not going to happen, is it?

Vladimir:

- Correct. I'll speak to our contact on the inside. I'll get her out. But why do you want to save Eileen? I thought Jing Xi was the objective.

Pierre:

- Jing Xi is still the objective. But James Winter wants to save Eileen and make her the puppet president of China. We got to keep James and the CIA happy.

Vladimir:

- Understood. I will get her out.

Vladimir hung up the phone and Pierre got changed. He was annoyed that he spilled his exquisite wine after James Winter had threatened him at gunpoint, but he would have to forgive James. Pierre was certain James had proof against him that he would release if Pierre sent Vladimir to kill him. In the end, it was all good. Pierre was certain he could also benefit from installing Eileen Lu as a puppet president of China.

Pierre returned to his armchair and enjoyed another glass of wine. He turned on the stereo and resumed enjoying classical music.

Chapter 30: Dying with his pants down.
17th May 2021.

Jing Xi met up with Tzi Cheng at the Ministry of State Security facility in Beijing. To his surprise his secretary Biyu Sang was also there. Jing turned to her and spoke:

- Biyu. What are you doing here?

Biyu:

- The presidential palace is under lockdown because of the Hei Bai virus deaths yesterday. So, I came here to work for you.

Jing sighed. He should have anticipated that the palace would be in lockdown after the Chancellor of China had died 'from the Hei Bai virus'. But what could he do? It would look very suspicious if he insisted to open the palace at this stage. Jing:

- Very well. Let's find you a room so you can carry out your duties. Do not disturb us. We have a very important prisoner to interrogate.

Biyu:

- Who is the prisoner?

Tzi Cheng:

- That's none of your business, stupid secretary!

Jing:

- Tzi Cheng. You cannot tell Biyu off. She is my secretary. I am
the one reprimanding her!

Tzi Cheng:

- Understood, Heavenly Master.

Jing turned to Biyu:

- We are interrogating the number 1 enemy of China, Eileen Lu.
We suspect that she and her Australian boyfriend was behind
the Hei Bai virus outbreak in Xuwan.

Biyu:

- But you are the leader of China, Chairman Xi. You can leave
the interrogation of Eileen to someone else.

Jing lashed out and slapped Biyu. Jing:

- Do not question me, Biyu. Now go make us some tea or I'll
lock you up in one of those cells myself.

Biyu rushed off towards the pantry without saying a word. Jing turned
towards Tzi Cheng:

- Let's go. It is time for me to force Eileen Lu into submission.

EILEEN LU WAS SITTING in a luxurious holding cell together with
Jared Pond. The room was comfortable, but since it was the rape room of
the genocidal dictator Jing Xi, neither Eileen nor Jared could appreciate it.

Eileen's thirst was driving her mad and she made her way to the drinks station, which looked very enticing to her. Eileen was about to open a bottle of water when Jared pulled her away.

Jared:

- Don't drink anything, Eileen. Remember what Jing said. Jing has contaminated the water and we'll get the Hei Bai virus if we drink it.

Eileen:

- He is playing with your mind, Jared. Besides what do you want to do? Stay here and die from dehydration? Sit tight until Jing comes back and rapes me? If I die from the Hei Bai virus, he can't rape me at least.

Jared:

- For all we know, Jing might be dead. Did you see the hurry he left in? I bet trouble is brewing within the Columnist Party.

Eileen:

- So, what do you suggest we do?

Jared:

- We stay put and hope someone comes by. If we can overpower the guards, we have a shot at escaping.

Eileen:

- That sounds like suicide.

Jared:

- Yes, but less suicidal than infecting ourselves with the virus.

Eileen:

- Very well. I'll stay away from the water for now. But I won't let
you force me to thirst to death!

Jared nodded. From what he had seen, dying from the Hei Bai Virus
was fairly quick, while dying from thirst took longer and caused more suffering.

Jared didn't have the time to ponder on the matter further as a group of
guards entered the cell, subdued him and Eileen, and chained them to their
beds.

JING XI ENTERED THE cell with a malicious smile on his face. "Get out
of here, you dogs!" Jing commanded and everyone except for Tzi Cheng left
the room. Jing turned to Eileen and spoke:

- You must be thirsty, Eileen.

- How lucky that I brought you some bottles of fresh, uncontaminated water.

After saying this, Jing took out a plastic bottle of water from his coat
jacket and handed it to Eileen.

Eileen threw the bottle away and spoke:

- Why would I trust that this water is not contaminated, you
monster?

Jing picked up the bottle, opened it, and drank a few sips:

- Would I drink the water, if I had poisoned it?

Eileen:

- So, what do you want?

Jing:

- I want you and Jared to admit that you caused the Hei Bai Virus outbreak, which killed more than 200,000 people in Xuwan.

- Furthermore, I want you, Eileen Lu. I want your luscious body and your warm wet pussy. If you submit to me, I might even let you live and take my late wife's place.

Eileen:

- I would never let you have me, you filthy murderer!

Jing sighed:

- I guess not even the emperor of China can have everything he wants.

Jing picked up the uncontaminated water bottle, poured the water over Eileen's crotch, and spoke again:

- Well, this is unfortunate, but I'll have to rape you and kill you.

Jared:

- Stay away from Eileen, you filthy pig!

Tzi Cheng ran up to the chained Jared, kicked him in the face, and broke his nose. Tzi Cheng:

- Shut up, white devil!

Jared didn't respond as Tzi Cheng's kick had knocked him out.

Jing put out a line of white powder, which was Viagra mixed with ground rhino horn. After snorting the powder, he beat his chest while chanting in Chinese to stimulate his erection.

Jing was about to enter Eileen when he heard the muffled sound of a silenced pistol and felt a sharp pain. He turned around and to his shock, he saw his timid secretary Biyu Sang. "Fuck you, Jing!" was the last thing Jing heard before everything turned black.

Chapter 31: The escape from China. 17th May 2021.

Vladimir Kravchenko was overlooking the prison where the Columnist Party kept Eileen imprisoned. He heard a multitude of sirens and distant gunfire, and the army seemed to be out in full force. This wasn't ideal. Vladimir called Pierre to discuss the situation:

Vladimir:

- The situation is not good, Pierre. Beijing has descended into civil war and chaos.

Pierre:

- And how is that not good? The chaos will make it a lot easier for you to extract Eileen Lu from the prison facility and escape the city. You wouldn't be able to do that if everyone was looking for you. Now they are busy killing each other.

Vladimir:

- What did you do?

Pierre:

- I told them the truth!

Vladimir:

- The truth?

Pierre:

- I listed everyone in the Columnist Party as an enemy of the Chinese people, and I released the video of how Jing Xi murdered Chi Wang.

- Now they are all trying to kill each other to rise to the top. It's beautiful, isn't it?

- But enough talk. Tell Biyu to hurry up

Vladimir:

- Understood.

Vladimir hung up the phone and messaged Biyu: "Move now. I am covering the back entrance. Hurry up."

BIYU UNCHAINED EILEEN and Jared in the cell. Jared was dizzy from Tzi Cheng's forceful kick and he was bleeding profusely. Biyu turned to Eileen:

- We need to leave. Hurry up.

Eileen hurried over to Jared to help him up on his feet. Jared's concussion made it difficult for him to get up. Biyu:

- Leave him behind. We need to go.

Eileen:

- I am not leaving him. It is not who I am.

Biyu shook her head, but there was nothing she could do. She couldn't threaten the woman she was there to save.

Eventually, Jared got up and they left the room. Outside there were a few dead guards, all shot in the head with millimetre precision. Biyu:

- Pick up their guns but don't use them unless you have to. It's better if we remain stealthy.

The alarm in the building went off, and Biyu shouted:

- Never mind that. Pick up the guns and don't hesitate to use them. Hurry up.

Having said this, Biyu contacted Vladimir via her radio:

- Vladimir! Create a diversion!

Vladimir:

- Copy that.

VLADIMIR TURNED ON 'combat mode: maximum casualties' on his Zetan Monocle. The following stats came up. 'Estimated casualties: 150. Chance of Survival: 98 %. The chance for Eileen's survival 52 %'.

'I can live with that!' Vladimir thought, and he fired off a grenade that hit the middle of the courtyard. The grenade didn't hit anyone, but that was never the intention. Instead, Vladimir intended to blow up the gas pipes that ran under the courtyard. The guards fired at him, and Vladimir took cover, reloaded the grenade launcher and fired another grenade. The second grenade blew up the gas pipes and caused a massive explosion, which set the whole area ablaze.

Vladimir contacted Biyu:

- Hurry up, run through the courtyard.

Biyu:

- The whole courtyard is on fire.

Vladimir:

- You'll survive running through fire for a few seconds. You won't survive fighting the guards that are approaching you from the inside of the building.

Biyu:

- Understood.

POOF *CLICK*

Biyu threw away her pistol as she ran out of ammunition. She could hear the bullets fired by her opponents hitting the wall behind her.

- Give me your rifle, and hurry through the door. I'll cover you

Eileen gave Biyu her rifle and she ran towards the door and she opened it. She squirmed when she saw the inferno outside. Eileen:

- We can't go out there.

Biyu:

- We'll have to. We can't hold them off for much longer.

Eileen felt a sharp breeze as a 50 calibre round passed narrowly to her ear and hit a Columnist Soldier at the far end of the corridor.
Vladimir radioed Biyu:

- I'll kill her myself if she doesn't hurry up. Go!

Biyu got up and Vladimir shot her through the shoulder without severing any arteries. The bullet continued and hit a soldier in the head.

Biyu:

- What the fuck, Vladimir.

Vladimir:

- I saved your life. All the soldiers are dead. Now hurry up and cross the fire-stricken square and meet me in this building.

Biyu pulled herself together and got to Eileen. Biyu:

- We need to get to the other side of the square.

Eileen whimpered:

- Through that fire? Your friend almost shot me.

Biyu:

- He did shoot me, but he knows what he is doing. Hurry up or we'll die.

Eileen nodded and she helped the concussed Jared and the crippled Biyu through the fire to the building on the other side of the square.
As they got through the fire and halfway across the square, Biyu heard another shot and saw a Chinese army helicopter crashing into a building.
Vladimir radioed her:

- Hurry up. Our odds of survival are shrinking by the second.

The trio managed to cross the square, and Vladimir was waiting for them and urged them to hurry into a van.

THE GROUP WAS ON VLADIMIR'S private jet headed towards Mongolian airspace when two Chinese fighter jets intercepted them. The radio buzzed and one of the fighter pilots communicated:

- Return to Beijing immediately or we'll shoot down this plane.

Jared sighed:

- Shit. We were so close to escaping China. Only a few minutes until the Mongolian border. What do we do?

Vladimir:

- We shoot down the fighter jets.

Jared:

- How?

Vladimir pointed at his 50-calibre sniper rifle.
Jared:

- Are you insane? How would you shoot down two fighter jets with a rifle?

Vladimir:

- Yes. I am crazy. But I live for these moments. If I succeed, it will be amazing. If I fail, I'll go down in a fiery explosion of glory. Whichever happens, I am happy!

Jared:

- Alright. Let's do this. What do you need?

Vladimir:

- Strap yourselves in, and be ready to pull me up.

After saying this, Vladimir attached himself to an abseiling harness and picked up the sniper rifle. He opened the door to the plane and jumped out, hanging a few metres under the plane. 'Shots almost impossible.' Vladimir's monocle displayed. "I like those odds!" Vladimir said to himself and aimed at the first pilot. He pressed the trigger and he noticed how the bullet shattered the windscreen of the plane, but he couldn't determine if he had hit the pilot.

Vladimir didn't have the time to reflect over this, as the second plane fired off a missile towards his plane. Vladimir acted instinctively. He shot the tip of the missile and caused it to detonate under the fighter jet. This blew up the hostile plane.

"Pull me up!" Vladimir shouted to Jared and a few seconds later he was back in the plane. They closed the door and they were gasping for air on the floor for a while. Eventually, Vladimir spoke:

- That's how you do it, Jared. Ha-ha

After saying this, Vladimir was rolling on the floor, filled with raging outbursts of excitement.

Chapter 32: Meeting between Pierre Beaumont, James Winter, and Eileen Lu. 18th May 2021.

Jared Pond woke up the following day in a private Swiss medical facility overlooking Lake Geneva. His head was still sore from the concussion and he had burns on his body from running through the inferno when escaping the Chinese prison. Yesterday's events felt so surreal. In particular, the episode where Vladimir shot down two pursuing fighter jets with a sniper rifle.

Jared pinched himself in the arm and realised he was alive. He heard that someone was in the shower and he admired Eileen's naked slender body covered in bath foam.

Eileen saw him and teased:

- Don't stand there peeking, Jared. Come join me.

Jared shook his head and smiled:

- I will join you in a couple of days. I have some pretty bad burns on my body.

Eileen:

- Oh really? Weren't you the horny one after we escaped those assassins in Shanghai?

Jared:

- That was different. That time I was unhurt but full of adrenaline. There is nothing more arousing. Now I am jetlagged, have a broken nose and several burns on my body. Believe it or not, I am not a machine!

Eileen:

- Then I better order one from China!

Jared:

- No, don't do that.

Eileen smiled:

- Don't worry, Jared. I am a big fan of the Aussie kind.

- You stay here and rest. I need to attend a meeting with Pierre Beaumont of the World Bank.

Jared:

- The World Bank? What does he want?

Eileen:

- I don't know. I think he was the one who sent Biyu and Vladimir to save us.

Jared:

- Okay. That makes sense.

Eileen:

- I still can't believe we got out of Jing's captivity alive. This feels like a dream.

Jared:

- Then live the dream. Jing Xi is dead and the Columnist Party is collapsing. This could be a new start for China and the World.

Eileen walked up to Jared, kissed him, and replied:

- You're right, Jared. I'll better get dressed and prepare for the meeting. Take care.

Having said this, Eileen put on some of the hospital clothes and left the room.

A WHILE LATER, EILEEN'S limousine dropped her off at Pierre Beaumont's mansion. Pierre's new butler, Jean, approached Eileen and bowed to her. Jean:

- Welcome, Mademoiselle Eileen. My name is Jean Valmont. Monsieur Pierre asked me to get you dressed for the meeting. Please come with me.

Eileen:

- Thank you, Jean.

Jean showed Eileen to a room full of expensive women's clothes. Eileen looked around and spoke in amazement:

- Wow. Does Pierre always have so many options for female visitors?

Jean:

- Monsieur Beaumont thinks a woman must look her best in a social setting. May I suggest the brown stiletto shoes, the black pants and the yellow blouse. I would recommend accompanying the clothes with this diamond necklace.

Eileen:

- That would be great. But I am not used to wearing high heels since I am pretty tall.

Jean:

- Yes, but of course. Silly me. How about these blue ballerina shoes?

Eileen:

- That will be great. Thank you.

Eileen got changed and she studied herself in the mirror. She loved the outfit and the diamond necklace, but at the same time she looked tired and worn out, having escaped from captivity.

Eileen:

- Do I need makeup as well?

Jean:

- No. Monsieur Beaumont is aware of your current circumstances. Besides, excessive use of makeup ruins the skin.

- Please come with me.

Eileen followed Jean and she reached the grand hall of Palace Beaumont.

EILEEN ENTERED THE grand hall of Palace Beaumont. It was newly built but the architecture borrowed many elements from the renaissance. Large panorama windows faced the lake below. Two men approached Eileen, and she noticed that they wore the same kind of monocle as Vladimir. Eileen studied the men. One of them was good-looking. He was a tall and muscular army guy with a crewcut hairstyle. The other man was balding and ugly with features that only a mother could love. The ugly man spoke to Eileen:

- Welcome to Palace Beaumont. I am Pierre Beaumont the CEO of the World Bank, and this is James Winter from the CIA.

Eileen:

- Nice to meet you, Pierre. I am Eileen Lu from the Chinese Civil Rights movement.

James:

- Yes, we know who you are.

Eileen:

- So, was it the CIA that freed me from China? I thought Vladimir was Russian?

James:

- The CIA has a widespread spy network and people of every nationality works for us. Vladimir Kravchenko, however, works for your host, Pierre Beaumont.

Pierre:

- Yes. Vladimir is the best in the world at what he does. Something I am sure you have already noticed. I only hire the best. That is why I hope to associate with you.

Eileen nodded with an afterthought and replied:

- So, what exactly do you want me to do?

Pierre:

- Take it easy, Eileen. Please have a glass of red wine and come with me on a tour of my palace.

Eileen objected:

- It's 10 in the morning. Isn't it a bit early for wine?

Pierre:

- You would have died yesterday if I didn't intervene. Please accept my hospitality and the excellent vintage.

Eileen accepted the red wine and she acknowledged Pierre's request. Pierre guided her around the castle and he spoke about the different artworks that he had acquired on auctions recently. The guided tour stressed Eileen. She knew Pierre had saved her for a reason and she wanted to find out why. Eventually, Eileen spoke:

- Pierre, I love your artworks and your passion for history. But you saved me for a reason and I need to know why.

Pierre cringed for a moment. He hated how Eileen had interrupted him when he spoke about the arts. He couldn't believe that James wanted to make such an arrogant bitch the new leader of China. Then again, James Winter was American, the birthplace of McDonald's, not the birthplace of classical music.

Pierre pointed to James and spoke:

- Bah. I saved you to help James and my American friends. James, please brief Eileen on what you expect from her.

James, who had remained silent during Pierre's guided tour, spoke:

- The Columnist Party is collapsing and their reign of terror is over. We will release evidence that Jing Xi was behind the outbreaks in New York and Xuwan.

- But we need to find a way forward to stabilise China. I believe you could be that way.

Eileen:

- What would you have me do?

James:

- There will be a global intervention to stop the budding civil war in China. After we have stopped the fighting, China will need an interim president. I want you to be that president.

Eileen:

- But you can't make me the president of China?

James:

- No, but President Mitchell Cent can. China killed a large number of world leaders at the United Nations summit in New York. The World and the Chinese Population will stand united against the remnants of the Columnist Party. You can lead the transition process. You will need to admit China's guilt, pay compensations, and dismantle the People Liberation Army.

Eileen:

- So, I will become the CIA's puppet president?

James:

- Yes, but you'll get what you want, and you'll avoid a global catastrophe.

Eileen sighed. She had wanted to free China from the Columnist Party, but she had never intended for western powers to humiliate her country.

This would be a replay of the Opium Wars in the 19^(th) Century. But Eileen understood why the world was vindictive after what had happened. Placating the world was the only way to save the Chinese people from complete destruction.

Eileen:

- I accept your proposal and I am willing to pledge my loyalty to President Mitchell Cent.

James:

- Excellent. I will make the arrangements.

- Please return to the medical facility and spend some time with your boyfriend. We have some busy days ahead of us.

After hearing this, Pierre rang a bell and a servant appeared. Pierre:

- Jean. Please take Mademoiselle Lu back to the Villeneuve Medical Facility.

Eileen nodded and she left Palace Beaumont.

Chapter 33: Bending One Knee to Theocracy. 22nd May 2021.

Eileen orgasmed and she got off her tireless lover, Jared Pond. Jared giggled at her:

- Are you tired already, Eileen? That was only 20 minutes.

Eileen:

- We need to prepare ourselves for meeting President Mitchell Cent.

Jared became more serious and replied:

- Yes, I know.
- How do you feel about all this?

Eileen:

- I feel terrible for all the deaths in my country. If I had bowed to Jing's tyranny many of those who've died would have been alive today. But on the other hand, what is the price of freedom?

Jared:

- It's a tough question.

- But don't feel guilty. It was Jing who chose to murder people with a new virus instead of debating politics. You can't allow yourself to cave in, to a tyrant like that.

Eileen:

- Yes. But even if I do become the president of China, I will still take orders from the USA and the World Bank. Am I then a president representing the people?

Jared:

- You can be the custodian paving the path for the one who will liberate China. Your goal was to liberate China. It can still happen in time. But you won't be the liberator.

Eileen:

- I guess you're right. For now, I must work to bring stability and save my fellow Chinese citizens.

Jared:

- And do you know what the best thing about it is?

Eileen:

- No?

Jared:

- I will be there for you on every step of your journey.

Eileen:

- Thank you, Jared.
- Let's head to the White House. We are meeting with Mitchell Cent soon.

Jared:

- I can't wait to hang out with that religious nutcase! But let's go.

After this, Jared and Eileen had a quick shower, got dressed and took a limousine to the White House.

EILEEN LU FELT A BIT uncomfortable when she reached the White House. She noticed that Mitchell Cent had erected a large crucifix in the Oval Office. Furthermore, he had placed a baptism chalice with water on a pedestal next to the crucifix.

Mitchell approached Eileen and spoke:

- Welcome to America. The nation of God.

Eileen:

- Thank you for receiving me, President Cent.

Mitchell:

- Miss Lu. Do you profess in our Lord, Jesus Christ?

Eileen:

- I don't follow any religion, President Cent.

Mitchell:

- You must. As a man of God, I can only help you if you do!

Eileen glanced at Jared and he nodded. Eileen sighed:

- Very well. If I must embrace Christianity to save China, so be it. I profess to Jesus Christ.

Mitchell:

- Excellent. I will baptise you at once.

Mitchell Cent splashed some water on Eileen and started chanting verses from the Bible. After half an hour, he shook Eileen's hand, blessed her, and he left the office.

After Mitchell had left the room, James Winter approached Eileen and whispered:

- Don't worry, Eileen. Mitchell's presidency is just to appease the stupid masses. Other people run the country in the background.

James' words didn't encourage Eileen. It drained her motivation realising that the President of the USA was a showpiece, while other people ruled the country in the background. This crushed her illusions. Her successful fight against Jing Xi had been for nothing.

Eileen hid her disappointment and replied:

- Of course, James. I am happy to discuss what steps we can take to ensure China's future.

James:

- Excellent. Come with me. There are better places to discuss our plans. The White House has too many prying eyes.

Eileen and Jared got up to follow James Winter who turned around and spoke to Jared:

- Nothing personal, Jared, but my associates want to speak to Eileen alone. Not everyone is keen to speak to an Australian Spy.

Eileen turned to Jared:

- It's okay, Jared. I will see you at the hotel later.

After saying this, she kissed Jared and left the room together with James.

Chapter 34: Eileen Lu Becomes a Puppet President for China. 15th June 2021.

A steamy summer day, a few weeks later, Eileen and Jared were in Beijing. Eileen was about to become the president of China, representing her party, the Chinese Civil Rights Movement. They had landed a few days earlier, accompanied by a large NATO force supported by every country, including Russia and Iran. The attack on the UN summit had killed leaders from every country, even former allies of China. This, combined with the infighting among the Columnist Party leadership, meant that China was powerless to fight. Thus, there was no resistance to the invasion aimed at punishing the Chinese leadership for their crimes against humanity.

Jared entered Eileen's room and he noticed she was crying:

- What's wrong, Honey.

Eileen:

- What is not wrong? I have landed in my home country escorted by a large foreign army. I have sold out China to foreign invaders. This was not how I envisioned the new China without the Columnist Party.

Jared:

- What if your dream was unrealistic? The Columnist Party would never give up without a fight. But with most of their leadership dead from infighting, they couldn't mount a defence against a foreign intervention.

Eileen:

- I know.

Jared:

- And at least you saved most of your followers from Jing Xi. If you hadn't acted, they would all be dead now. There was nothing more you could have done.

Eileen:

- I know. Life goes on. But I don't want to be the unelected president who carries out orders from foreign bankers.

Jared:

- I understand. But someone needs to govern China until there can be general elections. Would you rather have an American General running the country?

Eileen:

- I guess you are right.
- Hey. What do you think about these robes?

Eileen walked over to a mannequin featuring yellow and red silk robes with intricate patterns.
Jared:

- They are very fancy, but they don't look very stateman like.

Eileen:

- I think you're wrong.

- This mantle is a replica of a dress worn by Wu Zetian of the Tang Dynasty. She was the only reigning empress in Chinese history. She rose from nothing to ruling China during its peak in the 7th Century.

- I want to follow her example and restore China's glory.

Jared:

- But wasn't Wu Zetian a bloodthirsty tyrant?

Eileen:

- It's hard to tell. No ruler believed in human rights during the 7th century. As the only female ruler in Chinese history, she would have scared a lot of men. But the fact that she rose from nothing, and became the only female ruler in Chinese history, has always inspired me.

Jared:

- Very well, Empress Eileen. You better get changed then.

Eileen:

- Yes, and I want you to wear the red robe. The red robe is for the consort of the ruler.

Jared:

- Consort? Is that what I am?

Eileen teased:

- That is, if you want to marry me?

Jared:

- You're driving a tough bargain.
- Okay my empress, let's restore China to glory.

After saying this, they got changed into their Tang Dynasty clothing. Dressed in the exquisite garments they headed to the podium where Eileen would give her inauguration speech.

Chapter 35: Failing to Tame the Dragon. 15th September 2021.

Pierre Beaumont was watching the news reports in his Swiss mansion and he sighed. Eileen Lu had turned out to be impossible to control. This was a bit disappointing for Pierre but not the end of the world. His original plan had been to release the virus, make a fortune from shorting the markets and then blaming China for what had happened. This had been a success, and Pierre was now the richest man on the planet. The failure to control China via Eileen Lu was only a minor setback.

Pierre's servant Jean entered Pierre's lounge room:

- Monsieur Beaumont. James Winter from the CIA is here to meet you.

Pierre sighed. Bloody James coming unannounced again. At least this time he didn't sneak in with a gun! Pierre:

- Okay, please tell him to meet me here!

Jean left the room. Pierre put on his monocle. It was time to pay back James for threatening him four months earlier. Pierre grabbed a pistol and he hid behind the door when James entered the room. Pierre got out and aimed the pistol at James. Pierre:

- Looks like I am the one holding the gun this time.

James smirked back:

- Hmm. A Beretta 92D weighs 900 grams when it's empty. Your pistol weighs 900 grams. Why are you aiming an empty pistol at me?

Pierre put down the pistol on a table and sighed:

- Why are you here, James?

James:

- Eileen Lu is proving to be uncooperative. She urged the US to withdraw our forces within the end of the month.

Pierre:

- So, Eileen Lu is proving to be more capable than we gave her credit. That's nothing to worry about. You win some and you lose some.

James:

- Don't be so casual about this. We cannot let China disappear from our sphere of influence!

Pierre:

- I beg to differ. For the bank, there is no reason to soothe your ego by appointing puppet presidents. All that matters is the money and influence we can yield from a country.

James:

- Well, I want you to send Vladimir to kill her.

Pierre:

- But I won't. Why don't you go yourself?

Pierre smirked. While James could go to China and carry out the assassination, he didn't share Vladimir's insane disregard for his own life.

James:

- I can't. If a US agent gets caught on that mission, it would risk nuclear war.

Pierre:

- Yes, and we wouldn't want that.
- Goodbye, James. I hope our paths won't cross for a while.

James shook his head and slammed the door as he left.

After James had left, Vladimir entered the room from the other side of the building:

- He didn't seem happy. What did he want?

Pierre:

- He wanted me to send you to kill Eileen Lu.

Vladimir:

- What? After all the trouble I had when I dragged her out of China four months ago! What is wrong with him?

Pierre:

- It's the clueless American way. They do this all the time. First, they fund ISIS and then they spend four years bombing ISIS. Three months ago, they installed Eileen Lu as their puppet president, and now they want a new one. Pathetic!

Vladimir:

- So, what is your new evil scheme then?

Pierre:

- Summon Theodore Ahmadi. We will use media to terrify people about the Hei Bai virus. We will use this fear to sell the harmful cure at a grossly inflated price! Muahaha

Vladimir:

- Yes, Pierre. I will summon him at once.

Vladimir left and Pierre got seated in a leather armchair and he smiled to himself. Pierre always found new ingenious ways of hoarding money, and it filled the void within him!

Chapter 36: Forcing the Cure. 18th September 2021.

Pierre Beaumont was sitting in his office studying the molecule model he had built to cure the Hei Bai virus. With the help of the enhanced intelligence from his Zetan monocle, Pierre had made a great discovery. Pierre had found that a high dosage of a proprietary molecule of Ammonium Molybdate Tetrahydrate could draw the dormant Hei Bai virus out of healthy cells and kill it. The problem was that the cure was much more dangerous than the disease. The Hei Bai virus lay dormant in the body unless someone had a very high selenium intake. Ammonium molybdate tetrahydrate, on the other hand, could cause liver failure and infertility in high doses. To kill the Hei Bai virus, one had to take a large dose of the drug.

Pierre had a trump on hand. The corrupt GHA director Theodore Ahmadi was looking for a new hand to feed him, now that the bribes had dried up after Jing Xi's demise.

Theodore entered Pierre's office, and Pierre met him cordially:

- Welcome, Theodore. It's so good to see you. I hope my tokens of appreciation for your hard work reached your family.

Theodore:

- Thank you, Pierre. Yes, my family loved your gifts.

Pierre:

- Glad to hear that. I am happy to keep providing for your family if you can help me spread public health awareness. I have come up with a great breakthrough.

Theodore:

- Promoting public health is the basis for my entire organisation. Please share your findings with me, Pierre.

Pierre:

- Estimates based on serological testing infer that billions of people are infected by dormant Hei Bai Virus.

Theodore:

- Yes, I saw those studies. The same study also showed that one has to eat a lot of selenium to activate the virus. That's never going to happen unless there is a new bioweapon attack.

Pierre:

- But what if I showed you how dormant Hei Bai virus can break out without an excessive selenium intake?

Theodore:

- It can't. We haven't had any cases where a high selenium intake wasn't involved.

Pierre:

- Correct. But what if I pay some scientists to publish a fake study claiming that? Meanwhile, I'll fill all media with terrifying imagery from the New York and Xuwan outbreaks.

- Furthermore, I want you and the GHA to release terrifying statements about the new findings.

Theodore:

- Why would you benefit from this?

Pierre:

- Because I have released a new drug to cure the Hei Bai virus. A proprietary molecule of Ammonium molybdate tetrahydrate. The drug will contain the equivalent of 1mg of Molybdenum.

Having said this, Pierre handed Theodore a document. Theodore read the document for a while and replied:

- That's five times the upper limit for daily molybdenum intake. Such high levels could cause liver damage and infertility.

Pierre:

- But it does cure the Hei Bai Virus.

Theodore:

- Yes. But considering how easy it is to not trigger a dormant Hei Bai virus infection, this cure is a lot worse than the disease.

Pierre:

- Exactly and that's the purpose of any drug.

- If a drug has dangerous side effects, which another drug can reduce, one has created an endless spiral of drug use. That's great for business!

Theodore:

- That's very cynical.

Pierre:

- Funny how the man who covered up the first case of Hei Bai virus, is criticising morals. I know what you did, Theodore.

Theodore:

- There is a nice mansion in your neighbourhood that is up for sale...

Pierre:

- I can organise that.

- But you must be starving. Let's head to a nice restaurant and celebrate Global Health efforts!

Having said this, Pierre led Theodore out of his office. Pierre felt excited about the new evil plan, which would make him even wealthier and his malicious grin couldn't leave his ugly face!

The Banker and The Eagle
The End of Democracy.
Unhappy with the election outcome, the banker plots to kill the US president.
Martin Lundqvist

Chapter 37: The attack on the FNN Headquarters, 6th June 2028.

CIA director James Winter was sitting in the FNN Headquarters, overlooking Central Park in New York. The sun was shining outside, and James would almost have been humming on a tune if his business here wasn't so important. "Mr Bucker will meet with you shortly. Would you like a cup of coffee while you are waiting?", Geoffrey Bucker's secretary asked James.

James didn't bother answering and he waved her away. James felt annoyed that Geoffrey didn't consider him important enough to put everything else aside when he requested a meeting. This kind of contemptuous behaviour never happened to Pierre Beaumont.

James realised that wealthy plutocrats were more interested in appeasing the world's richest man, Pierre Beaumont, than appeasing him. James got distracted from that thought when his phone rang. It was Melinda.

James stared at his phone and hesitated. Melinda Barnes was James' subordinate at the CIA, and they had a secret fling. Although James felt closer to her than he had ever felt in his life, he also felt terrified at the same time. Melinda was a straight-and-arrow operator and a true patriot. James feared to get close to her as he had received a lot of money from Pierre for concealing the truth about the Hei Bai Virus outbreak that spread in 2021. The outbreak had killed 300,000 people in New York within a matter of days. Many of them had been world leaders, as the outbreak had coincided with a United Nations summit.

Pierre had orchestrated this biological weapons outbreak. He had caused it so that he could become the wealthiest man in the world from shorting the markets before the outbreak.

To make matters worse, James had not only kept his mouth about Pierre's crimes against humanity. James had also covered up the fact that Pierre's alleged cure for the Hei Bai virus, Reversogene, made by Pierre's pharmaceutical company Axil Azteca, caused infertility and serious liver damage. Millions had died worldwide from Pierre's shoddy drug, and many more had ended up sterile.

James picked up the phone:

- Hi Melinda.

Melinda:

- Hi James. I was worried about you. You are not in your office and you haven't picked up your phone all day.

James:

- I am sorry, Mel. I am meeting someone.

Melinda:

- Is this one of your many women that you're meeting?

A part of James wanted to answer 'yes' to this question. His feelings for Melinda was risky and he wanted to keep her away. But James couldn't make himself brush her off, so he replied:

- No, I am meeting someone for work.

Melinda:

- Who?

James:

- I am sorry, but that's above your pay grade.

Melinda remained silent for a few seconds, and James could imagine how annoyed she was. Melinda broke the silence and she hid her irritation:

- I understand. Are you still bowling with me, Jack, and Joanne tonight?

James:

- Yes, I can't wait to meet those cute troublemakers again. Got to go. See you tonight.

James hung up the phone. How could it have come to this? Why was he about to swap his life of partying and glamorous women, for being a monogamous boring old stepdad? It didn't make sense, but perhaps that was the way of the heart.

'Mr Bucker will receive you now.' The secretary informed James, who got up and walked towards Geoffrey Bucker's extravagant office.

GEOFFREY BUCKER SMILED as James Winter entered his office. The men shook hands and got seated by an antique mahogany table.
Geoffrey:

- I am sorry to keep you waiting. As the CEO of the Factual News Network, I must report on daily occurrences that affect our world. A great responsibility as you can appreciate.

James shook his head and mocked:

- Oh, I have always thought that FNN stood for Fake News Network. I learn something new every day.

Geoffrey:

- Fake or factual, these are just words. What matters is the impact my news has on the world.

James:

- That is true, and that is why I am here. I have heard rumours about your intentions to report that Reversogene caused a lot of deaths and suffering back in 2022. Tell me why?

Geoffrey:

- I haven't decided yet. But our sources are credible, so that scoop would be a good deed for once.

James:

- That's irrelevant. Revealing the truth would destroy President Mitchell Cent's chance of re-election.

Geoffrey:

- That's what I am after. Mr Damien Vanderbilt owns this media empire. He would be keen to run for president himself.

James:

- Revealing the truth could cause the opposition to win. We wouldn't want that.

Geoffrey:

- Damien is quite content with losing the presidency to Barry O'Connor. But he would rather give it a shot than allowing Mitchell Cent to run for president again.

James:

- And what if he loses to Eva Moreno?

Geoffrey:

- Eva Moreno doesn't stand a chance. It's impossible for someone who is neither Republican nor Democrat to become America's president.

James:

- It is not against the constitution and it can happen. That is something we ought to stop.

Beep, Beep, Beep

James Winter got distracted when his Zetan Monocle warned for danger. James got up, turned his back to Geoffrey and inserted the Zetan Monocle into his right eye. He squinted from discomfort as the monocle attached itself to his optical nerve, but it was a necessary evil. The monocle was the most intelligent AI on the planet, and James would be a fool to ignore this.

James' perception of time slowed down, as the Zetan Monocle displayed the following message:

'High threat level: Dozens of assailants from GAG, the Guns Against Globalism terrorist group have entered the building. Their objective seems to be acquiring the proof of the lethality of Reversogene. Suggested action: Destroy the security camera, subdue Geoffrey Bucker, steal the hard drive with stored evidence, and leave via the ventilation shaft. Probability of survival is 98 %, probability of success is 95%. Alternative options: Combat mode chance of winning is 72 %, Diplomacy mode 78 %'.

James resumed time and he chose the suggested action. He wouldn't risk his life to save Geoffrey, who supported another candidate than him. James pulled up his silenced pistol, shot the security camera, roundhouse kicked Geoffrey in the head, and picked up the laptop. James aimed his pistol, shot the hinges that held up the cover for the ventilation shaft, and got into the shaft.

There were a loud explosion and lots of gunfire. James set his monocle to 'avoid confrontation mode' and a hologram map of the air ventilation ducts came up in front of his right eye, guiding him to safety.

JAMES WINTER WAS BACK in his hotel room, a few blocks away from the FNN Headquarters. James had escaped before the SWAT team had stormed the building to fight the GAG terrorists. This was for the best. He didn't want anyone to know about his visit there, and he would need to tie up loose ends before the end of the day. James was examining Geoffrey's computer when he received a message from Pierre. The message read: 'Do you know anything about this?'

James opened the link. The link opened a video showing how GAG terrorists tortured and executed Geoffrey Bucker and other FNN executives. James felt a short burst of guilt. He could have stopped this from happening if he had accepted a 28 per cent probability of death and fought the terrorists.

James brushed off the guilt. Why would he risk his life to save those vultures on the executive level of FNN? Death was a suitable punishment for their deceit, and besides, they had proven to be uncooperative.

James had a bigger problem than guilt. He could not find the evidence about the lethality of the Reversogene drug. That proof could never see the light of the day, otherwise, Pierre would fall, and he would drag James with him. But where could the evidence be? James had hoped that it would be stored in Geoffrey's computer, but the Zetan Monocle had failed detecting it. Apparently, not even a genius alien AI could know everything.

James decided to come clean to Pierre. Pierre had real resources and Vladimir as an ally. These factors would make him better at finding and destroying the evidence than James. James wrote the following message:

'I couldn't find the evidence against us on Geoffrey's computer. I need help from your side. I will tie up some loose ends in New York.'

Pierre responded with:

- I will send Vladimir to have a chat with the GAG leader, Julienne Bessange. You can go back to playing stepdad for now. Be ready when I need you.

James sighed. He hated that Pierre was spying on him, but it was to be expected. Besides, he wasn't better himself, as the privacy of others were a danger to men that wanted to dominate the world.

Chapter 38: Pierre sends Vladimir to deal with the GAG leader Julienne Bessange, 10th June 2028.

It was a sunny Sunday afternoon, and Pierre Beaumont was sipping XO cognac on his terrace overlooking Lake Geneva from the top of a beautiful hill. He was annoyed that James Winter had failed to find and destroy the evidence for the adverse health effects of Reversogene. Sometimes, having the CIA director on his payroll was insufficient to convert inconvenient truths into forgotten falsehoods. However, Pierre knew who to send when James had failed. He would send his Siberian right-hand-man, Vladimir Kravchenko.

Pierre, Vladimir, and James were all members of the Monocle Conspiracy. The Monocle Conspiracy was not united by a single cause but by a single technology. In 2020, a group of nine individuals had found alien technology that elevated their minds while hiking in Nepal. The technology was in the form of a monocle that elevated the mind of the individual and made the wearer superior. The monocle allowed Pierre to anticipate future outcomes, and it enabled Vladimir to become the world's most dangerous assassin.

Pierre recalled the last meeting within the monocle conspiracy. The group had gathered in Colombia in February 2026 to find another Zetan Temple. They had hoped to unearth more marvellous technologies. Pierre had left Vladimir at home to avoid arousing the anger of Sandra Santiago, whose father Vladimir had murdered in Nepal. The mission in Colombia had been a fiasco, and Pierre had almost died when Zetan sentry bots had defended the temple. Worse yet, they had not found anything of value in the secret temple.

Pierre thought of assembling the Monocle Conspiracy again. It had been two years, and it was nice to meet with a group of people that shared the same experience and the same elevated mindsets.

Apart from Pierre, the other members of the Monocle Conspiracy were the following:

Vladimir Kravchenko was a sadistic Russian killer. Vladimir carried out assassinations for Pierre to fulfil his murderous desires. In return, Pierre used his wealth and influence to cover Vladimir's back, if he left incriminating evidence behind. Pierre and Vladimir had been occasional lovers over the years, but Pierre had left that part behind him. Vladimir was too dangerous, and Pierre did not intend to end his days, falling victim to a sadomasochistic sex marathon.

James Winter was the CIA director and the true power behind Mitchell Cent's presidency. Having the US president in his pocket was useful, and bribing the CIA director was less conspicuous than bribing the president.

Ben Yehuda & Szymon Yehuda were fanatic Zionists working for the Mossad. They wanted to commit genocide on non-Jews in Israel to fulfil a Zionist golden age dream. Pierre had funded these two brothers and their resurgence of the Templar Order, as they were too dangerous to be against him.

Martin Orchard was the man who had led the group to find the Zetan Monocles back in 2020. Martin was rash, unpredictable and dangerous. Pierre did not understand how Martin could be alive, after having returned from the dead several times. However, Martin was too fascinating to have Vladimir put him down permanently. Instead, Pierre had convinced the Yehuda Brothers to make Martin the leader of the resurgent Templar Order. Martin had gone missing in 2026 and Pierre had been too busy with his other schemes to find out about Martin's whereabouts.

Elaine Orchard was a middle-aged Indonesian business tycoon and Martin's estranged wife. Pierre had lent Elaine a fortune to make sure that her corporation, the Harapan Conglomerate, became the most powerful entity in South East Asia. Elaine's debts to Pierre made her controllable.

Josefina Fiero was a Brazilian femme fatale and business tycoon in her late 40's. Like Elaine's situation, Pierre had lent Josefina a fortune after the Hei Bai virus outbreak in 2021 had made him the wealthiest man on the planet. With Josefina indebted to him, her Avanço Verde-Ouro Corporation became the most powerful entity in South America.

Sandra Santiago was a pretty girl who was in her late teens. After Vladimir murdered Sandra's father in Nepal, Josefina took her in and raised her as her own.

Having contacted the members of the Monocle Conspiracy, Pierre went inside to have an afternoon nap.

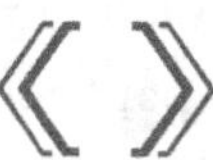

WHEN PIERRE WOKE UP, Vladimir stood silent in the room, staring at him. Pierre sighed:

- I hope you didn't hurt my guards.

Vladimir scoffed:

- Hah. I wouldn't do that to you. I know how difficult it is to find good employees these days.

Pierre:

- So, how did you get in this time?

Vladimir:

- I climbed the mountainside. It's a nice challenging climb. It's the perfect warm-up for bed.

Pierre sighed. He lived in a palace on the top of a hill to avoid unannounced visitors, not to encourage them to climb the hill for fitness. Pierre:

- This is not a booty call, Vladimir. I summoned you for a new mission.

Vladimir:

- I love going on missions. Especially if they entail death and mayhem.

Pierre:

- I leave that to your discretion. I need you to confront the Guns against Globalist leader, Julienne Bessange. She has information about our involvement in the Hei Bai Virus outbreak and about the Reversogene cure that we created.

Vladimir:

- I like this mission already. I have seen the videos of what she can do with a gun. I bet that she would rock the bedroom!

Pierre:

- I don't think seduction is your strongest suit. Stick to your strengths.

Vladimir:

- I will stick to my strengths, but I will fuck her, and you cannot stop me. I will carry out the mission the way I like.

Pierre sighed. It would be a complication if Vladimir, the sex-crazed bisexual, raped Julienne during the mission. But the main goal was that Vladimir destroyed the evidence against them regarding Reversogene causing death and infertility. For minor crimes like rape and murder, Pierre could pay off the authorities for cover ups, especially if the rape victim was a well-known terrorist and a wanted criminal.

Pierre:

- Very well. Do what you deem necessary but don't leave too much of a mess.

Vladimir:

- Of course. I will keep the scene clean. I will find Julienne for you and I'll report back once I have completed the mission.

Pierre:

- Great. Please leave via the front door. I can't have you die in a climbing accident. Stopping Julienne is far too important.

Hearing this, Vladimir smirked, ran towards the ledge, and jumped off the cliff. Pierre looked towards the ledge and stared at Vladimir who plunged towards the ground, opening his parachute in the last moment. "Merde, bloody idiot!" Pierre mumbled to himself as he returned inside.

Chapter 39: Vladimir ends up in a coma, 18th June 2028.

Vladimir Kravchenko stood outside a shoddy farmhouse in rural Tennessee. Using his persuasion skills and force, mostly force, he had located Julienne Bessange's hideout. James Winter had told him that all police agencies in the USA were looking for Julienne after the attack on the FNN Headquarters, 12 days earlier. It was imperative that Vladimir found her first. If Julienne got captured, she could use the evidence against him and Pierre, to strike a deal with the authorities.

Vladimir scanned the building with his Zetan Monocle. The monocle revealed that there was only one person inside the building. This surprised Vladimir, but it also allowed him to fulfil his desires towards Julienne. This would have been far more difficult if armed men surrounded her.

Before entering the building, Vladimir noticed something interesting. A custom-made luxury car made in Indonesia. Indonesian cars weren't sold in America, so how had it got there? He walked up to the luxury car and he checked it out. He recognized the model, he had travelled in this exact car, a few years earlier, when Pierre had told him to be Elaine Orchard's bodyguard for a summit in the USA. But why was the car here, and what was the connection between Elaine and Julienne? Vladimir decided to focus on the mission. Once Julienne Bessange was dead and the evidence secured, Vladimir could discuss Elaine's car with Pierre. For now, it was crucial to focus on the mission.

Vladimir chose a stealthy approach and he entered the building. He made his way upstairs to the room where Julienne's heat signal came from.

Beep, Beep, Beep

Vladimir's monocle beeped to warn him of danger, but it was too late, as a bullet shot through his hand. He dropped the pistol in shock, and he turned to his right. What he saw amazed him. Covered in wet mud, Julienne was aiming her pistol at him. Vladimir smiled, he had never been outsmarted before and this strangely aroused him.

Vladimir:

- So, I guess you are not alone, after all?

Julienne:

- I am. What you see in the bed is a life-size doll with artificial heating that emulates my body heat to trick the infrared sensor in your monocle. I have been expecting you, Vladimir.

Vladimir:

- So, what do you know about me?

Julienne:

- You are Vladimir Kravchenko, the world's most ruthless assassin. I guess that Pierre Beaumont sent you.

Vladimir nodded and replied:

- You seem to have it all figured out.

Julienne:

- Yes, we are freedom fighters, not goons that Pierre Beaumont can bribe.

Vladimir:

- So, why am I still alive?

Julienne:

- I need you. The attack on the FNN Headquarters was our desperate attempt at taking down the treachery that rules the world. But they are fighting back, and we are losing. You are part of the Monocle Conspiracy, but Pierre is using you as a tool.

- Besides, I can offer you something that he can't.

Vladimir:

- What are you offering?

Julienne:

- Great sex and a challenging mission. Taking down the rest of the Monocle Conspiracy would be your greatest achievement!

Vladimir nodded and replied:

- You got me. I'll serve you if you spare me.

Julienne:

- Prove it to me. Take off your monocle and hand it to me."

Vladimir did as Julienne commanded, and he threw the monocle to her.

Julienne studied the monocle for a while and almost put it on. Vladimir hoped that she would, as the Monocle would kill any unauthorised user. Instead, Julienne shocked Vladimir when she shot him in the leg. He groaned as he collapsed to the floor.

Julienne:

- You failed the test, Vladimir. The monocle would have killed me if I inserted it into my eye, yet you said nothing.

Vladimir:

- Hmph, funny that you knew about that. Did you expect me to change my loyalties at gunpoint?

Julienne:

- I could have given you everything. But now, all you'll receive is death!

Hearing this, Vladimir leapt towards Julienne. However, his injuries slowed him down, so she stopped him dead in his tracks with several bullets from her pistol. Getting shot in the chest, Vladimir stumbled a few steps backwards and fell out through a window.

KABOOM

Julienne didn't have the chance to hear the bullet from James Winter's sniper rifle that ended her life. After shooting Julienne from afar, James rushed towards the farmhouse, accompanied by a few CIA operatives. He told his associates to rush Vladimir to the hospital, while he entered the farmhouse and secured Vladimir's monocle. While James found Vladimir's monocle, he could not find the evidence Julienne held against Pierre. Frustrated over this, James slammed the door and left the scene in anger.

Chapter 40: Trouble in the Campaign, 23rd June 2028.

It was early morning, and the sun was rising in the northeast. President Mitchell Cent was sitting in front of the large crucifix that he had erected on the Rose Garden lawn at the White House. This was the best time of the day. Mitchell was almost alone, and he felt close to God. This was a feeling he could not get later in his hectic days as the president of the United States. Mitchell planned to become a piece of history through being the longest-serving president in USA's presidential saga.

Mitchell had replaced President Deidrick Dump who had died in the Hei Bai Virus outbreak in 2021. According to the constitution, Mitchell was ineligible to run again. However, with the help of God, and some rich benefactors, he had found a loophole to circumvent the term limit. Mitchell transported his mind into a state of trance and he almost reached the Holy Ghost when one of his Secret Service agents interrupted him:

- Mr President. Mr Damien Vanderbilt is here to see you.

Mitchell:

- Of course. Please bring him to me, Joseph.

As Joseph walked away, Mitchell felt puzzled. Damien was his biggest sponsor and they met frequently, but the timing was off. Why was the media mogul Damien Vanderbilt visiting him at 5 in the morning? How could he know that Mitchell would be awake this early? The whole occurrence was absurd. Damien approached Mitchell and spoke:

- Greetings, Mitchell. I trust that you found God this morning. Early bird gets the worm, after all.

Mitchell:

- Yes. Early morning prayers are the best solace. But why are you here? You haven't booked an appointment and you're visiting at a time when few would be awake.

Damien:

- I wanted to be away from the prying eyes of the press. I have some important matters to discuss.

Mitchell:

- You own the prying eyes of the press. They will never bite the hand that feeds them.

Damien:

- I own most but not all news and social media. One can never be too careful.

Mitchell:

- So, what do you wish to discuss?

Damien:

- The upcoming presidential election.

Mitchell:

- What's new? Thank you for rigging the Democrat's primaries so that I am facing the senile idiot Barry O'Connor. This will be a walk in the park.

Damien:

- Yes, but not for you, Mitchell.

Mitchell:

- What do you mean, Damien?

Damien:

- I came to tell you that I have decided to take your spot in the election. I have made my money. Now I want my shot at the presidency.

Mitchell:

- Are you out of your mind? You helped me winning the primaries and now you want me gone? That doesn't make any sense!

Damien:

- It makes more sense than your stupid Bronze Age biblical belief. I wanted you to win so I could take your place. Winning the primaries would have been difficult. Convincing you to step down will be a piece of cake.

Mitchell:

- I don't think so. I will run for president without your support if I have to. I'll defeat Barry without your help.

Damien:

- Not when the population finds out about your involvement in the Reversogene cover-up. They'll vote you out and you'll go to jail. This is the evidence Guns against Globalism was looking for when they attacked the FNN Headquarters. Fortunately, I had already moved the evidence before my mole convinced them to attack one of my TV stations.

Damien handed Mitchell the documents proving his claim. Mitchell stared at the documents in terror, unsure on how to proceed. Eventually, Mitchell spoke:

- So, what do you want? Why did you convince GAG to attack your own TV station?

Damien:

- I already told you what I want. I want your spot in the presidential election.

- As for orchestrating the GAG attack on the FNN, I had several motives. Firstly, the attack got rid of Geoffrey Bucker for me. I have wanted to fire him for a long time, but I worried over what evidence he has against me. GAG solved this pickle for me. Secondly, I wanted to drag GAG out in the open. After the attack, they have become the public enemy number one. Besides, their backing by the Chinese government doesn't strengthen their claim to be civil liberty fighters.

Mitchell:

- I see. It seems that you have it all figured out. So, if I comply with your terms, how do I give you my spot in the presidential election?

Damien:

- You'll blame your withdrawal on illness and your religious fervour, which demands your full focus on God. But don't worry about that for now. I'll brief you on what to say and when to say it before we'll make the public announcement.

- I need to head to my private jet. God bless you, President Cent.

Mitchell didn't reply and he watched how Damien Vanderbilt entered his car that drove him away from the White House. Mitchell sighed. He was in a mess, but there was also some silver lining to it. At least, he knew who held the evidence against him for the Reversogene cover-up.

Mitchell called James Winter to have the situation rectified.

James answered the phone in confusion since Mitchell woke him up:

- Hmm, President Cent. What is going on? Has something happened?

Mitchell:

- Damien Vanderbilt holds incriminating evidence against us. We need to deal with him, immediately. Oh, and allegedly China is funding Guns against Globalism.

James:

- When you say deal with him, you mean...?

Mitchell:

- How we normally deal with threats against national security. That evidence must never see the light of day.

James:

- Okay. I'll drive to the White House so we can discuss this. Don't make any rash moves, President Cent.

James Winter got out of bed and headed to his car. He knew that killing Damien Vanderbilt would be a disastrous move that could ruin everything. James needed to discuss this with Pierre before acting on President Cent's orders. Filled with doubts, James entered his car to drive the long way to the White House.

Chapter 41: Cloaks and Daggers in Indonesia, 24th June 2028.

Min Li, the former mistress of the late Chairman Jing Xi, smiled at the stern-looking Budi Sepulyat, who was the Head of Security of the Indonesian Harapan Conglomerate. Min Li felt terrified and she prayed that she could convince Budi to let her leave the Harapan Conglomerate Headquarters.

Budi:

- Miss Li. Where are you going?

Min:

- I am going to lunch.

Budi listened to a message in his headset and then he responded:

- Lunch sounds good. I am coming with you.

Min:

- Oh. I'd love to, but I have a date with someone else.

Budi scoffed:

- Bah. I AM coming with you for lunch. Would you rather come with me to the security office?

Min:

- Lunch is fine. I am sure my date won't mind.

Budi:

- I am sure he will understand.

- Let's go to the Pempek Bali restaurant across the street. I have heard they have great Gado-Gado salad.

Min nodded and forced a smile. She felt terrified. She had a USB memory with evidence that she had stolen from Elaine Orchard's office. The last thing she wanted to do was to have lunch with Elaine's terrifying beefed-up bodyguard.

They crossed the street in silence and got seated at the restaurant. A waitress arrived at their table and Budi ordered:

- Dua Gado Gado, ekstra pedas. Buat mereka cepat, aku tidak punya waktu seharian! *(Two Gado-gado, extra spicy. Make them quick, I don't have all day!)*

The waitress seemed a bit offended by Budi's commanding tone, but she nodded and rushed off.

Min:

- You don't need to be rude to the attendants, Budi.

Budi:

- Bah, time is money. I don't have all day. That's why I'll cut straight to the point.

- Why were you in Mistress Elaine's office?

Min:

- I was looking for her. I wanted to present my latest artwork.

Budi:

- You should have booked an appointment instead of stealing my access card.

Min:

- I am sorry. Harapan is a huge company and I wanted to get ahead of my competition.

Budi:

- Can you promise me I won't find anything incriminating if I check through your handbag?

Saying this, Budi grabbed Min's handbag and opened it. Min put her hand on Budi's hand, looked him straight into his eyes, and pleaded:

- Please, Budi. You must trust me. I'll do anything to please you.

Budi looked at Min Li's beautiful Chinese eyes with his heart full of desire. He licked his lips and replied:

- There is a hotel around the corner. I don't need to be at work for a couple of hours.

Min Li swallowed her shock. The mission was too important, and she feared Budi would kill her if she did not play along with his games. Besides, Budi was considered attractive compared to the fat and disgusting Chairman Jing Xi, she had been the unwilling mistress to, until Jing Xi's death in 2021. Min Li responded with a fake excitement:

- Oh, hee-hee. I like what you are suggesting. I also have a few hours to kill.

Hearing this, Budi smiled and showed off a few missing teeth and a golden grill. He walked up to the counter, left a couple of hundred thousand Rupiahs to pay for the food, and led Min away from the establishment.

EILEEN LU WAS RESTING in the presidential suite of the Manhattan Hotel in Jakarta. She had discussed a new trade deal with the Indonesian president, and she hoped this deal could restart China's struggling economy. She had to get the economy started, as a presidential election was looming in China, and the people were getting restless.

The collapse of the Columnist Party of China (CPOC) in 2021 had destroyed China's economy. Eileen Lu had destroyed the prospects of economic recovery when she refused to be the puppet president of the corporate giants. Eileen Lu standing up to the corporations had initially been immensely popular in China. For the first time in history, China had leadership that embraced the unique Chinese culture as well as civil rights and democracy. Riding on a wave of popularity from her reforms as an interim president, Eileen Lu had won a decisive victory in the 2023 presidential election.

Despite her successes, Eileen Lu was in serious trouble. After becoming the president and refusing to sell out Chinese assets to the World Bank, her former allies at the World Bank had turned hostile and put China under economic warfare. This in combination with the fighting that surrounded the regime change had brought China to the brink of financial ruin. The people who were used to an improving economy were angry with Eileen and she couldn't silence them. Silencing dissenters would make her the same evil that she had fought. Hence, securing a trade deal with Indonesia and improving the economy was Eileen's last chance at winning the 2028 Chinese election.

There was a knock on the door, and Eileen's bodyguard spoke:

- Mrs President Lu. You have a visitor requesting to meet with you. It's Min Li, the former Mistress of Chairman Xi.

Eileen Lu nodded and replied:

- Okay. Bring her in a couple of minutes.

Eileen closed the door and she turned on the kettle. She would drink the special tea variety her herbalist had composed. It was an exclusive blend that Empress Wu Zetian had developed during her reign, a blend that had been forgotten for over 1000 years. Eileen Lu had a sip of the tea and she smiled. The flavour was divine.

There was another knock on the door and Min Li entered the suite. Eileen studied Min Li. While Eileen's middle-aged beauty had faded somewhat from the stress of being China's president, Min was still a stunning beauty in her prime age. At first, Eileen had disliked Min Li, as she was Chairman Jing Xi's mistress. But when they had met face to face, Eileen had realised that they had experienced a comparable situation. Min Li had been repulsed by Jing Xi, but she had rather accepted his advances than risk getting raped and killed by the power-hungry tyrant, and having her entire family murdered.

Eileen looked at Min Li again. Her eyes were teary, and her body was shaking. Eileen walked up to Min, comforted her, and spoke softly:

- Darling, what happened? Did my guards mistreat you?

Min:

- I feel so dirty. I had to have sex with him, or he would have found out about our plan, and he would have killed me. He was so rough and disrespectful to me.

Eileen:

- Who is he?

Min:

- Budi Sepulyat, the Head of Security at the Harapan Conglomerate and Elaine Orchard's watchdog.

Eileen:

- Tell me what happened?

Min:

- I snuck into Elaine's office with a swipe key that I stole from Budi. I downloaded secret documents proving that the Harapan Conglomerate sponsored Guns against Globalism and made it look like our country was behind it.

- Budi found out, and he threatened to expose me unless I had sex with him.

Eileen:

- I see. Do you have these documents?

Min:

- Of course. That's why I hurried here. You're the president of China, I oblige to what you ask me to do.

After saying this, Min handed Eileen a USB drive. She inserted the drive into a laptop and opened the documents that proved her claim.
Eileen studied the files for a while and spoke:

- It seems that we must leave Indonesia at once. If the Harapan Conglomerate wants to harm China, it is not safe for us here anymore. You better join me, Min Li.

Min nodded:

- Thank you. I am sorry if the news is damaging the trade agreement.

Eileen:

- Well, it's better to not have an agreement than signing a trade deal with the enemy. You better stay in the guestroom. I'll organise a swift return to China for the two of us.

Min:

- Thank you. I would like to take a shower now.

Eileen:

- Of course. The bathroom is over there.

After hearing this, Min Li had a long shower where she scrubbed herself hard after the unfortunate rendezvous with Budi. Meanwhile, Eileen gathered her ministers to discuss the matter and plan for how to leave Indonesia immediately.

'WAS THE SEX ENJOYABLE?' Elaine Orchard smirked cunningly. She knew that Budi desired Min Li's beauty, and when she had realised that Min Li was a spy, Elaine would let Budi fulfil his desires.

Budi:

- It was great. She is an extraordinary beauty.

Elaine:

- Tsk, tsk, Budi. When are you going to find a woman who is not terrified by you?

- Anyway, everything went according to plan. So, thank you, Budi.

Budi:

- But I don't understand this, Mistress. Why did you instruct me to have sex with her and let her go? Now China knows that we are funding Guns against Globalism.

Elaine:

- Tsk, tsk. Are you complaining after having sex with the woman of your wet dreams?

Budi:

- Of course not. I was simply curious about your plan.

Elaine:

- The sex was to reward you, and to test her. Now I know that she is a spy that would do anything to complete her mission for her Chinese president, Ms Eileen Lu.

- But in saying this, I won. The document I allowed her to copy contained a virus that infected Eileen's computer. My spies are listening to the Chinese leaders as we speak. They told me that Eileen and Min Li are paranoid, and they are going to leave Indonesia.

- Eileen abandoning the upcoming trade meeting will insult our Indonesian president Fadhlan Azim. This will further the crisis in China, which will please Pierre.

- As for me, I will offer President Azim a better deal, which will bring us closer. This is a big win in just one day.

Budi:

- I see. Shall I kill Min Li for betraying us?

Elaine:

- No. Her betrayal was exactly what we needed. Besides, I assume the sex with you was punishment enough? Ha-ha!

Budi smirked but didn't say anything. Elaine spoke again:

- Now leave, I need to rest after a good day's work.

As Budi left, Elaine picked up her phone and messaged Pierre Beaumont:

- It's done. I have made sure that Eileen abandons the trade meeting with President Azim. I will put in a good word for your proposal to open a uranium mine in Aceh.

After doing this, Elaine leaned back into her chair, and she summoned a masseuse to massage her feet. A 3-hour massage and a bottle of expensive red wine was the perfect end to a productive day.

Chapter 42: Pierre visits the comatose Vladimir, 25ᵗʰ June 2028.

Pierre Beaumont exited his private jet in Washington. He worried about Vladimir Kravchenko, who had been in a coma since his confrontation with Julienne Bessange one week earlier. This worry annoyed him. Vladimir was just a tool to further his goals, by far his best tool, but still only one out of many. Pierre shed a tear. Did he still have feelings for Vladimir, after all? Pierre had been terrified of Vladimir's capabilities since the New York Hei Bai Virus outbreak in 2021.

In 2021, Pierre had intended to kill the world leaders at the UN summit to crash the world markets. But Vladimir had gone beyond Pierre's order and spread the virus across New York City, instead of killing only the world leaders at the summit, causing over 300,000 unwarranted deaths. After this, Pierre had realised that he and Vladimir were incompatible as partners, but Pierre had kept Vladimir close for his skills, and because the alternative, which was to be Vladimir's enemy, terrified Pierre.

James Winter met Pierre at the tarmac of the airport. James smirked and taunted Pierre:

- Have you been watching melodramatic movies again, Pierre?

Pierre:

- What are you talking about?

James:

- You are crying.

Pierre:

- Mon Dieu. It's my bloody hay fever.

James:

- Whatever you say. I picked up Vladimir's monocle from the GAG hideout. You'll need a new agent to wear it.

Having said this, James handed Vladimir's monocle to Pierre. Pierre looked at it for a while, nodded, and spoke:

- Yet, I don't know how to reprogram the monocle to a new user. The monocles tend to be lethal to non-authorised users. Such a mess and such a waste!

- Anyway, where is Vladimir? I would like to see him.

James:

- He is at the National Military Hospital. But there is no point. He is brain dead. I had to pull some strings to keep the respirator going. He is a foreign national with a fake ID after all.

Pierre:

- I see. I'll bring him back to Switzerland. I'll find a way to save him. If a Zeto Crystal brought Martin Orchard back to life, it can also bring back Vladimir.

James:

- Whatever you say, Pierre. Get in the car and I'll take you to the hospital.

After saying this, James and Pierre entered an armoured limousine. James Winter remembered President Cent's request to kill Damien Vanderbilt. He was against the idea, but he needed to discuss it with Pierre. James Winter cleared his throat and spoke:

- There has been a development regarding the upcoming presidential election.

Pierre:

- Oh really. Is Mitchell Cent unwilling to concede his presidential spot to Damien Vanderbilt?

James:

- Worse. He tasked me with killing Damien.

Pierre:

- That is unacceptable. Damien is one of my closest business partners, while Mitchell is a fool. Convince him to resign.

James:

- How do I do this?

Pierre:

- The monocle records all your interactions. Access the recorded conversation where Mitchell tasked you to kill Damien, transfer it to a portable hard drive, and show the video to Mitchell's chief of staff, Elise Santos. She will convince him to resign.

James:

- And what do I do if Mitchell targets me?

Pierre:

- Then you are allowed to kill him. But I want to keep the pres-idential assassinations to a minimum. It's too messy, unless you have a narrative to feed the people.

James:

- Understood, Pierre.

Pierre nodded and he closed his eyes while the limousine took them to the military hospital where Vladimir was in a coma.

PIERRE ENTERED THE hospital ward, where Vladimir was attached to a respirator. Pierre concluded that the technology in the room was obso-lete, and he felt angry that Vladimir wasn't given better care. Then again, to the Americans, Vladimir was just an unidentified thug and not the most valuable operative of the world's richest man. Pierre had kept his association with Vladimir as secret as possible. It suited them better. For Pierre, the advantage was that he could claim innocence if Vladimir was caught. For Vladimir, the advantage had been that he was less recognisable when he was outside of the spotlight, which decreased the risk of him getting caught.

Pierre walked up to the comatose Vladimir, pushed him gently, and ex-claimed:

- Vladimir! Wake up you big Russian bear. I know you can hear me.

Vladimir didn't respond to the touch or to Pierre's shrill voice. Pierre felt how desperation was taking hold of him. He had hoped that this would be one of Vladimir's morbid jokes, where Vladimir would spring up from the dead with a thundering laughter. This did not happen, and sorrow over-whelmed Pierre. Pierre's voice broke, and he snivelled:

- Vladimir. Please wake up. I know that I never told you, but I have feelings for you. I also fear you, but I will do everything to bring you back to life. I need to visit Elaine Orchard and find that idiotic ex-husband of her, Martin Orchard. If Martin could come back from the dead, so can you.

Hearing this, the unconscious Vladimir made a bit of sound. Pierre noticed this and spoke:

- Is Martin Orchard the key to bringing you back, Vladimir?

Vladimir remained silent, and Pierre tried again:

- Is Elaine Orchard the key to what happened to you?

Vladimir growled again, and Pierre understood that he needed to seek out Elaine to find out what her involvement was. Pierre left the room to speak to James Winter:

- Elaine Orchard must be involved in what happened to Vladimir.

James:

- Are you sure? She hasn't been to America for over a year.

Pierre:

- I doubt she travels herself to get things done. Can you check the whereabouts of her two closest men, Budi and Rexi?

James:

- Hmm. You might be right. There was an Indonesian-made car at the farm where Julienne Bessange shot Vladimir. But that car was registered as stolen.

Pierre:

- Why would Julienne steal a Harapan Conglomerate car if they weren't involved with her? I will need to discuss this matter with Elaine.

James:

- Okay. What do you want me to do?

Pierre:

- My lawyers will contact the Department of Justice requesting that they send Vladimir to our care-facility in Switzerland. I need you to make sure there are no legal problems with that request.

James:

- Understood. I'll contact you if the need arises.

Pierre nodded and walked away. He would need to find a way to bring Vladimir back to life, but first he needed to make sure that Elaine fell back in line. He had sponsored the Harapan Conglomerate with billions of dollars from his ill-gotten Hei Bai Virus outbreak windfall, and she shouldn't keep him in the dark.

Pierre reached his car and he turned to his personal assistant, Jean Valmont:

- I need you to organise a meeting with Indonesia's president, Mr Fadhlan Azim.

Jean:

- Of course, Monsieur Beaumont. When would you like me to book the meeting?

Pierre:

- Tomorrow. We are flying there today.

Jean:

- I don't understand, Pierre. Why haven't you mentioned this before? Has something happened?

Pierre felt irritated that Jean had the audacity to question his orders, but he decided to not act on his irritation. Jean's performance held an acceptable standard and she had served him for seven years. Getting another dimwit to replace her would only cause him more headaches.

Pierre:

- China pulled out from the trade meeting with Indonesia. I need to discuss the repercussions with President Azim. Besides, Indonesia owes me a lot of money, and he should beckon at my calling.

Jean:

- Understood, Monsieur Beaumont.

Pierre nodded and turned to the driver:

- Take us to the airport.

After that he entered the car and sat in silence.

PIERRE WAS ON HIS PRIVATE jet, and he tried to ignore Jean's annoying voice so he could enjoy his glass of red wine in peace. Meeting with President Azim was a diversion from Pierre's real goal in Indonesia, which was to confront Elaine Orchard about her connection with Guns against Globalism. However, it would seem very strange if Pierre visited Indonesia without meeting President Azim, since Eileen Lu's abandonment of the trade discussions had made worldwide headlines.

Pierre felt how his headache was getting worse. Listening to Jean's briefing was like hearing nails on a chalkboard, and Pierre wanted peace and quiet more than anything. While he could tell her to shut up, there was better ways of keeping her from talking.

In the last few years, Pierre had occasionally requested fellatio services from Jean. While he didn't particularly enjoy her talents, or the fact that she was a woman, he enjoyed the power he felt from fucking his secretary. Pierre turned to Jean and spoke:

- Enough of the briefing, Jean. I am tired and I need to relax.
There are better ways for you to use your mouth.

Having said this, Pierre tilted his seat back, while pointing at his crotch. Jean hesitated for a bit but eventually gave in to Pierre's request.

As Jean gave Pierre fellatio, he sighed of relief. Most of all, he was relieved that he didn't have to suffer listening to her voice anymore. After finishing, Pierre took a sleeping pill, flushed it down with red wine, and fell asleep with a smug grin on his face.

Chapter 43: Mitchell Cent concedes his spot in the Presidential Election to Damien Vanderbilt, 26th June 2028.

James Winter was waiting outside the oval office. He had booked an appointment with President Cent's chief of staff, Ms Elise Santos. James worried about the meeting, as there were two possible negative outcomes. Either Elise wouldn't believe him, or she would believe him but decide to silence him instead. James shook off his fears. With the Zetan Monocle inserted, he would be difficult to kill, although Vladimir had fallen a few days earlier, proving that the monocle did not make the user invincible.

Elise entered the waiting room and she approached James. James studied her as she entered. She was a Latina woman in her fifties. Like a large portion of the American population, she hadn't looked after herself, and she was sporting a "Type 2 diabetes" body shape. James pushed his judgemental thoughts aside and he forced a smile as he spoke:

- Thanks for seeing me today, Secretary Santos.

Elise didn't reciprocate James' fake smile. Instead, she gave him a stern look and spoke:

- Stop wasting my time with that disingenuous smile, CIA Director Winter. Tell me why you are here.

James sighed. While it was a relief that he didn't need to smile at the hideous Elise, he had hoped that his attractive looks would help him convince her to see things his way.

James took out his phone, and he played a video recording where Mitchell tasked him with killing Damien Vanderbilt.

Elise gave James a sceptical look, and after a few seconds she replied:

- So, I assume that you are not interested in the mission President Cent offered you.

James:

- Thanks for stating the obvious. My associates and I would like Mitchell to concede his spot in the election to Damien Vanderbilt.

Elise:

- I see. I will notify President Cent about your request. Was there anything else, Director Winter?

James hesitated. He couldn't read Elise, and he damned himself for not wearing his monocle to assist him. James felt how his chest went tight, and his worried mind gave him visions of how Mitchell's thugs would kill Melinda and her children. *'Damn. I should have thought about Melinda's family's safety,'* James reflected.

James:

- That is all, Elise. Thank you for your time.

After saying this, James dragged himself to the closest toilet and he purged from his fear. *'I hope my visions are not real.'* James thought, pulled himself together, and left the Whitehouse.

PRESIDENT MITCHELL Cent was kneeling in front of the crucifix in the Oval Office when Elise Santos entered. Mitchell turned his head, gave her a disapproving look, and turned towards the crucifix again. Elise hesitated for a bit, cleared her throat, and spoke:

- President Cent, there has been a dangerous development.

Mitchell turned around and reprimanded Elise:

- You should never disturb me when I am connecting with God.

Elise:

- But President Cent, this is important.

Mitchell sighed and replied:

- Very well. Tell me what's on your mind, Elise.

Elise:

- I met with CIA director James Winter. He showed me a recorded conversation of how you tried to convince him to kill Damien Vanderbilt. He demands that you concede your spot in the upcoming election to Damien.

Mitchell looked at the recorded video and he swore to himself. He had misjudged James Winter. He had believed that James was a true patriot who would do anything for his country. Instead, it turned out that James was a lackey of Damien Vanderbilt, who supported that Swiss faggot Pierre Beaumont. Mitchell grabbed a vase, chucked it into the wall, and exclaimed:

- Damn those unbelievers! Damn them all! They are all enemies of God's work!

Elise:

- Who are they?

Mitchell:

- James Winter, Damien Vanderbilt, and Pierre Beaumont.

Elise:

- But aren't you close to all of them?

Mitchell:

- Not anymore. Can we kill them all?

Elise:

- Mr President. This is unconstitutional and I can't believe that you are suggesting it.

Mitchell sunk into his chair. He sighed and stared into his palms. Eventually, he spoke:

- You're right. Please call a press conference and ask Damien Vanderbilt to get here. I will concede my spot in the election to him.

Elise:

- Understood, President Cent. I will make all the necessary arrangements.

LATER THE SAME DAY, Damien Vanderbilt arrived at the Whitehouse and met with Mitchell Cent before the press conference. Damien walked up to Mitchell and taunted:

- Thank you for conceding your spot to me, Mitchell. It would have been more worthwhile if you did so before considering killing me.

Mitchell grumbled:

- Wouldn't you have done the same thing, Damien?

Damien:

- Yes. But I am not hiding behind the will of God.

Mitchell:

- I know. Yet, to become the President of the USA, you must pretend to follow our saviour, like my predecessor Deidrick Dump did.

Damien:

- I am sure that I can partake in that ploy. Politics and religion are just stage performances for the masses. The real powerbrokers make the decisions behind the scenes. Even the Romans knew this.

Mitchell:

- Yes. So, what policies and ideologies are you planning to promote before the election?

Damien:

- I don't know yet. Policies don't interest me. All I care about is the power and wealth of my associates and I. But I know one thing, with my world-class campaign staff, it will be easy to defeat Barry O'Connor. He is senile and even his own party loathes him.

- Anyway, as much as I love chatting with you, we have a press conference to attend.

Mitchell nodded and the two men headed for the auditorium where the press had gathered.

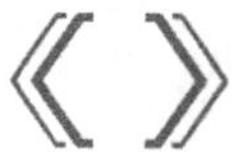

MITCHELL CENT WAS CRYING in front of the Virgin Mary bronze figurine in his bedroom. Damien was the devil, and yet he had conceded his spot in the election to him. As Mitchell looked at the figurine through his teary eyes, it seemed to him that the statuette was weeping blood. He heard a peal of menacing hissing laughter in the back of his head and he threw the figurine at the bulletproof glass window. The figurine bounced and came back to hit Mitchell in the head, cutting his chin.

Elise Santos rushed in together with a few nurses. She jabbed Mitchell in the neck with a syringe. The last thing that Mitchell remembered before passing out was Elise urging the nurses:

- Take President Cent to the medical ward in our bunker. For the sake of our nation, this episode must not become public knowledge.

Chapter 44: Pierre Beaumont pulls Elaine Orchard back in line, 28th June 2028.

Pierre was visiting the ARTsphere Gallery in Jakarta. He was watching a Javanese gamelan performance, and the beautiful intricate musical notes were driving him crazy. He didn't have time for this, he needed to discuss the issues that Elaine Orchard had caused at once. Elaine had allowed a Chinese spy sent by Eileen Lu to infiltrate her computer database and steal priceless evidence against Pierre. The evidence proved that the drug Reversogene was more dangerous than the Hei Bai virus that it claimed to cure.

Pierre had built his absolute fortune from releasing the Hei Bai Virus, shorting the market, and then releasing the drug that cured the virus. While Eileen couldn't prove that Pierre released the Hei Bai Virus, the evidence of Reversogene's dangerous side effects could still ruin and discredit him. It was crucial that this evidence did not gain popular traction.

Pierre also needed to discuss whether Elaine had supported the Guns Against Globalism attack on the FNN Headquarters. Pierre needed to make sure that Elaine fell back in line and didn't make these decisions on her own. Pierre had made Elaine wealthy with his ill-gotten gains, and he expected loyalty.

As Pierre thought that his eardrums were about to burst from the music, Elaine approached him:

- Come, Pierre. I need you to make a bid on an antique sculpture at the auction next door.

Pierre nodded and followed Elaine to the next room. As he closed the door behind him, he felt relieved as he needed to divert his mind.

The auction was about to start, and Pierre whispered to Elaine:

- You have kept me waiting for several days. I don't appreciate waiting.

Elaine shrugged her shoulders and replied:

- I wanted you to take your time with President Fadhlan Azim. He should be an important dignitary for the CEO of the World Bank to meet.

Pierre scoffed:

- I didn't come to Indonesia to discuss charity and school projects in Aceh. I have more important matters to discuss with you.

- What is your connection to Guns against Globalism?

Elaine looked away, took a deep breath, sighed, and spoke:

- Please make a bid on this sculpture, Pierre. I will tell you afterwards.

Pierre nodded and he bid on the Balinese sculpture of the demoness Rangda. Much to his dismay, there was another prospective buyer and Pierre ended up in a bidding war. After ten minutes of bidding, Pierre lost his patience and he bid USD2,000,000. This move deterred his opponent and Pierre finally won the auction. Elaine nodded at Pierre and spoke:

- Thank you, Pierre. Follow me to a private dining room upstairs and I will tell you everything I know.

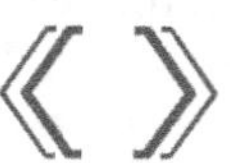

AS THEY GOT SEATED at the dining table, Pierre whinged:

- Why did you make me spend USD2,000,000 on that ugly sculpture?

Elaine:

- That sculpture was of the Demoness Rangda from Balinese mythology. Did you know my ex-husband believes Rangda is speaking to him via the monocle?

Pierre:

- Do I look like a person who doesn't know things? Of course, I know the origins of the Zetan monocles' power. I still don't know why you need that ugly sculpture. My Zetan monocle didn't give me any hints to its usefulness.

Elaine:

- I don't need it. That's why I sold it to you.

Pierre:

- Huh. Why would you sell me an ugly statue?

Elaine:

- Because I ran into some problems with my mining project at Taliabu Island. However, when my bank sees that this sculpture has sold for USD2,000,000; I can use my other 50 statuettes as security for a bank loan.

Pierre:

- I see. That is smart accounting.
- Now tell me about your connection to Guns Against Globalism.

Elaine ignored Pierre's question. She picked up a bakso beef meatball from the soup set menu with her chopsticks, slurped and said:

- These meatballs are divine. Do you want to try one?

Elaine didn't wait for Pierre's reply. She stuffed her mouth with the beef meatball and started chewing it, giving out a slight moan of pleasure as she enjoyed its meaty juices.

Pierre tapped the table in irritation, and after watching Elaine stuffing her face for a couple of minutes, he had enough. Pierre roared:

- Enough of this, Elaine. Tell me about your connection to Guns Against Globalism now!

Elaine nodded, swallowed her bakso and drank her soup, wiped her mouth with a napkin, and spoke.

- I met with Julienne Bessange a couple of months ago. She provided some evidence for Reversogene being a dangerous drug. I wanted to find out the truth, so I sponsored the GAG attack on the FNN Headquarters.

Pierre:

- Bah. The truth on Reversogene. What does it matter to you?

A tear ran down Elaine's chin and she sobbed:

- My niece died in 2022 after taking Reversogene. Julienne hinted that a lot of people had died from the drug and that Damien Vanderbilt was covering it up. I wanted the truth to come out.

Pierre hesitated. He wanted to scold Elaine for her stupidity that put them all in danger, but this was not the time nor the place. It was dangerous to taunt someone when they experienced grief. Besides, Indonesia was Elaine's backyard and the local law enforcement would take her side if there was a conflict. Pierre tried to use empathy to get out of this pickle and stop a dangerous situation from unfolding.

Pierre:

- I am sorry to hear that. I should have warned you about the dangerous side effects of Reversogene. I worried that the Global Health Association wouldn't approve the drug if I disclosed the truth. If it wasn't for the Reversogene drug, the Hei Bai virus would ravage humanity.

Elaine nodded:

- Yes, I guess you are right. The Hei Bai virus outbreak was terrible. Thank you for saving us all.

Pierre exhaled. He was lucky that Elaine didn't know the truth about the Hei Bai Virus. When someone had been infected, the Hei Bai Virus only became active when these infected people ingested large doses of selenium, and thus it was easy to avoid negative effects. Pierre put a hand on Elaine's shoulder and spoke:

- Look. I feel guilty about what happened to your niece. How about I pay off your debts for the Taliabu Island project?

Elaine wiped her tears and smiled at Pierre:

- Thank you, but I already owe you a lot of money and I don't want to be in more debt.

Pierre smiled:

- Don't be silly. This is a chance for us to get a fresh start. I am willing to forgive all your debts so you can use your money to form Indonesia as you envision it.

Elaine:

- That's amazing. Thank you very much. I can't wait to make Indonesia the greatest nation on Earth.

Pierre:

- That's who I am. A generous soul keen to help.

- Considering the fortune that I am about to give you, will you help me make sure that Damien Vanderbilt wins the US presidential election? I need help to cover up the Reversogene debacle.

Elaine:

- I will help you. But you must promise to be forthcoming with me in the future.

'Yeah right!' Pierre thought, but he responded:

- Of course, Elaine. I promise.

Having said this, Pierre got up from the table and corrected his tie. Elaine gave him a confused look:

- Are you leaving? But you haven't eaten anything?

Pierre:

- You have to forgive me, but I am attending a state banquet with President Azim in two hours. You know how slow Jakarta traffic can be.

Pierre didn't wait for Elaine's response. Instead, he turned around and strode for the exit.

PIERRE SENT THE INDONESIAN ladyboy away from his hotel room after he had done his deeds, and he collapsed on his bed. While it felt good being the one on the top in Vladimir's absence, Pierre worried about his Russian assassin and sadomasochistic lover. Apart from his love of money, Vladimir was Pierre's next greatest love. However, Vladimir's aggressiveness also terrified Pierre, who worried about his life every time they met.

'Maybe it is better if Vladimir stays where he is.' Pierre muttered to himself. Pierre leaned back and closed his eyes. Exhausted from the intense meeting with Elaine Orchard and the sex with the ladyboy escort, Pierre fell asleep.

Chapter 45: Eileen Lu Releases Crucial Evidence to Eva Moreno, 10th July 2028.

Eva Luisa Moreno was waiting in anticipation in a villa located at the Yuanyang Terraced Fields in Southern China. The afternoon was hot and humid, but a slight breeze made it comfortable. Eva sighed. While she didn't mind spending some time holidaying in China, her time was too precious for such pursuits. Her worst nightmare for America was about to take place. The corrupt media tycoon, Damien Vanderbilt, had replaced Mitchell Cent as the Republican candidate after Mitchell had withdrawn his candidacy. Damien would defeat the senile Barry O'Connor in the upcoming US presidential election. Eva couldn't allow this scenario to happen. She loved her country and democracy too much to allow this disaster. She needed to win the election herself.

Eva's problem was that she didn't have a large party nor any wealthy supporters. Besides, no independent candidate had ever become the president in the past. Yet, after witnessing the ludicrous debate between Damien and Barry, Eva knew that she had to become the first independent president. During the debate, Barry had fallen over and forgotten what year it was. His candidacy was blatant proof that the electoral college in his party had sent an unelectable candidate. Damien's candidacy was equally suspicious. Just two weeks earlier, the incumbent president, Mitchell Cent, had conceded his spot in the election to Damien due to unknown reasons.

Eva knew that she had to act fast to save American democracy. Through a strange twist of fate, Chinese agents had promised her crucial information about Damien if she went with them to China. It had been an offer that she couldn't refuse, at least Eva had felt so when several armed Chinese agents approached her house. After twelve hours on a private jet, Eva had landed in Southern China, fearful but confident about one thing. The Chinese agents didn't intend to kill her.

Eva sighed and took another sip of the exquisite tea the Chinese agents had served her. Whatever was about to happen, it was outside of her control, so she was better off living in the present. Eva cleared her mind and found inner peace as she enjoyed the beautiful views and a delicious blend of Chinese tea.

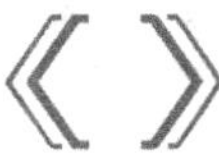

EILEEN LU:

- Welcome to China, US Presidential candidate Eva Luisa Moreno.

Eva woke up from her thoughts and she stared at Eileen in awe. Why on Earth had the president of China, President Eileen Lu, come to see her? Eileen smiled and she spoke again:

- Oh, I am sorry, how rude of me to not introduce myself. I am President Eileen Lu of China.

Eva:

- President Lu, what are you doing here?

Eileen:

- I am here to talk to you. I am sorry I didn't extend a formal invitation. However, it is better for your chances in the upcoming election if our association is not made public.

Eva:

- Your agents said that you have incriminating evidence against Damien Vanderbilt?

Eileen:

- I do. These classified reports prove that the Reversogene drug against the Hei Bai Virus killed a lot more people than the virus did. These reports can expose the top-secret scheme, which Pierre Beaumont and James Winter has been involved in. They are behind Reversogene, Damien Vanderbilt was using his media influence power to cover it up, and President Mitchell Cent was covering up their criminal conspiracy, which caused the deaths of millions of Americans.

Eva:

- These are severe accusations.

Eileen:

- Yes, and I urge you to do your own research. It is, however, the truth.

Eva looked away and gazed at the horizon where the sun was setting behind the picturesque rice paddocks. What a predicament she was in. Her only way to stop Damien Vanderbilt from becoming the president was to depend on China. If China's aid became public knowledge, Eva would destroy her chances of becoming the next US president. However, if Eva kept her association with China a secret, she would be no better than the candidates that she fought against. Eva decided to be honest to the American people, as the truth was more important than her ambitions.

Eva:

- I trust you, Eileen. But you should not have invited me to China. I do not intend to keep our association a secret.

Eileen:

- Admitting that China is helping you will destroy your aspirations of becoming the next US president.

Eva:

- That might be correct. What I do know is that I am not going to follow Damien's path of lying to the public to get elected. I want to make our association known. That is if you are willing to help me in my campaign.

Eileen:

- But wouldn't that breach the US laws against foreign interference?

Eva:

- I am sure that China had similar laws, yet here you are, being the president of a great nation.

Hearing this annoyed Eileen. She had never gotten over the fact that she became the president of China because of the same corporate enemies, which she had fought ever since. While she had won the election in 2023, history would never forget that Pierre Beaumont, Damien Vanderbilt, and Mitchell Cent made her the interim president of China in 2021, after the death of Jing Xi and the collapse of the Columnist Party. Eileen shook off her annoyance, stopping Damien and Pierre was more important than her ego.

Eileen:

- Very well. I am happy to announce China's support for you in the upcoming US election. I will assemble a press conference tomorrow evening. Until then, please examine these pieces of evidence about Reversogene.

Eva:

- Thank you, President Lu.

Eileen:

- You're welcome. I'll see you tomorrow.

Eva watched Eileen as she left the beautiful terrace as day turned into night. She felt excited to meet the inspirational Eileen Lu who had once been a prisoner of the genocidal tyrant Chairman Jing Xi. Rumours claimed that Eileen had killed Jing Xi when he tried to rape her, and Eva wanted these rumours to be true. Eileen's transformation from the rape victim of an evil dictator to the president of the world's largest democratic state served as an inspiration to Eva. Many hours later, Eva fell asleep after reading the evidence against Damien Vanderbilt throughout the night.

Chapter 46: Eva's Surge in the Polls terrify James Winter, 31ˢᵗ July 2028.

James Winter was drinking a glass of Macallan 25-Year-Old's 1962 Anniversary Malt whisky at the terrace of Palace Beaumont. Even though the whisky retailed at $10,000 a bottle, James could not enjoy the sumptuous taste. He needed to discuss some unwelcome news with Pierre, and he couldn't understand why the Swiss poof didn't take the issue seriously.

'Would you like some more ice for your Scotch, Mr Winter?', Pierre's assistant Jean asked. James lost his temper and yelled at her:

- No. I want you to fetch Pierre straight away. I have waited long enough.

Jean rushed off and James sighed. Although yelling at the servant hadn't helped, releasing his frustration was better than letting it boil over. James finished his expensive drink, and he looked at the blue lake from the hilltop palace. He turned around when he heard Pierre's annoying voice:

- Tsk, Tsk. Screaming at my servants won't help us against Eva Moreno.

James:

- If you were at home all this time, why did you make me wait for so long?

Pierre:

- For the same reason that you screamed at Jean. Because I can.

James:

- I don't have time for this. Eva Moreno is surging in the polls after exposing our and Damien's crimes.

Pierre:

- Who cares about polls? Ask Damien to release some fake polls. He controls 80 per cent of US media, so creating a narrative against Eva is a piece of cake. Particularly, since Eva admitted that China supports her.

James:

- Eva has exposed our crimes. This is going to have catastrophic consequences. Mitchell Cent suspended me as the CIA director when the news spread.

Pierre:

- Stop worrying. I will talk to Mitchell and I'll try to make him reinstate you. Otherwise, you can work for me. The main priority is to make Damien the next US president.

- As for me, the lawsuits that will follow Eva's announcement will bankrupt Reversogene Corporation. But I emptied that company of any money years ago, and the company has a figurehead CEO who will be my scapegoat.

James:

- At least look at the result of this polling.

Having said this, James transferred the polling data to Pierre's monocle and the results came up as a hologram in front of Pierre's vision. The following text accompanied the data: 'Predictive capability indicates a 72 % chance for Eva Moreno to win the election.'

Reading the monocle's prediction on the hologram vision unsettled Pierre. When the technology that helped him become the world's wealthiest man predicted that he would lose, he had reasons to worry.

Pierre sighed and replied:

- You might be onto something. We need to leverage our capabilities to discredit Eva. Her association with Eileen Lu and China should do the trick.

James:

- And what do you suggest that we do about the evidence against us?

Pierre shrugged his shoulders and replied:

- Who would dare to take us to court? Besides, with our control of the news and social media, people will focus on our enemies, while we can hide in the broad daylight.

- But to secure our future prosperity, we need Damien to win, and Mitchell Cent needs to protect us for the rest of his term.

James:

- Good. Will you visit Mitchell and ask for his support?

Pierre gave James a disdainful look. This was the best time of the year in Switzerland, and Pierre would not go back to America a few weeks after his last visit. Mitchell Cent would have to drag himself to Palace Beaumont to get his instructions. Pierre:

- I am not going back to America for a while. Mitchell will have to make his way here. Besides, do you want to go back to the

USA where everyone knows you as the suspended CIA director?

James:

- How are you going to make Mitchell Cent come here on your whim?

Pierre:

- Tsk, tsk. Everyone knows that the President is a puppet. He will dance after my tune. Now I will retreat to my chambers. I suggest that you stay in one of the guestrooms in my palace, away from the prying eyes of the public.

James didn't reply. He had escaped the USA before some overzealous judge decided to put him on trial. James suspected that Pierre feared the same fate would befall him if he travelled to the USA. For now, James hoped that the president would sign an executive order that protected him.

Not wanting to bother Pierre further, James turned around, exited the room, and went to the guestroom that Jean had organised for him.

Chapter 47: Pierre Strikes a Deal with Mitchell Cent, 7th August 2028.

Pierre Beaumont was looking at the guests arriving at the reception area of Hotel d'Angleterre, located at Lake Geneva. To improve his reputation after the uncovering of the Reversogene scandal, Pierre had decided to lead a fundraiser as a distraction to the public. The objective of the fundraiser was to raise funds for poor villagers affected by a volcanic eruption in the Philippines. While Pierre didn't give a fuck about the poor villagers, Damien Vanderbilt, Pierre himself and James Winter needed to appear in a positive light.

Another important reason for the fundraiser was to entice the American puppet president Mitchell Cent to visit Pierre. Pierre didn't want some renegade judge in the USA to order his arrest, knowing the Reversogene scandal had been rampant over there, so he needed to secure Mitchell's support before setting foot in America.

Pierre saw Mitchell Cent entering the small and luxurious Parquet Louise conference room. Pierre decided to ignore him. While meeting with Mitchell Cent was crucial, Pierre didn't want others to realise this. Instead, he walked onto the stage. He set his monocle to give him a speech that "sway hearts" and gave a passionate speech about the importance of helping the survivors of natural disasters in South east Asia.

Once Pierre had finished with his speech, he got off the stage. As the camera crew left, Pierre smiled. Who would believe that he had deliberately released a dangerous medication via his pharmaceutical company Axil Azteca when he pledged billions of dollars to charity for the sake of humankind? The news corporation and social media that his peer Damien Vanderbilt controlled would label anyone speaking against him as a conspiracy theorist. This would deter most people from criticising Pierre and keep politicians obedient.

With the damage control done, Pierre went to his table to enjoy the dinner and the socialising with other banking executives. His conversation with Mitchell Cent would have to wait until later.

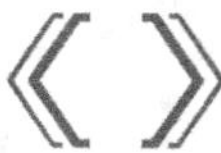

A FEW HOURS LATER, Pierre met with Mitchell Cent in a private meeting room at the hotel. Mitchell seemed a bit agitated and spoke:

- That was an impressive speech and display of charity from you, Pierre. Yet, I assume that it wasn't your true motivation for holding this fundraiser.

Pierre smirked:

- Public perception is everything. My emotional speech and my $2 billion donation to the survivors of the volcanic eruption will sway the masses in my favour. Who will believe that I've made my fortune from deliberately releasing the Hei Bai virus and the unreliable Reversogene cure of the virus itself? That would be preposterous!

Mitchell:

- I haven't heard any allegations about your releasing the virus. The consensus is that Chairman Jing Xi was the one that released it as a biological attack on us.

Pierre looked away for a second, and he bit his tongue. Why had he suggested that he might be behind the Hei Bai virus outbreak? There was no point in dwelling on it, so Pierre replied:

- You're correct. I read too much of what people say about me on the Internet. A bad habit of mine.

Mitchell laughed:

- You wouldn't last a day as the President of the USA if you cared about political rants online.

- So, how can I help you and the World Bank?

Pierre:

- I need you to sign an executive order that grants me, James Winter, and Damien Vanderbilt diplomatic immunity for the rest of your term.

Mitchell:

- Diplomatic immunity? I don't understand. James and Damien are American citizens and you are a not a diplomat.

Pierre:

- We are global citizens and spokespeople for a global movement. As such, we should have the same degree of protection as other diplomats.

Mitchell:

- I doubt people will appreciate if I grant you immunity, Pierre.

Pierre:

- Bah. You said that you don't care about political criticism. Besides, you are 69-years old and retiring this year. Why not live out the rest of your life in wealth and affluence. Money is, as you know, not a problem.

Mitchell shook his head and replied:

- I don't need your money. Too much wealth would only alienate me from God.

Pierre took a deep breath. He hadn't anticipated Mitchell refusing his bribe. Then again, everyone had a price, Pierre needed to find out what Mitchell desired. Could God be the answer? Pierre decided to give it a shot.

Pierre:

- My wealth can help you spread your religious doctrine. What better way to spend your retirement than preaching the true word of God?

Mitchell:

- You have a point. If protecting you and Damien can save countless souls, so be it. I need to spread the true words of Jesus Christ, for the sake of humanity.

Pierre:

- Excellent. We know that you are currently writing your own memoirs into a book. If you sign the executive order protecting us, one of Damien's publishing houses will offer you $10 million for your memoirs. In the book, you can share your views on the truth about your much-loved Jesus Christ.

Mitchell:

- We have a deal. I know that you are not a god-fearing person, but thanks for helping me spread God's words.

- I need to return to my room. As the president of the USA, I have a busy schedule tomorrow.

Pierre nodded and replied:

- Thank you. May God bless you.

As Mitchell left, Pierre sighed of relief. For a brief moment, Pierre had feared that Mitchell was incorruptible. As it turned out, Mitchell just needed another form of motivation. Pierre hoped that Damien would be willing to publish Mitchell's memoirs as it would be annoying to acquire a publishing company and do it himself. Pierre got into his limousine and went back to Palace Beaumont. He felt satisfied that the issues with Eva Moreno and Reversogene drug would soon be under control.

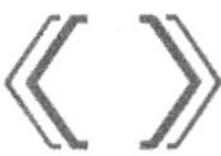

AS PIERRE ENTERED PALACE Beaumont, he noticed an unexpected visitor. Sandra Santiago, the adoptive daughter of his Brazilian business partner Josefina Fiero, walked up to Pierre and hugged him:

- Pierre, it's so nice to see you again.

Pierre didn't reciprocate Sandra's hug and instead he whinged:

- Stop this charade, Sandra.
- Tell me why you are here?

Sandra stopped hugging Pierre and took a step back. She smirked:

- I am turning 18 in a couple of months, so Josefina wanted me to learn how to become wealthy and influential.

Pierre shook his head. While he was certain that the young and beautiful Sandra would be a suitable partner if he wanted an heir, he had already organised that several years earlier. Pierre had paid a multitude of surrogate mothers to bear and raise his children, having lived an unmarried life for the past 58 years. This way, he could pick the most suitable successor when he approached the end of his days. As for Sandra's youth and beauty, Pierre couldn't care less. He liked mature men, not young girls.

Pierre taunted:

- I am afraid Josefina hasn't done her research. I prefer mature men over young women. Thus, while I am sure many men would find you seductive, I find your advances irritating.

- Now tell me what you want.

Sandra sighed and replied:

- Josefina wants to summon everyone in the Monocle Conspiracy to Brazil. She has heard about your aspiration to make Damien Vanderbilt the president of the USA. She is willing to help, for a price.

Pierre laughed:

- It is always about money, isn't it?

- Sending me an email would be easier than sending you to seduce me. Nonetheless, let me show you to a room. It is past midnight and it is too late to discuss business.

Sandra nodded and Pierre showed Sandra to a guestroom on the third floor. As Pierre walked back to his bedroom, he reflected over Sandra's beauty. She was extraordinary and if he hadn't been aligned the other way, she could have seduced him and exerted power over him. In the end, it didn't matter. Josefina's powerplay had failed, but he would play along, and he would give her the money it took to make her cooperative. Money was, after all, not a problem.

Chapter 48: The Monocle Conspiracy Meets in Brazil, 12th August 2028.

Josefina Fiero watched how one of her servants carried in a tray of cocktails. It was the dry season and the sun was shining; thus, it was the perfect conditions to assemble her associates. Josefina looked at the rare birds she had assembled in the large private park surrounding her palace. In this serene environment, she could forget about the turmoil that was affecting the rest of her home country.

Josefina's private palace was a replica of the white house and it was an extension of Josefina's ego. Although she would never rule over the actual white house, presiding in her replica was even better. Besides, she was more powerful than the American president. At least she had felt that way until her failed attempt at interfering in the Brazilian election the previous year. Since her chosen candidate had failed, the Brazilian president had disrupted Josefina's business with frivolous lawsuits. While Josefina felt certain that she could win in court, she wanted to make sure that she would win. Securing the support of Pierre Beaumont, the richest man in the world, was her best bet.

Josefina thought about the upcoming meeting. She hoped Vladimir Kravchenko would not attend. While Vladimir's murder of Jorge Santiago had played out in Josefina's favour, she knew that his presence would upset Sandra. Because of the murder, Josefina had been able to adopt Sandra, who filled her with pride, and would be the successor to Josefina's business empire.

While Josefina had upheld contact with the other members of the Monocle Conspiracy, this was the first time they assembled in over two years. During their last meeting, they had tried to uncover an alien artefact in Colombia. That mission had been a failure, and they had been seconds from dying when sentry robots had attacked them. They had survived the ordeal, however, and Josefina knew that she could never achieve her goals if she was too risk-averse.

A servant approached Josefina and spoke:

- A senhora Josefina. Elaine Orchard, do Conglomerado Harapan, está aqui. *(Ms. Josefina, Elaine Orchard from the Harapan Conglomerate is here.)*

Josefina:

- Obrigado, Evelina. Vou ótimo aqui na sala de coquetéis. *(Thank you, Evelina. Bring them to the cocktail room.)*

JOSEFINA APPROACHED Elaine Orchard, who was sipping on a cool Caipirinha. Elaine looked younger and fresher than ever and seeing this filled the slightly older Josefina with jealousy. When they first met in Nepal eight years earlier, Josefina had still maintained the stunning looks from her youth. But now when they were both in their mid-40s, Josefina's looks had faded while Elaine still looked fresher than ever. Josefina decided to fake it, as she needed to speak to Elaine in confidence before the meeting. Josefina:

- Oh my god. Elaine, you look amazing! What is your secret?

Elaine smiled and replied:

- I found the fountain of youth and my scientists at The Harapan Conglomerate managed to replicate the formula. This facial treatment will make you look a decade younger.

Having said this, Elaine passed a jar of Kalaotoa Island mud to Josefina, who smiled and replied:

- Thank you very much. I can't wait to try it.

Josefina put the jar aside, picked up a drink from a tray and cheered:

- Cheers to us. Together we will shape our continents to the better.

Elaine:

- Yes, indeed. The first step of our plan is working out. I allowed Eileen Lu's spy to steal the evidence against Pierre, to force him to finance our plans. With the world's richest man bankrolling us, nothing can stop our long-term plans.

Josefina:

- Yes. For too long the bankers have robbed our nations and made us weak. Now we can make our nations great while weakening our rivals.

Elaine:

- Yes. So, what is your opinion about Eva Moreno? Should we support her or Damien Vanderbilt?

Josefina:

- We should support Damien. Josefina would be a good president for the USA. She would crush Pierre and rebuild her country. But we are better off if the USA has a corrupt president that makes them weak while we siphon money from the World Bank. That's how we become stronger.

Elaine:

- So, are you saying that we should support Damien, knowing that he will destroy America?

Josefina:

- Yes. I hope that doesn't bother you?

Elaine took a sip of the Caipirinha and smirked:

- It doesn't bother me at all. Oh, and I love this drink.

Josefina:

- I am happy to hear that. Let's enjoy a few more and coordinate our business plans. We have so much to catch up on.

Having said this, Josefina rang a bell and ordered some more drinks. After that, Elaine and Josefina got drunk, socialised, and coordinated their business plans for the rest of the evening.

THE FOLLOWING DAY, Josefina's head felt like someone had punched her with a sledgehammer. She had enjoyed far too many drinks the night before. A meeting with Elaine was a rare opportunity for Josefina to socialise with someone with similar ambitions. Having a Zetan Monocle was both a blessing and a curse, as it altered the mind and made it harder to socialise with other humans. Since Elaine was in the same situation, they had drunk and gossiped late into the night. This was something that Pierre's whiny voice had some objections to.
Pierre:

- I am disappointed with you, Josefina. I had anticipated a proper reception when I arrived last night. Instead, I found the two of you blind drunk and gossiping.

Josefina didn't respond. She had drunk too much, and Pierre was too important to disregard. She lined up some cocaine and snorted it. As the effect kicked in, she felt better. Josefina:

- Relax with the attitude, Pierre. You are not the centre of the universe. Besides, we are here to discuss how to make your candidate, Damien Vanderbilt win the US election.

Pierre scoffed:

- Bah, I would prefer a hostess that didn't cure her hangover with cocaine.

Ben Yehuda intervened:

- Cut the crap, Pierre. My brother and I haven't travelled all the way here to listen to your bickering. Let's get back on topic.

Pierre nodded at Ben Yehuda. Ben and Szymon Yehuda were two Israeli brothers who had been on the same trip as Pierre when they found the Zetan Monocles in Nepal. Pierre had funded their mission to find the primordial Zeto Crystal, but it had been to no avail so far. Despite this, it was important to keep them on the payroll. Through James Winter and the Yehuda Brothers, Pierre controlled the Mossad and the CIA. Through this partnership, he had something that was even more important than money, which was information. Pierre sighed:

- You're correct, Ben. My apologies for wasting your time. Let's focus on the issue at hand.

Szymon:

- Not so fast, Pierre. We need to know where Martin and Vladimir are.

Pierre sighed and replied:

- Vladimir is in a coma after a botched mission. Martin is a broken man who has withdrawn to a secluded island in the Pacific.

Sandra taunted:

- Such a shame with Vladimir. Can I pull the plug on that bastard?

Pierre gave Sandra an angry look and replied:

- No, you cannot. Vladimir is an essential member of my inner circle and he has been crucial in aiding our cause.

Sandra:

- Whatever you say, Pierre.

Josefina brought the conversation back on track:

- So, how would it benefit the rest of us if Damien Vanderbilt wins the Presidential election?

Pierre:

- Well for starters, it keeps me out of prison so I can keep funding your operations. Besides, with Damien as the US president, all of you will receive lucrative US government contracts.

Josefina:

- That's all good, but I need something concrete. We have expenses, after all.

Pierre:

- Very well. If you choose to help me, I will give you $1 billion each. That should be enough to cover your conflict with the Brazilian president, Josefina. It will also be enough to fund the Templar order and our continued search for the Zeto crystals, Ben and Szymon.

Josefina:

- That should be acceptable. What do you need from us?

Pierre:

- For now, I need you to use your influence to support Damien and discredit Eva Moreno and Barry O'Connor in international media. I might need you to perform covert operations as well, but my generous donations will cover your expenses.

Josefina smiled at Pierre and replied:

- I agree to your terms, Pierre. What about the rest of you?

Ben Yehuda:

- We agree to this arrangement.

Elaine:

- I am also happy with this arrangement.

Josefina:

- That's excellent news. Let's enjoy some Churrasco. I have ordered my chefs to make it Kosher, to honour our Israeli guests.

After saying this, Josefina rang a bell to alert her employees. Chefs entered the room, carrying big platters with assorted grilled meats and side dishes. As the group feasted on the meats, and drank expensive wines, they made detailed plans for the months to come.

Chapter 49: Pierre and James travel to China to pressure Eileen Lu, 2nd September 2028.

Pierre Beaumont and James Winter were sitting on a private jet headed for China. Developments had been unsatisfying, and Eva Moreno had a large lead in the polls despite Pierre's and Damien's attempts at discrediting her. Due to the political situation, President Mitchell Cent hadn't dared to reinstate James Winter as the CIA director. This meant Pierre did not have access to CIA data, which was not ideal for his plans. With this in mind, Pierre had taken a gamble to travel to China and confront Eileen Lu. If China withdrew their financial support to Eva, her candidacy would drown in the media cacophony that Pierre and Damien organised against her.

Jean walked up to Pierre and topped up his glass with red wine. As she left, James complained:

- You shouldn't drink that much wine. We need to focus on our meeting with Eileen.

Pierre:

- Don't talk to me like that. I am a connoisseur and I can handle my drink.

James:

- Fucking hell, Pierre. We should discuss our plans. Instead, you're drinking and ignoring me. We are equals.

Pierre taunted:

- We are not equals.

- I am the world's wealthiest man, and you are a disgraced government employee who has been hiding in my palace. Now sit back and enjoy your wine in silence. Domaine Leroy Chambertin Grand Cru 1990 is too expensive to be left to go to waste.

James:

- I don't care about wines anymore. All I want is to get back to Melinda and her children.

Pierre:

- Bah. Trading a glamorous life of wine and women to raise someone else's progeny. Pathetic.

James:

- Look who is talking. You have a lot of children, Pierre.

Pierre:

- Yes, a dozen children with a dozen surrogate mothers. Six boys and six girls. All turning 4 this year. As a prominent man, my dream is to have a diverse pool of progeny so I can choose a suitable successor when the time comes. That doesn't mean I like children.

James:

- I could tell when I attended your quarterly inspection last week. You showed a chilling level of contempt for your children when you met them.

Pierre:

- Yes. I must admit my disappointment with the 2024 batch of surrogacy. Hopefully, I can master genetic modification and produce a better batch in the future. Genetics is an interesting topic, and we can only learn from our mistakes.

Having said this, Pierre recalled the latest quarterly inspection of his progeny. Back in 2023, Pierre had paid a dozen women to mother his children. Once the children were born, he had opened a centre where his employees worked to raise the children according to Pierre's desired specifications. The program had been an abject failure this far, and the only children with actual potential were the twins Lucien and Delphine. Pierre had thought of ending the program and culling the children, but he had stopped. The risk of detection was too high, and Pierre didn't want infanticide to be his downfall. Pierre spoke again:

- Thinking back to the inspection, Lucien and Delphine showed some potential. No matter, I have many years left, and I will revisit the program at a later stage.

James:

- You're a very sick and demented man, Pierre.

Pierre:

- Bah, there is a fine line between insanity and genius. Now shut up and enjoy your wine.

James did as Pierre instructed. After sculling his wine, he put on a blindfold and he fell asleep.

PIERRE BEAUMONT WAS tapping the glass table irritably, waiting for Eileen Lu to receive him. Pierre hated when people made him wait, as it was beneath him waiting for others. Yet, there was nothing he could do to make her hurry up. Pierre regretted that he had fast-tracked Eileen to become the president of China after the collapse of Chairman Jing Xi's Columnist Party. For seven long years, Pierre had suffered Eileen's ingratitude, and this was the last straw. By exposing Pierre's crimes and supporting Eva Moreno, Eileen had declared war on the man who made her.

Eileen Lu entered the meeting room, accompanied by a large group of bodyguards. As Eileen shook Pierre's hand, Pierre complained:

- I asked for a private meeting. Not to meet you and half of China's army!

Eileen shrugged her shoulders and replied:

- I have seen the capabilities that your monocles give a trained warrior. I assume that former CIA director James Winter is an accomplished warrior like the late Vladimir Kravchenko. Why else would you bring him here?

Pierre:

- Bah, Vladimir is not dead, and I wouldn't come here to kill you myself.

Eileen gave Pierre a cold stare. Pierre backed down and replied:

- Very well. We'll take off our monocles.

Having said this, Pierre nodded to James and they took off their monocles and put them in the inner pockets of their suits. When they removed the monocles, they revealed their purple predatory eyes on the righthand side of their faces.

Eileen:

- What did you do to your eyes?

Pierre stated:

- Our monocles' connection to the optical nerve changes the colour of the iris. It's a nuisance but in the grand scheme of things, it's insignificant.

Eileen:

- Where did you get those things from? I remember Vladimir wore one of them when he saved me from the wrath of Jing Xi. He shot down two pursuing fighter jets with a rifle during our escape.

Pierre joked dryly:

- Yes, he always spoke about that episode. It was the highlight of his illustrious career.

- Anyway, now that we have taken off our monocles, would you mind a private meeting?

Eileen shook her head and gestured towards most of her guards to leave the room. Pierre:

- Thank you, Eileen.

Eileen:

- Now tell me why you are here?

Pierre:

- Because you need to stop supporting Eva Moreno in her bid to become the US president.

Eileen:

- I won't withdraw my support from Eva. I have met her, and our values align. Eva would be a good leader for her nation and good for the world. She is the opposite of your candidate, Damien

Vanderbilt, who only seek to enrichen himself and his accomplices.

Pierre:

- This is unacceptable. I saved you and I made you who you are. You should obey me.

Eileen:

- I am not your puppet president, Pierre. If there is nothing else, please leave my office.

Pierre knew that he was better off not taunting the Chinese Dragon, but he couldn't control himself.
He yelled with his shrill voice:

- You must obey me, Eileen, or I will destroy China's economy.

Eileen:

- That's enough, Pierre. From this day on, I expel you and James Winter from China. You will not be allowed to return. Guards, escort our guests to the airport.

James Winter intervened and pulled Pierre away. Threatening Eileen Lu while they were in China was unwise and they were lucky that Eileen Lu was not a blood-thirsty tyrant like her predecessor. *Shut up and comply,'* James whispered in Pierre's ear. Pierre calmed down and Chinese soldiers escorted them back to their private jet at the airport.

JAMES AND PIERRE WERE back on the private jet when James shouted:

- What the hell is wrong with you? You almost got us killed.

Pierre:

- I was testing her. I suspected that she was a weak bleeding heart and this proves it. While we couldn't persuade her to stop supporting Eva, we can destroy her economy and force her out of the race.

James:

- And what if she had decided to kill us in her office?

Pierre:

- She wouldn't. If she had wanted me dead, she would have wanted a public trial. That would be disastrous for her.

James sighed. There was no point in arguing with Pierre, who believed in his superior intellect and would never admit any wrongdoing.

James:

- So, what are we doing now?

Pierre:

- I will make good of my threat. Eileen Lu and China will suffer as I will direct the World Bank's power of the international banking systems against China and use Damien's news and social media influence against her. I will stop all overseas banking transactions to and from China, bringing Eileen to the brink of ruin. This will force her to cooperate.

- Now please refrain from talking. I have plenty of important dignitaries to contact!

Having said this, Pierre inserted his monocle and he started contacting all the global banking dignitaries. It was time for Eileen Lu to experience the full extent of his power.

Chapter 50: Damien Vanderbilt visits Pierre Beaumont, 8th September 2028.

Pierre sighed as he closed the email from the Deutsche Bank chairman, Gunter Fritz. Another major banker had refused to help him in his economic crusade against China. This was not how Pierre had intended things to go. He needed compliance among the other bankers in his economic war against China. Otherwise, he would lose this war and China would be able to participate in the global economy. Jean entered Pierre's home office and spoke:

- Monsieur Beaumont. Damien Vanderbilt is here.

Pierre sighed. Why on Earth did people arrive at his mansion unannounced all the time? In the last few months, James Winter, Sandra Santiago, and now Damien Vanderbilt had arrived without prior notification. Pierre hoped that Damien would follow Sandra's example and go home after the meeting, as James Winter seemed to be impossible to get rid of. That uncultured Yankee had occupied one of the Palace Beaumont guestrooms for the last six weeks. Pierre:

- Well, it would be rude to keep him waiting. Bring Damien some refreshments. I will meet him in the dining room.

Jean nodded and left the room. Pierre got up and made his way to his bedroom where he got dressed in a tuxedo with the Beaumont family crest. He rarely wore clothes with the crest, but the attire was suitable for a meeting with the next American president.

Pierre studied himself in the mirror while he wore the tuxedo. He felt proud donning the family crest while being the epitome of success. Being the sole survivor of the family's line, Pierre had gotten expelled from Palace Beaumont as a young boy, growing up amongst foster parents. But he had worked himself to a position of considerable wealth and power and bought back the palace. Pierre's wealth and power had been amplified when he found the Zetan Monocle in 2020 and when he released the Hei Bai virus a year later. Since then, Pierre had been the wealthiest and most influential man in the world. Thanks to his breeding program, he would have enough progeny to create a dynasty that would rule the world. Pierre smiled; it was time to meet the next puppet president of the USA.

DAMIEN VANDERBILT WAS tapping on his smartphone when Pierre entered the dining room. Pierre gave Damien a quick look before speaking. Damien looked tired and his clothes, although expensive, looked unkempt and wrinkly.

Pierre cleared his throat and spoke:

- Welcome to Palace Beaumont. Apologies for the lack of entertainment. I never received your meeting request.

Damien:

- I never sent one. I have a very busy schedule with my election campaign.

Pierre:

- Bah, if you can't handle a campaign, follow Joe Bitten's strategy from 2020 and campaign from your basement, blaming the coronavirus pandemic.

Damien shook his head and replied:

- I am not elderly so I can't cite "avoiding the flu" as a valid reason to not campaign in person. Besides, Joe Bitten lost to that fuckwit Deidrick Dump, so it didn't work out for him.

Pierre smirked:

- He didn't miss out on much. He died from dementia the following year.

Damien:

- And Deidrick died from contracting the Hei Bai virus. Funny how things work out.

Pierre:

- Yes. But Mitchell Cent has served us well. Hiding behind a cloak of zeal, he has made sure to fulfil all our needs.

Damien:

- But he cannot protect us if Eva wins the election. If I don't win, we are toast.

Pierre:

- Agreed. Eva winning the election would be an unacceptable outcome.

Damien:

- So, why haven't you acted against Eileen Lu? You promised that you'd make her stop supporting Eva Moreno when I spoke to you last week.

Pierre sighed, walked over to his whiskey collection, and poured himself a drink. He hated admitting that his plan had faced a hiccup, but the truth was that he needed the other major bankers to wage economic warfare against China. Pierre:

- There has been a complication. My colleagues believe economic warfare against China will harm their interests.

Damien:

- That's ridiculous. When I become the president, I can make the Federal Reserve print trillions of dollars to finance their expenses.

Pierre:

- Yes, but money printing can't go on forever. My colleagues at World Bank federation need real assets and potential benefits to support you against Eva Moreno and her Chinese alliance.

Damien:

- What other assets do you have in mind?

Pierre:

- There are still large areas in the USA that are kept preserved as wildlife national parks. If you promise to cancel these land protections and transfer the land ownerships to private interests, I am sure we can reach an agreement.

Damien hesitated. Even though he was a dishonest man that spread lies and propagandas through his news and social media network, he still appreciated the beauty of nature. Besides, countries without environmental protections ended up facing wanton ecological and economic disaster. Damien shook his head and replied:

- I cannot agree to those terms.

Pierre taunted:

- What a shame. I am sure Eva would love to beat you in the election and throw you into prison.

Damien:

- No, she won't. We will convince her to pull out of the election.

Pierre:

- We? How are we going to do that?

Damien:

- Yes, you are coming with me. You have as much to lose from Eva becoming the president as I have. Even more if she finds proof that you were behind the Hei Bai Virus outbreak. If that's the case, there will be nowhere for you to run, Pierre.

Hearing Damien's statement filled Pierre with fear, and he struggled to contain his act of arrogance. He walked to the bar, poured himself some more scotch, and sculled it. Pierre:

- Very well. I am coming with you. Let's meet with this Eva Moreno.

Damien:

- My car is waiting outside, we are leaving at once.

Pierre nodded and replied:

- Understood. I'll go upstairs and fetch James Winter. We'll need his expertise and connections to stop Eva.

After saying this, Pierre went upstairs to fetch James. A short while later, the three of them walked to Damien's limousine for a transfer to the airport.

While they were in the car, Pierre sat in silence and thought carefully. Although he hated that Damien had arrived at his house and given him orders, he had to comply. Damien hinting that he knew about Pierre's involvement in the Hei Bai Virus outbreak meant that Pierre had to obey Damien. If the truth came out about Reversogene and the Hei Bai Virus outbreak, nothing could save Pierre from being sentenced to a lifetime in prison!

Chapter 51: Pierre and James try to influence Eva Moreno, 10th September 2028.

Pierre Beaumont exited his private jet at the small regional airport in Santa Fe, the capital of New Mexico. Despite the summer being over, it was still a sizzling hot day in this southern state of the USA. Eva Moreno had refused to meet them, but Pierre would not take no for an answer. He would sneak in and speak to her after her campaign meeting. He turned to James Winter and spoke:

- Are you ready to confront Eva?

James:

- I am not keen to assassinate Eva. There are cameras everywhere, and we better send someone else while we have an alibi.

Pierre:

- Tsk, Tsk. We are not going to murder Eva at this stage. Let's first investigate whether we can come to an agreement with her. Perhaps, a hefty sum for her retirement fund or a position in Damien's cabinet will win her over.

James:

- I don't think so. Her refusal to meet with you should be indicative to her predisposition.

Pierre:

- You might be right. No matter, I'd rather find a peaceful solution than resorting to violence. If we have Eva murdered, her voters might swing to the senile Barry O'Connor from the Democrat Party. It is better to win her over. That way, Damien will win the election, while we maintain the status quo at a minimal expense.

James:

- Very well. Let's head to the convention centre. Eva will speak soon.

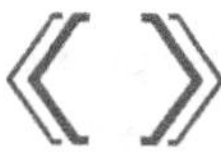

PIERRE WAS STANDING on the street watching the crowds cheering Eva's speech. He hoped Eva had paid the crowds to be her audience, because if all these people had come by their own free will, it would be hard for Damien Vanderbilt to beat Eva Moreno. Damien always had huge crowds, but he paid most of them to attend. This was an embarrassing fact that they worked hard to cover up.

Pierre queried his monocle of the best way to confront Eva and it showed 'Pretend to be catering staff.' He turned to James and spoke:

- Does your monocle also tell you to pretend to be a bloody waiter?

James:

- Yes.

- Those men over there look like catering staff and they have convention centre uniforms. Let's have a chat with them.

Pierre was disappointed. This was the reason that he preferred to send Vladimir on missions. Having to pretend to be a servant to meet a politician was below him, but it was crucial to the plan. James led the way, took out a bundle of $100 bills and they approached the waiters. James:

- Hey guys, how does five hundred dollars for not going to work sound?

Waiter:

- Sounds like the best plan ever.

James smiled and handed the money to the waiters. He spoke:

- The money is yours if you give me your uniform shirt and your passkey, and head home.

The waiters hesitated for a while, but they gave in to the temptation and shortly afterwards Pierre and James were waiting in Eva's greenroom.

EVA MORENO STARED IN shock when she entered her greenroom and she saw James Winter and Pierre Beaumont. Pierre spoke:

- Eva Moreno, we meet at last.

Eva:

- Why are you here? I told you that I did not want to meet you.

Pierre:

- If you had agreed to meet me, I would not come here dressed as a waiter.

Eva took up a two-way radio and was about to summon security when Pierre interrupted her:

- Please, Eva. Hear me out, it will be worthwhile.

Eva put down her radio, gave Pierre a cold stare, and replied:

- Okay. I'll give you one minute to state your business.

Pierre:

- Eva, even if you win the presidency, it will be for nothing. The Democrats and the Republicans will never accept an independent candidate, neither will the judges in the Supreme Court. You'll be stuck in limbo for four years and people will remember you as a failure.

Eva:

- I am aware of the difficulties, but I don't understand why you made all this effort to taunt me?

Pierre:

- Because I am offering you an alternative. Withdraw your candidacy and pledge your support to Damien Vanderbilt. Once he wins the election, he'll make you the minister for whatever department you want to be in. You'll have real power to change the world and you'll be financially secure for life.

Hearing this, Eva picked up the radio and called security:

- Eva Moreno to security, I have two intruders in my greenroom. Please remove them.

Eva put down the radio and spoke to Pierre:

- I would never sell out my integrity like this. You are going to prison, Pierre.

Pierre was about to say something, but security guards stormed in and expelled them. After that, the guards handed them over to the cops who drove them off to police custody.

Chapter 52: Pierre and Damien convince the Global Banking Cabal to engage in economic warfare against China, 17th September 2028.

Pierre was feeling uncomfortable in a cheap and ill-fitting waiter uniform. The idiots at the Santa Fe police department had 'misplaced' his property and he had lost his tailor-made suits and Swiss watches. The four days that Pierre had spent in jail meant that he didn't have time to go home and get his tailor-made outfits pressed and cleaned.

Pierre sighed. It had been embarrassing to spend four days with low-class criminals in jail. Mitchell Cent had certainly taken his time to pardon Pierre's intrusion at the convention centre.

Pierre entered the boardroom where he intended to gather the leaders of the major banking conglomerates in the world. The men in the room controlled 90 % of all overseas transactions, which would be enough to bring China and her president Eileen Lu to her knees.

Damien caught a glimpse of Pierre. He put down the cup of coffee he was drinking, and he taunted:

- Hello Pierre. How was jail? Was it like Four Seasons or like Swissotel?

Pierre frowned and replied:

- I would have preferred if Mitchell Cent had hurried up. I spent four days living and eating with peasants. Such a disaster!

Damien laughed and replied:

- I don't understand why you broke into Eva's greenroom with James? Did you lose your mind?

Pierre:

- Eva impressed me. She would have been invaluable if I could turn her to our cause.

Damien:

- That will never happen.

Pierre:

- That is correct. That's why we need to make sure that Eva will never use her talents as the next US president. To achieve that end, do you agree to revoke environmental protections and give up governmental ownership of the wildlife national parks in favour of the support from my fellow bankers?

Damien:

- I will do whatever it takes to win this election. If I need to give up our national parks to knock Eva Moreno and her Chinese alliance out of the race, so be it.

Pierre:

- Excellent. I will speak to the others and I am sure that we'll come to an agreement.

Having said this, Pierre rang a bell and a waiter entered the room. A short while later, Pierre was enjoying a peppermint tea while waiting for the other dignitaries.

PIERRE WATCHED IN CONTEMPT as the sweaty, obese, and caviar-smelling Gunter Fritz, the head of the Deutsche Bank, entered the board-room. Gunter was from the northern German-speaking parts of Switzer-land and there was no racial group that Pierre had more disdain for. How could anyone speak such an uncultured barbaric language when they lived in a country where French was also an official language?

Gunter and Pierre were the same age, and they had been rivals since they were both entry-level bankers at Deutsche Bank, 35 years earlier. Born into an ailing noble family, Pierre felt contempt for the lower classes, and it had destroyed him when Gunter got promoted instead of him. Pierre had left Deutsche Bank to work for the World Bank, and the rest was history. Pierre was now the wealthiest man on the planet and had numerous world-class international bankers under his grip.

Gunter got seated, turned to Pierre, and spoke:

- Pierre, I hope that you have secured the deal that you promised us. I would hate to travel all the way to New York to listen to more vague promises.

Pierre:

- I have discussed the matter with Damien. If he becomes the next President, he will repeal the protection of the wildlife na-tional parks. He will grant you the mining rights at Yellowstone National Park. The area is rich in rare earth minerals due to the vicinity to the volcano.

Gunter:

- That is not enough. I need the US government to guarantee all my future investments. My mines will be worthless if the volcano erupts.

Pierre:

- That shouldn't be a problem. The Federal Reserve can guarantee them by printing more money and provide you with investment funding.

Gunter:

- I don't want money. The way the Federal Reserve is printing money, the US dollar will soon have the same value as toilet paper. I want gold!

Pierre glanced at the Federal Reserve Chairman, Angus Brothschild, who shook his head. Pierre sighed; he would have to put his own gold on the line if he wanted a deal. Pierre:

- I will guarantee the gold from my personal reserves. How much gold do you need as a guarantee for your Yellowstone National Park investment?

Gunter smirked and licked his lips:

- 10,000 metric tonnes of gold will suffice.

Pierre stared at Gunter in disbelief. 10,000 metric tonnes of gold were 5 percent of all gold on the planet. All of this to guarantee the investment on one mining complex. "That bloody volcano better not erupt." Pierre muttered to himself. He turned to Gunter and spoke:

- I agree to your terms. I will guarantee your mining project at Yellowstone once your contribution has led to Damien becoming the president of the USA.

Gunter grinned slyly:

- Then we have an agreement, Pierre. I am sure that my fellow banker are looking for similar guarantees from you and the World Bank.

Pierre sighed. He knew that the others had ganged up on him and this would ruin him. However, he had to agree for now, but he would word the agreements so he would never have to pay.

A gruelling half an hour later, Pierre had agreed to guarantee the others with 50,000 metric tonnes of gold. Purchasing these amounts would drive up the gold price to astronomical levels, but he would find a way and the others would suffer for ganging up on him. For now, all that mattered was to crush Eva Moreno and drive her out of the American election, and to not let the truth of the origin of the Hei Bai virus outbreaks be known.

Chapter 53: Eileen Lu gives in to Pierre's demands, 4th October 2028.

Pierre was sitting in front of his fireplace in Palace Beaumont. He was in a great mood. The goose liver, the beluga caviar and the vintage wine tasted better than ever, and Pierre had turned the previous month's defeat into a great win.

Realising that he needed to acquire 50,000 tonnes of gold to guarantee the other world bankers' investments had terrified Pierre. But he had found a way to turn his predicament into success. Pierre had used Damien's media influence to spread fake stories about the discovery of abundant goldfields on earth, rendering gold worthless. The alleged discovery of huge quantities of gold had caused retail investors to panic-sell their gold at low prices. Thus, through creating a false narrative through Damien's social media and news networks, Pierre had turned his predicament into an opportunity to amass gold at a very low cost. The value of gold would skyrocket back to its normal high when people found out that the discovery of the massive amounts of gold were a hoax.

Pierre put down his wineglass, picked up a gold bar, and stroke it. What an amazing feeling it was to touch something so beautiful and priceless at the same time. Jean Valmont entered Pierre's lounge room and interrupted his passionate moment with the gold bar. Jean:

- Monsieur Pierre. Eileen Lu and a delegation from China have arrived.

Pierre smirked:

- How lovely! Please tell them to go to the Grand Dining Hall. My chefs have cooked a meal worthy of this occasion. I will see them after dinner.

Jean nodded and left the room.

Pierre clutched the gold bar to his chest, and he stroke it like a baby. This was his moment of glee. Eileen Lu had come to surrender in the economic war that she started by refusing to submit to his authority. It was poetic justice that the woman he had elevated to power, had come to admit his dominance.

EILEEN LU WAS EATING a beef eye fillet with potato gratin when Pierre entered the dining room. Pierre:

- How was the steak? Such a shame you couldn't wait for me to arrive. Such uncultured behaviour.

Eileen:

- Your employee told us that you would arrive after dinner.

Pierre:

- Oh, did she? Tsk, tsk. I guess you don't understand Swiss etiquette. Regardless of what my servant tells you, you are meant to wait for the master of the household before dining.

- No matter, we have a more important topic to discuss.

Eileen sighed. She regretted that she hadn't imprisoned Pierre when he had pressed her in China. If she did, this situation wouldn't have come to pass. Then again, if she allowed herself to be a tyrant that imprisoned and murdered people on a whim, she wouldn't be the leader that she aspired to be. Eileen spoke:

- Your unlawful economic warfare against my nation is causing great suffering among my people. Now all international bankers have put sanctions against Chinese financial transactions. It needs to end.

Pierre smirked:

- I am willing to discuss the sanctions the international banking community applied to China for influencing the American election. All you need to do is to stop supporting Eva Moreno. Political leaders should not interfere in foreign elections.

Eileen:

- Hold on. You lobbied to change the US law, so you were able to influence the 2024 re-election of Mitchell Cent. What is the difference?

Pierre:

- The difference is that I am not a politician and I don't represent a nation.

- I assume that you are here to achieve results and not to discuss philosophy. Stop supporting Eva Moreno, and I will discuss ending international banking restrictions against China with my peers.

Eileen:

- So, will the sanctions end if I stop supporting Eva Moreno?

Pierre:

- Doing so would increase the possibility of a favourable outcome. The Chinese elections are coming up in January. You should focus on your own election.

Eileen sighed. She looked at Pierre's face and tried to understand his intentions, but she was empty-handed. Supporting Eva came at an excessive cost for herself and her people. Pierre and the international banks were powerful foes, and this conflict could tank the Chinese economy. If the economy failed, her re-election hopes would come to naught. Eileen:

- Okay, I'll withdraw my support for Eva Moreno.

Pierre:

- Good. When I receive proof that you are fulfilling your promises, my colleagues and I will discuss the cessation of our sanctions against your nation.

- Now please leave. Your presence is as unwanted in Palace Beaumont, as mine is in China. Au revoir, Eileen.

Eileen got up and commanded her delegation:

- Gāi zǒule. Ràng wǒmen bùyào yúyuè wǒmen de huānyíng. *(Let's go now. Do not let these people treat us with disrespect.)*

After hearing this, everyone in Eileen's delegation left without a word.

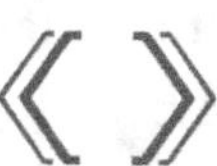

PIERRE WAS ENJOYING a glass of smoky whisky, while dressed up in a World War 2 uniform owned by his grandfather Vincent Beaumont. He looked at the portrait of his late grandfather and spoke:

- I did it, pépé. I averted the danger and I will bring our family back to greatness.

He stared in silence at the portrait and he spoke after a while:

- No. I will not end sanctions against Eileen Lu. She must fall for opposing me. It is the only way. She must fall in the same way that you brought down our family.

After saying this, Pierre shed a tear, and he recalled the day when his family fell from grace. Pierre's parents and his sister had died in a mountaineering accident. Destroyed by sorrow, Vincent had believed that their deaths were divine punishment for his crimes. To find peace, Vincent had admitted that the family fortune came from Nazi victims during World War 2. After this, the Swiss authorities had seized their assets, Vincent had killed himself, and Pierre had ended up in a foster home.

His fall from grace had convinced Pierre about his true purpose in life, to rise again and bring the Beaumont family back to glory. Pierre had almost reached his goal. He was the wealthiest man in the world, and if he could achieve success with his breeding program, the Beaumont's would rise and rule the world. That was a vision to fight for.

With tear still running down his cheeks, Pierre laughed a burst of hysterical laughter, then cried himself to sleep at night.

Chapter 54: A Sensational Victory, 3rd November 2028.

Eva Moreno was sitting in her campaign headquarters in Santa Fe together with her partner Angela Baker and her brother Andres Moreno. Despite the enthusiastic shouting by her supporters outside, Eva felt heartbroken. Since Eileen Lu had withdrawn her support, Eva had been exposed to relentless media attacks. Most of the attacks against her were absurd and fraudulent reports. However, with media and social media ownership concentrated to a small group, there was nothing she could do. Because of the relentless attacks, Eva's polling had collapsed, and she had fallen from a 40 per cent support level, to a level in the single digits.

Eva felt hollowed watching the exit polls on the television screen. She would lose, despite being the only candidate that actually cared about her fellow citizens. She would lose to a group of plutocrats who would stop at nothing when it came to killing democracy and oppressing their fellow citizen for their personal gains.

Angela hugged Eva and stroke her hair.

- At least you gave them a run for their money, sweetheart. History will remember the independent female candidate that almost ended the political duopoly in the USA.

Eva:

- I want people to remember me for my achievements. Not for being the closest candidate to shake up the status quo.

Andres Moreno:

- Don't say that! You scared those bastards for a while. You riled Pierre Beaumont when you revealed that Reversogene had killed a lot of people.

Eva:

- Yet the exit polls show that Damien Vanderbilt will get 48 per cent of the votes, Barry O'Connor 42 per cent, while I stand at just 8 per cent. I mean come on. Damien is the most corrupt politician in our history of corrupt politicians and Barry doesn't even know what year it is.

Angela:

- I know, love. But let's keep the hope up for now. You should speak to your followers. The night is young, and anything can happen.

Eva:

- You are correct. There can still be a miracle.

PIERRE BEAUMONT WAS following the presidential election in his home in Switzerland. He felt terrified about the outcome. Despite polls showing that Damien would win by a large margin, Pierre couldn't relax. Pierre knew that the polls were fake. Out of fear for a leak, none of his associates had dared to make an accurate poll in the weeks leading up to the election. In the last real poll that they had made four weeks earlier, Eva had maintained a large lead over Damien. Pierre could only hope that the sheepish masses had bought the fake narrative about Damien's popularity.

Pierre's phone rang. It was from Damien. Pierre:

- Hello Damien.

Damien:

- We are fucked! Eva has won in Maine. 46 % to her, 33 % to me, and 18 % to Barry.

Pierre:

- Don't publish the result in media. Instead, publish the article and the scripts about voter fraud. We'll need to delegitimise Eva as much as we can.

Damien:

- Understood. But the electoral college handles counting the votes, not my media empire. No matter what I do, it doesn't change the facts.

Pierre:

- Sow dissent and mistrust in Eva, delay her in the courts. Do everything to discredit her. I will come up with a solution.

- Claim victory at the end of the night regardless of the result.

Having said this, Pierre hung up the phone. In a bout of anger, he threw his phone at his bulletproof window. This shattered the phone but left the window undamaged.

EVA MORENO COULDN'T believe her eyes when the election results were published late at night. She had won the presidential election with 42 % of the popular vote, compared to 35 % for Damien Vanderbilt and 18 % for Barry O'Connor. Barry had already conceded his loss and congratulated Eva on her sensational victory. Damien, on the other hand, had released a statement in the news and social media where he accused Eva of voter fraud and stated his intent to take her to court for voter fraud. It didn't matter to

Eva.. Damien was desperate for her to lose because he knew that her first presidential order would be to arrest him, as well as Pierre Beaumont, and James Winter for the deaths that Reversogene caused to Americans.

Eva gathered herself and walked out to the stage together with her brother and her partner. She gave a speech to the cheering crowds:

- Today is a historical day. Today is the day when the deep state falls and democracy rises. Despite relentless media attacks in the last months, Damien Vanderbilt could not defeat us. This marks the end of his reign of fake news and propaganda. Yet again, the government should govern for the people and not increase the wealth of a small circle of billionaires.

- My first policy will be to break up the ownership of media and social media and give the rights of freedom of information to everyone at no cost. No longer shall a small group dominate the minds of our citizens, to the detriment of the people.

- My second order will be to file charges against Pierre Beaumont, James Winter and Damien Vanderbilt for the deaths caused by Reversogene. I will also order a full inquiry into the origins of Hei Bai Virus outbreak in New York. I am not satisfied with how that investigation was performed, as there was never a true set of evidence found that it had originated from China's ex-president Jing Xi, as we all have been led to believe.

- Thank you all. May God bless America.

After saying this, Eva walked off the stage and secret service agents took Eva to a secure location. Eva knew that she had put a target on her back by winning the election. Against the men who released unreliable drugs that killed millions, she couldn't be too careful. Eva sighed and reminded herself that once the conspirators were in prison, she could become the president that she strove to be.

Chapter 55: Pierre and James plan to assassinate Eva, 4th November 2028.

Pierre was recovering from a hangover. He had lost his cool upon hearing about Eva's election win, and he had drenched his sorrows with wine and whisky. In that sedated state, he had reached a level of clarity and found the solution that his Zetan monocle couldn't find for him. He would have Eva Moreno murdered, and he would pin the blame on Eileen Lu. While it was absurd that Eileen would murder the president that she helped getting elected, Pierre's plan would work. People were dumb and believed what they were told. In 2020 the media had succeeded in scaring 30-year-olds of a virus, which mostly killed elderly, so he could convince them that China had murdered Eva Moreno.

Pierre summoned James Winter, who came down from the guestroom where he had holed up for the last months.

James gave Pierre a long look. James:

- What is going on, Pierre? You look terribly ill.

Pierre:

- So, would you, if you drank for 36 hours straight in your late fifties. Age, I am telling you, is a merciless beast.

James shook his head and sighed:

- So, do you want something in particular or are you going to entertain me with nonsensical chatter?

Pierre:

- I know what we have to do to get out of our predicament. We must murder Eva Moreno and frame China's president Eileen Lu for the murder.

James:

- That's absolute nonsense. Why would Eileen Lu send someone to murder the president that she helped to win the election? No-one would believe in it.

Pierre:

- You're wrong. To understand lesser men, you must lower your intelligence. During my 36- hour stupor, I saw the truth. Given the attention span of average Americans and their bias towards Chinese people, it will make them believe in our message if we repeat it enough times. Damien controls the media and he will become the next president. People will soon forget about the re-al reasons behind Eva's death.

James:

- Even so, Damien is not the next in line if Eva dies. Her vice president candidate, Jonathan Xi Feng is next in line.

Pierre:

- Not if we convince people that Xi Feng conspired with China's president to murder Eva. Neither the Republicans nor the De-mocrats are happy with Eva's election. The congress would be happy to imprison Xi Feng and let Damien Vanderbilt become the President.

James:

- I am not too sure about this plan.

Pierre shrugged his shoulders, poured himself a whiskey, sculled it, and replied:

- What you think is irrelevant. I am your only hope. Eva will prosecute you for treason.

James sighed and replied:

- Whatever. What is the next part of your drunken plan, Pierre?

Pierre:

- We will contact Elaine Orchard from The Harapan Conglomerate to find a suitable hitman with ties to China. Her company operates in South East Asia and she knows the talent pool better than we do. We should also involve Martin Orchard. We need one of our own to make sure that the job gets done while Vladimir is still in a coma.

James:

- Why do we need Martin Orchard? He doesn't bring anything to the table. I can shoot Eva myself.

Pierre:

- I told you I had a plan. You will be with Eva when she dies. We'll make it look like you have defected to her side. Eva will love to attend when you are giving a speech to the press outlining the crimes of Damien Vanderbilt, Vladimir, and me. I want you to pretend to betray me, but before you reveal anything, our Chinese hitman will kill Eva. This will confuse everyone, and we can use this our advantage.

James:

- I see. This could work. I guess you'll short the markets on the day of the assassination?

Pierre:

- Of course. I would never let a crisis go to waste. It is the perfect time to short the markets.

- Now I must retreat to my bedroom. Alcohol abuse has damaged my body, and I cannot achieve my plans if my body perishes. I'll see you tomorrow.

After saying this, Pierre retreated to his bedroom. He took off his monocle, stared at the ceiling, and passed out from being drunk and exhausted.

Chapter 56: Pierre involves Elaine in the Assassination Plans, 6th November 2028.

Pierre felt jittery and nervous as his private jet prepared to land at Jakarta International Airport in Indonesia. The hungover was still encapsulating his head in a thick fog and he abstained from drinking red wine to allow his body to recover. Pierre recognised the tension from when there was an outbreak of the Hei Bai Virus seven years earlier, but this time, there was a major distinction. Back in 2021, Pierre had been an outsider, and the release of the virus which led to the mandatory imposing of the cure was his path to glory. Now he was on the top, so he had everything to lose and nothing more to win. Yet, being on the top, he had to eat or be eaten, and killing Eva Moreno was his only option.

Pierre opened the test profiles of his offspring, Lucien and Delphine, the artificially inseminated end products of his breeding project. They were excellent human specimens that excelled in both intelligence and ruthlessness. Yet, they were only four years old, so Pierre had to succeed in killing Eva for the future of the Beaumont Family. Pierre envisioned how the Beaumont's would rule the world. In his ideal world, all the power and wealth would stay with a small elite, while the ignorant masses existed to serve these rich elites.

Pierre woke up from his daydreaming when the plane touched down. The force of the landing was too much for Pierre and he threw up. He got up and had a hissy fit:

- Jean! Bring a fresh suit for me and tell the pilot that his terrible manoeuvring of the plane made me sick!

Jean nodded and rushed off to get Pierre a spare outfit.
James gave Pierre a curious look and spoke:

- Are you okay, Pierre? Can I be sure that you are up to the task
at hand?

Pierre threw his soiled suit jacket to the floor and gave James a cold
stare. Pierre:

- Never question me, James. Eva is coming after you as well, so I
am your only hope. Never forget that.

James didn't reply. Pierre wasn't his only hope, there was an alternative.
He could defect to Eva and sell out the others in return for a presidential
pardon. If he did, he could withdraw from the bureau and spend his time
being a stepdad to Melinda's children. As Pierre ran off to the back of the
plane to freshen up, James called Melinda. She didn't pick up the phone.
James sighed. The uncertainty nearly killed him, and all he wanted was an
answer to the question that had tormented him for the last month. He
needed to know whether there was still hope for their relationship.

ELAINE ORCHARD STARED at the scruffy-looking Pierre Beaumont
as he entered the dining hall of her mansion in Jakarta. While Pierre had always been an ugly man, he always strove for a neat and immaculate appearance. Yet, his jacket was wrinkly, his eyes were glary, and he smelled funny.
Could Pierre be sick? Elaine decided to voice her concerns:

- Oh dear, Pierre. What happened to you?

Pierre gave Elaine a cold-stare and muttered:

- What kind of question is that? I have faced a lot of stress because of Eva's election victory. You, on the other hand, are not in
danger from Eva.

Elaine ignored Pierre's tone of voice and replied:

- Neither are you. Eva has no power to prosecute you in Switzerland.

Pierre shook his head and replied:

- You're wrong. The moment Eva releases an international arrest order for me, my life is over. What would I do then? I can't hide away at Palace Beaumont hoping that the Swiss Government will protect me.

Elaine:

- Well, lucky you know me. I know the perfect man for ending Eva's ambitions.

Having said this, Elaine handed Pierre a folder.

Pierre opened the folder and studied the profile of the assassin. Lim Dao was the perfect candidate for the job. He was a former Taiwanese elite soldier who was currently working as a soldier of fortune. Lim Dao's most important qualification was not his skills, however, but that he had worked with Xi Feng, Eva Moreno's Vice President candidate. If all went to plan, all the evidence would point towards Jonathan Xi Feng as the perpetrator, backed by China and Iran. This would absolve Pierre and Damien of any suspicion in the murder enquiry.

Pierre nodded towards Elaine and spoke:

- This is an excellent candidate, but there is a problem.

Elaine:

- What is that?

Pierre:

- While his skills are impressive and Lim Dao's connection to Xi Feng and China is crucial, he is still just one man. The Secret Service counter-snipers would kill him in a heartbeat before he gets to shoot Eva. We need another person to locate these counter-snipers and kill them before they shoot our Taiwanese assassin.

Elaine sighed and replied:

- Why didn't you tell me about this? I guess I'll have to assemble a whole team, but that creates other problems. How will I conceal my association with a group of mercenaries killing the US president? At least one of them will talk.

Pierre:

- There is a man who would be useful. This man wouldn't get caught, nor speak to the Americans.

Elaine:

- Who is this man?

Pierre:

- Martin Orchard.

Elaine was shocked to hear that and said:

- I doubt that he would be willing to leave Kiribati where he is currently residing. Last time I spoke to him, he was happy sleeping with the housekeeper and writing his god-damn books.

Pierre taunted:

- Do I hear some resentment towards your ex-husband? How unexpected.

Elaine:

- That bastard caused the deaths of hundreds of people when we fought against the Juarez Cartel in Colombia back in 2022. While I am happy to be alive, I can't get rid of the nightmares from witnessing burnt children. Martin's actions burned down the entire Valla de la Muerte valley.

Pierre:

- Then I assume you have no issues if we put him in harm's way?

Elaine:

- No, I don't mind. If you think his participation is necessary to further our goals, then so be it. Do what you must do.

Pierre turned to James and spoke:

- Did you hear that, James? Gather some mercenaries and pay Martin Orchard a visit in Kiribati. A man with his talents shouldn't stay in retirement when we need him.

James nodded and replied:

- Understood. I know some mercenaries in this region. They did some jobs for the CIA a few years ago. Coming in force will convince Martin to be cooperative.

Pierre took out a USB memory with a cryptocurrency account and handed the key to James. Pierre:

- This crypto account should have enough money to cover your expenses. Find Martin and avoid violence, we need him on our side.

James nodded and left the room.
After James had left, Elaine turned towards Pierre and spoke:

- So, do you need to see Lim Dao yourself or should I leave the contact to my head of security, Budi Sepulyat?

Pierre:

- I shall not meet the assassin who will kill the American president. It would be disastrous if we get photographed together. I leave the brutish actions to others, such as James, Vladimir, and Martin. Now, is there anything else?

Elaine:

- Yes, I would like to discuss some of my business projects with you. In full confidence, of course.

Pierre sighed. He didn't believe that such a discussion could be fruitful, but he had to repay Elaine for finding a suitable assassin.
Pierre:

- Very well. Bring in some suitable refreshments and I will share my wealth of knowledge.

Elaine clapped her hands and shouted to her servants:

- Pelayan. Bawalah anggur terbaik dan keju-keju terbaik kami. *(Servants. Bring our best wines and best cheeses for us.)*

As the servant brought the fine wines and produce, Pierre noticed something that lifted his spirits. Elaine's servants had brought a bottle of Domaine Leroy Chambertin Grand Cru 1990 as well as a platter with delicate and exquisite Swiss cheeses. If Elaine preferred the same vintage, their conversation had potential.
Pierre:

- I love your taste in wine. If we share the same shrewdness for commerce, I am sure we will have a fruitful discussion ahead of us.

Elaine smiled to herself. She had done her due diligence and learnt about Pierre's favourite foods and drinks. It was the best way to manipulate a man that was so full of himself. While listening to Pierre's arrogant words was painful, Pierre was her best chance to finance the future of Indonesia that she envisioned. After indulging in the wines and cheeses, Pierre and Elaine spent the night discussing their future business projects.

Chapter 57: James Winter Convinces Martin Orchard to help, 9th November 2028.

James Winter was drinking a glass of beer at a bar overlooking the Pacific Ocean in the sleepy village of Tarawa, which was the capital of Kiribati. The locals looked at him and his entourage with a mix of curiosity and terror. James had hired a group of experienced mercenaries to make sure that Martin Orchard didn't cause any trouble. James and his associates looked menacing in the eyes of the elderly cruise ship passengers that usually visited Kiribati for a vacation.

James sighed. It would have been easier to hire someone else for the assassination, but Martin Orchard was the best hitman there was, in Vladimir's absence. Equipped with the Zetan Monocle set to combat mode, Martin had fought his way out of the captivity of the sadistic drug lord Andres Juarez in Colombia. Martin had annihilated the Juarez drug cartel and torched the entire valley. The fatalities had been in the hundreds and James hoped that history wouldn't repeat itself in Washington.

James' phone rang. It was his ex, Melinda Barnes. Melinda spoke with a direct tone:

- Hi James. I have a message from Eva Moreno. She is willing to give you a presidential pardon, if you reveal the Reversogene cover-up that your co-conspirators did to the world, during a public announcement.

James:

- Since when are you Eva Moreno's mouthpiece?

Melinda:

- I am not. Eva reached out to me knowing that I was in a relationship with you. I am relaying her message.

James:

- Well, are we still in a relationship?

Melinda:

- Don't be silly, James. There is a reason I haven't picked up your calls. I just want to give you the chance to do the right thing.

James:

- Tell her I will do it if she will be attending the public announcement.

Melinda:

- Okay, I will relay your message.

James:

- Thank you.

Melinda:

- James, please be careful. If Pierre or Damien find out about your betrayal, they will come after you.

James:

- Trust me, they won't know. Call me when you have the details.

Melinda:

- Yes. Take care of yourself.

James hung up the phone and a bittersweet feeling overwhelmed him. He had known all along that there was no hope left for him and Melinda, and yet she had called him. On the bright side, this would lure Eva out in the open for the planned assassination, while giving himself an alibi.

'I guess it's time for me to be extravagant with wine and women,' James thought and he walked up to the bar and put down a few $100 bills. James:

- I am looking for female companionship for the night. Preferably a good looking one.

Bartender:

- This venue does not provide this kind of services, you must be mistaken.

James:

- I'm asking you privately. I want someone fresh and young; I am sure $1000 will suffice. It's a yearly pay in Kiribati after all. There is even an added bonus for you if you fulfil my request.

The bartender got on the phone and made some calls. A while later, a cute but somewhat chubby young Gilbertese woman approached James. The young woman stuttered:

- Hi. I am Mawara. My brother said you were looking for company.

James looked at Mawara for a while. He thought of sending her away, but he realised that he wasn't spoiled for choice. James smiled at Mawara and spoke:

- Nice to meet you, Mawara. I am James and these are for you. Please follow me upstairs.

Having said this, James handed Mawara a few banknotes and he led her upstairs.

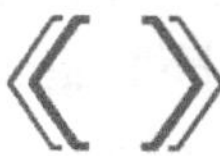

JAMES WINTER FELT CONTENT when he boarded the rented vessel accompanied by his mercenary entourage. While Mawara hadn't been a talented lover, she had been a virgin and James hadn't experienced sex with a virgin for many years. As he took Mawara's virginity, he felt reborn. He had overcome the infatuation and yearning for Melinda that had plagued him for the last months.

On the boat ride to Martin's secluded island, James was pretending to be friends with the Persian jihadist, Ervin Ghorbani. James planned to turn Ervin into a scapegoat, by killing him. There was nothing personal about murdering Ervin. However, killing the Persian jihadist and placing his dead body at Martin's shooting site would deflect the responsibility for the death of Eva Moreno. Once he had successfully framed America's biggest enemies, no-one would think of looking elsewhere for the perpetrators.

As James spoke to Ervin, he realised that they were alike, and James felt excited knowing that he would be the master of Ervin's fate. After what felt like a heartbeat, the boat arrived at Martin Orchard's mansion, which faced a secluded atoll.

MARTIN ORCHARD WAS writing one of his novels when James and his men arrived. Martin heard the boat's engine and decided to walk down to the jetty. At first, he hoped that his housekeeper and mistress, Alani, had come to visit him. While she wasn't rostered this day, he wished she would come because he liked her company. Martin sighed when he realised that his visitor was James Winter, accompanied by a group of shady operatives.

James spotted Martin and commanded:

- So, this is where you are hiding, Martin? Get on the boat! We got a job for you to do.

Martin paused and checked his monocle. It read: *'Combat mode: Odds for survival less than 2 %. The suggested course of action: Compliance.'*
Martin sighed:

- It doesn't seem like I have much of a choice, do I?

James smirked:

- That's correct, Martin. That's why I brought others to deter you from resorting to violence.

Martin:

- Okay, I am coming with you. However, there is something I need to do first.

James taunted:

- What would that be? You have lived alone and off the grid for two years.

Martin:

- I need to write a letter to my housekeeper, Alani. I will give her the house and access to my Kiribati bank account. She needs them more than I do.

James:

- Very well. Hurry up, I don't like waiting.

Martin didn't respond, and he retreated to his home office. After writing the note to Alani, Martin grabbed both his fake and real passports and walked to the jetty without a word.

As the ship took off, James had to contain his doubt of Martin's trustworthiness. While James surrounded himself with shady characters, Martin was the only one who posed a threat to him. *'Remember that this is the first day of the big plan!'* James mumbled to himself, leaned back into his seat, and fell asleep.

Chapter 58: The Assassination of Eva Moreno, 12th November 2028.

James felt nervous as he exited the private jet accompanied by Martin Orchard and his group of mercenaries. It was crucial that there was no record of James being in the same flight as the others in case border officials detained some of them. 'Is everything going as planned?' Pierre sent this hologram message to James via the Zetan Monocle. 'Yes.' James replied.

James had discussed their plan to go back to the USA with Pierre. They didn't want to attract any attention to themselves, but they didn't want it to be too shady either. Their solution was to hack the border customs at the private Washington airport where they landed. To the unknowing operator, everything looked in order, but none of the information were saved or sent to the database, so none of these mercenaries were recorded to have entered the country. "Welcome home, Mr Winter," an immigration officer said, and James felt how a big weight had fallen off his shoulders.

James was safe for now. He had lost his job, but the American president Mitchell Cent had banned all investigations into James' conduct and connections. James glanced at his mercenaries as they passed immigration. While Pierre had hacked the system, there was always a risk that some overzealous immigration officer would go beyond his or her duty. Satisfied that everyone passed immigration without incident, James turned to Martin and spoke:

- Martin, I have some preparations to make. Head to the Jefferson Hotel. I have booked a suite for you there.

Martin gave James a sceptical look and replied:

- Did you book it under my real name? You haven't told me why I am needed and why I had to leave Kiribati.

James:

- I booked your room in your real name. Your mission will not take place at the hotel, so there is no need to use a fake identity.

Martin:

- You still didn't answer the more important question. Why am I here?

James:

- You are here to do a job for the group. You owe us big time, since Pierre and I resurrected you after your silly escapade in Colombia.

Martin:

- Why won't you tell me?

James:

- Well, it is easier to learn something correctly the first time than to unlearn incorrect knowledge. Thus, I won't brief you until our plan is complete.

- I suggest that you head to your hotel. I have some things to deal with before briefing you.

After saying this, James got into a cab and ordered a ride back to his Washington home.

JAMES WINTER FELT EXHAUSTED returning to the home he hadn't been to since Eva Moreno exposed his involvement of the Reversogene cover-up. The house itself meant nothing to James, but it felt good to have roots to a place again. James had hated staying in Pierre's mansion, but it had been for the best. There were still independent media sources around, and they would have made James' life a nightmare if he had stayed in the USA. In his absence, the press had moved on to other more present topics than deaths that occurred seven years earlier.

James tried to focus on the task at hand, but he couldn't. The house was too messy and full of dust, after being unoccupied for four months. The pictures of Melinda and her children hanging on the walls made James feel resentful and heartbroken. She had betrayed him, and he needed to clear every trace of her out of his life. James wanted Melinda to be one of the people that took the fall for Eva Moreno's murder. He called Pierre:

- I have an additional objective I would like to add to the mission.

Pierre:

- I don't like last-minute changes. Why didn't you mention this before?

James:

- Nevertheless, it needs to happen. I want to frame Melinda for being the mole who sold us the positions of the Secret Service counter snipers.

There was a silence for a while. Eventually, Pierre replied:

- Have you organised the meeting with Eva Moreno yet?

James:

- Not yet.

Pierre:

- Then you should do that first.

- Don't worry, I will help you with your pointless revenge against your ex. I will make a few deposits into Melinda's account that appears to come from the Iranian government. Then, I will leak this information to the press.

- Now get back to what's important, Eva Moreno's assassination.

After saying this, Pierre hung up the phone.

James felt bad for going after Melinda after he made his request, and he had hoped that Pierre would refuse, but he couldn't change his mind again. James called Eva Moreno's aide, Aaron Smith, to set up a meeting. After that, he left his house to get away from all his old memories.

JAMES WINTER FELT INSTANT disdain when he met Aaron Smith at a fancy coffee shop. Aaron was an effeminate politician with purple hair, and James couldn't respect a man like that. In the end, it didn't matter. James hadn't come to join Eva Moreno but to draw her into a trap.

Aaron smiled at James and spoke:

- Welcome home, James. Thank you for reaching out. Would you like some coffee? The caramel hazelnut affogato is divine.

'Fucking hell, Pierre's homosexuality is bad enough!' James thought to himself, but he contained his homophobia and replied:

- A large cup of extra strong black coffee. No sugar.

Aaron exclaimed:

- Oh, how masculine. I'll be right back!

A short while later, Aaron returned with their beverages and James spoke:

- So, why the diversion with the coffee? Let's discuss our deal.

Aaron chuckled:

- Of course. Let's do business.

- Eva is happy to pardon you if you give up your co-conspirators during a public announcement.

James:

- Will Eva Moreno herself attend?

Aaron:

- I cannot guarantee it. Eva is a busy woman and she needs to prepare for her presidency.

James taunted:

- I doubt she'll pass up on the chance to gloat in the defeat of the man she referred to as an enemy of humanity.

Aaron:

- Eva doesn't gloat in the defeat of her enemies. Eva wants to create a better world for her fellow humans. People suffering the consequences of their actions is a necessary evil.

James thought of arguing back but he realised that he wouldn't do himself any favours criticising Eva. Instead, he changed the topic.

- So, when, and where shall I make the announcement? I am ready to dob in Pierre and Damien.

Aaron:

- I am not at liberty to say. The safety of the president-elect is paramount.

James:

- I have agreed to make a public announcement revealing Pierre and Damien's involvements in the Reversogene cover-up that killed many Americans in response to the Hei Bai virus. I will travel to the meeting on my own accord, but that will only happen if you tell me the time and place well in advance.

Aaron sighed and replied:

- Okay. How about making your public announcement at the steps of the Holocaust Museum on Friday at noontime? The Hei Bai Virus outbreaks and the Reversogene deaths were deliberate and cruel attacks on humankind, so the symbolism is clear.

James nodded and replied:

- Very well. I will be there. Enjoy your coffee, Mr Smith.

Having said this, James got up and left the cafeteria.

JAMES WINTER WAS SITTING in a boardroom in a Washington DC office complex. He felt tense and he hoped that the meeting with Damien would yield the desired outcome. The media needed to deflect all the allegations in the right direction.

Damien Vanderbilt looked sceptical towards James, as he told him about his plan. Damien:

- What if this is a trap? What if they are testing us? What if Eva won't show up?

James shrugged his shoulders and replied:

- In that case, I won't tell them anything. I don't have any credibility to lose, but Eva will look like an idiot for summoning the press conference.

Damien:

- I am worried that they will come after us for Eva's murder.

James:

- Why worry? It's a perfect setup. Neither the Democrats nor the Republicans want to end their political duopoly. So, everyone will accept the fake evidence blaming Eva's vice president-elect, Jonathan Xi Feng, for her assassination and you will become America's president.

Damien:

- What if you're wrong?

James:

- Pierre and I have thought of this plan very carefully. If we manipulate the news to divert people's attention, the nation will focus on other issues than following through with Eva's crusade against us. In any case, the situation can't get worse from eliminating Eva.

Damien:

- So, what do you want me to do?

James:

- As the news mogul, I want you to divert people's attention and release plenty of propaganda to create mass confusion. I will deal with the murders.

Damien:

- Understood. I agree that it is better if we focus on our strengths.

James didn't reply. It had been a while since he murdered someone. While his conscience didn't torment him, the concept of conspiring against the future US president was a stressful ordeal. Not keen to continue the conversation, James Winter left the meeting.

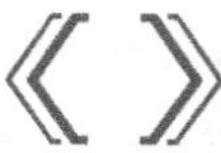

IT WAS FRIDAY AND THE time was 10 AM, two hours before the assassination of Eva were to take place. James Winter was sitting in a shady warehouse belonging to the White Brotherhood leader Randy "Hitler" McNeill. While James didn't like far-right white supremacists, Randy was his best bet for finding a prospective ally for the assassination.

James studied the inbred redneck opposite him. He had to hide his contempt for the man who lived in the century-old myth that one's race made him superior. He knew that it was a man's action that made him superior, not the colour of his skin. If someone could only claim superiority because of racial heritage, it proved that he was insecure and inferior. Randy spoke:

- So, you want to put a bullet in that bitch's head? How can the White Brotherhood help?

James thought about putting a bullet in Randy's head, and claim him to be the second shooter. James stopped himself. While framing the white supremacy movement for Eva's murder was an entertaining scenario, it was not what he had agreed with Pierre and Damien. James said:

- I need you to move the body of someone.

Randy:

- Who?

James:

- You'll soon find out.

A door opened and the Persian jihadist Ervin Ghorbani entered the warehouse. He looked at James and Randy in confusion and spoke:

- Hey, Mr Winter. Why are we meeting in this shithole?

Randy clenched his teeth and growled:

- Why the fuck did you bring the dirty sand nigger to my place?

James turned around and shot Ervin between the eyes with a silenced pistol. After that, he chucked his pistol to the floor, turned around, and smirked at Randy. James said:

- I want you to dump his body at a certain location. Take him to the roof of the Artisan Condominium building and hide him out of sight until I say so. Here is a cryptocurrency account with payment for your troubles.

Having said this, James handed Randy a USB-drive with cryptocurrency details. After this, he left the room while the flabbergasted Randy stared at him.

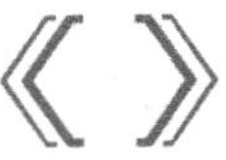

JAMES WINTER WAS FEELING tense as he stepped out on the podium that was set in front of the main entrance to the Holocaust Museum. His monocle showed that Lim Dao, the assassin that was tasked to shoot Eva;

Martin Orchard, who was tasked to shoot the American counter-snipers; and the American snipers were all in positions, but where was Eva? James walked up to the podium, looked at the crowd, and set his monocle to 'improvise and delay speech'. For what felt like an eternity, James was reading up gibberish that his monocle fed him to the public, lengthy eulogies to people he didn't even know about, while waiting for Eva's appearance.

Eventually, Eva arrived, walked up to James, put her hand on his shoulder, and spoke:

- I appreciate the touching tributes, but perhaps you should tell the press why you are here?

'Proceed now!' James sent this message to Martin via his monocle. His monocle entered 'time mode' and James perception of time slowed down. Martin shot the American counter-snipers at the same time the assassin Lim Dao pulled the trigger towards Eva from afar. Time slowed down to a standstill, when Lim Dao was hit in the exact moment he shot towards Eva.

'Danger, Danger. Incoming .50 calibre bullet is coming towards you.' The monocle beeped. *"Oh shit! Lim Dao shot towards me by mistake!"* James thought frantically.

James acted decisively. Still having his 'time mode' on his monocle, he faked a slippage while also dragging Eva's helpless body into the position where he had stood. James perception of time resumed, and he fell headfirst to the floor. James' nose cracked as his head hit the pavement and blood splashed into his eyes.

As James got up, he looked at what remained of Eva. The heavy-calibre bullet had left a huge gaping wound in her head, and her blood had splattered across the stage. Her assistant Aaron Smith had got hit by the bullet, which had taken off a few of his skinny fingers, and he screamed in agony. 'Serves the poof right!' James thought to himself and smiled before he faked fainting from his deliberate slippage.

Chapter 59: Pierre frames Jonathan Xi Feng and Eileen Lu for Eva's murder, 15th November 2028.

Pierre Beaumont wasn't bothered by the chilling wind that met his face when he exited his private jet onto the tarmac of a tiny airport in Washington DC. He felt more alive than he had felt for years, and everything was set up for success. Everything had gone exactly as he had planned. The counter-snipers killing Lim Dao had tied up a loose end and ensured that Lim would not be a future threat. Pierre had organised transactions to make it appear like China's Eileen Lu had paid Jonathan Xi Feng, Eva Moreno's vice president elect, who then hired Lim Dao and his supposed Persian accomplice, Ervin Ghorbani.

James Winter approached Pierre at the tarmac. James:

- What's with that big grin of yours? It's fucking freezing today.

Pierre:

- A small breeze will not take the joy out of our victory. My victory!

James:

- We are not there yet. An autopsy will reveal that Ervin Ghorbani died hours before the shooting, making him an invalid decoy.

Pierre:

- Yes, I know. But what will they make of it? It will suit the Republicans and the Democrats to keep their duopoly and follow our narrative. Damien's media will discredit Ervin's autopsy report and the coroner will fall in line.

James:

- What about accusations that I might be involved in this plot? People have been talking about the strange coincidence that I slipped just before the shooting and managed to drag Eva right into the path of the bullet.

Pierre:

- It's inconsequential. Evidence shows that China's Eileen Lu and her puppet Xi Feng had paid Lim Dao to carry out the shooting. If they intended to shoot you but shot the president by mistake, that wouldn't make a difference from a legal point of view.

- But do tell me, how did you anticipate the trajectory of the bullet with enough accuracy to get Eva into the right spot?

James:

- The monocle warned me and slowed down my perception of time.

Pierre:

- I see. These Zetan Monocles are impressive gadgets, aren't they?

James:

- Martin's story was even more impressive, albeit impossible. He claimed that he shot Lim's bullet mid-air to change the trajectory of the bullet towards Eva.

Pierre:

- That's absurd. Our friend Martin was only tasked to shoot the counter-snipers protecting her.

James:

- He needs a new purpose. I've sent him to Israel to help the Yehuda Brothers open the gate that blocks the primordial Zeto Crystal.

Pierre:

- Good plan. I will pay him a visit. But first, we need to meet Damien and congratulate him on his unorthodox way of winning the presidency.

Having said this, Pierre and James entered a limousine that took them to Damien's Washington DC mansion.

DAMIEN'S MANSION DIDN'T impress Pierre. He had hoped that a fellow billionaire would have an impressive dwelling full of exquisite furniture and expensive artwork, but Damien's newly renovated abode showed an extreme lack of taste.

Damien sensed Pierre's disapproval and he spoke:

- I am sorry for the state of my Washington mansion. I have focused too much of my efforts on creating presentable mansions in New York, the Hamptons, and the Bahamas.

Pierre:

- Don't worry. You'll soon have the most impressive dwelling of them all, The Whitehouse. The seat of power for the Western World.

Damien smirked:

- Well, the real power lies elsewhere.

Pierre:

- Yes. Yet, you'll control the armed goons and the drone strikes. With you in the Whitehouse, we can spread chaos without the fear of repercussions.

Damien:

- We are not there yet. Xi Feng's trial hasn't been finalised, and he might still get Eva's electoral votes if he can prove himself innocent.

Pierre shrugged his shoulders and replied:

- Well, that's where you come in. I need you to convince other American politicians that they need to sentence Xi Feng for treason and for you to become the president. It's in their self-interests, so it should be an easy sell.

Damien:

- I need some help with that.

Pierre smiled:

- That's why I am here. When big money talks, politicians listen.

Damien:

- Thank you, Pierre.

Pierre shook his head:

- Don't thank me, Damien. My support comes at a steep price. But not for you. Now let's sit down and discuss how I envision the future of America.

Damien clapped his hands and a servant came in. Damien:

- Please bring us food and drinks, Mr Beaumont has travelled far and needs refreshments.

As Pierre tasted the wine and food, he had to hide his irritation. Damien had done a lousy job researching Pierre's culinary preferences. Pierre faked a smile. While the wine tasted off, control over the US army and drone fleet were within his grasp, so there was no reason to cry over sour grapes. Pierre:

- Thank you very much for this exquisite dinner. Now let's discuss my vision on how to further the progress of the human species.

Chapter 60: Massive protests force Eileen Lu to resign, 2nd December 2028.

Eileen Lu looked at the crowds that had gathered on Tianmen Square. The table had been turned. Tianmen Square, once a place of reverence where her countrymen had stood up against the tyranny of the Columnist Party, was now a place where people stood up against her. Eileen Lu studied the masses that had gathered outside. Millions of Chinese citizens had resisted the icy winter winds and they were screaming derogatory terms about her.

Thin lines of riot police surrounded the palace. They would not be enough to protect Eileen if the demonstrations turned violent. Eileen hesitated, she could not bring in the army to disperse the protesters by shooting the innocents, it was not who she was.

The Chinese economy had struggled for years since Eileen Lu became the president. Initially, people had cherished the prospect of being free from the Columnist Party's tyranny. Yet, as the economy deteriorated due to Eileen's refusal to bow her head to the international banking regulations, people had turned against her. The last straw was the allegations that Eileen had financed the assassination of Eva Moreno, to make the American-Chinese Jonathan Xi Feng the president of the USA. The allegations were unfounded, and Eileen hadn't even met with Xi Feng. Jonathan's Chinese heritage was coincidental, but the rest of the world saw his ethnicity and assumed that he was a Chinese spy.

In the end, it didn't matter. The truth was of no consequence when fighting against villains like Pierre and Damien. Eileen knew she had lost. China was under a complete blockade from the rest of the world. Governments had frozen Chinese assets and deported Chinese citizens. War, both civil and foreign, was brewing unless Eileen Lu stepped down.

Min Li entered Eileen's office and spoke:

- Special Agent Min Li, reporting for duty.

Eileen gave her a resigned look and replied:

- Do you have any good news? Please tell me there is a way out of this.

Min Li:

- I fear not. I suspect the riot police will abandon you. If that happens, anything can happen. People are blaming their hardship on your involvement in US politics.

Eileen sighed. Helping Eva Moreno had been a crucial mistake. Eileen had shared Eva's convictions about stopping Pierre and the other powerbrokers that governed from the shadows. Eva was dead, and Eileen would follow in her footsteps unless she could figure something out.

Eileen pleaded to Min Li:

- Please don't let the mob catch me. Shoot me if you must.

Min Li:

- Don't say that. There is still hope.

Eileen:

- What kind of hope? I crushed the Columnist Party and I rejected the banking cabal. But the population are destitute and there is no relief in sight. I can't tyrannise the population I am meant to serve. Even if I wanted to, I don't have the army's support.

Min Li:

- Go into exile. The Emir of Dubai is offering you political asylum.

Eileen:

- Would the Americans agree to that? They allege that I killed their president.

Min Li:

- They know you didn't. It's a political play to stop reform from happening. Eva winning the election threatened the corrupt career politicians that have feathered their nests for too long.

Eileen:

- I guess I have no choice. I'll call Emir Aksam Al-Islam straight away.

Eileen got on the phone with Emir Aksam and after a short conversation, she turned to Min Li.
Eileen:

- He accepted me and offered me asylum. I will take you to Dubai as my protector.

Min Li:

- Understood, President Lu. It will be an honour to keep serving you.

Eileen:

- Glad to hear that. Let's head to the helicopter on the roof. We need to leave.

Eileen and Min Li rushed to the helicopter that took them to a secret army base for further transport out of the country. As Eileen watched the masses that had gathered against her rule, she felt heartbroken. Her life of good intentions had pawed her way to hell, and her only option was to flee like a criminal. How would she recover from this?

Eileen thought of Jared Pond. He broke her heart when he left her after she took out her vengeance on the Columnist Party politicians when she became China's leader. Jared was right all along. Eileen had been a great inspiration as a freedom fighter and dissenter against Chairman Jing Xi's tyranny. Yet, her tenure at the presidency could be characterised by incompetence at best, and tyranny at worst. Eileen sighed and she hoped she would see Jared one day in the future.

Their helicopter reached the airport. Eileen and Min Li rushed towards a plane that took them out of China, never to return.

Chapter 61: President Damien Vanderbilt writes the Monocle Conspiracy a blank check, 2nd February 2029.

Josefina Fiero was enjoying Caipirinhas in the shade of a rubber tree in the park surrounding her Brazilian palace. Her adopted daughter Sandra Santiago and her friend Elaine Orchard accompanied her. They were gossiping and sharing stories about men and beauty treatments. A heavy burden had been lifted off her chest the day Damien Vanderbilt became the US president. Damien had called his Brazilian counterpart, Jorge Santacruz, and the allegations against Josefina's business empire had disappeared. Josefina had considered going after Jorge, but she had refrained from doing so. Jorge had made himself look like a fool, and that in itself was a victory.

Josefina smiled towards Elaine and spoke:

- So, is Martin coming to our meeting?

Elaine:

- No, Martin and Szymon Yehuda are looking for a Zeto Crystal hidden somewhere around Lake Victoria in Africa. Martin claims that there is a Zetan Temple on Nabuyongo Island that is visible only once every 12 years.

Josefina:

- Such a waste of time looking for these ancient crystals when we can achieve so much if we work together for a worthwhile cause.

Elaine:

- I disagree. You must remember that our primary goal is to find and utilise the power of the primordial Zeto crystal. Even a replicated Zeto Crystal could power the monocles to their utmost supreme conditions, and the crystals even brought Martin back from the dead in 2022. Imagine the powers that lie within the primordial Zeto Crystal, the true ancient Zetan source of energy in this universe.

Josefina:

- So, what would you do if you got your hands on that crystal?

Elaine paused for a while to think before she replied:

- I wouldn't get my hands on it. I am not pursuing it; hence I am here.

Josefina:

- Yet you know more than me about the pursuit for the Zeto Crystal.

Elaine:

- It came up during my last conversation with Martin. I am happy that Martin found a purpose in life again. Now he can pursue his goal to 'stop the apocalypse'.

Josefina:

- The apocalypse that allegedly will take place in 2131, according to a Zetan artefact? What a joke, none of us will be around by then.

Elaine:

- Correct. But like religion, it gives a far-away purpose in life. I am happy for him. I would like to find God.

Josefina:

- What will you do if you don't find a higher purpose?

Elaine:

- I'll turn Indonesia into the greatest nation on Earth, built according to my visions. No poverty, no illness, no suffering.

Josefina:

- That's an unrealistic dream. It will never happen.

Elaine:

- Well, that's my ambition. If we convince the US president Damien Vanderbilt to give us unlimited funding, it can happen.

Elaine and Josefina looked towards the helicopter pad, as a US helicopter landed. President Damien Vanderbilt and his family disembarked.
Josefina:

- Damien Vanderbilt has landed, let's host a reception for him.

THE US PRESIDENT DAMIEN Vanderbilt, his first-lady Eloise, and his children Jane and Jeff approached Josefina as they arrived at her mansion. Josefina bit her lip in frustration. She had planned to seduce Damien to get herself advantages, but the presence of his family was a no go. As if Damien read her mind, he spoke:

- Thank you for having us, Josefina. We met with the Brazilian president and my advisors told me that it was beneficial to bring my family on my first overseas trip as a president.

Josefina:

- I didn't even know you had a family. You have never mentioned them before.

Damien:

- Don't be silly. An American President must have a family. That they loathe each other is of no concern.

First lady Eloise interrupted Damien:

- Can I take the children somewhere else? I have no interest in socialising with your latest play toy.

Damien:

- Mind your manner, Eloise. You might be my wife but you're not immune from the dangers in life. Quite the opposite!

Eloise was about to rush off when Damien interrupted her:

- Hold on, we need a happy family photo first. Josefina and Sandra, please join us for a photo.

Eloise sighed and moments later the presidential photographer had snapped some unnatural-looking photos for the Whitehouse propaganda channel. Eloise:

- Come, children, let's head to an amusement park while your father is discussing business with our fabulous host.

The children came to their mother, and moments later they left in a limousine. Josefina smirked:

- Woah, what a happy family you got there!

Damien ignored her tone and stated:

- The nuclear family is crucial for national morale. The family members hating each other is better left unsaid.

Josefina:

- Perhaps you should try to fix your relationship with your wife?

Damien shrugged his shoulders and replied:

- My wife cannot expect that a man in my position must choose between family life and other women. I can and will have both.

After hearing this, Josefina scratched her plan of seducing Damien. It had been an interesting prospect to have sex with the US president, yet his misogynism was a turn-off. Josefina gave Damien a cold stare and spoke:

- We will meet in the dining room when the others have arrived. My servants will look after your every need in the meantime.

Having said this, Josefina turned around and walked back into her mansion.

A WHILE LATER, EVERYONE had gathered in the dining room for an eight-course degustation menu. Present were Josefina Fiero, Sandra Santiago, Pierre Beaumont, Elaine Orchard, Ben Yehuda, James Winter, and Damien Vanderbilt. Damien was in a great mood and he proclaimed:

- I would like to thank you all for your contributions on my path to the presidency. As the US president, I have signed an executive order protecting James and Pierre from the Reversogene drug investigation. I have also agreed with the Brazilian president to stop his unjustified crusade against our gracious host Josefina. I have decided to reinstate James Winter as the CIA director for his outstanding efforts for my country. Finally, I have ordered that your respective companies should be preferred suppliers for US purchases in your regions. This will grant you lucrative opportunities.

Josefina:

- How did you deal with Jorge Santacruz?

Damien:

- I hinted that an Amazon-based indigenous rebel-group was underway to steal a US drone to kill him. I offered him the deactivation code for a price.

Sandra:

- So, you issued a death threat to our president?

Damien:

- Quite the contrary. I saved his life. It wasn't my fault we lost the drone in the first place. At least that would be difficult to prove.

Pierre:

- I like what I am hearing. Access to the US satellite and drone network will be a fantastic way to make troublemakers fall into line.

Damien:

- Yes, and with James Winter reinstated as the CIA director, we will find and eliminate these troublemakers pre-emptively.

James nodded and smirked. Damien continued:

- And to the rest of you, as US government preferred suppliers your business success is guaranteed. You'll become even more prominent than you already are.

- Cheers to my election victory and the future society we will build together.

After Damien finished his speech, everyone cheered. They spent the rest of the day wining and dining while dividing the world amongst themselves.

Chapter 62: Szymon Yehuda gives Pierre a Zeto Crystal. 12th February 2029

Pierre Beaumont exited his private jet at Tel Aviv International airport. He scoffed at what he saw. How could this impoverished desert be the most contested territory in the history of humankind? Yet Pierre knew that deep under the Solomon Temple lay his destiny. If he could get his hands on the primordial Zeto Crystal, the future was his.

Pierre had witnessed the miracles of the replicated Zeto Crystals in the past. These Zetan artifacts could bring back the dead and power up the hidden technologies in Zetan temples. Yet, these crystals were replicas, mass-produced like batteries by the Zetans themselves. The Primordial Zeto Crystal was the original. It was a true source of power and Pierre's Zetan Monocle informed him that he could gain immortality if he found it.

"Welcome to Israel."

Pierre turned around and he saw Szymon Yehuda and Martin Orchard. Szymon had a fresh scar across his face, and Martin had his hand in a gypsum cast.

Pierre:

- Did you find the Zeto Crystal?

Szymon:

- Yes, but we almost died. The Temple's defences caused the island to collapse and drowned several members of our entourage.

Pierre knew about this. The collapse of Nabuyongo Island had caused several hundred deaths in Tanzania the previous week. The media narrative had claimed that an earthquake caused the collapse, and no-one had questioned the narrative. Life was cheap and plentiful when it happened in far-away destitute countries.

Pierre:

- The collapse of Nabuyongo Island is of no concern. Quite the opposite. Helping people after natural disasters is an easy way for the World Bank to maintain positive public relations.

Martin snarked:

- Even when the World Bank's actions cause the natural disaster that you're alleviating?

Pierre smirked:

- Who would ever believe in such far-fetched theories? Now take me to the Templar Tunnels and the gateway that blocks the primordial Zeto Crystal. I want to succeed where you fail.

Szymon:

- Of course. Come with us, Pierre.

PIERRE SENSED AN IMMENSE power behind the indestructible gateway that blocked the primordial Zeto Crystal. Pierre, Szymon, and Martin were in the Templar Tunnels, far below the ancient Solomon Temple. This was it. When Pierre deciphered the code, he would become the most powerful man in history.

Pierre turned to Szymon and spoke:

- I guess this is it? Once I decipher the code, no one will be able to stand against us. You'll get your pure-breed Jewish nation, I will attain full global economic control, and Martin will get a chance to stop the future apocalypse.

Szymon nodded and showed off an evil grin. Szymon:

- Of course. We have a deal.

Pierre:

- Very well. Hand me the crystal and tell me how to activate the panels on the wall.

Szymon handed Pierre the replicated Zeto Crystal and spoke:

- Slam the replicated crystal in the hollow section of that wall. That will drain the replica and energise the temple and the control panel.

Pierre nodded, took the crystal, and was about to slam it into the wall when he received a message from his monocle. If he tried to get the primordial Zeto Crystal today, he would fail. There were two potential outcomes if Pierre tried to open the door. Either he would fail, get electrocuted and lose the replicated Zeto crystal as Martin, Szymon, and Ben had fared when they tried to open the door. Or worse yet, if he managed to open the door, he was at the mercy of Szymon and Martin. Pierre was the oldest and least accomplished fighter in the group. If it came to violence between the three of them, he was likely to perish.

Pierre put the replicated Zeto crystal in his pocket and turned around. Szymon ran up to him and shouted:

- What are you doing, Pierre? What is the meaning of this?

Pierre:

- I cannot open the door. Only Keila Eisenstein can open it.

Szymon:

- Keila Eisenstein? Who the hell is that?

Pierre:

- Ask Martin Orchard, or as you call him, Martin Al-Sham. Quite a fitting name for such a duplicitous liar.

Martin:

- I don't know what you are talking about.

Pierre:

- Yes, you do. You searched the CIA archives and you asked your fellow Templar Michael to help you look for her. This happened after you failed to open the gateway. You must have reasons to believe that Keila Eisenstein is the key to opening that door.

Martin:

- I don't know who Keila Eisenstein is. I just know that the name is of importance.

Pierre:

- Bah, you know more than you're willing to admit.

Martin looked away and didn't reply. Szymon looked at Pierre and spoke:

- So, what happens now?

Pierre:

- I will continue funding your operations if you let me leave with this Zeto crystal. With a bit of luck, you'll find this Keila Eisenstein during your travels.

Szymon:

- So, what are you going to do?

Pierre:

- I am going to visit an old friend capable of furthering our cause.

Szymon froze and examined his odds. If he were to enter combat mode: The monocle displayed: *'Odds for survival 43 %. Odds for finding the primordial Zeto Crystal 0.2%.'*
Pierre smirked:

- Do you like those odds, Szymon? Your odds of survival are better than mine, but it won't help you reach your goals.

Szymon didn't reply and Pierre swiftly left the tunnels. Martin approached Szymon and spoke:

- So, what do we do now? Why did you let him leave?

Szymon growled:

- Because you would turn hostile if I attacked Pierre. Besides, why didn't you tell me about Keila Eisenstein?

Martin looked away and stayed silent. Szymon shouted:

- Just what I thought. You better pull yourself together, Al-Sham. I'll debrief you about this later.

Having said this, Szymon strode towards the exit and left Martin Orchard, also known as Martin Al-Sham behind, to yearn for the primordial Zeto crystal, which was so close, yet so far away.

Chapter 63: Pierre resurrects Vladimir and reveals his plan for humanity. 15th February 2029.

Pierre was in a top-secret research lab in Switzerland. Pierre watched Vladimir who was still in a coma, connected to a respirator. Pierre walked up to the doctor who oversaw Vladimir's health and spoke:

- Do you have any news about our patient, Dr Gruber?

Erik Gruber shrugged his shoulders and replied:

- There is nothing new to discuss. The patient is brain dead and beyond hope. Why are you hiring me when there is nothing I can do?

Pierre:

- I wouldn't know that there was nothing you could do if I hadn't hired you to save him. Besides, I pay you a handsome salary, so quit standing around doing nothing.

Erik:

- I wasn't complaining Monsieur Beaumont, I was merely asking.

Pierre:

- In any case, your services are no longer required. I have terminated your employment and I will pay your redundancy according to your employment contract.

Erik:

- May I ask what you are planning to do with the patient?

Pierre:

- You may not. As you are no longer my employee, I urge you to leave my facility at once. My employees will send your belongings to your designated address.

Erik:

- But Mr Beaumont. I have unfinished projects. If I had known, I could have prepared a handover to my colleagues.

Pierre:

- If you had known, you could have stolen research data and prepared to betray me.

Pierre clapped his hands and two beefed-up security guards entered the room.

- Guards, please escort Dr Gruber to the exit and organise the audit and delivery of his belongings.

The guards nodded, grabbed Erik, and led him out of the room.

Pierre smirked. While he didn't distrust Erik, he didn't want him to steal any medical journals, which could have happened if Pierre notified him in advance. Pierre wanted to keep Vladimir's recovery a secret, as the world wasn't ready to know about the Zeto crystals.

Pierre connected Vladimir's monocle to Vladimir's right eye. As per usual, it wasn't enough to bring Vladimir back to consciousness.

Pierre then placed a replicated Zeto crystal on top of Vladimir's monocle. There was a bright flash of immense blue light, and seconds later, Vladimir opened his eyes and took a terrified gasp of air.

Vladimir:

- What happened?

Pierre smiled and said:

- You tell me. How was the world's greatest assassin outdone by a single woman?

Pierre knew the answer; Elaine Orchard had tipped Julienne Bessange on how to outsmart the monocle's AI. Pierre didn't intend to tell Vladimir. If Vladimir killed Elaine, Pierre would lose control over Asia and Martin Orchard would come after them.

Vladimir:

- I don't remember.
- Where is Julienne Bessange now? I must kill her to get my revenge.

Pierre:

- Julienne Bessange is dead. James Winter shot her in the head with a sniper rifle.

Vladimir:

- What about Julienne Bessange's body?

Pierre:

- Dead and cremated. You have been gone for seven months, Vladimir. A lot has happened in your absence.

Vladimir:

- Like what?

Pierre:

- We overthrew Eileen Lu as the president of China. I allowed the Emir of Dubai to take her in. Eileen must live in shame for defying us.

- Eva Moreno won the US presidential election and threatened to put us on trial for our crimes. This was unacceptable, so we killed her and blamed it on China and Iran. My friend Damien Vanderbilt is doing my bidding in the Whitehouse instead.

- Lucien and Delphine, the children born via my breeding program are showing enormous potential to become successful heirs to the Beaumont family. But they are still children and need more training before they are useful.

Vladimir:

- These are all good news. So why did you bring me back?

Pierre smirked:

- Because of my love for your great personality. Why do you ask?

Vladimir gave Pierre a dead stare and replied:

- Tell me the real reason.

Pierre sighed:

- I need your help to secure the primordial Zeto Crystal. I was close to finding it, but I realised that Szymon Yehuda or Martin Orchard would kill me the moment I opened the locked passageway. I need you to be by my side to stop them from getting any dumb ideas.

Vladimir:

- And what will happen once you have the primordial Zeto Crystal?

Pierre:

- With the power of the primordial Zeto Crystal, we will be immortal. Our breeding program will breed new generations of intelligent superhumans, formed in our image. We will change humanity forever. We will become gods!

After saying this, Pierre and Vladimir burst into a diabolical laughter of victory. The world was theirs. They had overthrown Eileen Lu, they had murdered Eva Moreno, and their lackey Damien Vanderbilt was now the US president.

AMID ALL OF THESE MISHAPS, a beautiful 9-year old girl who lived somewhere faraway, a lovely girl by the name of Sabina Hines had been awaken of her prophecy. Pierre and Vladimir were unaware of the existence of Sabina Hines, who was to be the only one who could save the world from their villainy.

THE BANKER
AND
THE EMPATH
After his daughter tries to kill him, the Banker sets out to steal an ancient artifact to bring his daughter back to life.
Martin Lundqvist

Chapter 64: Pierre Beaumont sets up a competition to find a suitable heir. 23rd October 2039.

Pierre Beaumont was holding the Zetan Monocle belonging to the fallen Ben Yehuda in his right hand. It felt poignant to him that one of the members of the Monocle Conspiracy had fallen, but Pierre had done what he could to bring Ben back to life. Pierre thought back on how Ben had died on that day, almost two years earlier.

Ben had reported that they had found Keila Eisenstein, who they believed to be the only one able to open the gate at Solomon Temple that blocked the entrance to where primordial Zeto Crystal was located. Keila Eisenstein was a fake persona, the real identity of the mysterious girl was the 18-year-old Sabina Hines, a lone traveller from Australia. The fact she had chosen the alias Keila Eisenstein had to mean something. Ben Yehuda and Martin Orchard had come up with a plan to lure Sabina Hines to the Templar Tunnels at Solomon Temple, so she could open the locked ancient gate. The plan had worked, and Sabina had managed to open the gate. Straight after that, things had turned bad. Martin Orchard had turned against his comrade Ben Yehuda and his fellow Templars and murdered them all. Martin had helped Sabina escape with the Zeto crystal and he had closed the gate, leaving the dead bodies of Ben and the Templars inside the temple. Mossad agents, led by Ben's brother Szymon Yehuda, had tracked Martin down and killed him, but the Zeto Crystal and Sabina Hines were nowhere to be found.

In the current time, Pierre was studying the lifeless body of Martin Orchard, which was frozen in a cryogenic tank. If Pierre chose to, he could resurrect Martin and punish him for his betrayal. Instead, he chose to let Martin remain dead in a permanent slumber. With Ben Yehuda, things were different. Upon Martin's betrayal, Vladimir and Szymon had been tasked to find a replicated Zeto Crystal to once again open the gate. Yet, as finding a replicated Zeto Crystal took time, they had come too late and Ben Yehuda's corpse had already decomposed when they got to him. Ben had been beyond resurrection, even with the powers of a replicated Zeto Crystal. However, a primordial Zeto Crystal could potentially still revive him. While Pierre had suggested that they would freeze Ben Yehuda's remains until they had the primordial Zeto Crystal, Szymon had been against it. They were too late, and Szymon felt compelled to continue his Jewish Supremacy plan on his own. They had cremated Ben Yehuda, and Pierre had kept Ben's Zetan Monocle for himself.

Pierre read the intelligence file on Sabina Hines. Sabina was now 20 years old, living in Sydney, running a charity to protect the environment. She had used the power of the primordial Zeto Crystal to make a fortune from trading the financial markets under a variety of fake aliases. Officially, Sabina Hines and her husband Alexander O'Neill were the directors of the environment-focused "Building a Better World" charity. Knowing that she owned the primordial crystal, Pierre suspected that she had other hidden motivations.

At first, Pierre had planned to send Vladimir to Australia to murder Sabina in secrecy. But then he had feared that all the other Zetan Monocle conspiracists that were also searching for the crystal would kill him if he attained it, and so he decided to let her go, for now. Having followed Sabina's actions for the last few years, he had foreseen that she was more gifted than any of his children. It would be ideal if she were to join the Monocle Conspiracy and serve him.

Pierre shook off the idea. Everything indicated that Sabina was a bleeding-heart do-gooder, and she was unlikely to serve him. To achieve his goals, he needed to get his own children more involved in his prime mission. The 24 children he had from the surrogacy breeding projects had turned 16, so they were ready to serve him and it was now time to choose a suitable heir.

Pierre creeped down to his old and musty-smelling wine cellar to fetch a bottle of vintage wine. His knee joints were creaking, and he realised that old age was catching up with him. He was 70 years old, and his body was in a bad shape from his stressful lifestyle and heavy drinking. *'I should have ordered the servants to fetch the bottle for me,'* Pierre thought, and brushed the thought off. He couldn't allow himself to be seen as weak to his obedient servants. How could he rule the world if he couldn't even fetch his own drink?

Pierre picked up a bottle of red vintage wine, dragged himself up the stairs, and poured a glass of wine in front of the warm and cosy fireplace. He turned on his hologram laptop, and organised an exciting competition among his 24 children, to find a suitable heir.

A 16-YEAR-OLD BRUNETTE girl, Delphine Beaumont, studied her reflection in the full-body mirror in her room, in Pierre's Swiss Alps heritage centre. *'This is where we will shape the future of House Beaumont and the fate of the world.'* Delphine mumbled. She sighed, hesitated, and shook off the thought. How could she be a future world leader, if she had lived the first 16 years of her life as a prisoner to her distant, cold, and awful father?

"Urrgh!" Delphine exclaimed as she picked up a glass and threw it at the mirror, shattering it into thousands of small fragments. She hated watching her reflection. It reminded her of her father, and in her eyes, she was as ugly as him. She remembered what Pierre had told her during one of their formal meetings in the last year. "I chose your mother as the IVF donor because she was my cousin, in order to preserve Beaumont heritage. Beauty is on the outside and it fades. You should feel proud that you have a true Beaumont bloodline."

Delphine hated her father. Pierre had spoken about herself and her mother, whom she had never met, as if they were racehorses that he bred genetically to serve a purpose to fulfil his wishes. Here she was, a 16-year-old girl produced genetically by artificial insemination, born through a surrogate mother, who never laid eyes upon her, and her purpose was everything she knew in her life. As much as she hated Pierre, her main purpose was to win the competition and become Pierre's ultimate heir, what else was there to live for?

The supervisor of the breeding facility, Constance Monet rushed into Delphine's room, looked at the shattered mirror, and reproached her:

- What is the meaning of this, Delphine?

Delphine:

- I hate this ugly mirror. I hate the way I look! I hate the way it reminds me of him.

Constance shook Delphine and spoke:

- Be quiet, spoiled child. You're living in a facility that prepares you for leading the world in the Beaumont legacy. Strength comes from determination and the willingness to succeed. It doesn't come from self-loathing and hatred.

Delphine clenched her jaw and looked at shards of the broken mirror. She wanted to slit the throat of her superintendent Constance, to get her revenge for all the torture and scorn she had experienced all these years. Constance spoke again:

- I know you want to attack me, Delphine. But it wouldn't serve you. If you kill me, my guards will kill you, and you'll lose your shot at the power you're so close to obtaining.

Delphine took a deep breath and swallowed her anger. Constance spoke again:

- Good. With that out of the way, please come with me. Mr Beaumont has summoned all his offspring to meet him at the grand dining room.

Delphine sighed and walked towards the door. Before she got out, Constance scorned her:

- Do you want to meet your father dressed like that? Dress appropriately. You are not a child anymore, silly girl!

Without another word, Delphine walked to her walk-in wardrobe, put on the Beaumont Family school uniform, and walked towards the dining room.

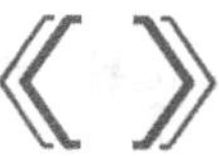

PIERRE FELT PROUD OF himself as he entered The Beaumont Family Heritage centre, where his loyal superintendent operatives raised his children. The construction of the centre took place in 2022, and it contained all the modern technologies, particularly surveillance technologies. Pierre's crew had built the centre in resemblance to the old boarding school he had attended when he was a child, before the Beaumont family's fall from grace. Visiting the centre, Pierre remembered his happy childhood years. Things were so different before the tragic accident that killed his parents and sister, and the suicide of his grandpa that followed.

Pierre looked at his children, who had lined up in unison at the dining hall. The tables were set in a U-shape. The facility supervisors sat at the centre of the table, all the boys were sitting at the right-hand-side and all the girls were sitting on the left-hand-side. The children were all facing the centre of the room and podium. It was a beautiful symmetry, which would be lost when he chose one child to stay with him. Such was the plight of life; perfect symmetry could not last forever.

Pierre walked up to the stand on the podium and spoke:

- Greetings, children.

- Today is a great day, because one of you will receive the privilege of leaving this facility and come to live with me at Palace Beaumont.

- I have put together a series of tests to determine who is the most suitable to become my successor. Do your best, but don't be distraught if you are not selected. The world is large enough for all of you to dominate it, together as a Beaumont family.

- I'll leave it to your superintendents to carry out the testing.

- However, I urge you to remember. Big Father is always watching.

Having said this, Pierre left the dining hall and walked towards the surveillance room where all the CCTV footage was available for him to see. This was his preferred way of interacting with his progeny, always watching from afar and giving them instructions via the speakers.

THE FOLLOWING DAY, Pierre was reviewing the competition results from the previous night's trials and tribulations. He smiled when he saw how Delphine had aced all her tests, closely followed by her twin brother, Lucien. The stupid and deformed Raphael had failed all tests, as usual. It was as if he intentionally failed on everything to gain Pierre's attention, which Pierre found bothersome. The emotive screening cameras didn't indicate that Raphael felt depressed, in fact he was happy that he failed. Genetic testing on Raphael hadn't found the cause for his deformity, lack of ambition and perceived unintelligence.

Pierre smiled when he anticipated the shock it would cause to his children when he announced that Raphael would be his winning selection. How they reacted to this announcement was the intention of the whole testing procedure. In actuality, the son or daughter who could rise to the occasion, the first runner-up to Raphael, was to be the one he would select as his real heir. Pierre had felt ashamed when he had been sidestepped in favour of the fat bastard Gunter Fritz while they were both working at the Deutsche Bank in Germany. Since then, he had come out stronger from the ordeal, and it was his burning desire for revenge to make Beaumont family the ultimate world leaders, that had made him the wealthiest and most powerful man in the world.

Having made up his mind, Pierre entered the auditorium to disclose his shocking decision.

PIERRE WAS WALKING to his car, accompanied by Constance Monet and Raphael Beaumont, when Delphine ran after them. She shouted:

- Pierre! Hold on. I need to talk to you.

Constance leaned in and whispered in Pierre's ear:

- Be careful, Monsieur Beaumont. Delphine is volatile and she was close to attacking me yesterday with a shard of broken glass.

Pierre smirked and replied:

- Thank you, Constance. But I have nothing to fear from the sweet and innocent Delphine. I am sure a few words will alleviate her worries.

Pierre turned to Delphine and spoke:

- Refer to me as Big Father or Father Beaumont. Addressing one's father by the first name is disrespectful.

Delphine:

- I don't care. How could you pick Raphael over me? I aced all the tests, while he failed everything!

Pierre:

- You are correct, Delphine. You did ace all the tests. However,
I never said that acing the tests was the desirable outcome. That
was something you incorrectly assumed.

Delphine held back her tears. She felt distraught knowing how unfair
Pierre was to her. Knowing that she was not the winner, she would never
get out of the horrible and cold breeding facility centre. How could it have
come to this? She fitted all the criteria of an excellent daughter, and he had
told her that she was his favourite daughter on one occasion. Pierre walked
up to Delphine and touched her face, a spitting image of himself. Delphine
sniffed and said:

- I hate you! How can you do this to me?

Pierre:

- You'll understand in due time. Besides, succeeding me is not
your true desire. Do what you truly desire, and you'll be free.

Hearing this, Delphine let out her tears. Pierre took his old and frail
hand away from her unappealing face, took a few steps back, and spoke
again:

- Unfortunately, our time is up for today, Delphine. I need to focus on Raphael now. But we will meet again. Take care, and keep
your faith in me.

Having said this, Pierre and Raphael entered his private limousine,
which took them back to Palace Beaumont.

Chapter 65: "Raphael is the worst part of me." 30th October 2039

Pierre Beaumont wrinkled in disgust, as he watched the CCTV footage of his mentally disabled son Raphael, sitting in his room by himself. Raphael had taken some lint from his own navel, tasted it, spat it out and looked at the camera with a silly grimace. Pierre turned off the computer. Observing Raphael's lack of intelligence would not bring more ideas to his evil mission. Pierre concluded that he had to interact with Raphael. "Mon Dieu, Raphael is the worst part of me," Pierre muttered to himself as he walked towards Raphael's room, on the top-level of the luxurious mansion.

Pierre walked towards the stairs, but his knees tormented him as he ascended the staircase in agony. He needed double knee surgery, and a long period of rehab to get them better, but he didn't have time for such pursuits. Age was catching up with him and he needed to achieve a lot more to secure his lineage. The Beaumonts were meant to rule the world, and it was Pierre's obligation to make it happen.

Pierre's assistant, Jean Valmont, approached him and spoke:

- Monsieur Beaumont! I am worried about your knees. Let me fetch Raphael for you.

Pierre gave Jean a sceptical look, and replied with a condescending tone:

- Hrmph! Don't worry about my knees. They are merely dysfunctional pieces of bone, ligament and muscle. The only thing that matters, my brain, is still in peak performance. As for fetching Raphael, I do not intend to let my knees stopping me from walking around in my own palace!

Jean:

- Apologies, sir. I didn't mean to offend you.

Pierre sighed:

- It's okay, Jean. You have worked for me for 18 years and you still haven't learnt how to respect me. I find small doses of your disrespect strangely refreshing. But don't go overboard, yes?

Jean:

- Alright, master. Perhaps we can install an elevator in here? That way you can move around in the palace without pain.

Pierre:

- Hrmph! The Beaumont family has inhabited this palace for centuries. Do you see any lift? My forebears could walk in these stairs, and so will I. Dismissed, Jean.

Hearing this, Jean bowed and rushed off. Pierre smiled as she went out of sight. Jean had been working for almost two decades and she was a fixture in his life. A source of annoyance for sure, but still a point of reference.

As Jean was often seen near Pierre, the tabloids were speculating that they were a couple. Pierre didn't mind, as a matter of fact, he encouraged it. If the media spent time speculating about his sex life, that meant they wouldn't investigate on more perilous parts of his life, such as how he had contaminated New York City's water supply with the Hei Bai virus; or how his drug manufacturing company had released a medication that killed the virus but also caused a lot of dangerous side effects; or how he meddled in governmental elections.

Pierre's phone rang. The display showed 'Danielle Anders, Australian Prime Minister'. Pierre ignored the call and kept walking towards Raphael's room. His puppet Prime Minister of Australia could wait a while.

RAPHAEL WAS LYING IN bed while watching a broadcasted video on his tablet. He was swooning over a press conference with the young, famous, and beautiful environmentalist Sabina Hines. The press conference described how robotic sea drones would clean up the Pacific Ocean. Raphael had never been to the ocean, but it looked beautiful and he hoped he could meet with Sabina.

Pierre entered the room and Raphael grinned and turned off the tablet. Pierre taunted:

- Are you watching porn, Raphael?

Raphael giggled and replied:

- No. Of course not.

Pierre:

- Very well. Then show me what you're watching.

Raphael turned on the tablet, showed the video to Pierre, and said:

- Isn't this amazing. She is so young and has such big dreams. I wish our tutors told us about her.

Pierre hid his disapproval. He had confined his progeny to a secret location and asked his superintendents to shape the children in his image. He had also programmed the AI to block all mentions of persons and events that didn't fit Pierre's future vision. As it would seem, nothing of this had worked as his son had become a teenage fanboy of the virtue-signalling Sabina Hines.

Pierre:

- Sabina is all talk. What has she ever done for the world?

- Your Father, on the other hand, saved humanity from doom when the evil Hei Bai virus ravaged our planet in 2021. We dispersed medication that helped the world.

Raphael:

- But I don't understand, Father. If you are such a benevolent man, why are your children confined to the boarding school in the Beaumont Heritage Centre? Why do you never show us any love?

Pierre:

- Don't engage in self-pity, Raphael. Sealing you off from the world was my gift to you. You grew up in a safe environment, where you received first-class care, nutrition, and education. That is more than most humans receive.

Raphael:

- I am in love with Sabina Hines. Can't we go see her, Father? I would love to travel to Australia to visit her. We can make Sabina's vision come true with our family's wealth.

Pierre thought of slapping Raphael, but he controlled himself. There was not a chance in hell that he would introduce his son to the fraud Sabina, who had stolen the primordial Zeto Crystal from him. Pierre:

- Hmmph. I just received an important financial news update via my monocle. I'll need to address this issue immediately. I'll speak to you later, Raphael.

Having said this, Pierre turned around, and strode towards the door, ignoring the agonising pain in his knees.

DELPHINE BEAUMONT WAS crying herself to sleep. She was furious with Pierre. He had dared to tell her to follow her dreams, while on the other hand keeping her as a prisoner at this boarding school / breeding facility. What had the old bastard meant by following her dreams? Delphine hated everyone, especially her indifferent siblings, and she wanted it all to end.

Delphine wiped away her tears and she forced a smile. There was one person she didn't hate in this facility. In fact, she adored him. It was her twin brother, Lucien Beaumont. When she was around him, she felt a tingling emotion and he had filled her with exciting wet dreams. Delphine held back. Was she in love with her brother, or was it the lack of other romantic options that caused him to be the focal point of her carnal desire?

Delphine opened a book about the pyramids and the ancient Egyptians. The Egyptians had always impressed Delphine. She loved their ability to build structures that could withstand the tests of time. Another thing fascinated her. The Pharaohs had married their sibling to keep the bloodline pure from the lower classes. Was this the reason she was locked up in this facility, together with her siblings?

Delphine studied herself in the mirror. Why had they put a new mirror in her room, a few days after she destroyed the other one? It didn't make any sense, yet she couldn't stay away from her reflection. Delphine stared in a mix of terror and fascination, as her reflection slowly turned to that of a hideous monstrosity. The monstrosity in front of her was no longer a shy 16-year-old little girl, it was now a humanoid creature with ugly fangs and purple predatoric eyes. The creature hissed:

- Delphine Beaumont, we meet at last. I have been observing you from a distance. Growl!

Delphine:

- Who are you?

Ugly Creature:

- I am Empress Rangda Kaliankan, and you have a rare gene that allows us to communicate to each other.

Delphine:

- What gene are you talking about?

Empress Rangda:

- Silence! Our connection is weak and our time is short. You need to fulfil your destiny. You need to breed with Lucien, kill your father, and then take his place. You'll create a dynasty that will rule humankind....!

Delphine:

- But how would I do any of this?

Empress Rangda:

- Your brother will accept your sexual advances. Seduce him, and murder the guard who will fall asleep in the guardhouse next Monday. Steal the guard's weapons, set the building on fire, and murder everyone as they try to escape.

Delphine:

- Who are you, and why are you telling me this?!

Delphine didn't receive any response. Instead, her reflection quickly reverted back to her usual self, and the voice was now gone. Delphine screamed and collapsed to the floor in shock. A few minutes later, the facility guards entered her room, gave her sedatives to silence her erratic behaviour, and put her to sleep in her bed.

'I CANNOT LISTEN TO Raphael talking about Sabina Hines any longer!!' Pierre muttered as he left Raphael's room in frustration. His son had petitioned that they should travel together to Sydney, Australia and meet with Sabina. Pierre had pretended to agree, since it was crucial to gain Raphael's complete trust for the next part of his malicious plan.

Pierre walked to his office, unlocked a biometric safe, and took out the deceased Ben Yehuda's Zetan monocle. It was time to give the Zetan gadget to Raphael, to silence his idiotic tendencies.

Pierre had postponed the testing of the monocle on Raphael's small head. If he failed to deactivate the monocle's automatic defences, it would identify Raphael as an unauthorised user and kill him. Pierre had thought of sparing Raphael's life by not making him wear it. However, having listened to Raphael's foolish ideologies for almost a week, Pierre had concluded that he would be the first candidate for the monocle, and thus the perfect test subject.

Pierre picked up the monocle and walked to Raphael's room. Raphael gave him a confused look when he entered the room again. Raphael said:

- Father, why are you back so soon? I thought you would make the arrangements for our trip to Sydney.

Spoiled brat. Treating his father as a servant to fulfil his whims and wishes, Pierre thought and replied:

- Before I can organise a meeting with Sabina Hines, Raphael darling, I need you to put this on. It contains an advanced AI that helped me become the wealthiest man in the world.

Raphael received the Zetan Monocle and he studied it carefully. It didn't look particularly impressive, although it looked like the one his Father wore, but Raphael sensed a mystical aura emitting from the monocle. *Don't put it on.* He heard a faint female voice whisper. He turned to Pierre and spoke:

\- Hold on. How did you get your hands on this monocle before you were wealthy? How is that possible? I thought your scientists made these for you?

'He is a lot more alert than meets the eye,' Pierre thought and replied:

\- When I got the monocle, our family was already wealthy and powerful, but the AI of this monocle made me the wealthiest man on the planet.

Raphael was excited with Pierre's answer and he replied:

\- So, when was it made, who made it for you, and what are the technical specifications?

'No point in lying to the boy, who has the potential to be my heir if he is able to activate it,' Pierre thought and replied:

\- I found it during an expedition in Nepal. We were a group of nine individuals that came across an ancient alien temple belonging to the Zetan race. One person from our group died a few years ago, and I am passing on his monocle to you.

Raphael shook his head and gave Pierre a funny look. Raphael said:

\- Stop mocking me, dad. If you don't want to tell me where you got it, that's ok. But do you promise that we'll meet with Sabina Hines if I try on this gadget?

'If you survive.' Pierre thought and replied:

\- Yes, we will. If you follow my directions, we'll go to Australia and meet that idol of yours. With a bit of luck, you'll realise that she is just a seller of pipe dreams and nothing else.

Raphael agreed and looked at the monocle again. *'It's a trap, you'll die, Raphael!'* The faint female voice whispered again. Raphael turned to Pierre and spoke:

- Is there someone else in the room? Is this one of your tests?

Pierre:

- Look, I don't have all day. If you don't follow my instructions, I won't organise the meeting with Sabina Hines.

Hearing this, Raphael inserted the monocle and Pierre sensed how his mind connected to Raphael. *'Unauthorised user connected to Monocle 005, preparing to terminate the user.'* popped up on Pierre's display. *'Monocle 001 demands to override usage restriction on Monocle 005.'* Pierre sent back. *'Usage changing request denied. A consensus is required to change user settings.'* Raphael's monocle replied.

Pierre's perception of time slowed to a standstill. A timer was counting down in slow motion. If he couldn't get the other members of the Monocle Conspiracy to approve Raphael as the Monocle's new owner, his son would die. *'I need to contact everyone at once'* Pierre thought, but he stopped himself. He would need Martin Orchard's approval to unlock the Zetan Monocle and that couldn't happen as Martin was frozen inside a cryogenic tank.

Time resumed and Pierre exclaimed:

- Raphael. You need to take off the monocle!

Raphael:

- Why, Father?

Time slowed down for Pierre. *'4 seconds to termination of the unauthorised user.'* Pierre's monocle showed. *"Mon Dieu, I don't have the time for this!"* Pierre thought. He would have to pull Raphael's monocle out of his small head, leaving him blind on one eye, but he would still live.

Time resumed and Pierre jumped towards Raphael and tried to grab the Zetan monocle. The attempt was unsuccessful, as the monocle's force-field electrocuted Pierre, and sent him flying backwards into the wall. Pierre looked in horror on the severe burns on his hand.

There was a shriek of pain and agony, and Raphael collapsed next to Pierre. The monocle had disfigured Raphael's face and blood poured out from his right eye.

Chapter 66: "It runs in the family", 1st November 2039

Pierre felt a little distraught as he studied the lifeless body of his son Raphael, who was now lying in a puddle of blood in one of the Palace Beaumont guestrooms. The first rays of the morning sun were entering through a window and Pierre had been sitting like this since the disastrous accident the previous night.

Pierre had planned to use Raphael to unlock the ownership, and then reprogram the monocle to a new user. This was the reason he had tested the Zetan Monocle on Raphael instead of his preferred successor, Delphine. Pierre had brushed off his concerns and he had felt convinced that he could disable the safeguards while also not killing Raphael. Not until the last seconds had he realised the terrifying truth. To disable the monocles safeguard, he needed permission from all other monocle users. With Martin Orchard dead in a cryogenic tank, this had failed miserably, and he had failed to transfer the monocle's ownership from the deceased Ben Yehuda.

Pierre knew what he needed to do. In order to give Ben Yehuda's monocle to Delphine and make her his true heir, he needed to revive Martin Orchard and make him agree to the transfer. This was the only way to achieve his goals.

Pierre's trusted assassin and occasional gay lover, Vladimir Kravchenko, entered the room. He walked up to Pierre and spoke:

- I have turned off our security cameras and sent our employees home. Let's get Raphael's body to the cryogenic tanks.

Pierre shook his head and replied:

- Take Raphael's body to the furnace. I don't want to revive him.

Vladimir gave Pierre a quick look and replied:

- Why? After complaining all night about how you lost your son, I thought we would drag ourselves across the world to find a Zeto Crystal and revive him.

Pierre:

- I will send you on a quest to find a Zeto Crystal, but we are reviving someone else. We are reviving Martin Orchard.

Vladimir:

- Why are you sacrificing your son's life to save that traitor? What is going on in that genius brain of yours? Tsk, tsk, tsk.

Pierre:

- I have to revive Martin Orchard to deactivate the monocle defences that stop me from giving Ben's monocle to Delphine, my true heir.

- Besides, I am doing Raphael a favour. The peace of eternal death is preferable to the terrible toll of survival in this cruel world.

Vladimir:

- Yet, you brought me back from the dead in 2029?

Pierre smirked:

- You are a murderous monster, Vladimir. You deserve to suffer after your countless crimes against humanity, so I'm letting you live longer.

Vladimir burst into laughter and replied:

- Ha-ha, thanks Pierre. Now get your needed sleep. I will cover up Raphael's death on your behalf. When you wake up, it will be like he never even existed!

Pierre nodded, left the room, and returned to his bedroom. Before he fell asleep, he thought. *I wish it was that easy. I wish I could convince myself that Raphael never existed. He was truly the worst part in me.'*

DELPHINE BEAUMONT STARED into her bedroom mirror. She wished to see the purple-eyed monster she had sighted the other night. She needed more guidance from this strange creature. The creature had told her to do the thing she desired more than anything in life. It had told her to fuck her twin brother, and kill the rest of her father's progeny so she could rule House Beaumont together with Lucien. But it was all too convenient to have this vision now, and she could not be sure that it wasn't a mental illness that gave her hallucinations. If she went through with her advances, the most likely scenario was that Lucien would reject her sexual advances. Even if he embraced her advances, it would still be difficult and dangerous to kill the guards and the rest of her siblings at this facility.

'It doesn't matter. I rather die than live like this!' Delphine thought and she prepared herself for her plan. The door to her room was locked, but she had petitioned Constance Monet to leave her window unlocked, stating her need for fresh mountain air to stay healthy. *'They must not consider me suicidal, or they don't care if I die.'* Delphine thought as she opened the windows and stared into the dark abyss.

The Beaumont Family heritage centre was built on top of a mountain and Delphine's room faced a scenery to the valley below. If she lost her balance while sneaking from outside her windows to Lucien's room, she would plunge to her death.

Delphine shivered from the icy mountain wind that chilled her to the bone, as she was scantily clad in a thin nightgown. *'I don't want to die.'* She whimpered.

Delphine pushed aside her fears. Her entire life had come to this, and her father had told her to pursue what she desired. This was it. Delphine climbed out of the window and stood on the narrow path that led to her only source of happiness. On her right-hand side, there was death, but on her left-hand-side, 50 metres ahead of her, was her salvation in the form of Lucien's chiselled body.

'Focus on your desires,' Delphine thought as she pushed through her fear of death and soldiered on. In no time, she stood outside Lucien's room. Delphine looked through the window. Her twin brother was watching sensual videos, and was masturbating. *'Rangda was right, this was the right time to make a move.'*

Delphine knocked on the window and her brother stared at her in shock, awkwardly covering his erect penis. He opened the window and exclaimed:

- What are you doing here, Delphine?!

Delphine smiled sweetly and replied:

- Are you going to let me in, dear brother, or would you rather let me fall to my death?

Hearing this, Lucien hurried to pulled Delphine over the window ledge.

Once inside Lucien's room, Delphine didn't waste any time. She dropped her nightgown to the floor, pushed Lucien to his bed, got on top of him, and rode him furiously until they came.

PIERRE BEAUMONT WOKE up as his secretary Jean Valmont called him on the intercom. "Bloody woman, can't she book an appointment before calling me like everyone else?" Pierre muttered and looked at the wall clock in the corner of the room. It was midday, and he had slept for over sixteen hours.

Pierre recalled blurry images from the day before. Mourning the loss of his son, Pierre had agreed to the drugs Vladimir provided and submitted to his carnal desires. The night had been rough, very rough, but it had been necessary to embrace the pain to get closure and move on. Pierre limped to the full-size mirror and studied his shrivelled old body. There were wounds and bruises all over his wrinkly torso, courtesy of Vladimir's sadistic whip and sadomasochism from the night before. "Fucking hell. That was truly a great night. Vladimir's malicious whip will be the death of me." Pierre muttered to himself while licking his lips quietly.

"Mon Dieu. Monsieur Beaumont, what happened to you?"

Pierre turned around, gave his assistant Jean Valmont a stern look, and exclaimed:

- Why are you sneaking into my room, Jean?

Jean:

- I needed to check in on you, Master. You are not answering the intercom. I have been calling for 30 minutes non-stop.

Pierre:

- Next time, don't come in without my approval.
- But since you are here, why do you need to speak to me?

Jean:

- Constance Monet is here and she refuses to leave.

Pierre:

- Bah! Bloody woman. Tell her I'll meet with her soon.

Jean:

- Understood.

- Umm. Mr Beaumont. May I humbly ask, what happened to your body?

Pierre:

- That's none of your business! But if you have to know, book an appointment with Vladimir. I am sure he'll be happy to show you.

Hearing this, Jean nodded and rushed off. "Bloody woman," Pierre muttered. Of all the pains he had to deal with, his secretary was his biggest headache. Pierre shook his head, got dressed, and headed to the lounge room to deal with the next headache of the day, Constance Monet.

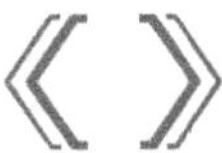

PIERRE FELT REFRESHED after doing a few lines of cocaine, before meeting with Constance. While drugs weren't the answer to his problems, they at least alleviated his migraine. As Pierre entered the lounge room, Constance Monet approached him and yelped:

- Master Pierre Beaumont! There has been a terrible development at the school!

Pierre gave Constance Monet a cold gaze and replied:

- Grummph. What's so terrible you can't book an appointment like my other employees?

Constance Monet handed Pierre a phone with the CCTV footage from Lucien's room, showcasing the incestual scene from the night before. Pierre looked at the video and struggled to hide his evil smile. Delphine had proven herself to be exactly what he wanted in his heir. She was a highly motivated risk-taker with her eyes fixated on the goal, willing to take any steps necessary to achieve it. This was her way of preserving the Beaumont bloodline, yet still satisfying her sexual needs. Pierre closed the video and turned to Constance:

- It runs in the family, Constance. I do not see this as a problem.

Constance:

- What do you mean?

Pierre:

- Never mind.
- Does anyone else know about this video?

Constance:

- No. I am the only one who has access to the videos from the student bedrooms.

Pierre:

- How convenient, I am sure you have a perfectly reasonable explanation for collecting secret videos from my children's bedrooms!

- In any case, if you don't like the copulation to take place, you should lock the windows to prevent further incidents.

Constance:

- But, Monsieur Beaumont. We need to deal with the issue straight away.

Pierre:

- Oh. Is that so? Alright, I'll just pop into my time machine, travel back to last night, and put a lock on Delphine's window.

- Oh, I don't have a time machine you say? Very well, then we'll have to live with what happened.

- Dismissed, Constance.

Having said this, Pierre turned around and left the room, ignoring Constance Monet's pleas for him to listen to her.

PIERRE WAS DRINKING red wine in a luxurious giraffe-leather armchair in front of the fireplace at the reading room of Palace Beaumont. He felt sleepy and exhausted. There were so many things that had happened in the last few days, and the drugs didn't make things better. Vladimir entered the room and spoke:

- I am afraid you'll need to find a new supervisor for your heritage centre.

Pierre:

- I wouldn't worry about that. Constance Monet is loyal and suitable for running the centre.

Vladimir:

- Constance Monet is dead. She died half an hour ago in a traffic accident. The AI in her self-driving car drove her off a cliff.

Pierre:

- What did you do, Vladimir? Did you kill her?

Vladimir:

- She was a threat to us, Pierre. She could have exposed what was going on at that place.

Pierre got up, slapped Vladimir, and spoke:

- You cannot kill my employees without my permission, Vladimir. I am their master; their lives are mine to decide.

Having reprimanded Vladimir, Pierre's perception of time froze. This could be it. Would he finally die by the hand of his lover, the Siberian gay sadist Vladimir Kravchenko? For what felt like an eternity, Vladimir stood silent and stared at Pierre. Eventually, he turned around and walked towards the door. "I'll be back to give you more punishments for your erratic behaviour." Vladimir stated as he left Palace Beaumont.

Chapter 67: Death and destruction at the Beaumont Heritage Centre. 6th November 2039.

Pierre Beaumont was enjoying the sunshine and the icy mountain winds at his terrace, wearing a bright-coloured skiing outfit. While his physique didn't allow him to do mountain skiing anymore, he still loved the refreshing feeling from inhaling the freezing air, and looking as fashionable as ever. Pierre looked at a photograph of his long-dead older sister Anna Beaumont. Anna had been beautiful, but at the time of her death, Pierre had been prepubescent, and he hadn't realised it. Once he reached puberty, he had become obsessed with Anna, and he couldn't make himself love another woman. Thus, instead of love, he had pursued wealth and the raw physical attraction he felt towards men.

Pierre picked up another photograph, the photo of his cousin, Luisa Beaumont, the unwilling biological mother of all his children. When Pierre had decided to run his breeding program, Anna had been dead and buried for over 40 years, and his younger cousin Luisa had been the closest Pierre could get to preserving the Beaumont heritage and bloodline. Luisa had not been interested in helping Pierre with his twisted scheme, but Vladimir had been. Together with Vladimir, they had kidnapped Luisa and kept her captive for six months while injecting her with drugs to make her constantly ovulate. Once they had made Luisa provide enough of her eggs, they had killed her to get rid of the evidence. They had used her eggs to then start a surrogacy foundation breeding program, using all of her collected eggs and Pierre's sperm to produce 24 children, forcing slaves to become the surrogate mothers.

Pierre sniffed arrogantly, thinking of Luisa's fate. Things had been so much better for her if she had agreed to help him. The Habsburg Family had been marrying cousins for centuries, while they had ruled Europe until the 18th century. Why was it immoral for House Beaumont to be the 21st-century equivalent?

Pierre wiped his nose; this was his ultimate goal. The Beaumonts were destined to rule the world. Yet, to reach that goal, he would need to find a replicated Zeto Crystal, revive Martin Orchard, and convince him to unlock the late Ben Yehuda's Zetan Monocle so Delphine could wear it.

Pierre picked up his phone and called Vladimir. There was no response and Pierre felt how his chest got tighter. He felt terrified that Vladimir would abandon him because of their trivial fight. If Vladimir abandoned Pierre, how could he ever achieve his goal of world dominance?

As Pierre watched the sun setting behind the mountains, he decided to go inside, have a nap, and clear his mind of his troubles.

"WAKE UP, DELPHINE. Your time has come."

Delphine Beaumont woke up with a twitch, as a harrowing voice was echoing in the back of her head. "What time is it?" Delphine asked the room's AI, but there was no response. How peculiar. Delphine heard how the door to her room unlocked, and she had a flashback from her passionate encounter with Lucien just a few nights earlier. As she came, her mind had elevated and she had spotted a tiny hidden camera in the room. When she came back to her senses from the exhilarating experience, she had been unable to find the camera. Yet she knew that Constance had been spying on her.

Delphine looked at the door. No-one was entering but she was certain she had heard the door unlock. Was Constance testing her?

Thinking of Constance, Delphine reflected that she hadn't seen her tormentor for two days. It was unusual for Constance to have days off, as her aging tormentor had nothing else to live for.

"Go Delphine. Your time has come." A voice echoed again. "Who are you?" Delphine asked, but there was only silence.

Delphine realised that it was past midnight and it was a Monday. She remembered the terrifying creature that appeared in the mirror, Empress Rangda Kaliankan, who had told her to seduce her brother and kill all of her siblings and her father. The very same creature had told her that tonight was the night she would kill her father and her siblings to become the true heir to the Beaumont family.

Delphine got to her wardrobe and got dressed in sturdy clothes, suitable for combat. Tonight, she wouldn't be a princess, tonight she would be a warrior, ready to take what was hers. She opened the door and snuck into the empty corridor, ready to convince her brother to join her.

LUCIEN STARED AT DELPHINE in shock as she put her hand over his mouth and spoke:

- Shh! Don't be afraid, Lucien. Tonight is the night we fulfil our destiny.

Lucien nodded, and Delphine removed her hand so Lucien could reply:

- Have you come to seduce me again, Delphine?

Delphine shook her head and replied:

- No. As much as I yearn for your body, tonight is about something much more important. We need to kill our siblings and our father. It is time for us to rule House Beaumont and the world. As brother and sister. As husband and wife.

Lucien:

- Is there no other way? I also hate our father, but our siblings are innocent.

Delphine:

- This is the only way. Once our father is dead, there will be a fight about his inheritance. The only way to avoid it is if we are the only ones remaining. If we don't kill the others, one of them will kill us. She has shown it to me.

Lucien:

- Who is she?

Delphine:

- Empress Rangda Kaliankan of the Xenos.

As Delphine mentioned Rangda's name, her eyes were flashing purple. Lucien flinched and stuttered:

- D...D..D..D... Delphine! what's happening to your eyes?!

Delphine:

- She is showing us the path to glory. Either you follow me on my path to magnificence, or you'll die here with the others.

Lucien:

- Very well. Lead the way, sister.

Delphine nodded, kissed Lucien, and hurried towards the guardhouse for the first step of her plan.

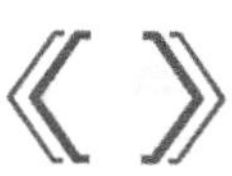

RODOLPHE BERGER WAS struggling to stay awake in the security office of the Beaumont Heritage Centre. The last few days had been stressful, since the head supervisor of the facility, superintendent Constance Monet, had died in a mysterious traffic accident. Rodolphe Berger felt uneasy and he wanted to quit his job. Yet, he knew the risks of quitting on Pierre and his terrifying associate, Vladimir Kravchenko. This conundrum had kept him awake for several days after Constance's death. During the night, Rodolphe couldn't stay awake any longer and he dozed off.

Rodolphe woke up as he was gasping for air. Not until it was too late, did he realise that he was under attack, as Delphine suffocated him from behind with one of Lucien's neck ties.

AFTER ELIMINATING THE security guard, Delphine grabbed his gun and rushed ahead to the boiler room of the Beaumont Heritage Centre. She ran fast and silent like a tiger, and Lucien struggled to keep up with her. Delphine used Rodolphe's security pass to enter the room, and she tampered with the boiler to cause a delayed explosion. After that, she rushed towards the corridor where her siblings lived. As the fire alarm went off, the doors unlocked and Delphine shot everyone who left their rooms with lethal precision. When the fire became too intense, she exclaimed:

- Let's leave, Lucien. Let our siblings choke and burn.

Shocked and fazed from seeing Delphine murder her siblings, Lucien didn't object and he followed her in a trance-like state, amazed at her sudden prowess and strength.

Delphine and Lucien reached the courtyard. Delphine stole the deceased Rodolphe's car, and she programmed it to travel to Palace Beaumont, to settle the score with Pierre. After that, she jumped on her brother and seduced him while the car was on auto-drive mode.

Chapter 68: The Beaumont Family Showdown, 7th November 2039.

Pierre Beaumont woke up as his monocle was beeping loudly to warn him of danger. He inserted it into his right eye, and it showed him a video feed from Rodolphe's car. Delphine and Lucien were copulating, and they would arrive at Palace Beaumont in fifteen minutes. Pierre turned off the video. As much as he wanted to watch them going at it, the fact they were heading towards him in a stolen car could only mean one thing, something disastrous had happened at the Beaumont Heritage Centre.

Pierre tried connecting to the security cameras at the facility centre, but the AI had malfunctioned and wouldn't let him access them. Instead, Pierre connected to a nearby traffic camera, and he deduced that the heritage centre was on fire. Pierre realised what this meant, Delphine was making a move towards seizing power, and she had gotten rid of her rivals to his inheritance.

Pierre screamed out a shocked cry. If he was correct, 22 out of his 24 children were dead. While it was one of the scenarios he had thought of in the past, he had hoped for a more cordial fate among his children.

Pierre called Sergei, one of his bodyguards, and spoke:

- I have visitors coming. Stay out of their way and let them into the palace.

Sergei:

- What about you, Mr Beaumont. Should we lead you to safety?

Pierre:

- No, I will be waiting in the reading room. This is a Beaumont Family matter that I need to deal with myself.

Pierre watched the CCTV videos as his guards hurried to take cover. It had come to this. If he could convince Delphine to join him, they could rule the world together, if not, he would punish her for killing his other progeny.

Pierre made his way to the reading room and poured himself a glass of Cognac. He got seated in a couch and he told the AI to set the music to Hector Berlioz - Dream of a Witches' Sabbath.

PIERRE SMILED CROOKEDLY as he saw his children Delphine and Lucien approach him in the reading room. Delphine was aiming a pistol at him. He turned off the music and spoke:

- Welcome, my children. Apologies for the lack of hospitality options. It's a work health and safety issue.

Delphine:

- What are you talking about, Father? Where are the rest of the people in the palace?

Pierre:

- I can't risk the wellbeing of my employees when my murderous children are visiting.

Delphine:

- So, you know why we are here?

Pierre:

- Of course. While I predicted this outcome in one of my scenarios, I am still disappointed. You could have achieved more if you cooperated with your siblings, instead of killing them, Delphine.

- Yet, killing me won't achieve anything. I have given Raphael access to my hidden bank accounts and he will inherit my estate. You two, on the other hand, will go to prison for murder of the Beaumont offspring. Unless Raphael sends Vladimir, to put you out of your misery, you will be in prison for life.

Lucien:

- Shut up! I don't believe you at all!

Pierre:

- Yet you know that I am telling the truth, Lucien. You shouldn't have followed your sister. However, I understand you. I felt the same way for my sister when I was young. Unfortunately, she died before I reached puberty, so I could never act on my desire.

Lucien:

- Fuck off. You don't know what you are talking about.

Pierre:

- But I do.

Having said this, Pierre snapped his fingers and a hologram video of Lucien and Delphine engaging in coitus appeared in the room. Pierre studied his progeny. The monocle determined Lucien to be a high threat, while Delphine was ambivalent. This suited Pierre. He needed Delphine to be his heir, while the loss of Lucien's life, was in the grand scheme of things, irrelevant.

Pierre:

- The affection you feel for your sister is perfectly natural, Lucien. The Egyptian pharaohs procreated with their siblings and they created the pyramids. The Hapsburgs married their cousins, and they ruled Europe for centuries. The Beaumonts can do it and rule the world.

Delphine interjected:

- We didn't come to seek your approval. We came to take your place. Where is Raphael?

Pierre:

- Do you think ignorance took me to my position?
- I'd be a fool if I told you.

Lucien:

- I don't care. All I see is a defenceless frail old man who is losing his edge!

Pierre:

- Oh, but is that so?

- I let the two of you in, and my bodyguards will kill you if any harm comes to me.

Pierre turned to Delphine:

- I will let you in on the family business and I'll give you the technology that made me the wealthiest man in the world. However, you need to be punished. Kill Lucien. The two of you need to suffer for what you did to my other children.

Pierre took out Ben Yehuda's monocle from his pocket and spoke again:

- This monocle contains an advanced alien AI. If you wear it, you can rule the world, Delphine. Kill your brother.

Delphine:

- Or we can take it off your dead body.

Delphine turned to Lucien and spoke:

- Lucien, seize the monocles from our father.

Lucien walked up to Pierre and try to pull the monocle off Pierre's face. Lucien shouted in pain and stumbled backwards as the monocle electrocuted him. Pierre laughed menacingly and continued:

- Tsk, Tsk. The monocle cannot be taken, it can only be given.

Hearing this, Delphine fired the pistol and hit the couch Pierre was sitting in, just below his crotch. Delphine shouted:

- Then give us the bloody monocle or we'll make your death excruciating.

Pierre sighed and realised that as much as he wanted the Beaumonts to rule the world, he was even keener on securing his own survival. He nodded, tapped on the top of his monocle to remove it, and he threw it to Delphine.
Delphine laughed and replied:

- That's it. Give us your real monocle instead of the booby-trapped one! Now let's find out what this one does.

Having said this, Delphine put on the monocle and as is it connected with her mind, she felt amazing. She felt so much sharper and so alert, she felt higher than a normal human, she felt like a goddess.
Meanwhile, Pierre was counting the seconds. When the anti-theft property of the monocle activated, he threw himself to the ground and

pulled out the pistol that he had strapped to the bottom of the couch. Lucien saw what was about to happen, and ran towards Pierre. A shot went off, and Pierre passed out as the force from Lucien's kick smashed him in the face.

"MR BEAUMONT, WHAT HAPPENED here?"

Pierre woke up with blood stinging in his eyes, nostrils, and mouth. He looked at his bodyguards Sergei and Vitali and replied:

- I had a problem with my children. Are any of them alive?

Sergei shook his head and replied:

- The boy, you shot him through the heart. The girl... It looks like the monocle drilled through her brain.

Hearing this, Pierre crawled over to Delphine's corpse, deactivated her monocle and inserted it into his eye. He took a deep breath of relief when the alien AI reconnected with his mind. The monocle was operational and he could still salvage this situation. Pierre turned to Sergei and spoke:

- Take the bodies of my children to the cryogenic tanks in my research lab.

Sergei nodded and replied:

- And what about you, sir?

Pierre:

- I will contact my medical experts. Any news about Vladimir Kravchenko?

Sergei:

- No. We haven't heard from our master in a few days. Should we keep looking?

Pierre:

- Yes. I need to speak to him. Now more than ever.

Sergei:

- Understood, Pierre. We will carry out your mission.

Pierre left the room without a word. His broken nose pained him, but not as much as the loss of his progeny. He hoped Vladimir would get back to him, because without Vladimir, there was no way for him to sort out this mess, and he might as well end everything.

Chapter 69: The Beaumont's must rise again. 12th November 2039

"I don't know anything about the tragedy at my boarding school for gifted children."

Pierre Beaumont felt stressed as he sat in a police interrogation room in Geneva. While the police were powerless to prosecute him due to his power over the Swiss government, the police investigation still impeded his plans. Instead of being cryogenically frozen in his research lab, the majority of his progeny were in the mortuary and would most likely receive a funeral.

Crime Inspector Cherise Villeneuve turned to Pierre and spoke:

- So, tell me Monsieur Beaumont. How come all of these children bear your family name.

Pierre:

- Because I adopted them all. Legally, they are all my children.

Cherise:

- Hmmm. They were all born the same year, 2023, and you adopted all of them at birth according to the legal papers. But do tell me Monsieur Beaumont, how did you know they were gifted if you adopted them at birth?

Pierre:

- I did not per se. However, the development potential in children increases through the power of positive affirmation. Thus, by calling the children gifted, I wanted to fill them with pride in their abilities.

Cherise:

- I see.
- What can you tell me about the mothers of these children?

Pierre:

- I assume they had their reasons for not wanting to raise their children. I didn't question their motives for putting their children up for adoption.

Cherise:

- Why did you decide to adopt 24 children?

Pierre:

- I wanted to give more children the chance of good schooling. The Beaumont Foundation is donating money to charitable projects all over the world, but I wanted to follow this group more closely. In any case, I don't see how this have any relevance to the investigation?

Cherise:

- It is very relevant to our investigation. Our forensic investigation concluded that all the children at the facility were siblings. Furthermore, their genetic markers were closer than average siblings, as if they were products of incest.

Hearing this, Pierre felt how panic was engulfing him. He had got away with many of his crimes against humanity, but would his top-secret breeding program be the end of him? He wanted to lawyer up and refuse to answer more questions, but he also wanted to talk his way out of trouble, like he had done many times in the past.

Pierre:

- That is impossible, I urge you to get an independent genetics lab to redo the genetic sampling.

Cherise:

- Yes, we have that on our agenda.

Pierre:

- I see. I would suggest you don't publicise your findings until you have performed an independent audit. I would rather avoid fruitless conspiracy theories risking the good work of the Beaumont Foundation and the World Bank.

Cherise:

- Of course. The Swiss government has classified the investigation for now.

Pierre:

- Good. Now if you excuse me, I need to leave. I must deal with the aftermath of this tragedy.

Cherise looked at Pierre and an awkward silence occurred. Eventually, Crime Inspector Cherise conceded and spoke:

- Okay, Pierre. We will be in touch in regards to this critical investigation. Au revoir.

Pierre didn't reply, grabbed his suitcase, and hurried to leave the police station.

"LE PDG DE LA BANQUE Mondiale emmené au commissariat de police après les morts mystérieuses au Centre du Patrimoine de Beaumont." ("The CEO of the World Bank, Pierre Beaumont, taken to the police station after the mysterious deaths of numerous children at the Beaumont Heritage Centre")

Pierre put down the tablet after reading an article including a photograph of himself at the Geneva police station. Pierre hated the independent press and that he could not completely control the flow of information, despite having power of the news and social media. Crime Inspector Cherise Villeneuve was a nuisance, and he should have crushed her by now, but instead, he felt weary and low. A few weeks earlier, he had anticipated a great future for House Beaumont, and yet here he was, an aging man, being the sole survivor of his great house.

Pierre walked out on his terrace and he overlooked the beautiful valley below. Normally, it would give him solace, but as he watched the steep fall on the other side of the ledge, he wanted to end it all. This was it. This was how the greatest man who had ever walked upon the planet would end his days, hated and alone after murdering his children in self-defence.

Pierre looked at the valley below. Should he write a suicide letter, exposing the crimes of the Monocle Conspiracy? He decided against it. Humans were sheep and they deserved to suffer for their weakness and stupidity. Allowing his co-conspirators to carry on with their schemes was the least he could do against the rotten masses that existed to serve him.

"Adieu la vie cruelle. Puissions-nous nous revoir, Delphine, mon amour." (Goodbye cruel life. May we meet again, Delphine, my love.) Pierre mumbled as he climbed over the edge and fell towards the valley below. 20 seconds of freefalling and it would be over.

After freefalling for several seconds, Pierre twitched as someone grabbed him mid-air and he felt the sudden deceleration from an opening parachute.

"You cannot kill yourself; you are mine to kill!" Vladimir yelled.

The duo landed relatively unscathed, although Pierre strained his ankle upon landing.

Pierre whined:

- Oh, mon Dieu. My ankle. That hurts a lot.

Vladimir taunted:

- Did it hurt more than breaking every bone in your body while bleeding out on the ground?

Pierre:

- I wouldn't know.
- What happened? Where did you come from?

Vladimir:

- I have been watching you since our fight, Pierre.

Pierre:

- How did you evade my guards and my building security?

Vladimir:

- I stole a personal cloaking device from the Harapan Conglomerate a while back. It's developed from Zetan technology.

Pierre:

- Bloody hell. Why didn't you tell me?

Vladimir:

- Because it was more fun not telling you.

- Anyways, you cannot die yet. The Beaumont's must rise again. I can't wait to see the mayhem Lucien and Delphine will unleash onto this world.

Pierre:

- But they are dead, and besides, the police are on to me.

Vladimir:

- The primordial Zeto Crystal can bring them back. I have already dealt with Cherise Villeneuve.

Pierre:

- Bah. I doubt killing Cherise will help me with my current predicament.

Vladimir:

- That's why I didn't kill her. Instead, I forged evidence that Cherise was a member of a conspiracy group that obsessed about you. To add some spice to her profile, I also faked evidence that she was involved with the Geneva Hei Bai virus outbreak that occurred last year.

Pierre:

- Oh, Vladimir. I don't know how to thank you. I am sorry about our silly fight after you murdered Constance Monet.

Vladimir:

- Apology accepted. Let's get back to Palace Beaumont and rest.

After saying this, Vladimir carried Pierre to a nearby road, and from there, they ordered a self-driving cab that took them back to Palace Beaumont, where they pursued a crazy night of romping and sadistic sex rituals.

Chapter 70: We must revive Martin Orchard and reclaim the primordial Zeto Crystal from Sabina Hines, 12th December 2039.

Pierre Beaumont was enjoying a glass of cognac in his top-secret research lab. The last month had been a monumental success due to Vladimir's faithful help, and Pierre questioned why he had ever fought with his long-time lover and partner in crime.

Cherise Villeneuve had been taken off the investigation on the mysterious deaths at the Beaumont Heritage Centre. Instead, the Swiss Government had appointed a politruk to oversee the investigation. As expected, he hadn't found anything that implicated Pierre. Instead, the blame for the murders had befallen an Islamic terrorist group that was an enemy of the World Bank.

Pierre had covered up that the children were his biological children conceived through incest, by having his associate Josefina Fiero purchase the laboratory and falsify the results. Remaining a free man, Pierre had got access to his dead children's bodies and he had staged a funeral. Their charred bodies remained in cryogenic preservation, waiting for Pierre to get hold of the primordial Zeto Crystal so he could revive them.

Vladimir Kravchenko entered the facility and approached Pierre. Vladimir:

- It seems that everything is under control. We should do our part to revive Delphine.

Pierre:

- Yes.

- Did you know that it was Martin Orchard's daughter, Sabina Hines, who convinced Martin to kill Ben Yehuda and help her steal the primordial Zeto Crystal in the Solomon temple?

Vladimir:

- Yes, but what does it matter to us? All we need to do is figure out where Sabina is hiding the crystal, and take it from her.

Pierre:

- No.

- I believe Ben Yehuda was on to something. The day before he died, he claimed that Sabina was a touch empath.

Vladimir:

- A touch empath? What the hell is that?

Pierre:

- According to legend, a person able to influence others through the power of touch.

Vladimir:

- Why do I care?

Pierre:

- Because we are dealing with a very powerful entity. When she was 18, Sabina travelled to Jerusalem by herself, met up with Martin, opened the ancient gate of the Templar Tunnels, and stole the Zeto Crystal in front of our eyes. Now at the age of 20, she is incredibly rich and influential. It would be unwise to put ourself on a confrontation course with Sabina.

Vladimir:

- So, what do you suggest?

Pierre:

- We should revive Martin Orchard and implant him with a remote-controlled nerve-pain-amplifier. That will make him our slave. We can use Martin's paternal relationship to Sabina to find out where she is hiding the primordial Zeto Crystal without confronting her ourselves.

Vladimir:

- Very well. So, where do we get the next replicated Zeto Crystal?

Pierre:

- The next Zetan temple that will be open is the Shankaracharya temple in Kashmir. It will be possible to open from midnight to dawn on the 4th January 2040.

Vladimir:

- Very well. This should be an interesting trip.

Pierre:

- Yes. I am coming with you.

Vladimir:

- Really? You have not been to a Zetan Temple since the incident in Colombia in the year 2026.

Pierre:

- Incorrect. I did go to the Templar Tunnels in 2029. In any case, this is about the future of House Beaumont. I cannot leave it to others.

Vladimir:

- Very well.
- I'll make the arrangements and I'll find a suitable crew.

Pierre:

- I am glad to have you, Vladimir.

After saying this, Pierre walked up to Vladimir and kissed him with a passion he hadn't experienced in decades.

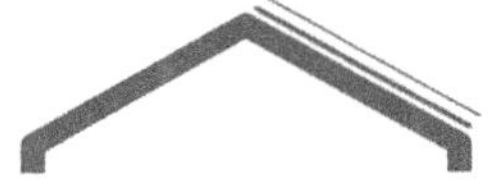

Chapter 71: Jared Pond, no longer a sex god. 24th December 2039

Jared Pond was sitting at a poker table at Crown Casino in Sydney. While his nick for poker was there, so much else had changed. He had lost his penchant for danger, booze, beautiful women, and he spent most of his days thinking about what could have been. He regretted that he broke up with the beautiful Eileen Lu, his one true love, back in 2023.

Jared Pond had never liked the spotlight he received from being the first gentleman to Eileen, who became the interim president of China after the collapse of the Columnist Party in 2021. At the time, he had convinced himself that he disliked the new policies that Eileen proposed. However, the whole debacle was about something else. Jared couldn't handle living in the shadow of his much more successful partner.

After the break-up, Jared's career as a field agent for the Royal Australian Kangaroo Intelligence (RAKI) was over. He had gained too much fame during his years as the first gentleman in China to be able to do reconnaissance in the field. Instead, he had focused on his poker playing and drinking, while occasionally doing some consultation work with RAKI. No longer doing fieldwork, Jared had turned rather plump, and this is in combination with the merciless effect of aging, had turned him into anything but a sex god.

Jared found himself stalking Eileen's social media account from his phone, and he realised that enough was enough. He needed to flirt with some fresh exotic women to get over his memory-induced melancholy.

Jared collected his poker winnings and he transferred them to his bank account. After that, he walked to a table where a few good sorts were drinking and gossiping.

Jared:

- The name is Pond, Jared Pond.

Bimbo:

- Who asked you, grandpa?

As the Bimbo turned to her friends and laughed, Jared decided to move on. He wasn't here to teach young women about proper manners. In any case, that would be a ridiculous proposition, since he had tried picking up a woman 30 years his junior. Jared walked to the bar and ordered a double scotch. An Eastern European woman approached him and spoke:

- Well played at the poker table, Mr Pond. I'll be yours for the night for 20 pineapples.

In his intoxicated state, Jared missed out on the $2000 price tag. Instead, he only heard the part about how his great poker playing made him irresistible to the semi-attractive lady. Jared smiled and replied:

- I love your enthusiasm, Ms....?

Woman:

- Svetlana Antonov, but you can call me Foxy.

Jared:

- Very well, Foxy. I accept your offer to spend the night. Please accompany me to room 7007. We'll keep the champagne cool and everything else hot.

After saying this, Foxy accompanied Jared to his room and they spent the night experiencing Jared's talent for lovemaking.

THE NEXT MORNING, JARED woke up full of confidence. How silly of him to spend time self-pitying and stalking his ex on social media, when he could pick up Russian bombshells half his age.

Jared tapped Foxy's shoulder and smiled as she opened her eyes. Jared spoke:

- Good morning, beautiful. Are you ready for another round of the Pond-train?

Foxy mumbled and replied:

- Sure, if you give me another five pineapples.

After that, she closed her eyes and fell back into slumber.

Foxy's response confused Jared. Why on Earth did she ask for pineapples? Could the woman be a prostitute?

Jared concluded that he was a sex god who wouldn't need to pay a woman of the night to get laid. Thus, Foxy's request for pineapples had to be for actual pineapples, five pineapples to be precise. He picked up the phone and called room service:

- Hello. I would like to order five pineapples to room 7007.

Waiter:

- Would you like them cut or whole?

Jared hadn't anticipated this question, as no one had ever asked him for pineapples after coitus before, so he replied:

- Cut half of them and bring the rest whole.

Waiter:

- Of course, Mr Pond.

A few minutes later, a waiter knocked on the door and delivered the pineapples.

As the waiter left, Jared smiled and he took a slice of pineapples to Foxy and tapped her on the shoulder. It was time for the Pond-train to have a morning departure. As Foxy woke up, she stared at him in awe and exclaimed:

- Why are you trying to feed me a pineapple, you crazy Australian? I am allergic to pineapples, are you trying to kill me?

Jared:

- How would I know? I hardly know your name. In any case, you asked me for pineapples 15 minutes ago.

Foxy:

- Pineapples, as in $100 bills you moron. I want 20 of them for last night.

Jared:

- What? I am not going to pay you! The sex was a privilege for you.

Foxy:

- You are an idiot!

Having said this, Foxy grabbed her stuff and stormed out of Jared's room.

JARED WAS REFLECTING over last night's events when there was a knock on the door. Foxy had returned, accompanied by two Russian goons. One of them spoke:

- Hey Mr Pond. Pay Roxy what you owe her, or else...

Jared realised that this was exactly the excitement he needed in life. First having sex with a beautiful woman and then knocking out the goons sent to kill him. Jared smiled and replied:

- I choose to fight.

Having said this, Jared swung at the closest Russian, but he shouldn't have. Jared was now past 50 years old and far from his prime. 20 seconds later, Jared lay on the floor after receiving a few knocks to the head.
One of the Russians approached him with a printed invoice and spoke:

- So, Mr Pond. Here is your invoice from today's encounter. $20,000. $2000 for the night with Roxy, $2000 for our callout fee, and $16000 to fix Alexis' missing tooth. Pay within seven days or we'll take you to court.

Jared:

- Wait, you came here to fight me and now you're threatening me with a lawsuit? What kind of Russians are you?!

Alexis:

- We are legitimate businessmen in the adult entertainment industry, who came here to deliver an invoice since you refused to pay Roxy as agreed. You were the one who resorted to violence, Mr Pond.

Jared:

- Very well. I'll speak to my accountant and I'll organise the payment of your invoice.

Alexis:

- Thank you. Please call our 24-hour-hotline if you have any questions. The number is on the invoice.

- Do svidaniya, mister Pond.

As the Russians left the room, Jared sighed. How had he, the greatest Australian secret agent to ever walk the earth, turned into a John who got knocked out while fighting debt collectors? Time and aging were indeed merciless beasts.

Chapter 72: Jared Pond receives a mission to investigate Pierre's actions in India. 28th December 2039

The prime minister of Australia, Danielle Anders, were throwing darts at a picture of Pierre Beaumont. She was mad at her former benefactor, who had helped her rigging the Australian elections the previous year. Pierre had refused to pay Danielle her Christmas bonus for 2039, and when she finally got hold of him, he had mocked her with these words:

"Why would I bribe the puppet who I helped rise to power? Setting you up as the prime minister was just a game for me, a game where I tested how much I could troll the public. You are, after all, the gender-corrected version of the most hated politician in Australia's history, Danielle, or should I call you Daniel?"

Danielle knew that Pierre was a terrifying opponent and she needed to dig up dirt on him. The signal-tracking from her phone call with Pierre showed that Pierre was in the contested Kashmir region of India. This was not part of his official itinerary and Danielle knew that he was up to something illegitimate. If she could find evidence against Pierre, she could blackmail him to avoid having her secret revealed.

But who would she send? It would be too obvious if she sent RAKI operatives to Kashmir. If she did, Pierre would know that she had betrayed him and he would use his powers over the media and corporate world to hang her out dry. But what about sending that old fool Jared Pond? He had stopped being a RAKI operative after his relationship with Eileen Lu back in 2021 had made him too famous to make him a viable field agent. Sending Jared would be unexpected, so Pierre couldn't anticipate that she was behind it if Jared got caught.

Danielle picked up the phone and summoned Jared to the Kirribilli House, the Sydney residence for the Australian Prime Minister.

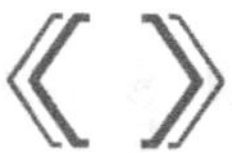

JARED POND WAS FEELING confused and sweaty in his Sydney apartment. It was a muggy day, the air-conditioning of his unit was broken, and he still had a headache from getting knocked out three days earlier. Worst of all were those police officers who had come to his place to interview him. The Russian debt collectors he had fought at Crown Casino had filed charges against him as they had photographic evidence that he started the fight. How had life come to this? How could Australia's greatest agent be charged after losing a fight to a group of shady Russians?

Ring, Ring

Jared Pond stared in disbelief when his phone showed an incoming call from Prime Minister Danielle Anders. Jared yelped and answered the phone:

- Hello, Daniel! How can I be of assistance?

Danielle:

- It's Danielle these days, and I would appreciate it if you got it right.

Jared sighed and replied:

- Oh, yes! Hello, Danielle. What do you want from me?

Danielle:

- I am summoning you to Kirribilli House. Be there in two hours.

Jared:

- There is a slight problem with that request. I have literally no desire to meet you.

Danielle:

- Tsk, tsk, tsk.

- I guess I'll just ask the police to stall the Crown Casino incident investigation. In the meantime, you'll be banned from leaving Sydney and barred from all licensed venues. Yes, that's right. No more poker for you, Jared.

Jared:

- Okay. I will be there in two hours.

Danielle:

- Excellent. I can't wait to meet with one of the legends of our intelligence community. Make sure to freshen up and dress well. You are meeting with the Prime Minister after all.

Jared hung up and went to the bathroom to take a cold shower. This day was on the trajectory to be really rotten.

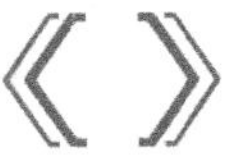

DANIELLE SMIRKED AS Jared entered her office. Seeing her smirk, Jared got reminded of a previous incident. He had played a poker tournament at Mount Druitt RSL and he had woken up next to a woman with a similar smirk. Had that woman also been a man? This thought, combined with alcohol withdrawal and untreated concussion made Jared vomit in his mouth, and he rushed off to the toilet.

As he returned to the Prime Minister's office, Danielle spoke:

- So, is this the fate that has befallen the once-great Jared Pond, a drunk who vomits in the Prime Minister's bathroom?

Jared:

- Cut to the chase, Danielle. I am only here to find out what I need to do to avoid an indefinite and unjustified police investigation.

Danielle handed Jared a photograph of Pierre Beaumont and spoke:

- Pierre Beaumont. My sources tell me that he is in the Kashmir region of India. I want you to find out what he is doing there.

Jared:

- What on earth does this have to do with Australian state affairs?

Danielle:

- It got nothing to do with Australia. It's a personal issue between me and Pierre, which is why I am sending a washed-up former agent instead of sending one of RAKI's top agents.

Jared:

- Why?

Danielle:

- Plausible deniability. Who would believe that I sent a washed-up former agent if things go south?

Jared:

- So, what's in it for me?

Danielle:

- I'll make sure that the police drop the charges against you for the Crown Casino incident.

- I also have crucial information regarding your old flame, Eileen Lu. Her life is in danger, and helping me is the only way for you to save her.

Jared:

- You're bluffing!

Danielle:

- Perhaps, but are you willing to take the risk?

Jared sighed. He hated Danielle Anders for figuring out that Eileen still was his weakness after all these years. But what would he do? He could refuse, but then Danielle would ban him from living any form of life for the foreseeable future. Besides, he did miss the sensation of being on a mission.
Jared:

- So, what would you have me do?

Danielle handed Jared a flight itinerary and spoke:

- The flight to Delhi departs tonight. From there you'll take a local flight to Kashmir. My trace on Pierre's phone call indicated that he is close to the Shankaracharya temple. Go there and find out what is up to. Be wary, your old friend Vladimir Kravchenko will be nearby.

Jared:

- Just the man I wanted to meet!

Danielle:

- He did save you from Jing Xi's captivity and certain death. Now leave my office, Jared. I can't handle the odour that is coming from your mouth.

Having said this, Danielle pressed a button and summoned two body-guards who confiscated Jared's phone and issued him with a new one. After that, they led him out of the office.

Chapter 73: Pierre secures a replicated Zeto Crystal and Vladimir captures Jared Pond.
4th January 2040

Pierre was enjoying the icy mountain winds that struck his face while he was waiting for the secret passageway at the Shankaracharya temple to open. The cold winds reminded him of the winters in Switzerland and it was far superior to the muggy heat which he had endured while meeting with various dignitaries in India. Pierre used his Zetan Monocle to do an infrared sweep of the surroundings. He had paid off the police to make a perimeter and keep away from the temple, but one could never be too careful.

Much to his dismay, Pierre's monocle detected a man in hiding, 500 metres away. The man was also equipped with an infrared camera. Pierre shouted to Vladimir:

- Vladimir. Come here!

Vladimir approached Pierre who spoke:

- Vladimir! A man is spying on us over there. The chief of police has betrayed us.

Vladimir laughed and replied:

- That's nothing to worry about. That's just the washed-up Australian ex-agent, Jared Pond.

Pierre stared at Vladimir and spoke:

- How long have you known about this?

Vladimir:

- He has been following us for days. Probably on the orders from your mistress, Danielle Anders. Let him watch. He'll be dead soon anyway.

Pierre whinged:

- Why haven't you told me, and what have you planned for Jared Pond?

Vladimir shrugged his shoulders and replied:

- I wanted to see how long it would take for you to notice it.
- You are getting very slow.

Pierre:

- Don't you dare to question my abilities. Hmmph!

Vladimir:

- Improve your performance and I won't have to.
- No matter, it's midnight and it's time to get that bloody crystal.

Pierre:

- What about Jared Pond?

Vladimir:

- As I said, I'll deal with it.

Having said this, Vladimir pulled a lever in the temple, and the whole wall lit up with bluish alien symbols. Vladimir's monocle gave him the secret code and he tapped the symbols in the correct order. This opened a secret door. Vladimir ventured through the door with Pierre in tow and they entered the inner sanctum of the temple.

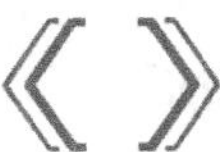

JARED LOOKED IN AMAZEMENT as the wall lit up with alien symbols after Vladimir pulled the lever. How had this happened and why had no-one ever discovered these strange symbols before? Jared tried taking a few photos from afar, but he couldn't get a clear shot. He hesitated for a moment. Did he want to disturb the volatile and dangerous Vladimir Kravchenko who was up to something? A part of him wanted to run away, but then he remembered Danielle Anders' claim that Eileen Lu was in danger. Jared couldn't let his cowardice endanger Eileen.

As Vladimir and Pierre entered the temple, Jared rushed to the wall to get a better look at the symbols. To his disappointment, the wall was no longer glowing. To make matters worse, he felt a heavy thump in the back of his head, before everything turned black.

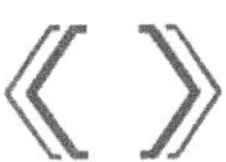

"WELCOME TO THE INNER sanctum of the Shankaracharya Temple, Mr Pond."

As Jared Pond opened his eyes, he noticed a glowing blue gemstone surrounded by the darkness of the rest of the temple. Vladimir Kravchenko smirked towards Jared and spoke:

- How do you like the replicated Zeto Crystal, Mr Pond?

Jared:

- I don't know what you are talking about. What is that, and what are you up to here?

Vladimir:

- The replicated Zeto Crystals are marvellous artefacts that were created by the Zetan species. An advanced alien race that altered our human genome and founded our first civilisations. These crystals can even raise the dead.

Pierre interjected:

- Why are you telling the Australian spy our secrets? Have you lost your mind?

Vladimir:

- Because he can join us. We have a slot to fill after Ben Yehuda's death.

Pierre:

- What makes you think you can invite Jared to our group?

Vladimir:

- Because I am the best fighter in our group and the only one with a pistol in this room.

Pierre was about to argue, but he held his tongue, not daring to stir the ire of the unpredictable Vladimir.

Jared:

- I am sorry, but I'll pass on your invitation, Vladimir. Threesomes with aging men have never been on my agenda.

Having said this, Jared tried to sucker punch Vladimir, who acted lightning fast, dodging Jared's punch and then flooring him with a kick to the knee. As Jared collapsed to the ground, Vladimir taunted.

- This wasn't an invite. It was a demand. However, I am in a good mood, so if you pick up the crystal and hand it to me, I won't kill you.

Jared realised that there was no point in keep getting knocked out from arguing with Russians. He complied with Vladimir's request and took the replicated Zeto Crystal from the plinth and handed it to Vladimir. As this occurred, Vladimir and Pierre looked tense for a few seconds until Vladimir exhaled, and laughed a burst of roaring laughter.

- You did it, Jared. Welcome to the group.

Vladimir's statement confused Jared and he replied:

- I did what exactly?

Vladimir:

- You did something amazing. Let's leave this place so we can celebrate.

Having said this, Vladimir and Pierre left the room and Jared tentatively followed them. He thought about trying to sucker punch Vladimir, but he refrained from doing so, as he wanted to avoid embarrassing himself by copping another beating.

As they left the temple, Vladimir turned around and knocked Jared unconscious. Pierre gave him a sceptical look and spoke:

- Can you explain what you are doing, Vladimir?

Vladimir smirked and replied:

- Normally, the person who picks up the replicated Zeto Crystal gets targeted by the sentry drones and gets killed before I manage to disable the drones. That was Jared's intended role. I don't know what happened in this temple.

Pierre:

- I understand. So, what do you have in mind for Jared?

Vladimir:

- A few of my local talents will keep him contained until I figure out what to do with him.

Pierre:

- I don't like that idea. Jared is a government agent. He might escape and cause trouble.

Vladimir:

- Don't worry about that. Jared is a has-been. He is nothing that Rajesh and Prakash can't handle. Now let's head back to Switzerland so we can bring Martin Orchard back to life. It is time for that bastard to start being useful.

Having said this, Vladimir closed the secret temple-entrance, tied the unconscious Jared to a railing, and called his associates for immediate extraction.

Chapter 74: Jared Pond escapes India. 11th January 2040

Jared Pond was not enjoying himself, as he was chained to the boiler in a dodgy shed, located somewhere in the Kashmiri wilderness. His captors were playing a cruel game on Jared. If the boiler was not on, Jared would freeze to death as the shed would reach the freezing temperatures outside. If the boiler was on, however, Jared would overheat due to being chained to the heating element.

The worst part of his captivity was the confusion that Jared felt. Why had Vladimir ordered his goons to keep Jared as a prisoner? He would understand if Vladimir wanted him dead, but what use was he to the villains alive?

Jared got some clarity to Vladimir's motives when a plump Asian man with a screechy high-pitched voice entered the shed. Jared recognised the man from his pathetic social media stalking sessions of Eileen. The visitor was Peng Yingxing, a Chinese businessman based in Dubai, who was Eileen's current husband. Peng walked up to Jared and spoke:

- Oh, the famous Jared Pond. How I have waited for this moment to happen.

Jared:

- Why? Is this a sexual fantasy of yours?

Peng punched Jared in the face, and Jared didn't flinch as Peng was much weaker than the henchmen that usually punched Jared. Peng gave him a disappointed look and spoke:

- You continue to insult me, Mr Pond, but I will get the last laugh.

Jared:

- I am not following you. Have our paths ever crossed?

Peng:

- You ruined Eileen for me. Whatever I do, I am not good enough at sex for her. This is your fault.

Jared:

- Thanks.

- Yes, bedroom activities have always been my strength. But why did you come all the way here to whine about your sexual inadequacy?

Peng:

- Don't flatter yourself. I came to oversee my opium smuggling business when Rajesh and Prakash revealed that they held you as a captive for Vladimir Kravchenko. I am paying them the double amount to kill you instead of keeping you as a prisoner. Thus, I will finally be able to kill the ghost from Eileen's past that has haunted me.

Jared:

- Viagra. The secret is Viagra.

Peng punched Jared again, this time with enough force to draw blood.

- I will kill you for your insolence, Guay-lo.

Jared:

- Oh well. Best of luck with Vladimir Kravchenko, I suppose.

Hearing this, Peng muttered something and stormed off.

Jared watched Peng as he left, and he sighed to himself. How could life have come to this? He would be murdered on the orders of a pathetic creature who couldn't compete with him for Eileen's favour. On the flipside, if he got out of this mess alive, there was still a chance to rekindle the flame with Eileen.

THE FOLLOWING DAY, the Indian henchmen Rajesh and Prakash entered the shed. They argued in Hindi and Jared heard them mentioning Vladimir several times. Jared presumed that they debated whether it was wise to double-cross the deadliest assassin in history to double their pay. Jared concluded that it wasn't. A much wiser option would be to not double-cross Vladimir and bet whatever he paid on red at the casino. That option entailed a 46 % chance of doubling the money and a 0 % chance of getting brutally murdered. After concluding their argument Prakash aimed his pistol towards Jared and Rajesh spoke:

- Mr Pond. Come with us.

Jared:

- I'd rather not. There is a blizzard outside, and after seven days you dimwits have finally set this shed to a comfortable temperature.

Boom
Jared flinched as Prakash shot next to him and threatened:

- Come now. I don't like asking twice.

Jared:

- I hate to be a letdown, but you do realise that I am handcuffed
to the boiler.

Prakash nodded to Rajesh, who uncuffed Jared. Jared knew that he
needed to time a daring escape, but he hesitated. He had lost his last two
fights, and against gun-toting adversaries, a third loss could be his last.

Not feeling that the moment was right, Jared obliged and walked outside the shed with his captors. They walked into a forest grove and they
reached a secluded spot. Prakash and Rajesh stopped. Rajesh threw a shovel
in front of Jared and spoke:

- There are two types of men in the world. Those with a gun, and
those that are digging.

*'What kind of idiotic assassin expects his victim to dig a grave when the
ground is frozen?'* Jared thought and realised that this was his opportunity.
He pretended to dig but the shovel couldn't break the ground. Rajesh got
closer to him and shouted:

- Dig faster, Australian dog!

'Now!' Jared thought and swung the shovel, hitting Rajesh in the head.
As the Indian henchman went down, Jared exclaimed "FOUR!" referring
to the cricket term for a good hit. A minor issue remained, Prakash was
outside of Jared's range, and he raised his pistol to shoot Jared. 'Please God,
give me a six!' Jared mumbled, closed his eyes, and swung the shovel.

A shot went off, and then Jared opened his eyes. He stared at Prakash
in disbelief. Against all the odds, Jared had swung the shovel in the way of
the bullet from Prakash's pistol. This had caused the bullet to ricochet and
hit Prakash in the eye. Jared wasn't about to wait for another miracle, so he
rushed to Prakash and kicked him in the head.

After that, he picked up the pistol and left the scene.

JARED WAS SITTING ON an Air India flight to Dubai. He felt a sense of excitement. Not only had he survived an assassination attempt, but he had also found out that Eileen's husband was a drug-dealing scumbag who failed to deliver in the bedroom. This was his chance to save the world yet again, as well as rekindling the long-lost flame with the beautiful Eileen. Satisfied with a good day's work, Jared helped himself to a lot of liquor from the inflight service and fell asleep, dreaming blissful dreams.

Chapter 75: A deadly reunion, 13th January 2040.

Eileen Lu was arranging a flower arrangement at her Dubai mansion for the umpteenth time when a maid approached her and spoke:

- Mistress, we ran out of Jellab and Qamardeen drinks. I fear how your husband will react if he doesn't have a good selection of drinks for the Emir's visit.

Hearing this, Eileen was about to scream in frustration. It was not because of the missing drinks, but that her life had come to this. After she was deposed from the Chinese presidency, the Emir of Dubai had granted her political asylum in Dubai. Unfortunately, this came with some strings attached, and she had reluctantly married the business tycoon Peng Jingxing due to the Emir's insistence. The marriage had been a loveless disaster from the start. Eileen had never liked anything about Peng, neither his looks nor his values. Peng had only married Eileen to improve his status, as it was the height of achievement in some circles to marry the former president. Things hadn't improved after her husband found out that she was unable to conceive. Eileen calmed down and spoke to the servant:

- Mariyah, I trust that you can make a few calls and find a suitable supplier of these beverages. Now leave me alone.

Having said this, Eileen left the reception area and retreated to her private office. She switched on her computer and opened a hidden file containing her autobiography and her political manifesto. Eileen had wanted to publish it for years, but even considering it, would be dangerous. The

Columnist Party reigned supreme in China once again, and the Emir of Dubai wasn't a fan of women having political influence.

Eileen closed the file. She was not motivated to write something that she had to hide from the world. She hated her life as a trophy wife to her fat and slimy husband. Eileen closed her eyes, and she wished that she had stayed and fought instead of running away, when the Columnist Party returned to seize power. Even if she had died, it would be better than living in this diminutive existence.

Eileen's phone made a beeping noise and distracted her from her thoughts. She had received a message from Jared Pond. She felt both shocked and excited hearing from him, and although it was dangerous, she couldn't resist the temptation to read his message. The message read:

"Eileen, I need to speak to you. I unveiled some of your husband's dark secrets. Meet me at Zahr El-Laymoun, Downtown Dubai in one hour."

Eileen hesitated for a moment. Could this be her ex-husband Jared? After all these years, why would he contact her again? Or, was it one of her husband's many tests?

'Screw it, I am going!' Eileen said to herself, and felt the excitement and adrenaline from straying from the boring and safe path.

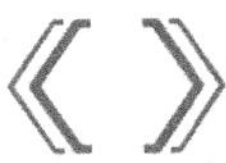

JARED POND WAS DRINKING Jellab (grape juice and rosewater topped with pine nuts) while reflecting over how much better the drink would taste mixed with alcohol. He refrained from finding out. The Dubai government shunned alcohol consumption, and Jared would rather avoid needless confrontation with the Emirati religious police.

He looked up as Eileen approached him cautiously. "Hi, Jared. I'm surprised seeing you here. It has been so many years since we last met."

At first, Eileen's reaction confused him. Hadn't she come to meet him as a friend? But then he realised that she might have people spying on her, and feigning surprise at meeting Jared was for her safety. Jared got up, bowed in front of her, and spoke:

- President Eileen Lu. It's an honour to meet you again.

Eileen:

- Likewise. Can I sit next to you?

Jared nodded, and Eileen got seated in the couch next to Jared. Eileen spoke again:

- So, do tell me. What are you doing here?

Jared:

- Oh, I am sightseeing and enjoying my holiday. I ran into your husband and his friends in Kashmir. It almost cost me my life.

Eileen came closer and whispered softly:

- No, really. What were you doing in Kashmir?

Jared spoke softly:

- I was spying on our old enemies, Pierre Beaumont and Vladimir Kravchenko. Vladimir caught me, ranted about some alien artefacts, and then he knocked me out. When I woke up, I was the captive of two bumbling Indian hitmen. That's when Peng visited me, to reveal that he had paid the hitmen to kill me for being a threat to his marriage.

Eileen:

- My husband wouldn't have travelled all the way to Kashmir for such a small reason, he never cared enough about me to show any kinds of genuine affection.

Jared thought for a second, then spoke:

- Well, he also runs an opium-smuggling operation in that region.

Eileen sighed and replied:

- Then it's true. I saw him meeting with the infamous Mexican drug lord, Jesus Ortega, when we were on a holiday in the Caribbean last year. He denied ever meeting him, but now I know. Peng's financial business must be a front for his drug empire.

Jared:

- You should leave him then.

Eileen:

- Yes. But where will I go? Columnist Party agents will kill me the moment the Emir of Dubai stops protecting me.

Jared:

- I can protect you.

"Eileen, you are not going anywhere!" shrilled a meek and wimpy voice. Eileen and Jared turned to the source of the noise, Eileen's husband Peng was accompanied by two beefed-up bodyguards.
Eileen:

- Peng. What are you doing here?

Peng smirked and replied:

- What kind of husband would I be, if I didn't have access to my wife's private messages so I can prevent her from cheating on me?

Jared:

- Ummm, the respectful and trusting kind?

Peng:

- Don't involve yourself in this, you Aussie scum. I don't know how you escaped India, but escaping Dubai will be even more difficult!

Jared thought about a good reply, but his mind went blank. The only thing he could think about was kissing the beautiful Eileen who sat next to him. As an answer, it wasn't too bad, at least not if she reciprocated his kiss, so Jared gave it a shot. He leaned over, grabbed Eileen and kissed her in front of her jealous and raging husband. For a moment, Eileen forgot all her troubles and she gave out a slight moan of pleasure. Aah!

As expected, Peng didn't appreciate watching another man kissing his wife. Burning with massive anger, Peng's blood pressure shot through the roof and he shouted:

- You shall die for this insult, Jared Pond! Ai-yahh!!

Jared didn't have the time to answer, as Peng's infuriating anger and elevated blood pressure caused the plump Chinese man to have a heart attack, when he was about to ask his guards to capture them both.

Jared turned to the bodyguards and spoke:

- We are leaving. I suggest that you save your boss, he looks like he's about to have a heart attack.

After saying this, Jared grabbed Eileen's hand and they left the coffee shop, while the bodyguards tried to resuscitate Peng.

"SO, WHAT DO WE DO NOW?" Eileen said and smiled as they left the shopping mall.

Jared:

- We are better off leaving Dubai. I doubt the Emir will be happy when he finds out the circumstances around Peng's heart attack.

Eileen:

- But where can we go? Can you protect me in Australia?

Jared reflected over Eileen's question. Bringing Eileen to Australia, which was led by the Columnist Party lapdog Danielle Anders, didn't seem like the best move. But where could they go? If they went to Mexico, they could help the Mexican government deal with Jesus Ortega. In return, the Mexican government could protect them.

Jared:

- No, CPOC operatives have compromised the Australian Government. You wouldn't be safe if you went there.

- However, we could offer our services to the Mexican government. Do you know much about your husband's dealings with Jesus Ortega?

Eileen:

- No, but I grabbed his laptop bag when his bodyguards tried to revive him. With a bit of luck, we can find some useful information on the laptop's hard drive.

Jared:

- Very well. That's our best bet then. Next stop, Mexico City.

After saying this, they grabbed a cab to the airport so they could leave Dubai before the Emir would learn about Peng Jingxing's fate.

Chapter 76: Don't forget about Mexico, 20th January 2040.

Pierre Beaumont was visiting the comatose Martin Orchard in his secret research facility in the Swiss Alps. He wasn't happy with the way things had developed. When Pierre used a replicated Zeto Crystal to bring Martin Orchard back from the dead, he had hoped for a quick recovery. He needed Martin alive and kicking in order to unlock Ben Yehuda's monocle. He also needed Martin to steal the primordial Zeto Crystal from the mysterious Sabina Hines, who had used the crystal's power to become one of the wealthiest and most influential persons in the world.

Pierre was shaking Martin's body, and was about to have a rant, when the chief scientist for the facility, Frank Van Stein, entered the medical room. He approached Pierre, smirked, and spoke:

- Monsieur Beaumont, your medical knowledge must be lacking if you think you can shake a comatose person back to life.

Pierre:

- Don't you dare to make snide remarks. Remember who you are working for.

Frank laughed and replied:

- I know who I am working for, and he looks damn silly shaking a comatose man.

Pierre sighed:

- Hmm. So, what CAN you do to bring back the comatose man in question?

Frank:

- Not much. It's a miracle that he is alive after being dead for years. What did you and Monsieur Kravchenko do to him?

Pierre:

- That's none of your business.

Pierre was interrupted by a phone call from Josefina Fiero. He sighed. Why did his South American associate have to disturb him at such an ill-timed moment? Pierre replied to the phone call:

- Yes, Josefina? What is it?

Josefina:

- Is that how you are greeting your important guest, Pierre? I am at your mansion and your employees don't know where you are.

Hearing this, Pierre recalled agreeing to meet with Josefina about their plans for Mexico and the La Prensa de la Muerte Dam project. The dam was crucial for their plans for their region. Officially, the dam would provide much needed clean hydroelectric power. Pierre's real motive, however, was to submerge prime agricultural lands to create a crop shortage in Mexico. Once the population were starving, it would be easier for Pierre and his accomplices to exert influence in the region.

Pierre:

- Very well. Please enjoy the beverage selection in my lounge room. I will be with you shortly.

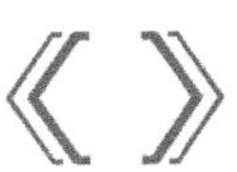

HAVING SAID THIS, PIERRE hung up the phone, turned to Frank, and spoke:

> - Monsieur Stein. Make sure to bring Mr Orchard to consciousness. Do not fail me, as failure often comes with adverse consequences.

Frank smirked but he didn't reply, and he gave Pierre a long look as Pierre left the lab to meet with Josefina.

JOSEFINA FIERO WAS smoking a cigarette and biting her nails while waiting for Pierre in the lounge room of Palace Beaumont. There had been complications with their plans in Mexico, and Josefina feared for the safety of her adopted daughter Sandra Santiago, who was on an undercover mission. Sandra was participating in the Monocle Conspiracy's scheme to overturn the Mexican government through having an affair with the drug lord Jesus Ortega. Things had turned dangerous when Jared Pond and Eileen Lu had approached the Mexican president, Ana Moreno, with evidence linking Peng Jingxing and Jesus Ortega. The evidence proved that outside forces were at play to overthrow the Mexican government and Josefina feared what would happen if the Mexicans found the connection to Sandra.

Pierre entered the room, coughed, and whinged:

> - What kind of behaviour is this? Why are you smoking inside my house? Such 20th century-like behaviour!

Josefina had a fit, threw a glass into the wall, and exclaimed:

> - Shut up, Pierre. Because of your incompetence, Sandra is in danger.

Pierre:

- Bah, how can I be responsible for the wellbeing of that spoilt child of yours?

Josefina:

- You and Vladimir captured Jared Pond the Australian spy, and you decided to keep him alive. He escaped and he is now collaborating with Eileen Lu to sell us out to the Mexican president, Ana Moreno.

Pierre reflected over Josefina's rant. It was an interesting twist of fate that Vladimir's desire to keep Jared alive was risking their objectives in Mexico. It was, however, a manageable risk. Pierre opened the file he had on Ana Moreno and he experienced a minor shock. Ana Moreno was the younger sister of the US President-Elect Eva Moreno, whose ambitions had ended with a .50 calibre bullet to her head, in the year 2028.

Pierre:

- I understand your frustration. Since this was Vladimir's mistake, it seems fair that he will need to fix it. I will send him to Mexico to remove Ana Moreno from the presidency, before she can cause us any undue problems.

- Now please let us enjoy some food and drinks. Despite your outburst, you are a valued guest at Palace Beaumont, and you deserve our best hospitality.

Having said this, Pierre rang a bell and a wait staff approached him and Josefina with a selection of exquisite food and drinks. They proceeded to make their plans for Mexico, but during the long discussion, Pierre could only think about one thing. He needed to make sure that Martin Orchard was to be revived. Martin was the only one who could steal the Primordial Zeto Crystal from Sabina Hines, which was the only thing that could bring his true heir, Delphine Beaumont, back to life.

THE FOLLOWING DAY, Pierre met with Vladimir Kravchenko in an upmarket restaurant in Budapest, Hungary. Pierre didn't like the way Vladimir had handled recent events, as it seemed like Vladimir had lost respect for his strategic brilliance. Pierre concluded that Vladimir was making a good call in sidestepping him. After all, only two months had passed since Vladimir saved him from his botched suicide attempt following Delphine's death. Vladimir followed strength, so Pierre needed to show strength to make things go back as they were.

Once they got seated, Vladimir ordered two steaks, extra rare, accompanied by a bottle of Russian vodka. Pierre gave him a disapproving look and spoke:

- Why would I eat barbaric food like that? Raw meat? Russian Vodka? You know me better than that.

Vladimir smirked and replied:

- You do not have to eat or drink anything. I have a mission for you. It is better if you stay sober and hungry.

Pierre gave Vladimir a curious look. 'It has come to this; Vladimir is taking over.' Pierre thought.
Pierre:

- What is the meaning of this? I am the one giving you missions, not the other way around.

Vladimir:

- You have gone too soft. You need to get your hands dirty from time to time. Doing this is the your only way to save Delphine.

Pierre:

- What difference does it make to you?

Vladimir:

- I don't follow weakness. Show strength or I'll take everything from you. Be the man I used to love.

Pierre sighed. He could see Vladimir's point, but how would succumbing to his demands affect their relationship and his future ambitions. Pierre decided to find out more:

- I am curious. What is the mission you have in mind for me?

Vladimir:

- The Romanian arms dealer Roman Ardelean owns a replicated Zeto Crystal. The crystal is weak and insignificant, in comparison to Primordial crystal, but it will be enough to wake Martin Orchard up from his coma. I want you to fetch the crystal for us. An easy task.

Pierre:

- What do I need to do?

Vladimir:

- Enter Roman's mansion, kill the guards and steal the crystal from his safe. Leave no survivors. Easy enough.

Pierre:

- Can't I buy the crystal from him? It's useless to him and I am the wealthiest man in the world.

Vladimir:

- That wouldn't get your hands dirty, would it? Do as I say or face the consequences.

Pierre nodded and didn't argue against Vladimir's demand. Mostly because he didn't want to anger the volatile Russian but also because Vladimir was correct. It was time for him to get his hands dirty. After sitting in silence while watching Vladimir drink and eat the rare steaks, Pierre finally spoke:

- I am ready. I will rise to the occasion. I will be strong so Delphine can have another lease on life.

Vladimir:

- Excellent. Let's go.

After saying this, the men got up and headed for the van where Vladimir had made the plans for the attack.

Chapter 77: The Budapest assault 22nd January 2040.

Dong, Dong, Dong

Pierre Beaumont heard the church bells from the nearby St. Anna's Church strike for midnight. It was time for Pierre to act. Pierre had always preferred to direct missions from the back, but this wouldn't be the first time he encountered action. He had survived the chaos that ensued when the Hei Bai-virus struck New York in 2021 and he had also survived when Zetan Sentry robots had attacked him in Colombia in 2026. This was, however, over a decade earlier.

Pierre was twiddling with the adrenaline shot he held in his hand. His body was frail, and he was unsure if the adrenaline was enough to help him succeed with the mission. However, he had one thing to help him on his quest, his Zetan Monocle, which in combat mode made him the equal of at least 10 elite soldiers.

Pierre toggled the combat mode interface on his monocle, and he programmed it to the parameters of success. To his expectation, the monocle showed him the infrared signature of all the guard in Roman Ardelean's mansion, as well as Roman's position and the location of his vault. At the bottom of the screen, there were two stats. Chance of success: 42 %, Chance of survival: 52 %. Pierre turned off combat mode, turned to Vladimir, and spoke:

- I don't like those odds that the monocle is showing me. There is only a 52 % chance of surviving the mission. I rather not flip a coin about my survival.

Vladimir:

- Hmm. My monocle gives me a 98.5 % chance of survival. Your odds would be much better if you weren't so frail.

Pierre:

- Bah, you know me. I am much more interested in expanding my mind, rather than expanding my muscles.

Vladimir:

- In any case, take the adrenaline shot. It should improve your combat performance.

Pierre followed Vladimir's suggestion, and he injected himself with the adrenaline shot. The adrenaline shot gave Pierre a huge surge of energy, but it also made him worry about his heart arrhythmia. As he entered combat mode again, his chance of survival had increased to 72 %, while his chance of success had fallen to 40 %. This confused Pierre and he turned to Vladimir:

- That's strange. Why has my chance of survival increased but my chance of success fallen?

Vladimir:

- Your monocle shows the odds for a snapshot of time. As time passes, things change, and the odds fluctuates. You should go now before your adrenaline wears off.

Pierre:

- Yes. But before I go, can you promise me one thing? If I die, please resurrect Delphine and rule the world together with my daughter. She is the future of House Beaumont.

Vladimir:

- Ha-ha. If you die you won't know whether I fulfil the promise
or not. However, you have my word. It would be my pleasure
shaping the future together with Delphine.

Pierre:

- Thank you.

Having said this, Pierre put on a mask and hurried to carry out the mission.

SWOOSH, BANG

Pierre felt an immense rush of adrenaline as he shot the first guard in
the garden of Roman's mansion. He dragged the corpse off the path into
the bushes, out of sight from the other patrols. Pierre followed the prompts
on his monocle, and he snuck past the guard who guarded the main entrance, and he sneaked into the mansion via an open window. This control
prompt perplexed him, since he intended to kill all the guards, so what was
the point of leaving one alive for now?

Pierre didn't want to second-guess the advanced Zetan technology, so
he followed the prompts and entered the bathroom of the palace.

Shclick, poof, bang

Pierre felt a deep sense of gratification that was almost orgasmic, when
he shot the second guard with a few bullets through the toilet door. Two
down, six to go. The control prompt on Pierre's monocle told him to keep
walking down the great hall and climb a set of stairs. When Pierre reached
the set of stairs, he was distracted by a half-open wardrobe, with the glimpse
of a naked body. Following his morbid curiosity, he opened the wardrobe
and he let out a loud shriek when he saw a mutilated female body hanging
from a rope.

Danger, enemy approaching flashed on Pierre's screen. Pierre turned around, but it was too late, and he flinched from pain and dropped his gun when a bullet hit him in the arm. Injured and unarmed, Pierre didn't stand a chance when Roman's henchman ran up to him and knocked him out.

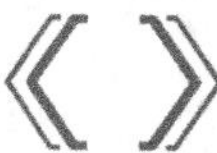

"PIERRE BEAUMONT. I would never expect us to meet like this."

Pierre opened his eyes and he was tied up to a chair in Roman's office in the mansion. Roman, who was dressed in a red velvet suit, smiled towards Pierre with his golden teeth and wicked grin. Roman spoke again:

- Why are you here? You must understand my amazement. In my line of work, assassination attempts are common, but I never expected the CEO of the World Bank to come himself.

- What could possibly be your motive?

Pierre paused and consulted his monocle. 'Telling the truth is the most favourable outcome.' The Monocle displayed. Pierre replied:

- I came here to kill you and steal one of your possessions. I want the blue crystal that you store in your safe.

After hearing this, Roman walked to his safe, entered the passkey, took out the replicated Zeto Crystal, showed it to Pierre, and spoke:

- Do you mean this crystal? What value does it have to the richest man in the world?

Pierre:

- There are things about me that you don't know, and which you don't need to know. All you need to know is that I am willing to pay you $10 million for the crystal and a safe passage from your mansion, if you let me go.

Hearing this, Roman walked up to Pierre, punched him in the face, and exclaimed:

- You greedy pig. You are insulting me. You planned to murder me, you killed two of my men, and now you're trying to pay me off? Fuck you, Pierre.

Pierre:

- Should I interpret that as you being uncooperative?

Roman:

- Damn right!

Pierre:

- That's unfortunate, then I will have to kill you.

Hearing Pierre's threat, Roman punched him in the face, and taunted:

- Don't make me laugh.

Pierre:

- Trust me, I will have the last laugh.

After saying this, Pierre contacted Vladimir via the monocle. A few seconds later, there was a loud noise of shattered window glass as Vladimir, attached to an abseiling rope, leapt through the broken window straight into the room. As he landed, Vladimir disconnected the rope and pulled his semi-automatic pistols from his holsters. It was all over in a matter of seconds, as the security guards lay dead on the floor and Roman collapsed in agony with bullets to his kneecaps.

Pierre looked at Roman and spoke:

- You should have taken my offer, Roman.

After Vladimir loosened Pierre's tied hands, he stomped Roman's head several times, until brain matter splashed on his shoes.

Vladimir smiled and looked at Pierre:

- Not exactly a clean crime scene, there will be so much cleaning up to do. Did you find the replicated Zeto Crystal?

Pierre:

- Yes, I got it.

Vladimir:

- Good. Let's burn down the place and leave. You failed the challenge as you didn't leave a clean crime scene. *wink*

Pierre:

- I didn't fail. Everyone is dead and we got the crystal.

Vladimir:

- Yes, thanks to me. Never mind, it was a pleasure watching you in the field. It's an exhilarating feeling when you're killing people up close and personal, isn't it?

Pierre:

- Yes, I haven't felt this alive for years.

Vladimir:

- I don't doubt that at all. Speaking of which, it's time to go back and revive that son of a gun Martin Orchard. He'll steal the Primordial Zeto Crystal from Sabina for us and victory will be ours.

Pierre nodded and smiled. Vladimir had done the right thing by forcing him to take part in the killing. He felt more energised than he had felt in years and he couldn't wait to see how the rest of his plans would play out. After initiating a fire to destroy evidence by burning the entire building, Pierre and Vladimir left Roman's mansion as quickly as they could.

Chapter 78: A meeting with the Mexican president, 1st February 2040

Jared Pond and Eileen Lu were sitting in the garden of the presidential palace in Mexico City. It was a lush tropical garden, full of exotic birds and animals. If it wasn't for the many military checkpoints on the way to the palace, Mexico would seem like a paradise. However, they knew better. Mexico was a country on the brink of civil war.

Eileen and Jared were drinking horchatas (a thick rice and almond drink) in the shade when President Ana Moreno approached them. Ana spoke:

- Welcome to the presidential residence. As I understand it, you have provided our federal police with important evidence linking the criminal Jesus Ortega with Peng Jingxing, who in turn relates to some very powerful people.

Eileen:

- Yes. Evidence on Peng's computer showed large amount of bank transfers to Mexican charities where Jesus Ortega's group is the beneficiary. Among their greatest sponsors are the World Bank, the Emir of Dubai, and a Brazilian business tycoon Josefina Fiero.

Ana:

- I know about this situation. What I don't know is whether I can trust the two of you. Eileen, you are legally married to

Peng, and instead of accompanying him in the hospital after his heart attack, you chose to run away with your former lover, Jared Pond. I am sorry, but that doesn't improve your credibility.

Eileen:

- I know what it looks like, but hear me out. The Emir offered me political asylum and forced me to marry Peng after the Chinese Columnist Party staged a coup against me. I accepted my fate, but I truly believed that Peng was nothing but a legitimate businessman. After finding out that he was involved in drug smuggling in Mexico and was in fact supporting terrorism, I couldn't stay with him any longer.

Ana:

- You're making some good points, but I am still not convinced.

Eileen:

- President Moreno, please listen. You've got to believe me. Now that I have lost the Emir's protection, Chinese Columnist Party agents will come after me. The only way for the two of us to survive is to cooperate. I knew your sister Eva Moreno well, when I was the president of China. We tried to make the world a better place through uncovering the dark elements hiding in the shadows. The conspiracy we are up against murdered your sister and forced me into exile and a forced marriage. We can set things straight if you believe me.

Being reminded of her sister's murder, Ana shivered, and a few tears ran down her cheeks. She poured herself a glass of water, drank it, and spoke:

- I never believed in the official narrative regarding my sister's death. Why would the then vice president, Jonathan Feng, collaborate with the Chinese and Iranian governments to have her murdered? It didn't make any sense. However, I had to move on, and I hope Eva's spirit can live on through me and my actions.

Jared Pond, who had been silent during the whole conversation, joined in:

- I believe that the Monocle Conspiracy was behind both the release of the deadly Hei Bai virus and the assassination of your sister. At the centre of the conspiracy, stands the evil mastermind Pierre Beaumont. Other notable members are the CIA director James Winter, the former US president Damien Vanderbilt, and Pierre's attack dog Vladimir Kravchenko.

Ana:

- Do you have any evidence for these claims?

Jared:

- If I did, I wouldn't be a washed-up agent, while evil men like Pierre rule the world.

Ana:

- I understand. This must be related to the La Prensa de la Muerte dam that Pierre wants to build in Mexico. There has been non-stop propaganda about the importance of building the dam to Mexican citizens wealth and prosperity. I believe doing so would actually diminish our prime agricultural lands and starve our people.

Eileen:

- If one repeats a lie enough times, it becomes the truth.

Ana:

- Yes, that's why I need you to do something for me. I need you to gather intel on Jesus Ortega and his group. My government agencies are compromised, but perhaps you can find out the truth.

Eileen:

- I would be honoured to help you, Ana. We need to find those responsible for Eva's death and stop Mexico from descending into chaos.

Ana:

- Thank you. I must leave now. My aides will provide you with all the assistance the presidential office can offer you.

After saying this, Ana walked away. Eileen studied the president intently. She resembled the late Eva Moreno, but she seemed more pragmatic and less idealistic in comparison to her. Perhaps that was a good thing. Eileen had a lot of great ideas but no means of implementing them during her years as China's president. Would things had been different if she had focused on strengthening her power before she tried to change things?

Eileen brushed off her thoughts. There was nothing she could do about her past, and the future was all that mattered. Whatever Pierre had planned for Mexico, she owed the Mexican population and the rest of the world to stop him. She turned to Jared and spoke:

- Let's head back to our hotel, hun. I am feeling a little tired.

Jared:

- What about seeking help from President Moreno's operatives? We should perhaps ask some of the intelligence officers before getting back to the hotel.

Eileen:

- You heard how she mentioned that our enemy has infiltrated her government? If we want to achieve our goal, we are better off acting without external assistance.

Jared:

- Very well. Let's leave this place.

After saying this, they finished their horchatas and they left the palace without seeking government help.

EILEEN STUDIED THE naked body of her lover Jared, who slept next to her in a muggy rundown hostel. The sex wasn't as good as she remembered it. Were her memories wrong, or was it simply the effect of aging? Eileen studied Jared's scars. They gave him character, and also reminded her about the past they shared. Jared had a lot of scars on his body, many of them had been caused by Chairman Jing Xi's thugs in 2021, before they escaped from Columnist Party captivity.

A cockroach crawled up on Eileen's arm, and she held back a scream of disgust while brushing it away. She didn't want to wake Jared up, and besides, she would have to settle for places like this for the time being. There weren't many hotels that accepted cash payments without any form of identification, and they needed to stay off the grid.

Eileen looked at her phone. A tiny part of her wanted to turn the phone on and contact her husband to tell him that she has regretted what she had done. If she could reconcile with her husband, she could resume her rich and easy life as a bored housewife, living in wealth and luxury. Eileen brushed off the idea. It was more likely that her husband would send someone to kill her than take her back, and even if he did forgive her, what life would it become. Did she want to spend the rest of her life in a gilded cage, being the property of her drug-smuggling and terrorism-financing fat husband?

Eileen kissed Jared's ear gently. She was right where fate intended her to be. If she could make the world a better place by stopping Pierre's evil schemes, it was her obligation to do so. If she were to fail, they could take her life, but they could never again take her freedom.

Chapter 79: Welcome back, Mr Orchard, 8th February 2040

Vladimir Kravchenko was testing a nerve-pain-amplifier on some unwilling test subjects in the Beaumont Science Centre in the Swiss Alps. Finding willing test subjects for the nerve-pain-amplifier was out of the question, as the pain this device could create was unbearable. However, Vladimir had found a workaround to this issue. He had recruited human traffickers to provide him with an infinite supply of refugees for his cruel human experiments. Thus, the people that ended up being Vladimir's lab rats inadvertently spent their life savings thinking they could get better lives, to receive an excruciatingly painful death instead. Vladimir couldn't stop himself from smiling wickedly when he thought about this cruel but humorous irony of fate.

"Monsieur Kravchenko. I have some great news. One of our test subjects survived all our pain enduring tests."

Vladimir turned around and looked at Chief Scientist Frank Van Stein. Vladimir smiled and spoke:

- Excellent. Can you take me to this test subject at once?

Frank nodded and he led Vladimir to another room, where five out of the six test subjects had died. He turned to Frank and spoke:

- Hmm, this is an interesting development. I thought everyone in this room had the same setting on their nerve-pain-amplifiers. Why did this one survive, when the others died?

Frank:

- I had a dream last night. In my vision, Akram had his nerve-pain-amplifiers set to setting 5B. I needed to find out if it works, so I changed his setting.

Vladimir:

- Setting the pain level to 5B? Wasn't that the worst setting in the past? Everyone died within minutes.

Frank:

- Yes. But somehow it seems to work better with our new proto-type of nanotechnology drones.

Vladimir:

- Interesting. I will go through another cycle with the surviving test subject. If your assumption is correct, he should survive the new process too.

Having said this, Vladimir walked up to Akram, who looked exhausted, drenched in cold sweat and with blood running from his nose. Vladimir spoke:

- Akram Hazaryan. Welcome to the Beaumont Science Centre. I am Vladimir Kravchenko, and I am the co-owner of this facility.

Akram:

- What have I done to you? Why are you torturing me? Why did you murder my family?

Vladimir:

- I can assure you, Mr Hazaryan, that this has do nothing to do with you or your family. Destiny has simply put you in the way of my marvellous creation.

Vladimir flipped a switch, and a hologram showed up next to them. The hologram showcased a schematic of the nerve-pain-amplifying nanorobots.

Vladimir:

- Behold the new nerve-pain-amplifier. With this device, I can afflict any form of pain to you through pressing a button on my smartphone. We have been developing this device for years, but you are the only survivor we have had this far.

Akram cringed and said:

- But why do you need this technology to torture us? What have we done to you?

Vladimir:

- You need to see the big picture. With this device, I can control people from afar. Not everyone fears dying, but everyone fears indefinite suffering.

Akram:

- What are you going to do to me, you wicked monster?!

Vladimir:

- I want to gain absolute control over humanity. My associate, Pierre Beaumont, has strived to control humanity through his power, money, and the media for the last decades. But it's ineffective and you'll always find dissent. I aim to develop the nerve-pain-amplifier and spread it across the globe using Pierre's money and influence. Once everyone has the nerve-pain-amplifier installed, I'll be in complete control of their pain response. Once I control people's pain, I'll control their behaviour.

- But enough of the wishy-washy talk. I got to run another test
to see if the device is working.

Having said this, Vladimir activated the device and pressed the 'Full
body On Fire' button. It was one of the most dangerous settings that killed
most of the test subjects, but he needed to find out if Frank had told him
the truth. Vladimir studied Akram, who was rolling around on the floor in
agonizing pain. Could Akram survive three minutes of this torture?

As three minutes had passed, Vladimir turned off the device, and he
watched how Akram got back to his senses. Akram whispered and said:

- Please make it stop. I'll do anything for you.

Vladimir:

- I did make it stop. Now enjoy your sensation of brain haemor-
rhage.

Having said this, Vladimir set the device to give Akram a sensation
of his brain haemorrhaging. He left his test subject writhing in pain, approached Frank, and spoke:

- Very well, Dr Stein. It seems like you have found the solution
to our little problem. Give me a set of the implants that Akram
has. I have a very special test subject for our next trial.

As Frank handed him the nanotechnology chips, Vladimir shone with
glee. It was time for the bastard Martin Orchard to pay the price for his betrayal in Jerusalem.

"FRANK TOLD ME YOU FINALLY got the nerve-pain amplifier to
work," Pierre said and smiled while he was slurping some oysters with beluga caviar for lunch.

Vladimir studied Pierre. At some point he would need to double-cross his partner and implant him with the amplifier for his plan to work, but now was not the time. Vladimir spoke cynically:

- Yes. How is the situation with Martin Orchard?

Pierre responded:

- He is slowly recovering, passing in and out of consciousness. I haven't spoken to him about our objectives for him to steal the primordial Zeto Crystal yet.

Vladimir:

- I want to use the nerve-pain-amplifier on Martin. We need to get complete control of him and punish him for his betrayal in the past.

Pierre gave Vladimir a slow look and replied:

- Hmm, you only had a single survivor from the group. I would rather not kill Martin again because of your experiments. It's too much hassle to bring him back to life again.

Vladimir:

- I will do more experiments on the technology once I have secured more test subjects. However, we cannot set Martin free and task him with stealing the primordial Zeto Crystal from Sabina Hines without complete control over him. He will betray us, and if they join forces, they can destroy us.

Pierre sighed and replied:

- You are correct. Let's do things your way.

Vladimir:

- With pleasure. It is time for Martin to pay for his duplicity.

VLADIMIR AND PIERRE entered a secret medical facility which was located under a luxurious resort near Lake Geneva. Pierre had used the resort to butter up greedy world leaders with luxuries such as expensive cruises, recreational drugs, and high-class prostitutes to collect dirt on his political friends and opponents. This was to make sure they complied with his wishes. Vladimir had greater plans for the resort, plans that he hadn't revealed to Pierre yet. Vladimir intended to use the resort as his staging ground for spreading the nerve-pain-amplifiers. Once he had the big wigs implanted with the nerve-pain-amplifiers, he would force them to spread the technology to the rest of the population. Then he would be in complete control of the world, and humanity would tremble at his power.

Vladimir snapped out of his daydreaming when he arrived at Martin's room. His Swedish former co-conspirator looked awful and weak when he was lying unconscious in the nursing bed. Vladimir had expected this. Although Vladimir and Martin were both in their early fifties, Vladimir had the advantage of not being dead and cryogenically frozen for two years.

Vladimir opened Martin's mouth forcefully and made him swallow a microchip with the nerve-pain technology. This was a less effective method than surgically implanting it into his skull, however, Vladimir wanted to avoid Martin from finding out about the microchip as it would give him a surgical scar on his head.

Vladimir smiled when the microchip came online. This meant that it had managed to attach itself to a nerve cell to operate on bioelectricity. "Let's wake him up," Vladimir exclaimed and sent a command to the nerve-pain-amplifier to give Martin a tingling sensation in his body.

Martin woke up with a shock, and Vladimir spoke:

- Welcome back, Mr Orchard.

Martin mumbled:

- What happened? What year is it? I remember that I died in Israel. Why did you revive me, Vladimir?

Pierre interjected:

- All very valid questions, Martin. As for your death, I had hoped you'd remember what caused it. Szymon Yehuda killed you for what you did to his brother Ben Yehuda. You betrayed us, Martin.

Martin sighed:

- So, why did you revive me then?

Pierre:

- We need your help. You will be the person to initiate the transfer of the late Ben Yehuda's monocle to a new owner.

Martin:

- Is that all? Did you bring me back from the dead to fix one of the damaged Zetan monocles?

Pierre:

- Not exactly. We have a more important task for you. You need to retrieve the primordial Zeto Crystal from Sabina Hines. We saw your background history, we now know that she is your biological daughter, so you must help us in retrieving the crystal from her.

Martin:

- What if I don't want to help you? What if I am pissed off that you disturbed my peaceful death?

Vladimir:

- Don't you dare to argue with us after all the hassle I had bringing you back from the dead.

Having said this, Vladimir activated Martin's nerve-pain-amplifier, and Martin screamed in excruciating pain, as if he was on fire. Eventually, Vladimir turned off the amplifier. Martin took a deep breath of relief, and Pierre spoke:

- We have been developing new technology in the last two years. Behold the nerve-pain-amplifier. It can cause you immeasurable pain through manipulating your nerve cells with pain sensory input. The best part is that the device won't kill you, so you'll face endless torture if you decide to oppose us.

Martin:

- What if I rather kill myself to fuck the two of you off?

Vladimir:

- Then we'll resurrect you. I have a specific torture chamber at the Beaumont Science Centre dedicated just for you.

Martin:

- Fucking hell, the two of you are real assholes. Okay, I'll submit to your demands. What do you need?

Pierre:

- Like I said, first you must unlock Ben Yehuda's monocle. As for the rest of the mission I am happy to discuss it over dinner upstairs. We are in the basement of the finest hospitality venue in the world after all.

After saying this, Pierre snapped his fingers and Jean Valmont brought a tailor-made suit for Martin and left.

Pierre:

- Don't just lie there, Martin. Get dressed. It's time to get some food.

The Swede got up from the bed and got dressed, feeling amazed that his pains had receded as quickly as they came. After that, the trio walked to the lift to enjoy some fine dining.

"I DON'T TRUST HIM. I want to follow him along the way and see what he is up to." Vladimir said as he and Pierre had a private rendezvous. Pierre smirked and replied:

- Of course, you don't. He is unreliable and bound to betray us. But he did unlock Ben Yehuda's monocle, and he will lead us to Sabina Hines and the Primordial Zeto Crystal. Once he does, we paralyse him from afar, and move in with our troops and secure the Crystal.

Vladimir:

- So, was this all a plan to deceive him?

Pierre:

- Yes, he hates us, and he will be more inclined to help his daughter. We should use this to our advantage. Take a group of your finest mercenaries. Keep him under surveillance but stay out of his way. We will know when it is time to strike.

Vladimir:

- Yes, Pierre. I will do your bidding.

Pierre:

- Excellent. I saw that he booked a flight to Copenhagen. Follow him there and see what he is up to. Dismissed.

Vladimir:

- So, you are not up for cuddles tonight?

Pierre:

- We can "cuddle" once the primordial Zeto Crystal is in our hands and both Martin Orchard and Sabina Hines are resting in their graves. Now go, my humble servant. Time is of the essence and we cannot allow Martin to disappear on us.

Vladimir nodded and left the room to assemble his team of lethal mercenaries to keep Martin under surveillance.

Chapter 80: "Who is that girl, Martin?" 5ᵗʰ March 2040.

Pierre Beaumont was sitting in one of the World Bank's offices in Sydney, Australia. He was having a meeting with his obedient Australian lapdog, Prime Minister Danielle Anders. He needed to investigate why Danielle had sent Jared Pond after him. There was, however, another detail that bothered him more than the ungrateful transgender Australian PM, he couldn't figure out who Martin Orchard's latest accomplice was.

Vladimir's men had taken photographs of the mysterious girl and she had matched the identity of a certain Sara Nilsson from Sweden. Pierre had suspected that something was amiss, and he had sent his men to question Sara Nilsson's parents in Sweden. They had confirmed his suspicions. Sara Nilsson had died a few years earlier, and whoever Martin was working with had assumed a false identity. Since it was extremely difficult to hack the global passport database in the year 2040, this meant that Sara was one of the best hackers in the world.

Pierre got distracted when the receptionist called him:

- Mr Beaumont. Prime Minister Danielle Anders is here to see you.

Pierre:

- Very well, send her in.

Pierre felt irritated when the ugly transvestite Danielle entered his office wearing an extremely thick facemask. Danielle who used to been known as Daniel, was the Columnist Party puppet premier of Victoria, just a few decades earlier. Unsurprisingly, after two decades of aging and her gender change, things hadn't improved, particularly not her looks.

When deciding to support Danielle's ambitions to become the Australian PM, Pierre had been trolling the Australian public. He had never anticipated that he could make a PM out of the man who escaped Australia after his ties to the Columnist Party became public. In any case, Danielle was now the PM of Australia and Pierre had to deal with her.

Pierre:

- Take off that bloody mask, Danielle. I want to see your face. Why are you wearing a disguise anyway?

Danielle spoke in a pretentious and unpleasant high pitch:

- Mr Beaumont. Your secretary told me that we needed to discuss the repercussions of the spread of Norovirus-40B to the general public. As per your instruction, I have asked media to spread terrible death scenarios to terrify the public of this mild virus.

Pierre sighed. He was getting old and it became more and more difficult keeping track of the lies he told the ignorant masses. Pierre said:

- Cancel it. I am sick of looking at people wearing masks and media fearmongering.

Danielle:

- Cancel the spread of the virus?

Pierre:

- Yes. Stop testing everyone and stop reporting about it. It was fun seeing so much mayhem and chaos escalated from unknowing fools. I no longer want to use a viral disease to scare the Australian public.

Danielle:

- Understood. So, what are we going to fearmonger about this year?

Pierre:

- I don't know. I will get back to you about that, when I feel like it.

Danielle:

- So, what is the purpose of our meeting then?

Pierre:

- You know why you are here. I helped you rise to power and you repaid my kindness by sending Jared Pond to spy on me. I want you to send your operatives to kill him. This is your mess, so you better fix it. You also need to support Jesus Ortega against President Ana Moreno in Mexico. We need that dam built in Mexico, to have power over the region.

Danielle:

- Understood. How can I help Jesus Ortega to usurp power?

Pierre:

- Send your best assassins to Mexico. After they've dealt with Jared, they can help Jesus assassinate Ana.

Danielle:

- Understood, Mr Beaumont. My sincere apologies for breaking your trust.

Pierre:

- Whatever. Get your unpleasant face out of here, I will summon you if the need arises.

Danielle held back her anger. Pierre should tread lightly. While he was the most powerful man in the world, Australia was her country, and he shouldn't dare to insult her looks. Danielle reminded herself that Vladimir Kravchenko was in Sydney, accompanied by a group of mercenaries. If she were to confront Pierre, she would no doubt lose her head. Keeping this in mind, Danielle put on her facemask, bowed to Pierre, and hurried to leave the office.

"WHO IS THAT GIRL, MARTIN? Remember that your mission to Australia is to steal the primordial Zeto Crystal from Sabina Hines." Pierre muttered as he met his Swedish co-conspirator in a restaurant in Barangaroo. Martin gave him a sceptical look and replied:

- Her name is Sara Nilsson. I decided to hire someone of similar age as Sabina to help me find out more about her. We are interviewing people surrounding Sabina to find out where she might hide the Zeto Crystal.

Pierre:

- Bah. Sara Nilsson is an assumed identity. My men cross-examined Sara Nilsson's parents in Sweden. She has been dead since November 2037.

Martin:

- Alas, I don't have the luxury and resources to do comprehensive background checks on my employees. Sara is a very talented researcher and crucial in helping me find avenues into convincing Sabina to give up the primordial Zeto Crystal to us.

Pierre:

- Bah, I don't believe a word you are saying. I give you until the end of the month. If you haven't given me the primordial Zeto Crystal by then, I will send Vladimir to take it forcefully from your daughter. That won't be pretty. Do we have an understanding?

Martin:

- Yes, Pierre. I understand you.

Pierre:

- Good. As for you, please enjoy the preview of what your life will entail if you fail me.

Having said this, Pierre sent a signal to Martin's nerve-pain-amplifier to emulate the pain of a few broken bones. As Martin collapsed to the floor, screaming in agony, Pierre smirked, left a few hundred dollars for the bill, and exited the restaurant.

"I NEED YOU TO GET MORE mercenaries." Pierre said to Vladimir as they were sharing a bottle of wine in the spa of an upmarket brothel. Vladimir gave him a curious look, sculled the wine, and replied:

- Why? I have an expert group with me, perfectly capable of dealing with the threat that Martin and Sabina pose. We have concluded that Sabina has no armed men working for her.

Pierre followed Vladimir's example and poured himself a glass of wine, took Vladimir's hand, looked him in the eyes, and spoke:

- I suspect that others might want to get involved. I had a confrontation with Danielle Anders earlier today. We need to make sure that she always has men following her, to prevent her from getting any disobedient ideas. But I am more worried about Elaine Orchard. She has the wealth to stand up to us and she controls the Harapan Conglomerate, the largest entity in South East Asia. She might want to get involved to save Martin and steal the Zeto Crystal for herself.

Vladimir digested Pierre's words. He didn't agree with his financier and mentor. Pierre was getting out of touch with reality. Engaging more mercenaries didn't do anything to promote their chance of success, quite the opposite. If they hired too many, it would be impossible to keep a tight ship and word would get out that they were up to something. This would attract the attention of other groups that also sought the primordial Zeto Crystal. Since Sabina Hines had unearthed the primordial Zeto Crystal two years earlier, the different factions in the Monocle Conspiracy had been watching each other waiting for someone to make the first move. If Pierre hired more mercenaries, they would attract the attention of the Yehuda's Mossad, James Winter's CIA operatives, the Indonesian Harapan Conglomerate led by Elaine Orchard, and the Avanço Verde-Ouro Corporation by Josefina Fiero. It was impossible to predict who would come out of this scenario alive.

Vladimir snapped out of it. Apart from his far-fetched dream of controlling the planet with the nerve-pain-amplifier, the scenario of an all-out battle in Sydney for the control of the Primordial Zeto Crystal also appealed to him. The greatest moment of Vladimir's life was when he freed Eileen and Jared from the Chinese Columnist Party's captivity back in 2021. He had levelled entire blocks in the carnage, and if he could experience that orgasmic chaos again, it was worth the risk of losing everything. Vladimir poured himself yet another glass and spoke:

- Okay, Pierre. I will get us more mercenaries. As for now, get us
a large selection of young fresh male and female dominatrices. I
am starving and this should be an orgy to remember!

After watching Pierre put through the order, Vladimir held him down and took him from behind forcefully, while Pierre moaned in exhilaration and pleasure. The thoughts of all the deaths to come made Vladimir insanely aroused, and this would be an orgy to remember.

Chapter 81: "We got to help Martin ASAP, Budi." 15th March 2040

The chief of Security for the Harapan Conglomerate, Budi Sepulyat, was checking out pro-terrorism photos online when Elaine Orchard entered his office. He panicked and turned off the screen, but realised that it was too late when Elaine spoke:

- So, this is how you are keeping us safe? It's a miracle that any of us are alive!

Budi:

- I am sorry, Ratu (Queen) Elaine. It won't happen again.

Elaine:

- In any case, I didn't come here to lecture you about your religious habits.

- Something is up. We got to help Martin ASAP, Budi.

Budi gave Elaine a confused look. He could swear that she had been very upset a few years earlier when Martin had been shot dead on a mission in Jerusalem. While Elaine never gave him the exact details of what happened to Martin, he was certain that Martin died. Budi said:

- I am sorry, Ratu Elaine. I feel so stupid, but isn't Martin already dead?

Elaine:

- Don't feel stupid. He did die. However, I found out that Pierre brought him back from the dead. Pierre and Vladimir have implanted Martin with a device that gives him insufferable pain if he doesn't do their bidding. They are moving in on the primordial Zeto Crystal. We need to stop them, save Martin, and steal the primordial Zeto Crystal for ourselves.

Budi:

- Understood, my queen. What do you need me to do?

Elaine:

- Bring your men to the presentation level. We are meeting our Chief Scientist Rexi Lembong in one hour. We'll present the plan for you then.

Budi:

- Understood, Ratu Elaine.

Elaine:

- Good.

- Oh, and don't let me distract you from your sick and twisted "religious dogmas".

Having said this, Elaine left the office while Budi was stuck with red cheeks from embarrassment, trying to figure out what to do about his "religious dogmas".

BUDI SEPULYAT MADE his way to the presentation level an hour later. Most of his men were already there, while Elaine and Rexi seemed to be debating over the structure of a 3D hologram building. Budi cleared his throat to alert Elaine of his presence:

- Security Chief Budi Sepulyat, reporting for duty.

Elaine:

- Tsk, tsk, tsk. Did I tell you to spend that much time with your personal hobbies?

Budi's cheeks turned red and Elaine spoke again:

- Don't worry about it. What matters is the mission at hand. Rexi, can you fill Budi in?

Rexi got up, stretched and corrected his posture. He spoke to the gathered group:

- We have a very difficult and dangerous task ahead of us. Vladimir Kravchenko and his group of mercenaries are in Sydney. They aim to murder Martin Orchard and steal a priceless alien artefact. It is our job to stop them. Our main concern is Vladimir Kravchenko who is equipped with alien technology that makes him the most dangerous warrior to ever walk the Earth.

Elaine added in:

- Don't fear. A single woman defeated Vladimir in 2028, and you are the best fighting group Indonesia has ever seen. You'll prevail.

The group chanted:

- Kami akan menang. Hidup Indonesia dan Konglomerat Harapan. (We shall prevail. Long live Indonesia and the Harapan Conglomerate)

After a while, Elaine raised her hand to silence the group, and Rexi spoke again.

- To defeat Vladimir's bloodthirsty devils, we will need discipline. You'll all be wearing Zetan invisibility suits to avoid detection. You'll also wear a suit that cools you down to ambient temperature to avoid detection via the infrared spectrum.

Elaine:

- Thank you, Rexi. You'll join Budi and his men on the mission.

Rexi gave Elaine a strange look and objected:

- But I am your chief scientist. What use can I be on this dangerous mission?

Elaine:

- You need to see how your inventions work in real life. That is the only way you can develop real-world applications. Besides, the group needs your brain as an addition to their brawl.

Rexi sighed and said:

- Understood, Ratu Elaine.

Elaine smiled and replied:

- My fellow men, let's have a feast. Today we celebrate, and tomorrow we go to war.

Having said this, Elaine clapped her hands. On this signal, a group of servants and concubines entered the room to fulfil the men's every desire.

ELAINE ORCHARD WAS watching the skyline from her penthouse in the Harapan Conglomerate Headquarters. She had left the feast early, but to no avail, as she could not sleep. She would soon be at the point beyond return. If she were to fight against Pierre and Vladimir, she would lose her benefactors and make herself some truly dangerous enemies. But what choice did she have? Her spies had told her that Vladimir and Pierre were developing a terrifying torture device that they could implant into people's heads, to control their pain from a distance. If Pierre and Vladimir could spread this technology, they would rule the world with terror. It would be even worse if they found a way to amass the almost limitless energy from the primordial Zeto Crystal. At first, Elaine had doubted her spy reports, but after seeing the CCTV footage of Martin collapsing in agony at a restaurant, she knew they were true. Pierre and Vladimir had implanted Martin with this terrible device to force him to do their bidding.

Elaine took a deep breath, and drank some warm mildly sedating tea. Under the influence of the sedatives, she felt at peace. She needed to stop Pierre and Vladimir. It was her purpose in life to stop them and build the paradise she envisioned. If she were to die trying to build that paradise, it was better than being alive in a dystopian future where Pierre and Vladimir ruled through terror and fear. Having made peace with the risk of dying in the war to come, Elaine leaned back into her bed and fell asleep.

Chapter 82: The Banker meets the Empath, 30th March 2040.

Pierre Beaumont was setting up a market manipulation scheme that would cause chaos on the ASX and make him a few hundred million dollars richer. Although Pierre's wealth was already in the trillions and he had no need to manipulate the markets, it was a pastime that never got old to him.

Pierre picked a few companies to short on the trading market and he risked a billion dollars in each company. The shorts would need to be repaid on Monday, and by then the shares would have plummeted and Pierre could close the shorts and make a fortune. Pierre sent out negative fake news articles about the companies he had shorted, and he would make his media empire push the negative news to bring the share value down. That would fool the unknowing sheep so he could fleece them for even more money.

Pierre checked his share trading account and he smiled when he saw how the share price of the companies he shorted had plummeted, due to his huge amount of propaganda to deliberate create fake news via social media. He was up $100 million from pressing a few buttons, from pushing his lies and debaucheries. Life was glorious on the top.

Pierre checked the list of dignitaries that he was meeting for lunch at the World Economic Forum. He hoped it would be someone interesting. At least the $100,000 he charged for a consultancy meeting would stop the rabble from accessing his valuable time. Pierre's jaw dropped when he noticed who had paid to meet him. Today's lunch meeting would be with Sabina Hines, the mysterious woman who had stolen the primordial Zeto Crystal from Ben Yehuda. But why had Sabina come to see him? The meeting request stated that Sabina needed funding for an ocean clean-up project, and needed to meet Pierre to get a sponsorship agreement. But Sabina was an incredibly successful trader who had made billions of dollars from online trading. She did not need to petition him for charity.

Bouts of paranoia struck Pierre. What if Sabina knew that he was coming after her and had decided to strike first? If that were the case, he needed Vladimir and the mercenaries to protect him, as he feared that his official bodyguards would not be enough against someone with Sabina's abilities. Pierre shook off the idea. He could not bring Vladimir and his armed mercenaries to the World Economic Forum. Bringing armed men to the International Convention Centre in central Sydney would cause too much attention. It would look obscene for him to pose with his private army, and besides, he didn't want the world to know that he did command a private army.

Pierre decided to meet with Sabina without revealing his plans against her. If she had come to snoop on him, he was better off if he knew about the official reason for her visit. Pierre opened the attached document to the meeting request. The proposed automated robot-technology for cleaning up the pollution of the oceans sounded impressive, but he couldn't see how it would benefit his goals, so he would give it a pass. After reading up on Sabina's proposed technology, he ordered coffee and watched his share portfolio, while waiting for Sabina to arrive.

"WARNING. THERE IS A powerful creature in front of you. Proceed with caution."

Pierre studied the message that popped up on his Zetan Monocle, as Sabina entered the meeting room. He had met countless world leaders in the last few decades, but he had never seen this warning before. He studied Sabina. She looked young, beautiful, and harmless. She had a tall and slender physique, and she wasn't carrying any weapons. Pierre doubted that she was a powerful fighter. Even if his bodyguards weren't around, he assumed that he could beat her in a fistfight if he activated combat mode on his monocle, despite his old age.

Pierre's eyes turned to Sabina's husband, Alex. He was also in his early 20's, and he was athletic and extremely handsome. 'Hmm, at least she has a good taste in men.' Pierre thought and reflected whether Alex was his key to forcing Sabina to submit to his will. Pierre turned to Sabina and spoke:

- As you know, my time is valuable, but I will give you ten minutes to make your case as for why the World Bank should assist you.

Pierre felt surprised when Alex started talking about their proposal and this annoyed him. Pierre knew that it was Sabina who had stolen the Zeto Crystal and made billions of dollars from using its supernatural powers. To send her husband who was nothing but a pretty face of her organisation to do the talking, was downright insulting and Pierre wondered why Sabina didn't speak herself. After listening to Alex's presentation, Pierre replied:

- Yes, I have heard about your utopian project and the bank's final answer is a NO.

Alex pleaded:

- But why, it could save a lot of marine life at a low cost.

Pierre:

- We do not prioritise marine life, and the World Bank has a lot of missions on its hands.

For the first time, Sabina opened her mouth and replied:

- Geez. We paid $100,000 to meet you. At least you can give us a proper answer.

'Oh, she is a fiery one,' Pierre thought and smiled. He got back to his cold personality and replied:

- While cleaning up the oceans is a worthwhile goal, the ocean is owned by everyone and it is nothing the bank can invest in. The bank does not deal with utilitarian means. We deal with assets.

Sabina:

- What about creating a better world?

Pierre:

- Everything good has a monetary value; clean oceans do not. Thus, it is not for us to pursue.

Hearing Pierre's arrogant and condescending tone, Sabina lashed out:

- Money is not everything in the world.

Pierre smirked and replied:

- That is where the bank must disagree with you. Money does not exist to serve humans. Humans exist to serve money. In the absence of deities, money becomes the new god, the raison d'être for humanity.

Pierre smirked at Sabina. His monocle indicated that her emotional state was approaching anger. *'Ha-ha silly girl. So young, idealistic, and easy to crush!'* Pierre thought to himself.

Pierre felt shocked when Sabina's emotional state changed from anger to love and compassion. She looked intently at Pierre and spoke:

- You need a hug. You must never have loved or been loved before.

Before he could object to this strange request, Sabina came closer and gave him a friendly hug. As Sabina hugged Pierre, he sensed something he had never felt before. His mind felt at peace, and he wanted to let go of his evil schemes.

"Warning, the girl is breaching your mind. Your secrets will be compromised."

Pierre got back to his senses when his Zetan Monocle flashed in front of his eyes. How long had he been gone? He felt how memories were flashing in front of his eyes, jumbled up in an incoherent order. *I got to break free.'* Pierre thought and pushed Sabina away. Much to his relief, she allowed him to slip from her grip. As Pierre broke free, he took a deep breath and yelped:

- I did not like that at all. Hugging is not a part of these proceedings. Your time is up, please leave the meeting room now, Sabina and Alex!

Sabina was about to protest, but Pierre signalled his bodyguards to expel them, so they left without a fight. After Sabina and Alex had left, Pierre took a deep breath and asked his bodyguards to wait outside, so he could rest and gather his thoughts about what had happened.

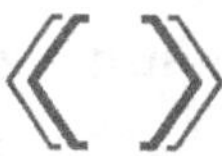

PIERRE WAS CHEWING his fingernails raw and his body was shaking too much to drink his whiskey when he tried to recap the day's events. He was in his Sydney property, which he had bought for the mission to have a secure location where his competitors couldn't spy on him. "Ah, I hate those ugly tapestry on the wall!" Pierre shouted to himself and realised that his mind was in disarray. Sabina posed a serious threat to him and his organisation, and yet he worried about the decorations in his temporary accommodation.

Pierre tried to calm down. Perhaps he had imagined it all. The only thing that had happened was that Sabina had believed that a hug would change his opinion about her proposal to charity funding. After all, she was young and beautiful, so seduction would seem like an effective method to sway elderly men. Then again, why would she bring her doofus husband, if that was her goal?

Pierre calmed down. Sabina had tried to seduce him. The thought that she would use a hug to extract information from his mind was preposterous. Feeling a bit better, Pierre took the whiskey glass to his mouth and enjoyed a sip of its strong smoky flavour.

"Warning, excessive stock market loss detected."

The warning brought Pierre back to an alert and terrified state, when he saw the news that someone was increasing the price of the shares he was shorting. On Monday, he would have to close his shorts as soon as possible and if this continued, he would lose billions. While the loss itself was not the biggest issue, it did prove one thing. Sabina had read his mind, and she was coming after him.

'I BETTER GET VLADIMIR to eliminate that girl at once. We can worry about finding the primordial Zeto Crystal later.' Pierre thought and tried to contact Vladimir via the monocle. There was only silence, as Harapan Conglomerate agents had attacked Vladimir and his group, just moments earlier.

Chapter 83: Do not underestimate the power of the Harapan Conglomerate, 30th March 2040.

Elaine Orchard was feeling tense as she sat in the fortified headquarters of the Harapan Conglomerate in Jakarta, Indonesia. The war with Pierre and Vladimir hadn't started, but yet she hadn't dared to leave the building for two weeks. She needed to secure the support of the other members in the Monocle Conspiracy, but she was afraid of taking the step forward. She couldn't know how they felt about her and Pierre, or which side they would be on.

Elaine knew that Josefina Fiero and Sandra Santiago would be on her side if it came to war. Vladimir had murdered Sandra's father in Nepal back in 2020, and there was no way that they would support Pierre and Vladimir's doings. Apart from them, what about the Mossad leader Szymon Yehuda and CIA's director James Winter? It would be extremely difficult for the Harapan Conglomerate to win a shadow war against the World Bank, the Mossad, and the CIA, even with the help of Josefina and her organisation, Avanço Verde-Ouro Corporation.

"Sabina Hines has left the meeting with Pierre Beaumont at the World Economic Forum. Miss Hines seemed upset."

Elaine looked at the news feed that her Zetan Monocle provided from the hacked CCTV cameras at the Convention Centre. If Sabina Hines and Pierre had come into a conflict, it was likely that Pierre would make a move and send Vladimir to attack her. Elaine needed to stop this from happening. She picked up an encrypted phone and called Budi Sepulyat.

Elaine:

- Budi, it is time. You need to attack Vladimir and his men today. They are going to make a move on Sabina and try to steal the Ze- to Crystal.

Budi:

- Understood. Have you secured the support from the other factions yet? Who are we up against except for the World Bank?

Elaine hesitated. She didn't want to lie, but it wouldn't boost the morale to tell Budi that he was up against overwhelming odds:

- Josefina Fiero and her company will help us.

- Do not underestimate the power of the Harapan Conglomerate. We will prevail.

Budi:

- Kami akan menang. Hidup Indonesia dan Konglomerat Harapan. (We shall prevail. Long live Indonesia and the Harapan Conglomerate)

Elaine:

- Good. I have faith in you, my son. Now make me proud.

After hanging up the phone, Elaine felt worried. She had sent her adopted son on a hazardous mission to kill the most dangerous man on the planet. Yet, it was the only way to stop Vladimir's evil scheme to use nerve-pain-amplifiers to terrorise humankind. Uncertain if he would listen, Elaine went down on her knees to send some prayers for Budi's safeguard.

BUDI SEPULYAT WAS SHIVERING from cold as he was hiding in the ventilation shaft in the World Tower, while watching Vladimir

Kravchenko. Vladimir and his crew were presiding in the penthouse level of the building, which was the highest residential building in Sydney. The cold from the heat-reducing suit was necessary to avoid detection from in-frared cameras, but it caused severe hypothermia. Budi hoped he would be able to stay focused before his body reached a state of shock, at which point the suit would turn-off to save his life.

Once he was in position, he took aim for Vladimir and waited for his men to move in place. His shot would be the starting point for the battle, and it was crucial that he felled Vladimir with his shot, otherwise anything could happen.

VLADIMIR KRAVCHENKO was drinking Russian vodka to deal with the boredom. He couldn't understand why they had spent weeks in Sydney without moving in on Sabina and steal the bloody crystal. They had con-cluded that she was unarmed and harmless, and yet Pierre wanted to give Martin Orchard the time to figure out the Zeto Crystal's location.

"Ura!" Vladimir exclaimed as he raised his glass of vodka. Vladimir was knocked back when something hit him in the face. Time stopped, and he saw the bullet that was centimetres from his eyes, frozen in time. *'So, this is how I'll die,'* Vladimir thought and smiled. Time resumed and Vladimir fell to the ground. While still injured, he looked up and glanced at the room. Muzzle flashes were everywhere, and his fellow mercenaries fell in droves to their invisible enemy. *'This must the Harapan Conglomerate's doing, but I will not fall here.'* Vladimir concluded and tried to make his way to the rooftop, while still in pain. He got hit several times, but his body armour took the brunt of his internal damage and he could pinpoint the direc-tion of the invisible opponent that blocked his path to the stairs. It pleased Vladimir when he saw blood streaming out from the thin air, as his enemy went down. Vladimir didn't have the time to study the scene. He made his way to the rooftop and tried to get his monocle to blow up the explosives he had hidden in the penthouse for scenarios like this.

"System crash. Command not available" the monocle showed him. "Damn it to hell!" Vladimir muttered as he pulled up his controller to blow up the penthouse. As he got the controller up, he heard how his pursuers were coming after him up the stairs. 'I rather live to fight another day.' Vladimir thought. He dropped the controller and ran to the hang glider he had parked on the rooftop and jumped off the building.

Budi and Rexi reached the rooftop the exact moment that Vladimir jumped off the building. They shot after him, but were unable to hit him with a killing shot.

Budi picked up the phone and called Elaine:

- We carried out the attack, but Vladimir managed to escape.

There was moment of silence, as Elaine checked on Vladimir's system connectivity via her own monocle. He had disconnected from the network, which was both good and bad. Good, as he wasn't nearly as dangerous without the help of his Zetan Combat mode, but it was also bad as they couldn't trace his location.

Elaine:

- How many dead and wounded?

Budi:

- Three on our side. We killed all of Vladimir's soldiers. We also found out that they rigged the whole level with explosives.

Elaine:

- Get out of there and set off the explosives. We need to cover up the evidence of this battle.

Budi:

- Ratu Elaine, but what about the innocents that will die from the explosion and the debris? They do not deserve this.

Elaine:

- We cannot worry about the few, just carry out my order!

Budi:

- Understood, my queen.

After saying this, Budi gathered his men and set the explosives to blow up the penthouse level. After that, they used their invisibility suits to escape the scene and the approaching sirens of police patrols.

Chapter 84: Pierre requests backup from the Mossad, 1ˢᵗ of April 2040

Pierre was hiding inside his Point Piper mansion. His mind was full of fear. He had lost his private army of elite mercenaries in the fight at World Towers. The forensic specialists had found 40 bodies at the scene, of which 8 were from the NSW police force who had perished when the building exploded. The number of injured was in the hundreds. This was real war.

Pierre had defied the odds by attending the races the previous day to give Martin Orchard an ultimatum. The show had to go on, and under Pierre's order, the media had not covered the massacre at World Towers on the news. For now, the fact-checkers would label anyone reporting about the recent attack as a deluded conspiracy theorist. Eventually, the truth would come out. Before it did, Pierre needed to cover up his ties to the dead mercenaries.

During the Sunday morning, Pierre had caved in to his fears and asked Prime Minister Danielle Anders for protection. Danielle had been happy to comply, and Pierre's residence resembled a fortress rather than a home. Despite being protected by large groups of police officers and army troops, Pierre still wasn't feeling safe. It was humiliating to hunker down like this, under Danielle's "protection". It also made him fearful of the Australian PM as their latest interaction had been less than cordial.

Pierre looked up when an Australian soldier approached him and spoke:

- Hi mate, you've got some visitors.

'Address me as Master Beaumont, you lowly brute!' Pierre thought to himself, but refrained from scolding the soldier and replied:

- I see. Did they identify themselves?

Aussie Soldier:

- They are on this screen here. Their leader introduced himself as Szymon Yehuda.

Pierre:

- I know this man. Please let their leader in. Tell the others to wait outside.

Aussie Soldier:

- Understood. Consider it done.

The Australian soldier left and Szymon Yehuda entered the room. Pierre sneered at him:

- Why did you bring only four men to help me? Do you know what we are up against?

Szymon:

- Tsk, tsk, tsk. Less is more. Assigning only four men to this mission attracts way less attention. Besides, what good are numbers if your men are getting drunk and get slaughtered like pigs?

Pierre:

- Point taken.
- So, do we have an agreement?

Szymon:

- Yes, we will locate Sabina Hines and Martin Al-Sham, kill them both, and steal the primordial Zeto Crystal for ourselves. Once we have secured the primordial Zeto Crystal, we will enact our glorious plan of expelling the infidels from the Holy Land. After that, we'll aid you in your crusade against the Harapan Conglomerate and bring House Beaumont to fame.

Pierre sighed. It was far from ideal that Szymon Yehuda would get temporary control of the primordial Zeto Crystal. But what else could he do? He was at war with the Harapan Conglomerate, Vladimir was nowhere to be found, and Elaine's manoeuvres had Pierre pinned down in this mansion. If Elaine Orchard, Martin Orchard, and Sabina Hines were to join forces, that would be the end of him. Pierre said:

- Yes, we have an agreement.

Szymon:

- Good. Our Sydney branch associates can track Martin, as he has our hidden nano-technology tracking device implanted. We will keep him under surveillance and intercept him when he meets with Sabina.

Pierre:

- Good. Any news on Harapan Conglomerate's activity?

Szymon smirked and replied:

- As I said, we will help you with those inferior South East Asians once the primordial Zeto Crystal is under our control.

- I am leaving you now. We will be in touch if anything changes.

Having said this, Szymon mock-bowed to Pierre and left the room. Pierre sighed. If he could only get hold of Vladimir. Or in case if Vladimir was dead, find out the truth, so he would know how to proceed.

Chapter 85: We must help Martin Orchard, 3rd April 2040

Budi Sepulyat was spying on Martin Orchard using a nanotechnology drone. Martin was standing close to Barangaroo Wharf. Budi got a sense that something was up when he saw a group of Mossad operatives led by Szymon Yehuda sitting at a nearby coffee shop. Considering that Martin had killed Szymon's brother, betrayed the Mossad, and had given Sabina Hines access to the Zeto Crystal at the Solomon Temple, a confrontation was imminent.

What happened next surprised Budi. Martin Orchard took off his Zetan Monocle and put it in the inner pocket of his suit jacket. Why would he make such a stupid move? Budi knew that the Zetan Monocle gave the user superhuman combat capabilities. Unless Martin wanted to die, it was idiotic to take off the monocle when a fight was imminent.

Budi switched to the screen of the security camera of another drone, and he saw how Martin was approaching Sabina Hines. As he got closer to her, the Mossad agents moved in the direction of them with their guns. Budi turned to Rexi and spoke:

- We got to help Martin Orchard, as instructed by Queen Elaine. The Mossad is coming for him and Sabina Hines.

Rexi:

- Yeah, but they are out in the open. There are tonnes of people out and about today. Do we want a war with the Mossad in front of a massive crowd?

Budi:

- It's unavoidable. We cannot allow the primordial Zeto Crystal to fall into the wrong hands.

Rexi:

- Understood, Budi.

After saying this, Budi and Rexi got out of the van they had been in. They activated their invisibility suits and rushed towards Martin's location, where the ruckus had started.

'That must be the Zeto Crystal,' Budi thought, when he saw Sabina Hines take a luminous gem out of her pocket and attack Szymon Yehuda with it.

What happened next occurred in very quick succession. Sabina back-flipped into the harbour and with the primordial Zeto Crystal still in her hand. The Mossad agents started shooting after her under the water. Martin Orchard jumped forward, inserted his monocle, pulled out his pistol, and fired off four quick shots which killed the four Mossad agents. Martin got up and exclaimed "Fuck you, Szymon," and offloaded his remaining bullets into Szymon's face, ensuring that he died permanently and would never be able to be revived again.

"Let's go. We need to sedate him and get him out of here."

Budi said and walked behind Martin undetected, while still wearing his invisibility suit. Rexi followed suit, and in a matter of seconds, they had attacked Martin from behind and injected him with a sleeping serum. They had sedated Martin to unconsciousness with their potent sleeping drug, to bring him back to safety. After that, they took out an invisibility blanket, wrapped it around Martin, and hurried back to their van for an immediate escape.

"GIVE HIM ANOTHER SHOT of the Tranquilizer, Budi"

Budi injected Martin with another shot of the high-grade tranquillizer. They needed to keep Martin unconscious, to perform some surgery on him. In order to leave the country undetected, they needed to find and remove the nerve-pain-amplifier chip that Vladimir had implanted.

"I have detected the whereabouts of the microchip, be steady with the scalpel." Rexi urged.

Budi was about to make an incision, when the sudden sound of gunfire distracted him. One of their men, hurried into the warehouse where they based their Sydney underground operations.

- Budi, we are under attack by the Mossad! They are bringing a large cohort of soldiers!

Budi:

- Understood. I'll join you in the fight after we are done with this.

Having said this, Budi turned to Rexi and spoke:

- I hope you can remove the microchip on your own. We will need to leave sooner than we planned.

Having said this, Budi ran to put on his invisibility suit. Once the suit was operational, he picked up an assault rifle to start the hunting.

Budi got out from a backdoor and he saw a few Mossad agents shooting towards his men. He resisted the temptation to shot them. Instead, he ran in a large semi-circle to reach the Mossad agents' vehicles. Budi twisted the neck of the driver of the large van, and he put a rock on the accelerator to make it go straight ahead. After that, he went ahead to the roof of the building. As the van crashed into a concrete pillar, he used the crowd's confusion to break the neck of two Mossad agents. The destruction of their vehicle caused other Mossad agents to run towards to the van to check what had happened. Budi used this opportunity to throw a hand grenade towards the van to take them out.

The sound of several more cars approaching caught Budi's attention. He had never anticipated that the Mossad had such numbers in Sydney, and retreating was the only option. He ran back to the warehouse, where Rexi had successfully removed the tracking chip from Martin's body.

Budi:

- Let's go.

Rexi:

- How? We are surrounded by enemies.

Budi:

- Put on an invisibility suit and wrap Martin in an invisibility blanket. We'll carry him to safety. I'll rig explosives to the rest of our gear; we cannot let our enemies steal our technology.

Rexi:

- What about the rest of our group?

Budi:

- They knew the risk. Let's go.

Rexi did as Budi instructed. He put on the invisibility suit and wrapped Martin in the invisibility blanket. After that, they carried Martin out of the building, while doing their best to stay out of the crossfire.

After carrying Martin a few hundred metres, Budi pulled up his phone and ordered a self-driving cab. It wasn't the best plan as it would implicate them, but he couldn't carry Martin to the airport. Besides, with a bit of luck, they would be out of the country soon.

A WHILE LATER, THEY arrived at Bankstown airport where the Harapan Conglomerate had hidden a Gulfstream private jet. They got on the plane and prepared to take off. They didn't contact air traffic control as they didn't want to bring attention to themselves. Instead, they dragged Martin onto the plane and set a course straight to the east to leave Australian territory.

Budi:

- Make sure to fly straight to the east until we are outside Australian territory. Fly at a very low altitude, it's the only way to avoid radar detection.

Rexi:

- That would wake up every suburb between here and the coast.

Budi:

- Yes, but it's night, and if we travel without our lights on, the low altitude will stop Australia's radar from finding us. Or would you rather take your chances with the Australian Airforce?

Rexi:

- Understood.

Rexi did as Budi commanded, and although their low flight path woke up half of the city, it stopped the air force radar from detecting them. Once they had reached international waters, they continued their low altitude flight to Indonesian territory. It was a bumpy ride, but it was better than being detected by the Australian Airforce.

Chapter 86: "Must I do everything myself?"
4th April 2040

Pierre Beaumont felt a sense of both worry and relief as he entered the Royal Prince Alfred Hospital in Sydney. He was worried about his recent financial losses. Sabina Hines had, through pumping the stocks he was shorting, caused him a loss of $7billion. While this was only a fraction of his total wealth, he worried what would happen if she kept targeting his investments. He needed to eliminate her as soon as possible, but first, he needed to find out about her whereabouts.

On the flip side, the Mossad's attack on the Harapan Conglomerate outpost had killed or disabled all known enemy agents in Sydney. There were reports about a low-flying private jet that had escaped Australian airspace. This aeroplane would have belonged to his enemies, as one had to be desperate to try such manoeuvre. It was just as good. While it was annoying that Elaine's closest men, Budi Sepulyat and Rexi Lembong had escaped Australia, Pierre was free to move again, albeit surrounded by bodyguards.

Pierre entered the room where the doctors had attached Vladimir to a respirator. His Russian partner was weak but conscious, and Pierre felt less worried about his partner than he had been the last time someone beat Vladimir. 'At least, he won't need nine months in a respirator and alien technology to bring him back to life this time.' Pierre thought.

Upon seeing Vladimir, Pierre felt a burst of irritation. Pierre had reviewed the CCTV cameras from the night of the attack. He had noticed that Vladimir and his group of mercenaries had been intoxicated and taken by surprise. How could they be so careless when a lethal confrontation was imminent?

Pierre reprimanded Vladimir:

- Wake up you big bear. How could you lose all our mercenaries? Why did you get drunk and let those Indonesians take you by surprise?

Vladimir:

- Drunkenness was not why they beat us. Those shifty bastards have developed personal cloaking devices. They butchered us before we even saw them.

Pierre reflected over Vladimir's statement. If the Harapan Conglomerate had developed cloaking devices, they would be difficult to defeat in shadow warfare. But what could he do? Should he opt to research countermeasures to their cloaking devices, or was it better to act fast, and have his agents detonate a nuclear device in Jakarta to destroy the Harapan Conglomerate Headquarters? Pierre turned to Vladimir and spoke:

- What about your Zetan Monocle? Surely it could help you detect them even if they wore cloaking devices.

Vladimir:

- They hit my monocle with the first shot and disabled it. It has been malfunctioning ever since, urging me to find a replicated Zeto Crystal to repair it. I can't even take the damn thing off.

Pierre:

- Well, you should find a replicated Zeto Crystal as soon as possible then.

Vladimir:

- How? I have eight bullet wounds in my legs and the malfunctioning monocle is jumbling up my mind. I won't be going anywhere.

Hearing this, Pierre had one of his hissy fits and exclaimed:

- Must I do everything myself!?

Vladimir kept calm and replied:

- So, it would seem.

Pierre calmed down and apologised:

- I am sorry, Vladimir. I will stage an expedition to get you a replicated Zeto crystal so we can get you back on your feet. There are many of them scattered around the world. It's us against the world now, and I need you by my side.

Vladimir nodded but didn't say anything.
'Jesus Ortega's men have caught Sabina Hines in Mexico.'
As Pierre saw this notification, he knew that he needed to act. He needed to gather a group and travel to Mexico at once. If Jesus Ortega came into possession of the primordial Zeto Crystal, he needed to hand the primordial Crystal to Pierre instead of giving it to Josefina or Sandra. If Josefina were to acquire the primordial Crystal, the situation would get even more complicated!
Pierre:

- I need to go. Jesus Ortega has captured Sabina Hines and I need to convince him to give me the primordial Zeto Crystal!

After saying this, Pierre gathered his Mossad agents and hurried to the airport where he chartered an Orbit Flight to go to Mexico.

Chapter 87: We need to help Sabina Hines. 4th April 2040.

Jared and Eileen were drinking coffee at a small private Mexico City airport, waiting for a flight to leave the country. They had struggled with their mission and had not gotten anywhere. They had failed to blend in, and thus they hadn't been able to find evidence that linked World Bank operatives in Mexico with the drug lord Jesus Ortega.

Jared had convinced Eileen to come with him to Australia. While Columnist Party agents had infiltrated all levels of the Australian government, the same applied to Mexico. By going to Australia, they were at least less likely to get caught in the crossfire between rival gangs, or actual warfare if the Mexican Civil War were to take place.

Jared felt tense when El Gaucho, the right-hand-man of Jesus Ortega, and a group of armed men approached them. He sighed in relief as the Narcos walked past him.

Eileen noticed Jared's tension and spoke:

- What's going on Jared? You look like you saw a ghost.

Jared:

- I thought we were in danger. That man was El Gaucho. He is Jesus Ortega's right-hand-man and one of the most dangerous men in Mexico.

Eileen looked at the group and she noticed that they were all carrying weapons. She whispered to Jared:

- How can they be carrying weapons? What happened to airport security?

Jared:

- I guess airport security officers are not paid enough to argue with the men of the most ruthless drug lord in Mexican history. Our flight is boarding soon. This is not our war anymore.

Eileen shook her head and got up:

- I got to find out what they are up to and warn Ana Moreno. The coup might be taking place today.

Having said that, Eileen walked up to a window and she watched as the men approached a private jet on the tarmac.
Eileen:

- They are kidnapping someone.

Jared:

- Please Eileen. We have done everything we can. This is not our fight anymore.

Eileen:

- Yes, it is. They are kidnapping Australian citizens. They are kidnapping Sabina Hines and her husband Alexander O'Neill.

Jared Pond ran up to the window and stared in disbelief. Why had the famous environmentalist Sabina Hines come to Mexico when a war was about to break out? It made no sense. As the Mexican militiamen were holding Sabina and Alex at gunpoint, it was not a cordial reception. Yet, her folly of coming here was not his problem, and he had little desire to die for it.
Jared:

- They are probably taken as hostages to solicit a ransom. Stupid influencers, what were they thinking?

Eileen:

- We got to help them.

Jared:

- There is nothing we can do for them.

Eileen:

- We can't, but Ana Moreno can. We cannot let Sabina die. Her environmentalist zeal is exactly what the world needs for a better future. We cannot let Pierre and his type crush the forces of good.

Jared sighed:

- What do you suggest we do?

Eileen:

- We must follow the kidnappers to their hideout. Once we know where they are hiding, we can ask Ana Moreno and the Mexican army to help us.

Jared:

- I doubt they would care about an Australian environmentalist when the country is descending into civil war.

Eileen:

- Correct. But she will care about stopping El Gaucho. We must follow the militia and find out where they are hiding. After that we call Ana and give her the coordinates. It's the only way to save Sabina.

"Last call to Sydney for Mr Pond and Miss Lu"
Jared grabbed Eileen and tried to get her to their flight on time. She stood firm and replied:

- No. I am not leaving Sabina Hines to her fate. I am staying. If you leave, this is goodbye.

Jared sighed but he also felt how his love for Eileen had rekindled to how it was when they first met. This was the Eileen he had fallen in love with two decades earlier. She was the brave idealist who risked her own life to uphold her ideals and make the world a better place.
Jared nodded and replied:

- Okay. You win. Let's get a vehicle and follow them to their hideout.

After saying this, Jared and Eileen hurried to the airport drop off area and bought a run-down car with cash to continue their pursuit.

JARED AND EILEEN WERE hiding in the bushes at a hill overlooking the complex where the militia had taken Sabina. The mosquitos, insects, and humidity made their lives uncomfortable, but Jared had bigger problems. They had missed their flight to Sydney, and they were hiding in enemy territory.

As they studied the complex below them, they realised that they couldn't get in to save Sabina and Alex. There were too many guards to even consider that idea.

Eileen picked up her phone and turned to Jared:

- We'll need to give Ana Moreno, Sabina's location. It's the only way to save Sabina.

Jared:

- No. The Mexicans might consider Sabina Hines to be collateral damage and attack the building with artillery and fighter jets.

Eileen:

- I trust Ana. She wouldn't do that.

Jared:

- Very well. Follow your instinct.

Eileen nodded and she picked up her phone to call Ana Moreno:

- Ana, I need your help. An Australian environmentalist, Sabina Hines, is being held hostage in the Valle de la Cantimplora.

Ana:

- I am sorry, but I cannot help you. The capital is a powder keg, and I must focus on the situation here.

Eileen:

- I understand your situation, but she is being held by El Gaucho. I can send you a photo to prove it.

There was a brief silence before Ana replied:

- I understand. This changes things. Can you repeat their location?

Eileen:

- Yes. Valle de la Cantimplora in el Parque Nacional Cumbres del Ajusco.

Ana:

- Understood, thank you, Eileen.

Eileen:

- Ana, please bring her out alive. Sabina is crucial to building a better future.

Ana:

- We'll do our best.

After speaking to Ana, Eileen turned to Jared and spoke:

- We did it. Ana promised to send help. Everything will be okay.

After hanging up the phone, Eileen sent the photos she had taken of El Gaucho kidnapping Sabina. Jared smiled at Eileen, but he didn't say anything. Deep down he feared that involving the Mexican army would condemn Sabina and Alex to their deaths.

Chapter 88: "She made the dogs kill Jesus." 4th April 2040

Jared and Eileen were overlooking Jesus Ortega's militia complex from a nearby hill when artillery shells and rockets started raining down on the complex. In the ensuing chaos, a car sped through the gate, but due to the smoke and fire, Jared couldn't make out who was in the car before it disappeared from his view. Eileen felt upset and exclaimed:

- No! Ana, what are you doing?

Jared:

- I am sorry, but I anticipated she would do something like this.

Eileen sobbed:

- But she promised...

Jared:

- She must protect her country. To her, stopping el Gaucho is more important than saving Sabina. What would you have done?

Eileen sighed and replied:

- I don't know. I was never a good president, was I?

Jared:

- Let's reflect on that later. We need to get Ana to stop bombarding the complex if Sabina is to have any chance of getting out of there alive.

Eileen:

- Yes, I'll call her now.

Eileen picked up her phone and called Ana. As Ana answered the phone, Eileen heard gunfire in Ana's background:

- Eileen, I cannot speak to you now, the fighting has taken to the streets of Mexico City, and Jesus' men are in the outskirts of the city.

Eileen:

- Can you please stop the bombing at Valle de la Cantimplora?

Ana:

- We already have, we are focusing on other, more important targets. *Beep, Beep, Beep*

Eileen stared at her phone as the connection broke. In the distance, she heard artillery bombardments in the city, 20 kilometres to the north. Eileen turned to Jared and spoke:

- We need to move. We need to go down there and find out if Sabina is still alive.

Jared:

- I'd rather not. We carry no weapons and there must be surviving militiamen down there.

Eileen:

- Aren't you the greatest agent Australia has ever seen? Isn't danger your second name? Are you going to let the girl save the day? I am going in!

Jared sighed. Being 'the greatest agent Australia had ever seen' had given him an interesting life of booze and sexy women. But now, it was a dangerous title that forced him to do something he rather wouldn't do. Jared got up, started walking to the complex, and said:

- I'll lead the way. Let's save Sabina and Alex from El Gaucho!

Eileen smiled. Jared was still a doofus, but a lovely man, and she felt more alive than she had felt for many years.

SANDRA SANTIAGO WAS feeling terrified as she was hiding from Sabina and Alex in a shed in the jungle. Sandra had taken off her Zetan monocle to visit Sabina in Jesus Ortega's basement. She had taken it off to hide her real associations and to gain Sabina's trust. Sandra had planned to convince Sabina to give her the primordial Zeto Crystal. Once she had the crystal, she would get herself to safety in Brazil while the Mexican Civil War played out.

Sandra's plan had come to naught. Somehow Sabina had gained control over Jesus' attack dogs and directed them to become silent and deadly assassins, who used coordinated attacks to kill everyone in the complex, including Jesus Ortega. To make matters worse, the government had started bombing the complex. Sandra had barely escaped with her life when she drove Sabina and Alex away from the complex. Sandra called Josefina Fiero via her Bluetooth headset.

Sandra:

- She made the dogs kill Jesus.

Josefina:

- What are you talking about? Is something wrong?

Sandra stammered:

- The Aussie girl, Sabina Hines. She controlled the minds of Jesus' attack dogs to kill everyone in the Valle de la Cantimplora complex. I had to pretend to be her friend to get out of there alive.

Josefina:

- Good. You are doing things according to plan. Is there anything I can do for you?

Sandra:

- She is forcing me to drive her to the Sun Pyramid. Send people to help me.

Sandra didn't pay attention to Josefina's answer as she heard terrible screams outside. She grabbed a pistol from the shed and ran outside to inspect the noise. What she saw shocked her. Blood covered Sabina's face, and Sandra's monocle lay on the ground with Sabina's bloodied eyeball attached to it. Sabina placed her primordial Zeto Crystal on her right eye socket, and it instantly grew back and she was unhurt. Sandra was shocked at this and stuttered:

- What's happening? You are not a normal girl. You lost an eyeball, and yet you have two healthy eyes? You look unhurt!

Sabina:

- I am sent by the True Maker to save the future of humankind. There is still time to save yourself, Sandra. Tell us why you have this monocle and repent your sins.

Sandra:

- No. I don't believe you. I saw what you did to Jesus' men. Even if you kill me, the others will deal with you.

Alex, who stood close to Sabina, shouted:

- This is your last chance, Sandra. Help us and save yourself.

Sandra lost her nerve and shot Sabina in the kneecap. Before Sandra had the time to shoot again, a misfired artillery shell impacted with her body and knocked the others to the ground. After a while, Sabina and Alex got up, and Sabina used the primordial Zeto Crystal to heal them. Once they had healed their wounds, they got into Sandra's car to resume their drive to the Sun Pyramid.

"WHAT HAPPENED HERE?" Eileen exclaimed as they entered the complex and saw a militiaman with a ripped throat.

Jared studied the wound. It looked like an animal had slit his throat with its teeth, but the man was armed with an assault rifle, so how had this happened? Jared picked up the gun and spoke:

- We are not here to investigate. We need to find Sabina and Alex.

They hurried to a building on the other side of the courtyard. It was the only building that hadn't been partially destroyed by rockets and artillery fire. Jared had a foreboding feeling when he saw blood flowing down from the stairs. Eileen saw it and exclaimed:

- Devils must possess this place. I am not going up there.

Jared:

- Devils or militiamen, in any case, you are not safe standing here out in the open.

Eileen nodded and she followed Jared upstairs.

They entered the room, which was full of dead militiamen and dead attack dogs.

Jared saw the dead bodies of El Gaucho and Jesus Ortega in the room. He heard the dying breaths of another man:

- Jared Pond. I can't believe you are here.

Jared looked at the man. Despite the man's mauled face, Jared recognized him. The man was Matthew "The Jackaroo" Warner, a RAKI agent specialised in overseas assassinations.

Jared:

- Matthew. What are you doing here?

Matthew coughed up some blood and wheezed:

- Danielle Anders sent me to kill you, and to help Jesus Ortega
kill Ana Moreno. Please forgive me, Jared.

'I thought people asked God for forgiveness when they were dying.' Jared thought but he held back his sarcasm and replied:

- I forgive you, Matthew.
- Do you have any evidence against Danielle Anders?

Matthew:

- Yes, it's on a secret server. You'll find the link on my phone. My
code is 4645.

Having said this, Matthew closed his eyes, and his breathing became weaker. Jared exclaimed:

- Eileen. Please help me, he is bleeding out.

Eileen shook her head and replied:

- No. We must broadcast the evidence of Jesus Ortega's death to the world. It's the only way to stop the Civil War.

Jared realised that Eileen was right. "Rest in peace, Matthew." He mumbled, got up and started filming Eileen Lu for a live stream where she announced that Jesus Ortega and El Gaucho had perished.

After filming the stream Jared collapsed to the floor and started crying. Eileen kneeled next to him, stroke his hair, and spoke:

- I am sorry for your loss. Who was he?

Jared:

- His name was Matthew "the Jackaroo" Warner. I was his mentor at RAKI. He was the closest I ever had to a son.

Eileen:

- And he came to Mexico to kill you?

Jared:

- Yes, my life story feels like a bloody Shakespeare play now.

Eileen:

- At least the Jared I know would find it funny that Mexico's deadliest man, and Australia's deadliest man, had nicknames that meant the same thing.

Jared smiled a sad smile and replied:

- Yes, it's like I have always said. It's not the sharks you need to worry about, it's the cows.

Eileen smiled as she comforted Jared. With a bit of luck, they had saved the Mexican population from senseless war and killing. If that was the case their trip to Mexico was worth it. Once Jared had calmed down, they stole a car and drove to a peaceful village far away from the capital to wait for the war to end.

Chapter 89: The face-off in the Sun Pyramid. 4ᵗʰ April 2040.

Pierre Beaumont was feeling exhausted as he sat in a World Bank office in the Northern outskirts of Mexico City. This was the longest day ever, as Pierre had travelled past the dateline, and thus, Tuesday 4th April 2040 had already lasted 30 hours for him.

Pierre looked at a tactical map outlining the fronts in the Mexican Civil War, which had started today. 60 kilometres to the south, in the southern suburbs of Mexico City, chaos had broken out. Pierre hoped that he could trust Jesus' promise to not attack the northern parts of the city.

If everything went according to plan, the battle between Jesus Ortega and President Ana Moreno would be a one-sided affair. While the Mexican army was a lot stronger than Jesus's rebels, the troops that protected the capital wasn't. This was because World Bank operatives had bribed Mexican generals to withdraw their troops from the southern part of the capital. Pierre followed the advancement of Jesus' rebels on a tactical screen. They had advanced and were only 20 kilometres away from the presidential palace. Would Ana stay in the palace or would she try to escape? Pierre had prepared for both scenarios.

Pierre picked up his phone and called Jesus Ortega. It bugged him that Jesus hadn't answered his call one hour earlier. If Jesus became the president, he would need to prioritize Pierre's phone calls.

'Incoming priority information. Transferring data.' Pierre's Zetan Monocle displayed. After that, it showed a live feed where Eileen Lu declared that Jesus Ortega and his right-hand-man, El Gaucho, were dead. Pierre panicked. If Jesus was dead, the revolution against President Ana Moreno was leaderless and likely to fail. What would then happen to La Prensa de La Muerte Dam project?

Pierre's mind got back to a more urgent issue when his monocle intercepted a phone call between Sandra Santiago and Josefina Fiero. Apparently, Sabina Hines was behind Jesus' death, and she was heading to the Sun Pyramid. Pierre didn't know what she was after at the Sun Pyramid, but he did know one thing. He needed to kill her and steal the primordial Zeto Crystal. He could not allow her to interfere with his plans any longer.

Pierre walked to another room and spoke to the Mossad agents that had accompanied him from Sydney. Pierre:

- We have located the woman who caused the deaths of Ben and Szymon Yehuda. Bring torture devices, it is time to get vengeance and find out who she works with.

The agents nodded, and a few minutes later, they were in a helicopter for the short flight to the Sun Pyramid, where Sabina and Alex were heading.

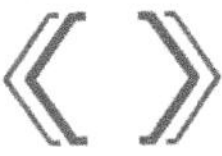

AS PIERRE'S HELICOPTER landed on the temple grounds of Sun Pyramid, a few security guards approached him. One of them shouted:

- No puede aterrizar su helicóptero aquí. Este es un monumento protegido por la UNESCO. (You can't land your helicopter here. This is a UNESCO protected monument)

"Fuck this shit!" Pierre muttered to himself, initiated combat mode on his Zetan Monocle, and shot the security guards in quick succession. After that, he shouted to his men:

- Anyone else got something to say?

The agents looked away, and a short while later they entered the inner sanctum of the temple area. The needless killing of the security guards had filled Pierre with adrenaline. Under normal circumstances, he would have used his money and power to bribe the guards. However, since he was in a country during a civil war, it was more satisfying to eliminate the problems.

Pierre directed his monocle to search for Sabina, and it showed him three potential heat signatures underground in a tunnel. 'I see, she is going to the Royal Tomb.' Pierre reflected and he directed his men to follow him. As they reached the Royal Tomb, Pierre shot the guide that waited outside the tomb and he entered the room accompanied by the Mossad agents.

Pierre stared in awe at the room and the primordial Zeto Crystal, which Sabina held in her hand. The primordial Crystal was glowing of a beautiful blue shining light, and the room looked so bright and luminous, different from Pierre's last visit to the complex. Pierre spoke to Sabina:

- What a beautiful sight. I love what you did to the room, Sabina.

Sabina gave Pierre an angry look and replied:

- So, we meet again. Why did you murder our guide?

Pierre sneered sarcastically:

- Well, we can't leave any witnesses behind for our little ordeal, can we? Like a speck of dust, his puny little life on this planet is now over. But it doesn't matter. By tomorrow this country will have descended into civil war and chaos. Hahaha!

Sabina:

- So, are you starting a war just because I am here?

Pierre:

- Don't be ridiculous. This war was long in the making. It is a consequence of the Mexican government's refusal to pay back what they owe us.

Sabina:

- But they won't be able to pay you back if you destroy them.

Pierre laughed hysterically:

- Ha-ha! Money is an artificial human construct. There is something even more important than money itself, and that is the power that money symbolizes. Besides, I have an unsurpassed ability to generate wealth from any forms of disaster.

Sabina:

- So, why are you coming after me?

Pierre continued with his sarcasm:

- You started this conflict between us, dear Sabina. You should never have pumped the shares that I was shorting and won against me. But an even more important reason for me to be here is the primordial Zeto Crystal, which you have stolen from us.

One of the Mossad agents walked up to Pierre and spoke:

- Mr Beaumont, we need to wrap this up, the frontline in the civil war is moving towards us.

Pierre nodded, turned to Sabina, and spoke:

- Mrs Hines. While I enjoyed speaking to you, we need to wrap things up. Give me the primordial Zeto Crystal or I'll kill you and your husband Alex.

Sabina:

- I am not giving you the primordial Zeto Crystal. You'll try to kill us no matter what I do.

Pierre smirked and replied:

- I won't just try to kill you. I will succeed as I always do. Neither of you will leave the Sun Pyramid alive!

Sabina shook her head and defied Pierre's taunt:

- No, you won't! Your evil reign ends tonight, Pierre Beaumont. This is your last chance to repent and save yourself.

'Hmmm... She seems so assured of herself, is she bluffing, or have I walked into a trap?' Pierre thought to himself. One thing was certain. He couldn't back down now. He had to double down on his threats. Pierre aimed and shot Alex in the kneecap. Pierre laughed as Alex collapsed in pain:

- Oh, that looks like a nasty wound. Tsk, tsk, tsk, lucky I got some medicine.

Having said this, Pierre took out a vial of poisonous acid and threw it into Alex's wound. As the acid dissolved into Alex's kneecap, it started to boil, and Alex screamed in excruciating pain from the toxic acid burn. Pierre taunted:

- I don't have all day, but I can spare some time to make Alex's death a painful one.

The same Mossad agent as before spoke again:

- Why don't we just shoot her, Monsieur? If the pyramid gets hit in the bombardment, this tunnel will collapse, and we are done for. We must hurry!

Pierre smirked at the agent and replied:

- Silence, Melchior. There is a method to the madness. You'll see.

"Very well. I accept your demands. Give me the antidote to Alex's poison."

Having exclaimed this, Sabina threw the primordial Zeto Crystal to Pierre, who instinctively caught it.

As Pierre caught the primordial Zeto Crystal with his hand, Sabina chanted some alien language prayers: "*Simba.... Zetani..... Humanis!*" This activated the Crystal's auto defence mechanism and set Pierre ablaze with a white luminous flame. As the Mossad agents stared at Pierre's ghastly death, Sabina bent down to pick up the primordial Zeto Crystal and Pierre's pistol. A short firefight broke out, and afterwards, everyone in the room except for Sabina were dead.

Sabina collapsed to the floor and uttered a short prayer to her deity, The True Maker. After that, she used the Zeto Crystal to revive and cure Alex. This self-blasting procedure that killed Pierre and the healing powers that cured Alex had drained the energy of the primordial Crystal, so Alex and Sabina left the Pyramid and hurried to Pierre's helicopter. They highjacked the helicopter and forced the pilot to take them to the airport where their private jet was parked. After that, they quickly left Mexico. Sabina's mission was still ahead of her, but she couldn't stay in Mexico any longer as she had more important things to do.

Chapter 90: Deaths and a new beginning, 10th April 2040.

Jared Pond and Eileen Lu were waiting at Mexico City airport. The civil war was over, as Pierre Beaumont's sponsored coup led by Jesus Ortega had died when their leader was mauled by his own attack dogs. Jared had found the evidence that Danielle Anders had sent Matthew Warner to kill him and President Ana Moreno. He had published the evidence online, and the news had viralled like wildfire. This had forced Danielle to resign, with a pending investigation on her coup against President Moreno. The ordered assassination of Ana Moreno was a huge scandal, as it was an unprecedented act of war between Australia and Mexico. Jared smiled. Even though Danielle Anders seemed to have more lives than a black cat, she would not find a way out of this mess. Particularly not since Pierre Beaumont and the media would no longer support her.

Eileen Lu was drinking Bloody Mary and Jared a glass of Long Island tea when a few guards from the Mexican presidential office approached them. One of them spoke:

- Senor Pond and Senora Lu. Please come with us, President Ana Moreno would like to speak with you before your departure.

Jared:

- Why isn't she coming herself?

Guard:

- Please Senor Pond. Which President in her right mind would show herself in the open six days after a failed coup, which ended thousands of lives? There are plenty of Jesus Ortega supporters out there, looking for revenge.

Jared:

- Very well. We are coming with you.

Jared and Eileen followed the guards to the VIP section of the airport, which was behind a bulletproof one-way-mirror. Eileen flinched when she saw what was on the other side of the mirror. President Ana Moreno was accompanied by several agents from the infamous Ministry for State Security from the Columnist Party of China, seemingly in agreement with each other. Ana smiled at Eileen and spoke:

- Miss Lu. Thank you for saving me and my country from Jesus Ortega's coup.

Eileen:

- And this is how you are rewarding me? By handing me right into the hands of the people who seek to murder me.

Ana:

- It is not as simple as that. Li Jing Xi from the ministry will explain it to you.

Li Jing Xi spoke to Eileen:

- First of all, let me be forthcoming with you. You murdered my biological father, Chairman Jing Xi. Shortly afterwards, you took the presidency which ended in a massive catastrophe.

Eileen tensed up. Was this the end of her? Couldn't fate let one good deed go unpunished?

Li Jing Xi gave Eileen an unexpected smile and spoke:

- Don't worry, Eileen. Murdering the tyrant Jing Xi was in fact a good deed. My mother was one of the many unwilling concubines he forced himself upon during his reign of villainy.

Eileen:

- I assume you did not come to thank me for murdering him, so why are you here?

Li Jing:

- Your situation is a conundrum to the Columnist Party. On the one hand, we want to eliminate you for deposing us from power and murdering Jing Xi back in 2021. On the other, I am glad that my cruel father died by the hand of an ex-journalist.

Eileen:

- I did not do any of this. I was Jing's prisoner, and he was about to rape me when his secretary turned on him to save me.

Li Jing:

- Debatable but irrelevant. However, there has been plenty of water under the bridge and we are thankful that you stopped Pierre Beaumont from taking control over Mexico.

Jared:

- So, why don't you let her go? Cross Eileen off your hit list if she promises to not involve herself in Chinese politics anymore.

Li Jing:

- Well, it's not that easy. The two of you are wanted in Dubai for the murder of Peng Yingxing, Eileen's deceased husband.

Jared:

- We didn't kill him. He had a heart attack.

Li Jing:

- Also, debatable. Regardless, the Emir sees things differently. You've embarrassed him, Eileen. He can't accept women disobeying his orders, he wanted you to stay married to Peng for political reasons. Even if he can't get you extradited to Dubai for a mock trial, he will send assassins to kill you.

Jared:

- So, no matter what, we'll have assassins coming after us.

Ana:

- Not necessarily. I've discussed the issue with Li Jing Xi and together we found a solution. We'll give you both new identities and Mexican passports while China will provide you with wealth that will last you a lifetime. Jared Pond and Eileen Lu both died as heroes, stopping the drug lord Jesus Ortega from overthrowing the Mexican government. From now on, Mr Jakob & Mrs Ellie Bond can live a happy life as retirees in the Caribbean.

Eileen:

- But our faces are known worldwide, it will never work.

Li Jing:

- The Ministry for State Security has some of the best plastic surgeons in the world. The Australian Prime Minister Danielle Anders used to be a man working for us, we have excellent cosmetic surgeries which will make you look completely different.

Jared:

- I knew that Daniel and Danielle were the same person.

Li Jing smirked:

- Yes, but less than 50 % of the Australian voters did. Some even thought he had been kidnapped by aliens and woke up as a female.

- Anyways, this is the best we can offer you. If you refuse, we won't do anything to protect you from the Emir's men.

Jared had a look at Eileen. Could he imagine retiring and spending his remaining days on a Caribbean paradise island with her? Yes, he could.
Jared:

- I would be happy to accept this offer and retire together with the one true love of my life.

Eileen:

- I am sick of fighting and I am sick of people around me dying. I would also be happier with a new identity as Jared's wife.

Ana:

- Excellent. We will take you to a medical facility to do the cosmetic procedure. Your new life should be due in 6-8 weeks.

After saying this, Eileen and Jared followed Li Jing Xi to a discreet plastic surgery clinic.

JAKOB BOND WAS NOW having a quiet night at their secluded mansion in the Caribbean together with his wife Ellie Bond. He had been going on a spin on the jet ski to get the adrenaline up, but apart from that, there was no danger in his life anymore. Jakob looked at his reflection in the mirror and sighed. "Look what they did to my face. No-one would believe that I once was Jared Pond, the greatest agent Australia had ever seen.

Ellie smiled, kissed Jakob, and replied:

- That was the point of the surgery, my love.

Jakob teased:

- At least they let me keep one good part...

Ellie:

- Indeed, that part is still the best Australian agent that no one else sees. *wink*

For a moment, Jakob felt melancholic that his past excitement of espionage, booze and great looking women was now over. But then he remembered that he retired with his one true love, and that he could always relive his prime years with her every night.

Chapter 91: Epilogue.

Below is the ending for all the main characters throughout the **The Banker Trilogy**.

Sabina Hines went on a holiday in Hawaii to recuperate. The holiday didn't last for long as Elaine and Martin kidnapped Alex to force Sabina on a daring mission. Sabina travelled with Martin to the Sunken Pyramid of Kiribati where she opened a portal to another dimension to confront her nemesis, the Xeno empress Rangda Kaliankan. After killing Rangda, Sabina activated the kill switch on all the monocles. This killed everyone in the Monocle Conspiracy except for **Martin Orchard** who vowed to get revenge. Sabina and her daughter, Keila, lived until Sabina was 112 years old, when they sacrificed themselves through letting their bodies absorb the gamma-ray-burst that was destined to destroy Sydney. To read more about Sabina's adventures, please check out my book **Sabina Saves the Future Trilogy**.

Martin Orchard felt convinced that Rangda Kaliankan was a threat to mankind, so Martin forced Sabina to come on a quest to stop Rangda. After surviving Sabina's attack on the monocle users, Martin swore to avenge Elaine's death and his own disfigurement. He did this through trying to destroy Sabina's reputation and convincing Sabina that Rangda possessed her daughter. After getting his revenge, Martin retired and stopped committing atrocities. Martin died from a morphine overdose after contracting terminal brain cancer in his late 60's. To read more about Martin's lifetime of villainy and adventures, please check out my book **The Fall of Martin Orchard.**

Jared Pond & Eileen Lu lived cushy lives as retirees under their new identities. Eileen involved herself in charity projects but stayed away from politics. Jared got his adrenaline from jet skiing, Scuba diving, and hiking. They led active lives and they died together in their late 80's from a flu that wasn't hyped.

Vladimir Kravchenko had barely recovered from his wounds when authorities arrested him for causing the Hei Bai virus outbreak in 2021. Mass arrests followed and the World Bank was dismantled for the organization's crimes against humanity. Vladimir died before facing court as Sabina activated the kill-switch on his Zetan Monocle.

Elaine Orchard rekindled the flame with her ex-husband Martin and died when Sabina activated her kill-switch. The Harapan Conglomerate passed on to her adopted children Budi and Rexi, and they focused on utilitarian projects to heal the damage that the company had caused.

Josefina Fiero was busy destroying evidence and contesting an extradition when the kill-switch put her out of her misery. Her company was split up into smaller parts after her death.

James Winter was facing court for his involvement in the 2028 assassination of Eva Moreno, when the monocle kill-switch ended his days.

Damien Vanderbilt served two terms as the US president after Eva Moreno's assassination. When the truth came out, Damien was pardoned by his successor, but that didn't help against the angry mob that lynched him.

Ana Moreno resigned as the Mexican president six months after the civil war had ended. She sought refuge in China under a new identity and she started writing left-wing-literature until her death many years later.

Danielle Anders hung herself while awaiting trial for her treasonous act to send an assassin to murder a foreign head of state. People speculated for a long time whether Danielle committed suicide or if she was murdered.

Frank van Stein died while using Vladimir's technology to resurrect **Delphine Beaumont**. Delphine continued her father's legacy of villainy and murder. However, without his technology and wealth she didn't last long, and she ended her days admitted to a psychiatric institution.

Please review:

If you got this far, please review my book. I don't care if it's a negative review if it points out why the book is bad and what can be improved. Of course, you might not score many brownie points from giving me one-star reviews, but on the other hand, what do you need brownie points for?

Don't miss out!

Visit the website below and you can sign up to receive emails whenever Martin Lundqvist publishes a new book. There's no charge and no obligation.

https://books2read.com/r/B-A-QIOG-LYPLB

BOOKS 2 READ

Connecting independent readers to independent writers.

Also by Martin Lundqvist

Divine Space Gods
Divine Space Gods: Abraham's Follies
Divine Space Gods II: Revolution for Dummies
Divine Space Gods III: Rangda's Shenanigans

La Trilogica Divina Zetan
La Divina Disimulación

Sabina räddar framtiden
Sabinas jakt på den heliga graalen

Sabina Saves the Future
Sabina's Pursuit of The Holy Grail
Sabina's Quest to Open the Portal in the Sun Pyramid
Sabina's Expedition to Stop the Apocalypse

The Banker Trilogy
The Banker and The Dragon
The Banker and the Eagle: The End of Democracy

The Banker and the Empath

The Divine Zetan Trilogy
The Divine Dissimulation
The Divine Sedition
The Divine Finalisation

Standalone
Matt's Amazing Week
James Locker The Duality of Fate
The Portal in the Pyramid
Money Laundering in the Laundromat
Pyramidportalen
Matts Fantastiska Vecka
Divine Space Gods Trilogy
Sabina Saves the Future: Complete Trilogy
Diez Historias Aleatorias y Muy Cortas
Ten Random and Very Short Stories
10 zufällige Kurzgeschichten Volumen 1
Dieci Storie Casuali e Molto Brevi
Dix Histoires Aléatoires et Très Courtes
Cinco Historias Aleatorias y Muy Cortas
Five Random and Very Short Stories
The Fall of Martin Orchard
Masa Depan Putri Sabina
La Caída de Martin Orchard
El Banquero y el Dragón
A Sedição Divina
Dieci storie casuali e molto brevi. Vol 2
Δέκα Τυχαίες και πολύ Σύντομες Ιστορίες Volume 2
The Coldvir-20 Killer
10 zufällige Kurzgeschichten Volumen 2

Förkylningsmördaren
The Banker Trilogy

Watch for more at martinlundqvist.com.